# GERÁLD B. GÁRDNER

# HIGH MÁGIC'S ÁID

**AURINIA BOOKS**

GERALD B. GARDNER, "HIGH MAGIC'S AID"

Published by Aurinia Books.

Cover artwork: Oliver Hahn
Cover photo: Divine Female Fantasy © Deviant/fotolia.com
Typesetting: Robert B. Osten

ISBN 978-0-9566182-0-7
1st revised edition 2010.


Please visit our website: **www.auriniabooks.co.uk**

# CONTENT

# INTRODUCTION

"AGIC! Witchcraft! Stuff and nonsense. No-one believes in such things nowadays. It was all burning evil-smelling powders, muttering words. The Devil jumped up, and you sold him your soul. That was all there was to it."

But was that really all? Would any sane-or insane person for that matter-sell their souls to eternal fire for nothing, or nearly nothing?

Our forefathers had faith. At least about nine millions of them suffered a cruel death, mainly by being burnt alive, because of this belief.

Magic is sometimes defined as attempting to do something contrary to the laws of nature, to bring success to various undertakings.

Now the Church taught this could be done by prayers and offerings to the Saints. It was also an article of faith that King Solomon evoked great Spirits and forced them to perform many wonders. Books were also written on similar subjects. "The Key of Solomon the King", the most widely-used book of Magic, was believed to be written by King Solomon himself. Perhaps the next most widely used was the Enchiridion of Pope Leo III.

If the great ones of the earth practised it and taught you to do likewise, should not the lesser ones also believe it could be done safely, if they only knew the way?

Art Magic was taught more or less publicly at various universities, and, secretly, almost everywhere.

You might ask: "But did it work, if not why did they believe it?"

But they saw innumerable cases where magical ritual seemed to work. When France was prostrate at the feet of England, her King had no men, money, hope, or followers. A young peasant girl, The Witch of Domrémy, apparently drew armies from the ground, and drove out the invaders; that she was burnt alive as a witch for so doing, only strengthened the belief that it worked, if one only knew how and dared risk it.

Pope Innocent III was made Pope some time before he was even a priest. Stephen Langton, an utterly unknown man, suddenly became Archbishop of Canterbury overnight. This smelled of Magic to our forefathers.

Would you know what they believed and at-temped to achieve ? Then come with me into the past.

*Note.* The Magical Rituals are authentic, partly from the *Key of Solomon* (MacGregor Mather's Translation) and partly from Magical MSS. in my possession.

# CHAPTER I
## HIGH MAGIC'S AID

"RPHIAL, *Anial, Oramageon, Adonai, Tzabaoth, El, Elothai, Elohim, Shaddai, Tetragramatton, Anaphoditon,*" so the names in the great incantation boomed on.

Olaf Bonder swayed slightly. Blindfold and helpless he stood in the Triangle, outside, and cut off from the Protecting Circle, medium between the pleasant world of man and the Dread Lords of the Outer Spaces. He had been instructed by Thur Peterson to make his mind a blank, to empty his mental vision, to create in himself a vacuum to be filled by the Spirit which would speak through him, and tell them how to set about their great enterprise.

Olaf's receptivity was as yet by no means complete. By blindfolding his eyes, his mental vision was tremendously stimulated, so that pictures of his life and intimate history over a period of many years rose unbidden and raced through his brain, unnaturally vivid and illuminated with flashes of flame like the jagged lightning in some frightful storm. For a moment he was almost paralysed with terror because he was not accustomed to such intense mental stimulation, or to the fearful rapidity with which the pictures succeeded one another.

He was barely sixteen years of age, and, were it not for his brother Jan, not greatly pre-occupied with their sadly fallen family fortunes. For the first time these terrifying pictures were showing him the sacking and burning of his grandfather's fortified house set high on the inaccessible rock, the murder of the good Thane Edgar Bonder by the hated Norman Fitz-Urse, the escape of his own father from the slaughter, and the steady rising of the Norman stronghold on the ashes of the old homestead.

Why should this be so vivid to-night, even to the death of his father away in the wars? Why should he see his mother so clearly when the news was brought to her by Thur Peterson, Olaf himself a little lad of three clinging to her rough skirts and Jan, so much older, standing by sullen and purposeful, as though even then he had resolved to regain their lost dignity by hook or crook. She had wiped away a tear with the back of her hand, and returned to her place behind the plough, with its yoke of oxen stolidly awaiting her word of command. There was no time for mourning, with the farm to run and their daily bread to be scratched from the reluctant earth, and a moiety to be salvaged from the clutching hands of the Church

"*Chiaoth, Ha, Qadosch, Beraka!*" Each name struck like a hammer on Olaf's brain. He must clear his mind from this clutter of the past, and go through with this task he had set himself to perform for Jan, that he might be head of a family with lands, castles, followers, instead of a skulking outlaw, grubbing a foul living among churls twenty miles away on the outskirts of the great woodlands.

"*Anphaim, Aralim, Chashmalim, I shm!*" Would it never stop? The events of the day flashed before him. Some act of petty tyranny from one of the Brothers had set Jan off, and he had come stamping to where Olaf was hoeing his endless patch.

"I will have no more of it!" he had stormed.

"This very night will we seek out Thur Peterson and ask his aid."

"What aid may he give, a simple leech?"

"Not so simple by far."

"Has he money? We would need a bushel of great gold pieces for this business, Jan."

"Aye, 'tis true."

"And has Thur so much, or even the Abbot himself?"

"Thur has better, as you will see. We ride to seek High Magic's aid! Wilt come?"

"Where you go, I will go, what you do, I will do."

The furious headlong ride at night to the tall house of Thur, and their subsequent talk seemed to have happened years ago instead of a matter of hours. Thur had protested:

"'Tis all so many years ago, Jan, well about twenty. I loved your father, he was my friend and companion, and had he made the attempt many years ago all would have followed him, but now 'tis nothing but an old wives' tale and even though by a miracle the castle could be stormed and taken, how could it be held? How establish yourself in a hostile country? You would need an army, and gold to pay and provender it."

"You vowed to help my father with the Arts you have at your command!"

At this Olaf looked from one to the other wild-eyed. Jan, fair-haired, grey eyes brooding, his tall, slender and muscular body taut with repressed energy sat astride a rush-bottomed stool with out-stretched legs resting on his heels. He searched Thur's face with keen attention, while the elder man, bigger than Jan and stouter, his dark thin face inset with darker, steady eyes hinting of unseen fires, stood looking down at his visitor, his jutting nose a bleak promontory or a black shadow in the weaving light of the guttering lamp.

"Sorcery!" muttered Olaf hoarsely, and crossed himself. Thur glanced at him whimsically and shrugged, turning again to Jan.

"Yes, yes, I know, but truth is I am more than a little fearful. I have the Parchments which give instruction, with the use of the right instruments ... but I lack them."

"Instruments!" gasped the horrified Olaf.

Jan gave an impatient half-gesture which bade him to be silent and not interrupt.

"Without them there is much danger. Firstly I must make a circle with a properly consecrated sword."

"How may one come by that?" asked Jan.

"It can be made, but the means are lacking, that is the trouble. To make the Sword I need the Burin, to make the Burin I must have consecrated white-hilted knife, the witch's Athame. They in turn must be made by the Burin."

Jan drooped hopelessly on his seat, sitting hunched with bent head. Thur looked compassionately at him.

"'Tis all in a circle, and I know not the way in."

A heavy silence fell. Jan's disappointment was crushing. His childlike faith in Thur's powers had made expectation soar, and though he knew he must fight and work hard to regain his lost possessions and to retain them, yet he had staked his hope upon guidance and direction through Thur and his Art Magical. With impatience at his own impotence Thur added:

"Fools, think I have but to wave a wand? Not so. Can I make bricks without clay and fire? A Magician must have the proper instruments of Art."

"I thought ..." Jan wavered, and tailed off into silence.

"True, the power lies in himself," Thur continued in a ruminating tone, "but he must have peace and quiet to inflame himself to the highest might of frenzy. How can he concentrate his will to draw down the most powerful forces when one ear is cocked for fear my Lord Abbot's men come thundering at the door?"

"A pox on all busy-body priests!" commented Jan.

"As for me, I cannot work in silence. To summon the spirits be they in Heaven or Hell, I must call loudly, and if I do so, will not the neighbours hear and word go to the Abbot straight away? ... and he loveth me not."

"Whom doth he love but his own belly?"

Thur laughed. "Nay, I know not how I may help you, boy. I would truly give my heart's blood for your father's son, but I know not how to do it to any purpose."

"You have the parchments, Thur, of which you have often told us when we were but toddlers."

"Yes, I have them, for what they are worth. I studied High Magic in Spain in the University at Cordoba, but what of that? Any may teach there do they but teach what attracts students to their lectures. A teacher with many students is a great man, but they teach only the theory, not the practice."

"But if you know the theory, surely you may practise?"

"Nay, therein lies the snag. They say, 'Take this and that' ... but 'tis ever what a man may not obtain. Give me the tools, and I will use them to thy best advantage. Yet ever they teach that if you have not the exact tool, 'tis danger to life and soul to meddle. Otherwise why should I, having the knowledge, be but a poor leech scraping a bare living in a tiny town? Think, man, had I the power, would I have not made myself rich ere now?"

"I see," said Jan, dejectedly. He had based all his hopes on Thur and now found him a broken reed.

"But, Thur, is there *no* way at all? I fear not to risk *my* life; must I, as the monks say, sell my soul?"

"That is but a priestly lie," said Thur. "The God whom the Magicians invoke is the same One that the monks pray to, but we are taught to pray differently, that is all, using the methods of King Solomon, of whom the Lord said, 'I have given thee a wise and understanding heart so that before thee there was none like unto thee, nor ever shall arise.' Solomon performed many wonders and great deeds by the use of the knowledge that the Lord had given him, but when old age came o'er him, he wrote to his son, 'Treasure up, oh my son Roboam, the wisdom of my words, seeing that I, Solomon, did do and perform many wonders, and I have written a certain Book wherein I have rehearsed the secret of secrets, and in which I have preserved them hidden. I have concealed also all secrets whatsoever of Magical arts of any Masters, and I have written them in this key, so that like a key it openeth a treasure house ... so this key alone may open the knowledge of the Magical arts and sciences.

'Therefore, oh my son, let everything be properly prepared, as set down by me both day and hour, and all things necessary, for without this there will be but falsehood and vanity in the work.'

'I command thee, my son Roboam, to place this key beside me in the sepulchre.'"

"And," continued Thur, "it was so done, but in time came certain

Babylonian philosophers, who dug out the Sepulchre, and they made copies of the key, and with them worked many marvels."

"And you have this key?" gasped Jan, while Olaf goggled.

"Aye, lad, and that is the fix. It sayeth so clearly that without the right instruments 'twould be but death and worse to try. 'Tis but to raise mighty forces which may not be controlled."

"So it seems there is no hope at all," said Jan. Thur answered slowly: "There *may* be a way."

He turned to Olaf and said sharply: "You … hast thou loved a woman yet?"

"Woman? I loved my mother when she was kind."

"Not that," said Thur. "Hast thou ever cast eyes on a young girl with thoughts of love … or any other woman for that matter. Answer truly!"

"Not me," said Olaf promptly. "All girls be silly things. I have no use for any of them."

"Then I may help," said Thur. "There is a way by which a spirit may be called up to enter the body of a young person, and so communication can come across the veil, as only the spiritual essence is present, and a circle made by an ordinary sword would suffice … at least, I have heard so. But the young boy, or girl must never have known bodily love in any form, for therein would lie danger to us all. Other dangers there still are … burning if we be caught, but we can risk that. I have never dared to try anyone else, lest they be frightened and blab and bring death to us all, but you I can trust. Remember though that the danger to the young person is greater, for he must form a link as a medium between the two worlds, and for his protection there is but a triangle … for, were he within the protecting circle, the spirit could not cross to enter his body. Or, should he release such a force, to enter it would slay all within the circle, for it be only a partial protection unless made by the tools which we lack."

"I perceive your meaning," said Jan slowly.

"If Olaf here be not afraid …"

Olaf hitched himself forward. "I am willing," he said.

"Nay, nay," expostulated Jan, "that I will not have…my own brother…"

"I am resolved," repeated Olaf quietly, and Jan fell dumb.

"If Olaf has the courage it is not dangerous (or so they say)," said Thur. "Let not the terror seize you or drive you into a panic, and if we be not disturbed we may succeed. If not…at least we will gain advice that may benefit us."

"I am truly afraid," said Olaf stoutly, "but I will drive out fear, and for Jan's sake, and that of his great desire, you may do with me what you will. I will obey in all things."

"Then fear not, brave boy. I will give thee a potent Talisman," said Thur, already busy with an ewer and a large tub. "Now strip we all, and bathe in this consecrated water."

This done, Thur next drew great circles on the floor, one within the other, and outside of them a big triangle. All were circumscribed with mystic names. After this he poured water over Olaf's head, saying:

"*Aspergus Cam Domini, Hyssop Mundabitur, Lavabus Eam, et Super Nivem, Delabatur,*" and then hung an iron Talisman round his neck.

The words had a comforting sound, and Olaf felt fortified by them, but the terrible words which followed struck terror into his very soul, echoing round his brain as though it was a vast cavern; and the voice not Thur's, but a thundering one which boomed and battered down all resistance, laden with an awful power to command obedience.

"*Orphial, Anial, Ormageon, Come, O Bartzebal, Bartzebal… COME!*"

Olaf was led into the Triangle, and Thur bound his eyes with a strip of black linen and tied his hands and feet together invoking him:

"As thou art blind save for what light I can give thee, so I bind thee for a space that thou mayst be subject to my will alone. With this sword I invoke upon thee the protection of Bartzebal, so that no force of Heaven or Hell or from under the Earth may act upon thee, save only the forces which I shall invoke within thee.

"With this sword do I prick thy breast that thy body be a Temple of Mars and I command thee to repeat after me ... 'I invoke the powers of Mars that manifest themselves within me, Ancor Amocramides.' "

Olaf's young voice rose clearly, adopting involuntarily a chanting tone: "I invoke the powers of Mars to manifest themselves within me, Ancor Amocramides." He stood erect and steady inside the Triangle.

Then began a ritual which seemed to have moaned and boomed around him since the beginning of time. The band round his head, so lightly tied, seemed a clamp of iron. His head seemed bursting and liable to split open, as were his lungs, and the thudding of his heart seemed as if it would shatter his breaths. This was sheer and unadulterated fear of such magnitude that a man could not experience it and live.

Fear!

And, should he die, caught in the toils of this unholy rite, even sweet Christ Himself could not save him from everlasting damnation. A great black pall assembled at the root of his spine and began to creep upwards, slowly ... slowly ... reaching his nape, until the hairs rose and crawled ... coming higher until it hovered over him like a canopy borne by all the devils in Hell. If he could have put up his hand it would have been tangible to the touch, thick, black, and suffocating like a cloth. This was fear made manifest ... and now the cloth began to descend over his head ... stifling him ... if it reached his mouth he would be lost.

This was the fear he had been warned against, that could blast Jan and Thur and kill him. It must not ... it *should* not! The black pall seemed to reach his nostrils ... in a matter of seconds it would be over his mouth. He began to drive it back, and it stopped. For endless-seeming moments it remained stationary, while he agonised at grips with himself, fighting now for all their lives. As slowly as it had advanced the black thing retreated and vanished, leaving him trembling and sweating, but master of himself again.

He had conquered! Never again, he felt, would the powers of Darkness assail or prevail against him.

Thereafter came more of those flickering visions, though with diminished frequency and intensity, until they vanished altogether, leaving him with a sense of exhaustion and dizziness so that he reeled again, and only mastered himself with a supreme effort. In spite of himself he began to mumble, as though in delirium, words whose import he knew not. He became aware of Thur's voice, which had changed into persuasion, and was charged with welcome and ... yes, was it also relief?

"Hail, O Bartzebal, Thou Mighty Spirit, welcome who come in the name of Elohim Gibur. Tell me with truth how my friend Jan Bonder here may gain his wish!"

From Olaf's dry, cracked lips came a rushing babble of words, the only intelligible ones being:

"Seek the Witch of Wanda." But then followed a terrible drumming sound that thundered through his head, and in a flash it came to him that someone was battering at the door. The Abbot's men! In a minute the door would be down ... then it would be the stake and the fire for them all and he was bound, blindfold and helpless.

# CHAPTER II
# BROTHER STEPHEN

"**S**EEK the Witch of Wanda!"

For a second or two Jan and Thur stared at each other through the swirls of incense curling up from the bowls on the floor. As for Olaf, striving to keep a grip on his fast-reeling senses, uncomprehending the words he had uttered and half smothered by the incense, he was aware only of the increased drumming in his head.

"What noise is that?" Jan demanded, by no means sure of either his own senses or courage, for he had experienced terrifying things.

"Someone seeks entrance. Plague seize the whole creation of curious men!" muttered Thur, then in answer to the thunderous knocks: "I come. I come! May the Devil damn thee!"

Olaf, his head seeming to split open, tottered and fell, the blood streaming from his nose and foam frothing his lips.

"Thur!" cried Jan, raising his voice to be heard above the din, as the door sounded as though it was being battered down.

Thur retained his presence of mind.

"Silence!" he warned, and then spoke rapid words of mystic dismissal.

"Now, O Spirit Bartzebal, since thou didst come to my aid, I license thee to depart in peace. I charge thee in departing not to harm any person or thing, and most especially him in the Triangle.

"Depart in peace in the name of Adonai!"

Then to Jan: "Drag Olaf into the circle, remove the kerchief but do not unbind him yet. Scuff out the Triangle on the floor, and I will see who knocks," and shuffling slowly through the front shop, purposely overturning a stool and damning heartily the noisy intruders, Thur made as long a play for time as he dared, though the battering still continued. To his surprise the door still held, though he had expected from the hubbub to find it smashed in. With a grim deliberation he unbarred and unchained as softly as possible, then with a quick heave swung open the studded oak in time to see a stout sandalled foot levelled at it.

"May the Devil stub thy toes!" he remarked genially. "What now? What urgency clamours so rudely?"

"Are we dogs to be kept shivering at thy door?" hiccoughed a voice almost quenched in liquor.

"God knows! 'Twould be spitting evil upon His good creatures to name thee such. Be silent and respect your betters, if this is not a tale for my Lord Abbot's ears."

"Thou blasted damned fox!" spluttered the other, too astounded at Thur's truculent boldness and too drunk to do otherwise than abuse, but Thur, who knew that meekness would not meet the situation, and that he must either bully or be bullied, directed a level glare of some potency into the drink-stupid eyes. Moreover, the success of his recent experiment and the tail-end of his late mood of mental exaltation was yet upon him, giving him a majesty of demeanour which he did not ordinarily portray, a fact which was not lost upon a pair of shrewd eyes at the back of the little group.

There were three men, brothers of the adjacent Abbey of St. Ethelred, each clad in white cassock and ample white gown and hood of the Benedictine order. Each carried a torch whose flame see-sawed amid its smother of flaring pitch in the gusty wind, giving more fog than light. Thur discerned through the murk a string of heavily-laden mules, each carrying two sacks of grain for the main portage, with an added litter of such varied oddments that the result bore some resemblance to the sack of some looted villages, as indeed it was. Thur looked and sniffed, and was silent, while the grin was wiped off the ruddy faces of the two nearest him and was succeeded by a look almost of discomfiture.

"How now, Thur? We bring some good sack and a venison pasty," said the man at the back.

"Always welcome, Brother Stephen, and you too, James and Thomas," Thur replied, holding the door wider.

"I smell incense," sniffed Stephen.

"Better that than drink sodden breath," Thur replied equably.

"Incense!" Stephen repeated idly. "Raising Venus, eh? We have been collecting tithes... with success. Do we disturb your practices?"

"Nay," Thur replied carelessly, "I have but a sick boy inside, and am casting out devils, not raising them, Master Stephen."

Brother James put in: "If we return now we shall disturb midnight service, which is unseemly."

"And be forced to participate," Thur commented dryly. "I understand. Pray enter, brothers all."

Brother Thomas began to giggle feebly.

"We have been dancing at Hob the Miller's. Good hefty wenches there, and thirsty work. When the beer ran out he thrust us forth, though I doubt the quality of his beer"

"Thomas was ever a doubter," James belched.

"It goes to the head rather than the legs," reproved Thomas, with dignity.

"If thy legs must wamble, let me pass. I shiver in this blast. We will leave the beasts where they stand."

"Aye, do, for some night-farer to stumble into, or to drive off," jeered Thur. "But enter, brothers, in God's name, if you have a mind to. There is beer and to spare."

"And Venus?" leered Brother Thomas.

"Venus is a pestilent heathen strumpet and no fit company for honest monks. I am an apothecary, not a pimp. Enter!"

By now the three men had staggered into the back room, Stephen alone walking straight to his objective. Thur locked and barred the door behind them and followed slowly. With no gentle hand he pushed James and Thomas on to a settle, then taking a big pitcher, went out of the back door to a shed to draw beer. When he returned Stephen was standing with hands on hips and legs astride, cowl thrown back and head bent forward so that the light caught his face, bringing into strong relief bold, handsome features. He was looking curiously and far too knowledgeably at Olaf, still bound and lying moaning within the circle. Jan knelt beside him, supporting his head with his arm, and wiping the blood-stained foam from his lips with the kerchief that had recently bound his eyes. He ignored the presence of the monk, and as Thur re-entered Stephen turned away abruptly. He had deposited his pasty on the table. The surgeon poured beer liberally and handed round mugs, quietly cutting huge portions of the pasty and dispensing them. Stephen took his own serving and resumed his staring at the prostrate Olaf, while Thur took the lamp and went into the shop to concoct a restorative.

"What ails the lad?" inquired Stephen, his mouth full.

Jan growled much like a surly dog, and Stephen nodded as sagely as though he had received a courteous and intelligible reply.

"Oh, indeed?" he commented. "'Tis a sad pity!"

Jan glared open hostility. He loathed all churchmen, whom he regarded as little better than highway robbers, but Stephen ignored his incivility, knowing he could do naught else. The indecorous behaviour of his companions gave the stripling the advantage.

Thur returned with the potion, bringing the lamp with him. Gently he examined Olaf and persuaded him to swallow the draught. Presently the moaning ceased and Thur began to loosen the bonds.

"The frenzy has passed, and we can safely unbind him."

At this Brother James's curiosity was aroused, and he got tipsily to his feet and came over to stand beside Stephen, a mug in one hand and pasty in the other at which he gnawed and drank alternately, eyeing the patient owlishly the while. Stephen maintained a pregnant silence, though his eyes missed nothing in the room.

"Hup!" ejaculated James. "If he is sick, unbind him by all means, I say, but this smells of witchery, or I'm a mole."

"So you say!" barked Stephen, frowning.

"The Evil Eye, to my seeing," pursued James.

"Can a mole see?" retorted Stephen, who seemed in some way put out and was waspish. James crammed the last piece of pasty down his throat and pointed a wavering fore finger to the floor.

"Perceive that circle, Brother Blockhead?"

"Circle!" echoed Stephen. "The bottom of thy mug is so stamped upon thy vision, it repeats itself on the earth and in the heavens. Circle!"

"That's a circle."

"So's thy belly, and thou canst not see beyond it."

"Circle or no circle, forbear," James said to Thur, "loose him not. Bring him to the Abbey tomorrow, unless he be recovered. I have cured many like him. Holy water and a heavy birch-rod works wonders at casting out devils."

Brother Thomas lurched forward to join in the argument, while Thur glared angrily from one down-bent face to another.

"We have easier and better cures if his skin is tender. Canst pay? Holy water and the rod costs but a penny, but for ten pence he may touch the toe-nail of the blessed St. Lawrence."

"But we have a better still," cut in James, "some of the original Plagues of Egypt, the plague of darkness, brought direct from the Holy Land by a sainted palmer."

"For twenty pence only a sick man may pull out the plug in the lid of the casket and put an eye to the hole. There shall he see the Holy Darkness."

"Aye," said Thur. "I saw the wonder being made by Will the carpenter to the order of the Sub-Prior. Was it not painted black inside, tight as a cask, with no way to open and fitted with a small hole filled with a plug?"

"The very one!" cried Thomas. "It has brought much money to our coffers. The Sub-Prior puts gums and sweet spices and some dung through the hole, and thus is the mystery and smell of the East created. Many a pilgrim has sniffed and sworn he was in the Holy City again !"

"Peace, fools ! Must Holy Church herself be at the mercy of such foul tongues ? Be silent for very shame's sake."

Stephen's sudden, cold anger was both unexpected and surprising. Thur studied him intently and even Jan vouchsafed a glance of appraisal. James and Thomas contemplated him with wide eyes and mugs half raised to their sagging jaws. At that moment Stephen looked formidable, as though he had received some personal affront and was about to enact swift retribution upon the offenders .. The two monks sat down quickly as the best means of protecting their posteriors, while Stephen's eyes threatened, and his strong jaw was out-thrust, emphasising its lean contours, promising execution of threat. His mobile, tolerant mouth had lost its sweetness of expression and become one grim line. An unusual face ... an unusual attitude for a commonplace monk to adopt, Thur decided. Perhaps there was nothing commonplace about Stephen at all ? But Thur was in no wise abashed. He coolly proceeded to cast oil on incipient flames.

"Let Holy Church cast a little of her pretended holiness and adopt honesty in its place and she will not lack for respect and love," he observed silkily, the while he bent over Olaf, seeking his pulse with deft fingers. Stephen did not distract his eyes from the erring brothers as he replied sternly:

"That is a purely Pagan utterance."

"Yet was the Lord Christ honest before he was Holy ... the world's mark for honesty in all things," he pursued, pushing the hair back from Olaf's damp forehead and drying it with the kerchief.

"This is the rankest heresy !" declared Stephen, snatching his eyes from the discomforted brothers to look at Thur in some wonder.

"A heresy much on men's tongues in these rebellious days. Note that, brother, if you have the prestige of your Church at heart. Why, man, honest Magic would stoop to no such arts, and that is another thing for you to mark well."

The boldness of this retort, together with its truth, plainly flabbergasted Stephen, whose eyes had lost their menace to be replaced by something enigmatic. James and Thomas, released from apprehension, and somewhat sobered by their recent experience, which seemed to them some personal danger, plunged hastily into speech to hide their discomfiture and seek safety.

"Truly I like not the look of that boy, Thur," said James, sagely shaking his head.

"He reeks of witchcraft," Thomas added.

James peered at Olaf without the risk of rising from the settle. "Aye, clearly he is bewitched. I know of no witch hereabouts, but there may well be. I believe a witch to be behind every haystack, though the people love them so they will not breathe a word to betray them."

"Hast thou heard of the Witch of Wanda?" Thur asked.

Stephen shook his head. "I know of no witch, and no Wanda."

"Did the boy babble of the Witch of Wanda?" James thrust in eagerly. "Did *she* bewitch him? There is such a place, some fifty miles off through the forest and up in the marsh lands. We had a brother come from the place. It lies on the shore of a vast mere, a wild and desolate spot, and the men who live among the reeds are little better than the beasts that perish. A fit spot for witches."

Stephen made a restless movement. "Have done with witches. Drink up. I hear the last chant, and we had best be gone, so we may sleep in our beds until dawn. Good night to you, Thur, and a speedy recovery to the lad. Many thanks. The brew was good and liberal."

Thur made no protest but ushered them out.

They returned, however, to thrust their half-burned torches into the fire and so went, leaving a trail of pitchy smoke behind them and a great smell of spent beer. The light patter of hooves died away in the distance.

Jan was still sitting beside Olaf on a low stool when Thur returned to the back room. The boy's white, exhausted face was alarming in its stark austerity of suffering. He was barely conscious and his breathing was still laboured.

"Damn the Abbey and every lousy, drunken pest inside it … nothing but a nest of robbers and a hot-bed of lechery … "burst out Thur, beside himself with anxiety and fury at the idle interruption which had cost Olaf so dear. He spat venom like a furious cat. "They have almost killed him!"

"Curses on myself rather for letting him risk his life," Jan lamented, but another voice in the wail of woe roused Thur to action quicker than anything else.

"Help me to strip him, he will be better without this confinement of clothes, and then to bed with him. Sleep and quiet alone will restore exhausted nature."

Obeying with hands that were far from steady, Jan revolved in his mind the terrifying events of the last hours.

"Never again!" he exclaimed with an involuntary shudder. "There must be some other way. I know not what to do, Thur. Counsel me! Shall I abandon my purpose? Shall we remain small farmers until he is older, when we can ride together to the wars, or join ourselves to some powerful baron?"

Thur considered his answer in silence.

"We have learned nothing by this awful rite," Jan pursued.

"Nothing, say you? Why, we have succeeded beyond all my fondest hope. Reach me that cloak yonder."

Jan obeyed, and together they wrapped the now naked Olaf in the fur-lined mantle and between them carried him out through the back door and up the spiral staircase to the chamber above, which Thur used as his sleeping quarters. There they l:lid him on a rough truckle bedstead which held a straw-stuffed mattress, then covering him with a coarse blanket, both stood watching him intently and anxiously.

Presently, as though aware of their regard, Olaf opened his eyes, and smiled with a faint reassurance.

"I shall do very well now," he murmured drowsily, "I shall sleep."

"And when he is himself again, we three shall seek the Witch of

Wanda before we pronounce upon our future course," Thur whispered to Jan." *That* is my advice to you, lad !"

# CHAPTER III
## SEEKING A WITCH

TWO miles outside the town on the next morning Jan and Olaf were awaiting Thur. Slipping out while it was still dark, swimming the encircling ditch, they thus avoided the danger of passing the guard at the gate. Because of their resemblance to their dead father it was ever Jan's fear that somebody would note the likeness, and while he knew that no townsman would betray them willingly, yet the countryman's love of gossip constituted an ever-present danger. If they were recognised, word would, sooner or later, get to Fitz-Urse, resulting in a search and a trumped-up charge, and they would both be hung as outlaws. So, in the first Bushings of a May dawn, they sat among the bushes by the wayside, basking in a feeble and watery dawn sun. The icy blasts that had recently harried the land were gone, but not until nine of the clock did it get really warm.

"This be a proper day for spring," said Olaf, sprawling at full length. He was still pale and drawn from his recent experience. Jan agreed:

"Aye, it has been a long and weary winter. I thought it would never pass. How I hate the churlish drudgery of our lives!"

"Yet we are better off than some."

"True, but that does not make our lot any easier. We were born to better things."

"That is the question," laughed Olaf. "Our mother was but a farmer's daughter, and father a wandering soldier."

"Our grandfather was Sir Edgar, knighted by King Henry's own hands, and we were lords of lands throughout the ages before that. All was well until the accursed Fitz-Urse spoiled us."

Olaf sighed. It was a pity to ruin a fine May morning by such dismal recollections. For his part, he deemed the past better forgotten since there seemed to be no immediate remedy.

"It was the fortunes of war," he commented soothingly.

"War!" Jan hissed, in suppressed fury. "It was a foul and bloody murder, for which I will be avenged before I die."

"With God's help, brother."

"If He has forgotten us, then I will seek other aid."

"This wild and reckless talk is more likely to seal our doom than to advance our fortunes. Where is Thur? He should be here by now."

"I can hear the beat of hooves some way off. This must mean that he is near."

"This witch we seek. Can she help?"

"That is a question for Thur. He has something on his mind; I am not his keeper."

"That was an awesome happening, Jan. I mean that dastardly crawling fear which seemed to smother and crush the life out of me, as if I were caught in some vast serpent's coils. I tremble to think how near I came to yielding my spirit to it. I can remember nothing but that, and how nearly I failed you both."

"Forget it, lad," Jan urged. "I shall never cease to blame myself for letting you do it. Your courage was amazing, and earned all my gratitude, but the fault was mine." A speech which caused Olaf to give a little smirk of satisfaction. He pulled a grass stem and began to chew it.

"I did it of my own will and you could not stay me. Yet, ere we commit ourselves we should know a little more of what is in Thur's mind. Witches are kittle-cattle folk to consort with."

"Do you question him then? Your achievement gives you the right, but for my part I do not doubt him."

"Nor I. He was our father's friend, and that is good enough for me, but I like not to walk in the dark"

Jan turned to look at Olaf as he lay on the grass. Certainly he seemed aged and more thoughtfully inclined since his experience. He hoped fervently that no harm had been done to the boy's mind, but at that moment Thur came swinging round the bend of the road and drew up beside them.

"I was hindered…"

"By what of all misadventures?"

Thur laughed. "By a man with the face-ache! So I yanked out his tooth and dispatched him, yawling like a wolf with the belly-ache! Then I had to arrange it with young Tom Snooks to physic any sick while I was absent. I told him I was called to my young brother who was ill."

"I was afraid that some of those pestilent brothers had come smelling round again," laughed Jan. "Well, to our saddles. We have a long journey before us!"

They started off in something akin to holiday mood. Their horses were healthy, stout animals and the party had equipped themselves with all needful for a long journey, since they did not know how long they might be on the road. Though the day was hot they carried heavy cloaks rolled and strapped to their saddles, bread, cheese, and ample meat pasty, and beer in a leathern bottle which swung at Thur's knee. Jan and Thur were well clothed in good russet cloth, with jerkins and boots of soft leather, while Olaf, beneath his jerkin, was clad in Lincoln green. In the matter of hoods they had rather let themselves go, Olaf's being of the same green as his clothes and faced with scarlet, which accentuated the clear bright-ness of his skin and yellow curling hair. Jan's hood was of match-less Virgin blue, a present from his mother on his last birthday, in the hope that it would turn his mind from thoughts of ambition and make it soar heavenward. Thur's hood was of more sober hue, and in the same shade as his red-brown suiting, but· despite the glory of these hoods, the warmth of the weather caused them to be pushed back and the men rode bareheaded. Each was armed with a strong sword and dagger, for in these troubled times of King John's reign no man dared ride unarmed. So they rode in the bright May sunshine over the rolling country of the cleared lands, where here and there a coppice smudged the sky-line with purple and left screens to protect crops against bitter prevailing winds. It was not long ere they reached the end of cultivation, and neared the great forest which at that time sprawled closely over that part of England. A broad grass track ran northward between the overhanging branches of mighty trees, while away to the right the river wound its way to the sea, which lay about forty miles east.

Oxlip and violet, hyacinth and anemone bespangled the sward, and the murmur of ring-doves made music in which the whirr of a startled pheasant was the only reminder of man's menace to wild creatures in all that fragrant place.

So thought Olaf, as his alert eyes lost nothing of his surroundings. They were silent, as is the habit of most men in forest-lands, for to the average mind there is a sombre and unfriendly atmosphere in the neighbourhood of dwarfing trees where Nature runs riot both openly and covertly in her hostility towards mankind, and soberness, if not actually melancholy, is apt to descend upon the wayfarer when he feels that he is an intruder in secret places. Each man was pre-occupied with his own thoughts. Thur with his unexpected success in magic … he was a man given much to mental pursuits, of a thoughtful and analytical turn of mind, who conscientiously performed his duty and did his utmost to relieve suffering as a good physician should. But noW a door had opened to him which had hitherto been closed, and through that door he could enter into such an exercise of power that the mere thought of it filled him with an internal excitement such as he had never known before. This power stretched before him in a series of intoxicating vistas. He was like a connoisseur, savouring it expertly and delicately. Yet Thur was not an introvert, and his mood soon switched to his silent companions.

How great was the difference between the two brothers. Jan was sunk in dreams of self-aggrandisement, possessed by desires not to carve out a great future for himself, but to snatch fortune from the remote past that would raise him to a position he had in no way earned. These ungratified wishes paralysed his mind to all but their own insistence, robbing him of all initiative. Loving Jan as a son, Thur felt he could not rest until he had done his utmost to help the boy achieve this almost impossible thing, so that Jan might be rid of his incubus and so freed to pursue the healthy vigour of his natural life.

As for Jan...his head was in a whirl of questioning. Who was this witch? Would they find her? What good would she be to them? What had Thur in his mind? Was there anything but a wild fantasy in their experiences? These thoughts chased themselves round his head like squirrels in a cage.

And Olaf, so alive to everything around him, wished that Jan could forget his grandfather for a space and all he did or did not represent, and so give his mind to this joyous May day. Truly it was the only time when woods were gay and filled with dappled sunlight, and the knots of bronze springing from the chestnut branches were better far than witches. Clusters of pink-flushed petals backed with green against the bleached austerity of ancient apple trunks were something a man might look at while living and remember when dying.

Olaf would have liked to have been able to transfer the beauty on parchment, as did Brother Jerome up at the Abbey, only Jerome thought such things were sinful, although he loved them, and so would portray only a little view of them through a window, while he portrayed the black and white robes of the monks. For a while Olaf pondered the possibility of learning to do all this from Jerome, but rejected the scheme upon reflection that in exchange he must give up freedom to roam at will.

Jan broke the silence with:

"This witch. Do you think we will ever find her?"

"I have been asking myself that question until I am weary," Thur shrugged, "but at least we can look for her."

"And what then?" demanded Olaf.

"I don't know," said Thur. "All depends on what we find, but before we doubt I think we must obey the message we received."

"That seems reasonable enough."

"All wonder is idle and beside the mark," Jan sighed.

"Take heart, Jan!" Thur advised cheerily.

"There may be great things before us, and Hope is the best of companions."

"You do well to advise me of that," replied Jan, making an effort to shake off his gloom. "I must sound an ungrateful dog, but you know I am not. Truth is, I can bear my present life no longer, and if this fails, or leads nowhere, I shall go to London and seek service with some powerful lord. A stout man-at-arms need never starve."

Olaf was silent. This was a threat he had heard too often to be impressed by it, and Thur smiled.

"Be patient, lad, I feel sure that our errand will not be in vain," and at the conclusion of his words another silence fell as their horses carried them ever deeper into the forest. They stopped to eat their midday meal under the boughs of a wild cherry tree which grew upon the banks of a river tributary which crossed their path at this point. A flat bridge spanned the stream. It was but two great slabs of granite laid across the water, and this structure aroused Thur's curiosity.

"'Tis a marvel to me how these stones came to be here," he said.

"The spirits must have dragged them straight from Hell itself," chaffed Olaf. "I am for a swim in the pool yonder. Come, Thur, 'twill wash away the cobwebs."

They all stripped and plunged in, and half an hour later lay on the bank drying their bodies under the sun. Then, while Olaf watered the horses and replaced their bits, the other two packed the food, and presently they resumed their journey.

"Thur," said Olaf, after a pause, "do you believe this tale of witches, how they dance round the Devil on a black Sabbath?"

"Aye, I believe what I have seen!"

"Surely you haven't *seen* it?"

"I have that, and danced with the best of them."

"Thur, you dared not!" gasped Olaf, gazing at him with awe and wonder, while Jan gaped fearfully.

"Indeed I dared, when I was a student at Cordoba. We were studying Magic under the very learned Doctor Henriques Menisis da Mendosa. I will tell you more of him another time. My friends and I wished to put our studies into practice, but we lacked the instruments and the means to make them. Our master, Doctor Henriques, hadn't the instruments either, as he taught only theory ... "

"Much as a farmer without a spade or plough," interrupted Olaf.

"Even so. We needed the witch's Athame to fashion our tools, so we went to the Sabbath to try to borrow one ... The gathering was held in a secret place, a different one being used each time. We were sworn to secrecy and conducted there blindfold by a masked guide. When we drew near we were bidden to put our staves between our legs and to ride them like hobby-horses, and so on to the dancing ground."

"Why this ?" asked Jan.

"Because their god, whom they call Janicot, is the god of all crops and cattle, and the god of Fertility, demanding that all perform this act of worship before him. Women oft use a broomstick because it is the handiest, though any pole will serve, even an axe-handle or stick at a pinch."

"'Tis simple," breathed Jan, while Thur laughed outright.

"What happened ?" Jan prompted.

"We looked on, keeping together, for our minds were uneasy. There was a rock, or other great stone set up as an altar on which sat the chief priest of Janicot, clad in a hairy skin. He wore a mask, horned, and a lighted torch was set between the horns. Naked children were brought to him and initiated, then knelt before him to do him homage. He blessed them and gave them the Freedom of the Brotherhood."

"Did they kiss his tail ?" asked Olaf eagerly.

Thur seemed slightly annoyed. "Nay, how could they ? He was *sitting* on it, and even a witch may not kiss through solid stone. 'Tis all a silly fable invented by the Church !

"Then followed some rites which we could not see, since they love not strangers who are not initiated, and kept us at a distance. After these rites, which I would have given much to see, we sat on the ground feasting on what we had brought. Much wine was passed around and there was great talk and a singing of songs in a strange tongue of whose origin we knew not ... the ancient tongue of the witches. Great fires had been lighted, and by their flames when we had feasted and sung for some time we danced naked, some in pairs, some back to back, others in a great ring round the fires. There was much love-making and the dancing grew ever more wild and furious."

"How did it all end?" Jan asked, eyeing Thur with great respect as the hero of this amazing adventure.

"I never could remember ... then ... or at any other time, but it was good while it lasted and we all slumbered soundly in class the next day. I well remember that."

"Did you go again?" whispered Olaf.

"A mere twice or thrice, but there was much danger, the risk of torture and the stake if we were caught, and as we could not come by what we sought, we went no more."

"I knew not that Magic was taught in schools," said Jan after a pause, in which he tried unsuccessfully to digest Thur's amazing experience.

"Nor I," cut in Olaf, assuming more and more the manner of a man full grown. "Does Holy Church permit such things? It seems strangely at variance with her teaching."

Thur laughed: "Yet the answer to that is simple. Art Magic can only be performed by the learned, and learning is centred only in the Church. Brother Stephen ..." He stopped.

"What of Brother Stephen?" prompted Olaf. "He has but newly come' to the Abbey."

"Even so. Brother Thomas tells me that he has been made Clerk to my Lord Abbot, who thinks highly of his learning. It seems he set up a school of Theology in Paris but had little or no following.

He is a native of Lincoln, and returned to visit his home. Little is known about him."

"Then Brother Thomas will invent much," commented Jan. "I liked the man."

"He has a way with him," Thur agreed. "And unless I mistake, we shall see more of him ... much more."

Both lads gave a startled look.

"Does he suspect us?"

"Nay, Jan, he *knows*."

"Do you fear him, Thur?"

The elder gave that hearty, reassuring laugh of his which warmed and cheered all who heard it.

"Not I! The more I know and can impart to Master Stephen the safer I, and all connected with me, will be. Be civil to Stephen, Jan, for he is a man to be reckoned with, even though he be but the Abbot's clerk in an obscure monastery. He may rise to great dignity, for he has many gifts. He showed me his horoscope; he will go far."

Jan pondered this with some discontent. He did not like Thur to praise so well or to speak with such warm approval of another, and especially when that other was a priest. Thur was aware of his discomfiture and eyed him with amused tolerance, but to aid the lad he spoke of other things, and in desultory talk they came out of the forest and into the open country. It was now evening. The flaming crimson of the sky gave promise of the fine weather continuing.

On a bend of the road before them stood a two-storied house built of stone and mortared rubble, surrounded by a huddle of thatched mud hovels. To its gable was attached a bunch of alder, that being the only tree in leaf hereabouts, and from this sign they knew that the house was an inn. They decided to spend the night within its walls, and there to make discreet inquiries as to their proposed destination. They drew rein at the door. A shockheaded youth opened the door. The accommodation afforded by the inn was simple to the verge of starkness, as they had expected. The youth who had opened the door gave vent to a yell of "Father!" rather as avenging some real or fancied slight than summoning assistance, and led off their horses to a big shed containing some dozen stalls. Olaf followed to see that the beasts were properly fed and watered. Thur and Jan accosted the landlord, who appeared in the doorway at his son's summoning yell.

"Good even, sirs," he said hastily, tucking a clean towel which had been draped round his middle into his belt. "Welcome, sirs, supper is ready."

"And smells excellent, friend," Thur assured him, while Jan looked palpably cheered, and occupied himself with looking around.

The interior of the inn consisted of one large room, furnished with stools, and boards on trestles. In the centre of the room was a circular place of stone, on which was a glowing fire, above which was suspended a huge black pot. A woman was busy here with a sheet of iron which she had rigged up with two stones over part of the large fire, and on which some cakes of bread were baking. She turned them with a long-handled two-pronged fork-like instrument, her face red and sweating with the heat, but good humoured enough as she greeted them.

The woman was an inspired cook and her stew had a savouriness. Thur quickly established good relations with host and hostess by his enthusiastic praise and excellent appetite, while Jan and Olaf seconded his every plaudit.

It chanced that they were the only travellers, but as twilight fell the labourers from the fields dropped in for beer and a gossip before going to bed with the darkness.

"What call you this hamlet, friend?" Thur asked, addressing no one in particular. A chorus answered him:

"Eyeford."

"Eyeford," he repeated ruminatingly. "Now where have I heard that name before?"

"Nowhere, I should say, Master," the landlord grinned. "We be stuck in the woods hereabouts, and no man knows aught of us."

"Yet I have heard it." Thur shook his head.

"No, 'tis gone. Wait, I have it! Brother John spoke of it ... he was talking of Wanda."

"Wanda! 'Tis more dead and alive than this ... a wild spot on the shore of the great mere, eastward."

"Aye," said Thur indifferently. "How far to the city? Are we on the right road? We would see the great cathedral a-building when we have done our business. Come, we must to bed ... the lad already sleeps and we have travelled far."

"Where from, Master?" the landlord ventured.

"St. Albans," Thur told him. "We go to buy madder in the city." They roused Olaf, and were conducted to the sleeping chamber above, a large room furnished with rough truckle beds in rows, on which were straw-stuffed mattresses and coarse blankets. After their long ride the beds looked inviting, and they stripped off their clothes, stretching at ease until sleep overtook them.

# CHAPTER IV
# THE WITCH

HEY lost their way and found it, lost it again and wandered far through fertile corn-lands and fields of mustard and madder. In the late afternoon they came to the shores of the mere. It stretched as far as they could see in that flat country, its waters blue as the sky above, glinting in the sunlight, its verge fringed with deep beds of osier, purple and delicate green in their spring dress. The silence was immense, a profound silence brooded over all, such as they had never before experienced.

"This is the mere, undoubtedly," said Olaf.

"Maybe. But what now? Do we swim?" asked Thur.

Olaf pointed to the left. They followed the direction he indicated and saw a narrow track between two sheets of water, and upon this they had no choice but to venture. Finding it firm to the tread they went on with greater confidence until they had crossed the mere and reached the fields on the farthest side.

"So far so good ... but where is Wanda?" Thur demanded, looking round. A rough track lay ahead which seemed to run into a group of willows. Olaf suggested that they should ride forward, and he would climb into the boughs of the tallest and reconnoitre from there. This done, he reported that there was a cluster of hovels two fields ahead, into which the track led, and more water beyond.

"We can but ride on," said Thur.

A few more minutes riding brought them to the hovels, where their appearance excited much curiosity. The people were wild-looking, and poverty had bitten deeply into their miserable lives. They were ragged and half-starved, and stood staring through their matted hair, or peered through the holes of the huts which served as windows. They seemed as fearful of strangers as they were savage. One hut ... a little larger than the rest proclaimed itself an inn by a bunch of leaves hanging over the door, and there they drew up, dismounted and went indoors, glad to get away from the people outside. The landlord sullenly lurched forward and stood waiting without speaking. Thur ordered beer, explaining that they had lost their way, that they were strangers in these parts and were going to the city on business.

Beer was brought and thumped down before them as they sat at the rude table.

"May we reach the city this way, or must we go back and take another road?" asked Thur civilly.

"Aye, follow the track. It joins the road two miles away."

"What is the name of your hamlet, friend?" Thur asked again.

"Wanda, Master," was the brief response.

Thur studied the man as he drank his beer. His extreme taciturnity seemed to be the result of some oppression of the mind rather than a disinclination to talk. He could barely swing his mind from what was troubling him to carry out his duties. After several attempts to draw him into talk and extract some information from him had failed, and a dismal silence had fallen, Jan's desperation drove him to what proved to be a brilliant stroke of intuition.

"And where is the good wife?" he asked.

"Dead," the man grunted. "This five years gone."

"Oh."

Thur, however, had seen a gleam of intelligence in the man's eye, what might be termed a lifting of the veil which obscured him mentally and morally, and he swiftly pursued the glimmer.

"Hast never thought to take another ... a lusty man of your youth," he insinuated.

"'Tis clear against human nature," his host declared.

"What? To take another wife?"

"Nay, Master, to live alone."

"Well, your remedy is not far to seek."

"But she will not all alone ... away from every living soul 'tis against nature now, ain't it, sir?"

At this juncture Olaf rose and went out.

"Why, is she a witch?" Thur jested, while Jan watched him wide-eyed with admiration for his adroitness.

The host jumped, spat disgustedly, and crossed himself.

"The Good God forbid," was his fervent plea. "Speak not of such abominations, Master."

"I did but jest, man," Thur apologised, but the track of his host's mind could not be switched.

"What may folk do? No holy priest comes near us from year's end to year's end. How can it but grow and fester?"

"What?" asked Thur coolly.

"Witchcraft!" again he spat and crossed himself. "Yet only yesterday did come a priest. He spoke to the people of the sin of witches, and said he would come again."

Thur could make neither head or tail of this
jumble, and he tried another shot at a venture.

"Well, won't she have you?"

"No. 'Tis clear against nature."

"Ask again, man."

"Seven times have I asked."

"You know what the blessed Scripture says "Until seventy times seven," said Thur flippantly.

"Seventy times seven ... seventy times seven," repeated the host. "'Tis clear unnatural. Huh!" And with this dismal grunt he lapsed again into gloom like a quenched spark. Meanwhile Olaf was lounging outside the closed door, looking around him. A young girl and a smaller child were playing in a pool of muddy water, floating chips of bark on it. He crossed over to them and sank on his haunches beside the tiny craft. Presently the girl peered at him sideways from under her tangled hair, noting his bright curls and smart clothes. Olaf puffed out his cheeks and blew strongly, ruffling the water into tiny waves. The little barque rocked and the child screamed with delight, clapping her hands, while the girl smiled.

"I will show you a better," Olaf offered. "Fetch me a twig and a leaf." The child scampered away, returning with a leafy branch which she had torn from a neighbouring bush. Olaf broke off a twig, fixed a leaf to it by spearing it on in two places and deftly fitted the twig into the chip with the point of his dagger. He then replaced it on the water, a little ship with sail and mast.

"Oh, oh," said the child, in ecstasy, and again the girl smiled, but seemed too shy to speak. Olaf searched his mind for something to loosen her tongue, and bethought himself of two cakes of bread given him that morning by the hostess of the inn. He drew them forth and saw with pity the avidity in the eyes of his companions. Silently he bestowed them and watched them eat.

"There is an old woman in our village at home. She hath a black cat and rides on a broomstick. Men say she is a witch. When she comes into the street we all cry: 'Witch! Witch!' and when our elders be not by we throw stones at her."

The last vestige of bread was devoured, but the girl had found her tongue, reticence overpowered by this fascinating subject, and as the child returned to her boat she volunteered:

"We have a witch too, at least, the women say she is, but the men will not hear of it."

"Is she old?" said Olaf, goggling his eyes.

"Not so very old ... not more than a hundred years. She lives in the hut by the water, a bow-shot away yonder, and she is an out-lander. Her husband brought her hither three years since, but he died in two weeks and she lives there alone."

"Is she in truth a witch?"

The girl shrugged, her eyes never straying from his face.

"Maybe. The women hate her."

"Do you?"

"No. She is kind, and heals the sick. Some men have asked her many times, but she will not. John Landlord would marry her, but she will not."

"Has she killed aught?"

"O, only her husband."

She went on to tell him how a priest had come among them the day before questioning them narrowly whether there was a witch in the place, and he told the people how sinful it was to have witch-craft, and that witches should be given up to be burned. The men had stoutly denied the existence of a witch, telling the priest that there were plenty in the next village.

"And are there?" Olaf asked, breathlessly.

"Nay, I know not. Vada is the woman's name. She does no harm, but the women say she hath bewitched the men, and call her worse than witch. I know not."

Olaf learned further ... that the priest had gone his way, dissatisfied by his inquiry, and had promised to come again shortly. At this juncture a tousled head was thrust from one of the huts, and a voice shrieked: "Maud!"

The girl started. "My mother calls," and seizing the child by the hand she snatched her up and bore her off protesting, but with the little boat clasped tightly. Olaf laughed and waved to them until they disappeared into their wretched home.

"Poor mites," he said aloud, then, dismissing a train of thought which distressed him, swung round and re-entered the inn. Thur looked up as he entered, and seeing by the significant smile (not to call it a smirk which Olaf habitually displayed when, all went well with him), that he had the information they needed, rose instantly and finished his beer standing.

"Come, Jan, it grows late."

He paid the score and some over, but even the sight of coin did not cheer their host.

"The way to the city, friend?"

"Follow the track to the left, my masters, a matter of eight miles over the fields."

"Many thanks, friend, and good luck attend you. Remember ... "

"Aye, seventy times seven. 'Tis a powerful many ... more than a man may count. Clear against nature." And still grunting and shaking his head he closed the door on them.

"Never saw I a man more crossed in love," said Thur, compassionately, then turning sharply to Olaf.

"Well, lad ?"

"She dwells in yonder hut beside the water."

"Art sure ?"

"Without a doubt 'tis she, and the woman who has our host's heart, to boot."

"I supposed as much, but could get nothing from the fellow. Well done, Olaf."

They mounted, and turned their horses back upon the track, whereupon the landlord re-appeared in a great flurry.

"Not that way, masters! To the left ... the left ... you go back upon your tracks."

Thur turned and waved re-assuringly, calling:

"We go first to view the waterside, friend," and the landlord drooped once more. As they rode the short distance, Olaf told of his encounter with the children and what they had revealed.

"You are right, of a certainty, but I mislike this story of the visiting priest. We have no time to lose. The pestilent fellow may be back at any time and he will not come alone. A witch-hunt looms too near to be pleasant."

They soon reached the hut, a wretched cabin built of flints and mudmortar, set by the mereside in the midst of a patch of cleared land. A woman was digging the patch with a wooden spade. She was thin and active in body, but wasted, and when she raised her head they saw a gaunt face which might have been any age beyond forty, having that transparency of skin born either of long illness or of semi-starvation. She looked at them with great amber eyes, set in cavernous sockets deeply marked and shadowed beneath. Her eyelashes were thick, long and silky, and of a luxuriant growth that was almost repulsive on that stricken face, though the brows above were thin and delicately arched upon the stark, hollowed front of her skull.

Her hair was strained back and confined in a snood, so that not a tendril escaped. Her body was pliant and her movements graceful under her coarse single garment of what looked like sacking. Her feet were bare, white, and beautifully proportioned as they pressed the dark earth, but oh, the woman was thin beyond everything the men had ever before seen.

Such was she whom they had sought so arduously, an object of compassion, which grew in their heart as they looked at her. The enormous eyes grew even larger with some hidden fear. She was so different from what they had expected to find that they were dumb for a moment. Thur marvelled, his mind in a whirl of conjecture. What had been the object of his injunction to seek this woman? Had he been made the sport of some devilish sprite?

"You miss your way, sirs. This leads nowhere. Go! Go back two bow-shots."

The voice, though strained with anxiety was musical, and had elements of even greater beauty.

Thur pulled himself together smartly, clearing his mind (with an effort) of all but the matter in hand, but Jan and Olaf still stared incredulously.

"Good morrow, Mistress," said Thur, with gentle courtesy. "With your permission we would speak with you, indeed, we have ridden far to find you."

"Sir, I shun strangers," she answered, leaning on her spade, her eyes searching each face in turn. "I thank you," she added.

"Your name is Vada?" Olaf asked, remembering what the girl had called her. The woman's mouth was so bloodless that the lips were almost invisible, but such as they were they parted in a shadowy smile, revealing small, white teeth.

"Yes, my fine youth. What then?"

"We would ask your help, Vada," said Thur.

"Help?" she echoed. "What help can such as I give such as you?" and her eyes roved shrewdly over their good clothes, and then sank involuntarily to her own bare feet.

"Mistress! Know you, 'a Tolado?' "

"Tolado?" she echoed curiously. "That is in foreign lands. Master, I have never been in them."

"But mayhap you have knowledge of them?" Thur pursued: "*Ab Hur, Ab Hus.*"

"Oh, what do you speak?" she gasped, drawing back a step and looking huntedly over her shoulder. "I have no knowledge of foreign tongues."

"Yet I think you *have* a knowledge. *Emen Hetem.*"

"I know not. I KNOW NOT!" she groaned. "Go, sirs, go your way. I cannot help you. I cannot help myself, even." Her tone was desperate in its fear. "You know not these people. They spy and talk. You have done me ill by coming here, my life was bitter enough. I dare not.... "

"Nay, nay, poor soul. We mean you no harm," Thur interposed soothingly. "We wish you well, indeed we do."

But she seemed almost distraught. "You know not what my life is." Her voice was hard, and dry with tension. "I dare not even own a broom, but must sweep my cot with a branch. For ever they peep and mutter. How can I help others who cannot help myself?"

"Dear Mistress, calm yourself. Listen, I beg. We would have you come with us. I am an ageing man, a leech in a far-distant town. I have a good house and maid-servant. Come with me and live there in all honour. I need one like you to grow my herbs and tend my garden, to help me prepare my simples and potions. You are skilled in such work?"

She nodded, soothed by his gentle tone, her mind arrested in spite of its torment. Olaf, who alone had remained mounted, now leaned from his saddle.

"Hasten! I see men mustering ... armed with bows ... some with bills," and though he spoke low, Vada heard.

"Go! Go!" she screamed. "See what harm ye have done me already."

Thur laid a firm hand on her arm.

"Quiet, Mistress. 'Tis not we who harm you, that was done last even when they came witch-smelling. They have come back for you. Hasten, you cannot stay here, or if you do you perish. Come with us to safety and comfort. Put your faith in me and I will never fail you."

There was so much of conviction in his tone that again she was arrested. She pointed to Jan, who had remained silent.

"Does he help you?"

"Nay, Mistress, *he* helps me and I pray you to help me also," Jan answered. Here Olaf thrust in again.

"The crowd is leaving the green and coming hither. Some have torches."

"Decide now!" urged Thur. *"On Thebal. Gut Gutini!"*

"Come, Mistress, is there aught you need in the cot? If not, swift!" Jan swung to the saddle. "Put your foot on my boot and mount before me!"

"They are coming in good earnest," Olaf warned. "Thur, hasten for the love of God."

"Mistress, Mistress, you seal your doom by this delay. Think what it will be!" cried Thur.

Suddenly Vada seized the spade, rushed to a corner of her garden and started to dig frantically. The ground had hardened in the late bitter winds, and the spade was clumsy. Thur ran to her.

"Come," he cried, "I will buy all you need."

"My mother's two knives!" she gasped.

In a flash Thur understood. The next moment his sword was in his hand and he was beside her, digging with it.

"One has a white handle and the other a black?"

She nodded. Between them they unearthed a rough box made of a split log of wood. Inside were the white and black handled knives for which Thur had sought during the past twenty-five years. They were wrapped in fresh white cloth, and Vada clutched them to her breast. Thur put up his sword, took her by the hand and, seizing her round the waist, swung her up in front of Jan, then sprang to his own saddle.

"Which way?" said Jan, in Vada's ear.

"You lead, Jan," cried Thur. "Bend low!"

"Straight ahead. Follow the shore," she directed.

Many voices yelled to them to stop. Two arrows whizzed overhead as the excited horses sprang into a mad gallop, but they had rested well, and were mettlesome. Fortunately too only two of the men had their bows strung. Two more arrows hissed ... one sticking in the back of Jan's saddle, the other just missing Olaf's thigh. It took half a minute for those who had bows to string them, then came the vicious whirr ... whirr ... kaplock ... kaplock of arrows, followed by the deeper whizz of a cross-bow bolt. With their heads almost touching the horses' necks they galloped on. Jan was in the greatest danger since he had Vada before him and their pursuers singled him out for their target. The rain of arrows was continuous, but they escaped a hit by the miracle of bad shooting ... or was it that most of the archers wanted to miss?

Then they came to that part of the mere which bent round before them, cutting them off. Thur groaned in dismay, Olaf whistled, Jan gritted his teeth.

"Straight through the reeds," gasped Vada. "'Tis but shallow, and safe." Jan plunged in recklessly. His horse sank over his girths in water, but found his legs, and recovering, staggered on, followed by the others. The reeds now impeded and slowed down their progress, and they had to force a way through while arrows whizzed overhead in an ugly way. Jan had the nervous feeling that a bad marksman might be a more deadly danger than a good one, but soon they were beyond the reeds and though the water was deeper, forcing the horses to swim, yet the osiers formed a screen for which they were thankful. The baffled pursuers stood on the shore~ yelling fury, death and damnation at their escaping quarry.

By now the party were out of range, the water was getting shallower and the shore lay only a quarter of a mile ahead, fringed by another osier belt. This last quarter of a mile presented no great difficulties, and soon the horses were wading ashore. As they landed

Thur turned to look back, and saw with satisfaction that he could no longer see the group on the shore. Wet and uncomfortable, but safe, they rode abreast. Vada pointed ahead.

"Across two fields and we are on the road to the city."

"Now, Mistress, how is it with us? We depend upon you for our guidance," said Thur.

"When we reach the road we shall be four miles ahead of the point where the other track joins it. They will follow because they know no other way lies open to us, but since they have no horses, they must needs return and take up the other track."

"Good. We have the advantage of four miles then. How far to the city?"

"A matter of eight miles."

"To go through the city in this trim would raise talk," said Jan.

"'Tis not to be thought of," said Vada hastily. "You all wet, with a beggar-maid before you drenched and barefoot. We should be held for questioning."

"The wench is right," said Thur. "What can we do, Vada? Know you the country?"

"As much as I can walk. A mile from the city is a road leading westward. We must ride far and fast until we come again to the forest. Where that is I know not ... and we must travel by night."

"Plague take this flat country!" Thur exclaimed. "I should not fear the men of Wanda, but there were two monks among them, and they will not drop this witch-hunt until they have secured some victim," Olaf informed them glumly.

"Monks, say you?" asked Thur, frowning in consternation. "That indeed puts another complexion on the affair. They will rouse the country against us and spread the tale from point to point ... and get help from every religious house."

"But as yet they are on foot and four miles behind us," said Jan, trying to draw comfort from this fact.

"Aye, but they are hunters, and can keep a steady pace," Vada told them bitterly.

At this Jan hastily turned his horse towards the broad grass verge of the road, and along this they fled at full stretch. The city lay before them, a fair and gracious sight in the evening light. Thur pointed to a group of poplars growing a hundred yards down the road to their left.

"You three take shelter beneath those trees until I come to you. There you will be well hidden. I go into the city to buy food and drink and a man's dress for Vada, here. If I return not in an hour, ride on without me. Olaf! You dismount, and let Jan take your horse while you hide in a ditch and keep watch for those oncoming louts, but I think 'they cannot come up in less than an hour and a half. They have exhausted themselves with too much bad shooting and running about and yelling."

"Thur, let me go," Jan entreated.

"Nay, I am inconspicuous, and have more experience."

So saying, he rapidly made off, while Olaf sought a safe place to spy from, and Jan and Vada rode slowly to the poplars, leading Olaf's horse. There they dismounted and sat beneath the trees, with their backs against a fallen trunk. Silence fell between them, and Jan sought for something to talk about in vain. He feared that Vada would resent his silence, but the more agitated he grew, the further speech fled from him, until a little sigh caused him to turn, and he saw that Vada had fallen asleep. Even in her slumber the lines of privation and suffering were not erased, and he averted his eyes because the sight was not a pleasing one, and the little starts and groans she gave afflicted his ear. He was thankful when Thur relieved his vigil, riding towards them with Olaf running at his stirrup. Vada was gently roused:

"You have not been gone an hour, Thur," said Jan and noted that Thur was in high spirits, and had secured a fourth horse, which he led by the bridle and upon which his purchases were packed.

He threw a bundle at Vada's feet.

"Here, Mistress, get behind the bushes and don this gear. Aye, there is no quicker man at a purchase than I in all England!"

When Vada had vanished, Thur began to transfer his belongings to the new horse. "Poor Nan has had no rest," he observed, "and she can do with a lighter weight than mine. This mare is fresh and hearty and I have taken a fancy to her."

"Where in fortune did you come by her?" queried Olaf.

"By a stroke of luck there was a horse-fair holding within five minutes' walk of the gate. 'Tis better to be born lucky than rich ... who comes here?"

A trim figure clad in russet-brown approached them, .still clasping two knives to its breast.

"Those knives are our most precious possession, Vada, since we can do nothing without them," Thur said gravely. "Yet, they are most dangerous to you, and if found in your possession would seal your doom. Will you trust them to me?"

"I will indeed," she answered readily.

Thur took them, still wrapped in the white cloth, and bade Olaf unstrap his cloak from the saddle. When this was done he wrapped the knives within its folds and fastened it securely back in place.

"Thank you, Vada. Your faith is not misplaced. Now, you, Olaf, hearken, and obey without question. I give these knives into your charge to be brought safely to my house and there restored to Vada. It is a solemn charge, lad, and if we are pursued, you must make good your escape, and hide them safely. Only after that must you return to see if you can aid us. These knives have marks on hilt and blade that shout Magic to all who look, and 'twill be the stake for us all if they are found on us. Without them, we may pass as peaceful travellers. It is, therefore, your duty not to let that evidence fall into their hands, but bring the blades safely to my house. You will do this faithfully?"

"As God is my witness," replied Olaf solemnly. "Good. We have wasted much precious time. Let us be gone. There are yet two good hours to nightfall."

They mounted, and were about to ride from beneath the poplars when a sound of voices raised in dispute came from the road. Waiting, they saw a tattered and foot-weary mob scuffling along in the dusk, and two monks in the midst of them, walking each side of landlord John, whom they seemed to have in custody.

"There they go," breathed Thur. "What luck we had not ridden out." The landlord appeared to be reluctant, and the monks had some difficulty in urging him along. This was the cause of their acrimonious urgings to proclaim himself a good son of Holy Church by aiding her to slay most barbarously the woman he loved. By his mutinous obstinacy he was delaying the whole procession and centring all attention upon himself. Perhaps he was not such a fool as he looked, John Landlord.

"Oh, the poor wretch! What will they do to him?" whispered Vada, wringing her hands.

"Very little," chuckled Thur softly, "I defy the Pope himself and all the Assembly of Cardinals to extract a word of sense from him."

"I found him not so."

"Oh, you have a power which His Holiness lacks," grinned Thur, and they stood silently, watching the procession pass with never a glance in the direction where they were concealed.

Thur unfastened his cloak and flung it to Olaf.

"Muffle it over your head and hide that green garb of yours," he commanded, and as Olaf obeyed Jan hastily removed his blue hood. Then, cautiously they emerged from their shelter, and cantered for half a mile. None pursued, and taking to the crown of the road they stretched into the hardest gallop their horses could take.

# CHAPTER V
## MOON'S AID

HEY rode through the night, stopping neither to rest nor eat until dawn was breaking. The moon was two days past its full, and never before had Thur appreciated how important it was for the "second luminary" to be favourably aspected in a natal horoscope. With the happy knowledge that it was so aspected in his own, he looked to the silver lady to aid him in this most dire extremity.

Nor did she fail him. She rose clear, and shone with splendour, and, if she appeared later every night, she was but restricted by an immutable law and at least her punctuality was unhindered by cloud. She guided them off the road, down grass tracks, over fields and through belts of May woodland where her light could penetrate the swinging branches as it could not have done a month later when the foliage would be heavier. Ever southwestward she led them, through all that week of flight, and never did she break her promise of that first night, when, by dawn, she led them into a thick belt of woods, wherein safety promised, and there they dismounted.

"We must stay here till nightfall," said Thur.

"Hey, Vada ... "and flung his arm about her, for as she got to earth her knees gave way beneath her in sheer weariness and she would have fallen. "Hey, wench, lean on me. We have tried you too far. Come! Bear up! 'Tis but a short step before we rest and eat. Here, Jan, take her, help her. Lay her down for a while. I must first scout. You come with me, Olaf," and Thur returned to the roadside, where he selected a post from which he could see the road for more than a mile each way, and was himself concealed.

"One of us must always be watching here," he said.

"Why?" queried Olaf. "If we be inside the wood, none can see us."

"'Tis sure that you were never a soldier," laughed Thur. "A soldier ever wants to know who pursueth! Men-at-arms I fear not, but if they send Foresters they will mark our tracks where we left the road, and be upon us in the woods as softly as they track game. Or, if it be a Sheriff with his mounted archers, they have ever smell-dogs with them who can track us anywhere, but what I fear most is swift messengers, sent ahead of us to rise the country against us. So, if you watch here, Olaf, keeping out of sight, and report to me if any such should come, we must fly swiftly. I will relieve you presently."

With that he returned to Jan and Vada, who tried to struggle to her feet on his approach, only to collapse into his arms again, saying with a wry smile: "If I can get aught to eat, I will be all right," at which Jan clucked with annoyance at his own carelessness. Vada had ridden at his side throughout the night, unspeaking, but tactily seeking his company, and he had been blind to her growing distress, nor would she voice it, knowing their danger. Though Jan was unobservant and self-absorbed, he was kindly disposed to all mankind, with the exception of the Fitz-Urse.

"Fool that I am," he said to Thur. "I forgot that she was but a woman."

"Her spirit will suffice for any danger, but her body is sick with hunger, I misdoubt. We might have known had we stayed to think."

Jan hastened to Vada and half-carried her along, murmuring words of encouragement and selfreproach for his lack of understanding. Glancing down at her face, more blanched than ever in the wan light, he saw tears glistening on her cheeks, for the men's compassion had so moved and softened her, unused as she was to pity, that she could not restrain them. And progressing in this way they came to a tiny glade almost surrounded by great forest trees, with an outer scattering of bush. In the middle was a woodland pool, beside which grew a yew tree, and the ground was covered with the orange of dried beech leaves which the recent wind had whirled and driven into heaps.

"We cannot do better than this," Thur decided, "and if we build a fire from dry wood beneath that yew it will hide our smoke. Vada can rest here while we prepare food."

He laid her gently on a heap of leaves, and she lay with closed eyes, lids smarting with her driven-back tears. She could not shame her comrades or herself by this weakness which had come upon her so suddenly, and she forced down the sobs which convulsed her throat, wondering at the inward storm which shook her and not in the least understanding that it rose from the effects of excitement, fear, and apprehension of what she very well knew awaited her if she was caught, or these men failed her. All these, acting upon her mind and body, had robbed her of self-command, though not of fortitude.

Not that she doubted these strangers.

She had implicit confidence in their willingness to defend her with their lives, but if they were over powered and taken, they would inevitably share her fate. This was the conviction that shook her with terror, and a fit of shuddering seized her so that she could not stay her limbs, and if the men had not been busy with their horses, collecting wood for a fire and unpacking food, they might have seen her condition.

Vada's agitated mind could see nothing but her mother's white face, gleaming now and then as the fitful wind blew aside the flames and dense smoke which rose around it. As she lay there in the wood, with birds beginning their dawn song, her quivering body felt the searing of those tongues of flame, and she writhed in agony, and turned over, burying her face in the cool and fragrant leaves.

"Oh, Janicot, Great God, have pity on me!" she sobbed. "Give me forgetfulness. Oh, God in Heaven, have mercy on my mother. Give her happiness and peace of mind and spirit. Comfort and bless her, and have her for ever in Thy safe and loving keeping."

The storm of horror passed, soothed, or perhaps exorcised by the prayer. Perhaps she lost consciousness for a merciful spell, for she lay still and silent, and when Thur came to her she seemed to be asleep. He spoke lightly, touching her on the shoulder.

"Come, Vada, we have fire and food. Let me raise you." She submitted, smiling fleetingly up in his face. There was some element of wonder that she, who had known nothing from men but desire, lust and cruelty should now receive from these nothing but respectful kindness. Already she felt the reaction of a condemned wretch who had reached sanctuary.

"Thank you, friend, you are kind," she murmured, as she went with him to the fire. He placed her in a sheltered spot, for the dawn was cold and cheerless, and they all observed her eyes as Thur split a small cake of bread and cut a wedge of hot sausage with his dagger and gave it to her.

"When did you last eat, Vada ?" Jan asked sternly, for he was still vexed with himself.

She smiled, knowing that his severity was not for her.

"Two days ago I ate the last of my bread and my flour was gone. Since then ... "Her hand made an expressive gesture as she opened it and held it palm downwards " ... naught but grass."

"Grass !"

Even as he spoke, Thur noted the grace of the gesture, but said, gruffly, "Why did you not speak of it ? We had food in plenty."

"I had not thought of it," she replied simply. "Give her beer," said Jan hastily, "'twill revive her."

"Nay, let her eat first, poor soul," said Thur. "Beer on an empty belly is a calamity," and at this all laughed heartily. .

They made a leisurely meal, and after they had eaten lay down to sleep the greater part of the day, the men taking it in turns to watch. None came near them, and when darkness fell they stole out of the wood and picked their way across fields along the hedgerows until the moon rose, pursuing their southwesterly direction, and avoiding all villages and hamlets. This obliged them to make many detours, for where the land was cleared of forest it was thickly populated, and men could not ride for miles without encountering any habitations as they can do now. Food and rest had already much restored Vada, and this night she showed none of the weakness which had troubled her the night before. She kept her place beside Jan, telling him from time to time a little about herself.

"A hard life has been yours," Jan observed, stealing a look at her, and marvelled the quick flush which rose in her gaunt cheeks. He longed to ask her age, but contented himself with guessing it at about forty years.

"Most hard," she agreed. "Famine pursues most of us for half the year."

"Aye," he assented bitterly, "no matter how good I the harvest, it will not suffice when the greedy hands of Mother Church snatches three times her share. Were she content with her tithe we should do well enough. So you starved much, Vada?"

"At times, yes, but you know how these things be. There are whiles when a coney can be caught ... I can snare with the best ... and others when they seem to have vanished from the face of the earth. The cold winds drove them underground."

"And did none help you?"

"John Landlord would have me marry him. He would bring me gifts of flour and meat, but I could not take them and always refuse him. He is a good man, but ... "

"'Tis plain against nature!"

She laughed outright, and then cried in wonder at herself: "What have you done to me? You have driven me to laughter, and I have not laughed since my mother died, three years agone."

Jan maintained a sympathetic silence as a fit of melancholy seemed to descend over Vada, but presently she roused herself from it, and asked him some question about himself. He told her of his life on the farm, and of the attack upon his grandfather, though he said nothing of his ambitions, but she put them into words for him by exclaiming: "Were I so placed I would never rest until I had snatched back their ill-gotten spoil!"

"I think of naught else," he admitted.

But that dawn, as they rested and sat by their fire in the heart of another wood, Vada told them more about herself in answer to Thur's question if she was a native of Wanda.

"Not so. I was born fifty leagues north of it, by the sea at Hurst-wyck. My father and his folk were sea-faring, and had dwelt there long. My mother was an outlander. My father was drowned at sea when his ship foundered in a storm. He was a master-mariner."

"You were but young then?"

She nodded, smiling that brief smile of hers, and pleased at his interest.

"We lived well. My mother had the old knowledge of her people. She knew simples and cures. Folk came to her in sickness from many miles around. She was a priestess of that old faith that came from overseas."

"The East," Thur supplemented.

Again she nodded, staring at him penetratingly.

"In the Ages of Ages. From the Summerland."

"Hm," muttered Thur, considering this at his leisure.

"What do you know of it, Thur?" she asked at length.

But Thur appeared to be sunk in thought and gave no answer.

"Somewhat, I am sure," she persisted, her great amber eyes try-ing to find and hold his, "but 'tis garbled. I deemed you a spy come to trap me at first."

"I know but little," Thur answered, at length, "and that little only theory; but I have been to the Sabbath in Spain. Tell me truly, *have you*, Vada?"

"My mother first took me when I was a child of five years. The meeting was held close to the town, and all went in those days."

"How did you go? On a broomstick?" Olaf cried eagerly, glanc-ing across at Jan.

"We walked. How proud I was of my brave new shift which my mother had made and embroidered, and how I wept when she stripped it off and we both bestrode a broomstick as a hobby-horse to ride naked into the midst of the assembly."

"And then?" Jan spoke dryly, unable to comprehend whether he approved or did not of these proceedings.

"All laughed and clapped their hands to see me. Then the Chief Priest, whose name it is unlawful to speak but whom fools and priests dub the Devil, laughed too when I was brought before him and said: 'What shall I do with such a little one?'"

Jan was, in truth, aghast now. "The Devil *spoke* to you?"

"Were you not terrified beyond reason?" asked Olaf, remembering his own much less hair-raising experience.

Vada threw back her head and gave a ripple of genuine amusement.

"It seemed naught, for he took me on his knee kindly, and put one hand beneath my feet and the other upon my head, saying:

"'My pretty little one, swear to be faithful to the old gods, who are love, and goodness, kindness and pleasure,' and I lisped, 'Aye, Master,' whereupon they all laughed and clapped louder than ever, so I too laughed and clapped my hands ... and he laughed again."

"This passes all," Olaf affirmed. "*Did* you not fear? Truly, Vada?"

"Children know not fear, Olaf. I was full of wonder. I well knew the goat's mask and shaggy hide were false, but the strangeness, the lighted torch between his horns, and the power which radiated from him frighted me a little but delighted me more. My mother had told me of fairies and animals who were part men, or who talked like men, and one tale was of a cat who wore great boots and with his cunning helped his master wed a princess. All children dream of beasts who talk to them. I only felt that my dream had come true."

Jan smiled, as if at some childish recollection and prompted:
"And then?"

"The god took his seat on a throne of stone. Many priests and priestesses assembled round him, and rites that were strange but very wondrous were performed. We feasted, and sang with much music. They took me into their ranks and danced in great circles, and I too danced with them, and was so happy I thought I was in heaven. After that I always went with my mother. Many people came from afar, and all were welcome, for all are brothers. We did all the wicked and beautiful things, knowing that they must be done if we were to have health and happiness and good crops."

"Did all the townsfolk go?" asked Thur.

"Yes, all, even the gentle and nobly born. Some wore masks and took no parts in the rites, standing aside, feasting and dancing among themselves, although many of the younger sort would join in our dances. But when our Lord, Sir Mortimer, died, all was changed. His lady had ever been a cold, hard dame, and a lover of priests. She never came to our meetings. She founded a nunnery and a monastery to save her lord's soul from hell, and forced her daughter (who had ever been the merriest at our gatherings), forced her with blows to enter the nunnery, where she grew cold and waspish as her mother."

"There were persecutions?" Thur inquired.

"Even so. The two parish priests, leaders of the dancing at our meetings, were taken before the Lord Bishop. Then many shipmen came to Hurstwyck from foreign ports, and merchants with their wives from Germany. These were devoted to Mother Church and declared our meetings a deadly sin."

"But did you in truth make the crops grow well and bring good weather?" was Olaf's shrewd question.

"What else were our rites for but to bring rain when needed, and dry days for harvest? When the sun was at its lowest, did we not have a Dance of the Wheel, when all danced in a circle with torches to show the sun the way to come back and conquer Winter: To rise high and bring back Summer?"

"And then?"

"Always did he come back and the crops were good. We desired only friendliness and brotherliness with all, rich and poor, gentle and simple alike, for how can one scorn those with whom one has danced naked the night before? But gradually all changed. The noble scorned the merchant; and he scorned those less rich and prosperous than himself. Even the poorest townsman grew to scorn the people who lived on the heath and never visited Church, dubbing them the Commonherd. We, who had little money, needed it not. When a man would wed, the brothers assembled and built him a house, aye, and furnished it with the necessary gear. But when scorn waxed and love died, help waned, or had to be bought. More and more money was needed.

"Church grew, and with her growth came taxes and yet more taxes, with the added cry to, 'Repent and forsake wicked ways.' Then did the Church spread false tales that our feasts were sweet only because we ate the flesh of unbaptised babes; so that whenever a poor soul bore a babe she would hasten to the priest to get it baptised. From her fear he would extract money, and yet more money, with a promise into the bargain that she would never suffer her husband to frequent our gatherings. So it was they dwindled."

"So that was the way of it," said Jan. "What think you, Thur?"

Thur did not immediately reply. He took some time to think over his answer, and then said:

"It seems to me that Holy Church has grown swollen with pride and wealth. She has robbed rich and poor in her greed for power. She has destroyed Love, which her Master preached and taught, and has put Fear in Love's stead."

"You say briefly what I must say at length," Vada replied.

"Brevity is the pith of any matter and speaks most easily to the understanding," he told her gently.

"Fear! You have the pith of the matter there. The Lord of the Manor feared the Church, and feared to let any brother of ours have land on which to dwell, so that he and his were outcast and starving. Many such were tempted to seek the Abbey for relief. Money was lent to them, and so they became thrall to the Church. Any man could gain favour from Church by bringing a charge of witchcraft, no matter against whom. So much iniquity was worked, many spites gratified, and much robbery went on. Many a noble and rich merchant was stripped of all he possessed and his life made forfeit, while his goods were shared between accuser and persecutor ... though Mother Church ever took nine-tenths of the spoil. *Mother* Church!"

She spat her contempt.

"So did we decline, and our meetings became dangerous beyond belief, and so more and more secret. Then the shipmen brought the Spotted Death to Hurstwyck. Many died, many went mad from fear and caught the plague the more easily. My mother toiled among the sick night and day, never resting. She cured many, and, in the midst of her labours ... they took her."

There was a long pause before she added, so low that they scarcely heard her, "She died."

"Of the pestilence?" Jan inquired.

"No, *of the fire. Mother* Church took her, *my* mother, and they forced me to watch her burn. Two holy monks held me between them, while a third held open my eyelids ... with pins."

There was a shocked silence, and at that moment the first rays of the rising sun came stealing through the wood, lighting the trunks around them with ineffable beauty. Yet they shuddered, for the contrast between that moment and the darkness of man's dreadful deeds was too appalling.

"And you?" ventured Olaf, at last.

"They spared me for I was then not yet sixteen, yet they put me sharply to the question."

"They ... ?" Jan faltered.

She nodded. "Yes, but I would not speak, and they threw me into the town jail. There were many poor wretches, and they would have burned us all earlier or later, and we languished awaiting this fate, and so passed some weeks. Then, at night, came a brother of my faith who knew me. His name was Peter. There was a little window with an iron bar through which we talked. He promised to come again the next night. I was very thin, and what with pushing, and pulling, and stripping off my clothes (and much of my skin in the process) he managed to pull me through the bars. We rode hard all night and hid by day, much as we do now, and Peter brought me with him to Wanda. But he too caught the pestilence, sickened, and died."

"Was that long ago?" asked Jan.

"It seems many years to look back upon, but in actual time ... only three."

Jan's wondering eyes roving over her face brought a flush to her cheeks, but she maintained a dignified silence which they did-not intrude upon. When they spoke again it was of their journey and prospects of escape.

"They must be sorely perplexed," Thur said. "No one has set eyes on us since we rode clear. We have vanished into the blue air."

"The Devil has aided our escape and smuggled us into Hell," Olaf declared.

"Doubtless that is what they are saying," Jan shrugged contemptuously, "and the tale is being recounted by every bibulous brother in every monastery in England."

As was indeed a fact.

# CHAPTER VI
## THEY LEAVE THE WILD WOOD

O passed two nights of hard going. On the third morning of their adventure they lay concealed in yet another of those mercifully concealing woods. Their beasts were jaded, for they had ridden far the previous night. The time was about the eighth hour of the morning and they had fed well on rabbits roasted over a clear fire, and now, replete and lazy, they sprawled on a thyme-strewed bank, basking in the sunlight, with the symphony of the forest in their ears.

"I ask nothing better of life than this," said Olaf, rolling over on to his back and staring into the sky.

"Aye, it's been a rare holiday," agreed Jan, "and mother will have plenty to say about it."

Vada contemplated the speaker in silence, seemed about to say something, and then changed her mind. Jan smiled at her.

"Why must women scold?" he asked idly.

"Does your mother scold?" she inquired. Jan nodded, and Thur thrust in:

"She used not. A prettier, kinder wench never lived when she married your father. I envied the fellow."

"Infinite toil sours a woman," Vada urged, pleadingly. "With no mate to aid her these many years.... "

"That is why I would regain our heritage," Jan interrupted her hastily. "Yet she is most solidly set against me. 'Tis her opposition makes half our disputes. I seek only her good ease, yet she will have none of it."

"Because she fears for you and Olaf, and because you seek to thrust upon her a strange way of living in which she would find little content."

"Vada has the sense of it," said Thur. "Mother Church bids her live in contentment and to work hard, and she, being a devout daughter, obeys. Her fathers before her lived so, and she knows no better. *Your* father was no lordling when he wooed and married her, but a rough man-at-arms with little in his pouch. How should she comprehend your discontents and schemes, Jan?"

"Yet I wish she did not scold," Jan maintained stubbornly, "and, as for my schemes, they are my own and I will pursue them."

"I like not a scold, yet I think she hath a just cause. While we idle here happily she labours in our stead to feed us next winter. For my part I wish I could be in two places at once...here, where I find enjoyment, and there, helping my mother."

They laughed at this, and Olaf, rolling back on to his stomach to examine an insect in the thyme added:

"But I vow by all the saints I'll work twice as hard, nay, thrice, when I return."

"And that is not yet," interpolated Thur, while Vada smiled at them both.

"Though," Thur added with an open laugh, "'twill be all the worse for you when you do."

The boys joined in rather ruefully, and Olaf said with a shrug:

"Sufficient unto the day is the evil thereof, or so Brother Stephen tells us, but whyfore do we delay, Thur?"

"For our safety's sake. Do but consider for a moment! We have committed the gravest crime against Mother Church...in that we have frustrated her action and have given aid and comfort to one whom she deems a witch, and will never cease to pursue. Word will go forth from abbey to abbey throughout the length and breadth of Christian England, and *her* messengers will travel fast and straight. Whereas we have had to go slowly, and by devious ways. Is it not so, Vada?"

"Indeed you speak the sorry truth," she corroborated with the utmost gravity. "Not only am I in the direst peril, but you also share it with me because of your aid and comfort. There will be no relaxing of the pursuit, and no mercy when we are caught.

We had as well hang ourselves on yonder tree and make an end of it."

"Not so!" protested Jan stoutly. "I hang myself for no woman, and least of all for Mother Church. Rather would I seek the depths of the wild wood and live there to despoil her on any occasion I may."

"And I," from Olaf. "I despair for no woman, Mother Church or no. But I believe that the Blessed Virgin will be our guard. She is a true Mother, and is compassion incarnate to all children of earth, whether sinners or whole."

This pious statement brought comfort only to Olaf.

"Thy faith is like thee, lad, and shall be our guard, but for myself, I have it not."

"Nor I," said Jan.

Vada said in a low voice: "I have no reason for faith."

Thur's look was compassionate as he replied:

"That will pass, wench, never fear. With restored health will come first forgetfulness, then happiness and peace. But about our dangers … there I must depend on my wits and cunning. Olaf here shall pray for us and sustain us with his faith, but I will plan our course. Now, let us think of our situation. I think that from the time we left Wanda, none have marked us. We have watched the roads all day, and none have passed ahead of us, but then we have fetched a wide compass, and now I make for London."

"London!" came a shout from all three.

"Aye, London. 'Tis the one place where men may disappear into the crowd, and not be marked by any, and more than that, I must be seen on the London road. When I left home I was put to it to explain my absence. An ordinary man may go where he lists, but a leech hath patients. So, not -knowing where I was going, or for how long, I had to tell a story that would pass, and I said I was going to a sick brother in London."

"London!" said Vada, with longing, "I would see London."

"Aye, wench, and thou must, for if questioned, thou must be

able to tell of it, just as I myself must know what be wagging there should I be put to the query about it. Now, you all wait here. There seems a large village ahead, and I will ride there and try to buy a woman's weeds for Vada."

"Woman's dress!" exclaimed Jan.

"She cannot live the rest of her days as a man. 'Tis a good disguise at night, or at some distance, but any with eyes would note the cheat if they came close enow. Vada must again become her natural self, and there lies her danger, and ours! Remember, the slightest slip anywhere may betray us, and our foes are relentless and cunning and know we are alive and riding somewhere.

"We are coming to thickly settled country and will be marked if we ride by night, or hide by day, and I deem it best that we ride boldly to-morrow in the sight of all men, as if we were honest travellers."

"Aye," said Jan, "but if any come asking for news of a party of four travellers? 'Tis a significant number."

"Perchance I may help there," said Vada. "Many of the farm folk who see us may be 'of the brotherhood'. Let us each wear a bit of white cloth behind us, like rabbits' scuts."

"To what end?" asked Thur.

"Any brother who sees us wearing them will know that we wish to travel unseen, *and even under torture will swear that they saw nothing but four rabbits on the road.* Long ago we found that if a man swore under torture that he saw none, his eyes betrayed him, *but if he believed that in some mystical way we are transformed into rabbits, he will maintain that he saw naught but rabbits to his death!* Aye, 'tis queer, but 'tis so."

"It will not hurt us to try, Vada," said Thur, "and so we are agreed? No more going by night for us, but on the morrow we ride out boldly?"

And so it was done.

By consultation together they perfected Thur's plan in detail, which was that they should ride boldly to the great city, and there lose themselves in its heart. From thence Jan and Olaf were to ride home alone after seeing the sights, and Thur and Vada were to follow in their own good time, Vada travelling as Thur's niece, where she was left as a charge upon his charity by his dying brother.

"And," said Thur, when he had finished telling his plan, "if any of you can think of a better story, then let me hear it."

There was a moment or two of silence, then each solemnly shook a head, and Vada said:

"Truly this is a sorry world. Here you are, three honest men, and I a poor wretch whom you have rescued, yet have you no reward but added danger. Without me you might go in peace. I would as lief be dead!"

"Nay, 'twas we who sought you, Vada," Olaf stoutly objected; but Vada pursued: "Yet the danger was mine ere you came."

"As small as makes no matter," Thur thrust in with energy. "It ill becomes you, wench, to speak so, who are the object of so ardent a love. Never saw I a man with such deep and unselfish devotion."

"You speak of John ... Landlord?"

"Yes, Vada, I do. And since he hath served you so well, you can but repay him .... "

"Nay, that I never will!" she broke in with a wild look.

"With gratitude at least for the life he has saved for you," Thur continued, equably. "'Tis a poor return to sit and wish for death, even though he cannot hear you. But for him that rabble of persecution would have met me at the city gate. He delayed their coming with no thought of the consequences, nor for his own skin. Therefore, be merry, and cast off these dolours."

Vada's clear mind acknowledged the truth and wisdom of this admonition. Jan and Olaf looked awkward, but Thur maintained his judicial bearing, fixing her with a look of kindly guardianship. The colour rose in her cheeks as she said at length:

"I crave forgiveness. It was no way to speak, yet I meant no ingratitude. Rather would I give my life than that harm should come through me."

Thur smiled warmly.

"That we each believe, Vada, but now to another matter. It is in my mind that your name be changed, for by it you may be captured. 'Tis a strange name, and one I never heard before, and I think it sticks easily in the mind." He spoke a little doubtfully, for he expected resistance, but she gave a ready nod of assent.

"That also is true. Thur, you have much wisdom and you see further than any. My mother had a secret name for me. She used it always when we were alone together, and it is dear to me for her sake. 'Twas the name I received when I took the oath in the Circle."

"But would it pain you, wench, to use it now?"

"No, rather would it comfort me. Call me Morven."

Yet, as she spoke it, her eyes filled with tears; but she smiled courageously at Thur and repeated more firmly: "Morven."

"So shall it be," he said, refraining from saying it after her.

Olaf broke the little silence that fell by remarking:

"It has been much in my mind that Churchmen are also Magicians, Thur. How can that be?"

"Because all learning is in the Church, and Magic demands much learning. Many bishops practise it, even popes have been known to do so. All the books of Magic come from Rome or Spain, where Holy Church is all-powerful."

"There is much more Magic in the East, from whence it derives," Morven interposed.

"True, but I speak of that which has been given to the West."

"How came you first to study Magic, Thur?" asked Olaf eagerly.

"When I rode from Fitz-Urse with your father, and the Normans were in hot pursuit. We had but little chance of our lives, and went hard for three days, at length doubling into a wood, and by that throwing off our enemies and making our escape. We boarded a ship bound for Spain. Your father was but twenty-two, and I ten years older, and we joined a band of mercenaries, and with them fought up and down. After a while your father itched to return home, so we did, and he married, but I went off again to fight. It was some years before I encountered your father again. He was killed in our next engagement, and once more I returned, to carry the sad news to your mother."

"Mother has told us many times of your comfort and goodness to her," said Olaf, with his wise, kind smile unusual in one so young. Thur noted it, with that fresh surprise which it always aroused in him.

"Soldiering was a good life while it lasted, and so thought I when I went back to it again, though I missed your father sorely. But all too soon it came to an end. I had little enough money for my pains, and I desired to learn to become a leech, having had much experience in the bandaging and tending of wounds, and the care of fevers. That is how I came to be a poor student at Cordoba, and to study magic and astrology, along with the lore of herbs and their preparation."

"Did this Don Menisis teach you much?" Jan asked.

"Aye, he lectured lengthily, and taught the theory of magic and none could have done it better, though he showed us nothing of practice."

"Tell us in substance what was the theory."

Thur laughed. "'Twould take a hundred years of steady talking, but to encompass the matter in a nutshell: ... The priests tell us that Messire God is in his high heaven among the Holy Saints and cherubims. He is too great to bother about we poor worms. We may pray and do reverence to His Holy Son, and His Mother, Our Lady, but even they are of too high a rank to heed *our* petitions, though Kings and Emperors may commune with them, perhaps.

"So, for we humble people, God in His wisdom devised the Saints, and to them we may address our petitions, and give them rich gifts ... and promise them more ... if they help us."

"Do they help you?" asked Morven.

"Well," replied Thur, "that is the trouble. Sometimes, by the tales you hear, a Saint may perform a miracle themselves, but more often they address a petition to Messire Christ, or Madame the Virgin.

"They, in turn, may grant it, or, as it were, pass it on to Messire God himself, who, should it be His Will, is gracious. The priests tell of many petitions being granted."

"My mother be for ever praying the Saints and giving them rich gifts, but never have I known any result, and the Saints (or rather the priests on their behalf) take the gifts, and give naught in return," growled Jan.

"Whereas, in Magic," continued Thur, "by the appropriate words of power and their allied spells one can call the attention of (and to a certain extent, constrain) powerful spirits and demons, and, by asking their aid, oft-times get it."

"Yes," said Morven, "there be not much difference, really, except for this. That if the spirits grant thy wish, thou are not the poorer for having made rich gifts."

"It seems to me from what you tell, Thur," said Jan, "'tis as if, when one wishes a boon from some mighty lord, thou hast first to see the bailiff, ahd give him a rich bribe. After that he, in turn, speaketh to my lord chaplain, who speaketh to his lady, and she, when her lord be in a good temper, speaketh of the matter to him and persuades him, perchance, to grant the boon.

"But in Magic, 'tis as if thou went straight to the under-bailiff and, by attracting his attention, he is prevailed upon to grant the plea himself, and without bribe."

"Aye, it is somewhat like that," agreed Thur, "but also as if thou saidest to him, 'I know thou hast been stealing the Lord's corn (or juggling with the rents) *and unless I get what I want,* thou wilt surely suffer.'

"Spirits are constrained through knowledge of how to attract their attention, and, after that, by making known your wishes in a way that they can understand, and *also by having the power to make them suffer.* Should they not grant your request, by the strange powers of sympathy, they do suffer, from the pains you inflict on their Sigil *they feel in their proper bodies.*"

"Tell us now, Morven, how it is in witchcraft," begged Jan.

"Of much I am sworn not to speak," she replied. "But this I may say. In the Christian belief you have a good God, or One who is good to you, so you say, and Who is All-powerful, and who greatly desires worshippers ... and yet you may not ask Him directly for what you want, but must ever petition some Saint, who, as I understand, is but a dead man. Also you must give money or other rich gifts before you can hope to receive favour. Now, I cannot conceive of an All-powerful God who is eternally in want of money!

"We witches have our gods also, and they are good, at least, to us, but they are not all-powerful, and so they *need* our aid. They desire fertility, for man, beasts, and crops, but they need our help to bring it about, and by our dances and other means they get that help."

"But your gods are but devils!" expostulated Olaf.

"Who may say what are gods and which are devils!" Morven snapped. "My test of a goodness of a god is this ... if he *does* you good."

"Aye," argued Olaf. "But what heeds it if he gives you good in *this* world, and casts you into burning Hell in the next?"

"True," said Morven. "Let that be a test of the goodness of our gods. Now, if what the priests told me be true, your God so loved the world he made that He devised a burning purgatory of everlasting fire, into which He casteth all the peoples He had created for many thousands of years ... except a few of a chosen race. Then, it seems, He changed His mind, and casteth all that chosen race into this fiery pit ... all, save a few ... who embraced a new faith which He had made!"

Thur and Olaf started back with horror, but Jan said:

"By Heaven, you are right, lass! Why should a poor babe who dieth ere it hath had a chance of baptism, burn in Hell for ever through no fault of its own?"

"But," said Thur, "Hell be a terrible country, and the only way to evade it be by obeying the commands of Messire God and His priests ... even though it be sometimes hard to understand."

"Aye," agreed Olaf. "Answer *that*, if thou canst, Mistress! Your gods cannot save thee from Hell. What when thou diest?"

"Why," said she, "having rested for a while in the lovely country on the other side of life, we come back again, and are reborn on this earth. We ever progress, but to progress we must learn, and to learn oft means suffering. What we endure in this life fits us for a better existence in the next, and so we be heartened to endure all the troubles and trials here, for we know that they but help us to higher things. Thus the gods teach us to look forward to the time when we be not men any more ... but gods!"

"As gods!" gasped Olaf. "Men as gods! I oft wondered why the priests would burn all witches ... and now I KNOW."

"So that is it," said Thur, softly. "I often wondered at the courage with which you and the others suffered so much without breaking under the strain. But it seems to me that we may talk of these things for ever without reaching a conclusion."

"Now it is your turn," said Morven. "Won't you tell us about the Magic you studied, and how it is supposed to work?"

"'Twould take weeks," said Thur.

"Nay," said Morven. "Tell the main in a nutshell, and leave us to chew on the kernel," and she smiled at him with her great eyes of liquid amber, so that he could refuse her nothing.

"Briefly then, it is this. Don Menisis taught us that in the beginning God made the world by a Word of Power ... let there be light ... and there was light. Then he made the seven planets of Sun, Moon, Saturn, Jupiter, Venus, Mars, and Mercury, setting them in their places in the firmament of heavens, and each one of them controlled by a mighty spirit whose name they bear. To each of those controlling spirits, serving under him, and subservient to His will are various Archangels, Angels, Spirits and Demons. Do I make it clear?"

He was talking now only to Morven, and watching her face as she absorbed his words. She nodded.

"I have heard my mother tell of that."

Thur continued: "If the student knows the word of power that controls each spirit, *he may call him up,* and compel him to do his will; but every spirit has his own name and sigil, or sign, and he can be summoned *only by that sigil.*"

"There is much to learn," she commented sagely.

"So much that there is little time for practice."

"You have the truth of it, dear wench. Each type of Archangel and his satellites has charge of only one type of work, and no other, and may be summoned only in his proper hour. The student must learn to observe the times and seasons and the special work ruled by each planet."

"My head swims," Jan complained, looking as bewildered as he claimed to be, while Olaf grinned and tossed a few small stones backwards and forwards in the palm of his hand with considerable dexterity.

"Nor is that all," went on Thur. "Our student must learn the names and powers, the sigils and words of power of each Planetary Spirit. Then he must learn the method of using those words, or, what is termed 'Ritual Art Magic', and that is a long and complicated business."

"Could a man hold so much in his mind?" Morven asked.

"He must remember, or have writings of it. Don Menisis had many books of Magic on his shelf amongst his treatises on Theology, but he never used them. I would look at him as he droned on in one of his lectures, and to my fancy these books cried out to be used, and read, and loved, instead of being left to moulder away useless there."

"Truly it is a marvel to be able to read and write," sighed Morven wistfully.

"I will teach you, if you have the will to learn."

"The will I have, but lack the ability."

"Only the will is needed, dear child."

"Wherefore did not the ancient Don practise what he preached?" Jan demanded. "Was he like the rest of his kidney?"

Thur shrugged. "New students were always arriving, and the Don was a precision of the first order. Each youth must start at the beginning, and the learned Doctor would drone on, repeating long lists of Angels, and Powers, and Principalities, while the flies swarmed in the heat, and the stench of garlic rose from the breath of snoring students. I recall it but as an happening of yesterday.

"So," Thur concluded, "naught came of it. 'Twas then that some of us went to dance with the witches, as I told you. Witchcraft is different. It is a rival religion to Christianity, a religion of love, pleasure and excitement. Therefore does the Church suppress it with fire and many huntings, lest the people forsake in numbers the Saints, and the stony way of life they preach. The Church fears a mass return to the old gods, whom they call devils. So, with the growing strength of Christianity as expressed by Holy Church, harshness and cruelty have come upon mankind in a greater degree than any yet known. 'Tis little wonder many return to witchcraft, and seek relief from the hardness and misery of their lives, and the cold austerity of the Church's preaching. Frail human nature needs a little warmth and comfort for its starved body on earth … not some distant Paradise beyond the grave."

This was so obvious a truth that no one commented on it, but Olaf asked: "What did you do then, Thur?"

"War came again, so I buckled on my harness and went into the classroom to bid farewell to Don Menisis, but he was not there … so … "

"So?" Jan echoed, as he paused so long.

"So, as I thought that they called to me, 'Use us! Read us! Love us!' … so … I stole the manuscripts!"

# CHAPTER VII
## THEY COME TO LONDON

UPPER was in active preparation as they rode up to an inn, situated in a fair-sized village. Serving men and women were setting up trestles and taking boards from their places against the walls, and with them they erected a long table down the middle of the room. Stews and roast meat, cakes of bread baked on an iron flap over glowing embers with that nutty taste that only bread baked so has, and beer ... rich, brown and strong, a meal in itself.

Pewter dishes, platters, cups and bowls ... all were of the roughest description, but there was plenty to eat and drink, and the food had been well cooked and was most appetising. In the middle of the long table was a huge cellar of salt, and the company ate with their fingers after cutting up the viands with their daggers.

The bustle of service broke up conversation, and, for the most part, the guests ranged themselves round the walls to give the servitors fair play. Thur and Morven stood just inside the door. As Olaf crossed the room he was impressed anew by the change in Morven. She was still thin to the point of attenuation, but her skin had lost its muddy look, and, though still colourless, was growing clear and transparent. Her mouth was no longer dragged with pain, but looked composed and patient, well modelled, and generous in its lines, but still pale as a shadow. He noted anew the good lines upon which her features were moulded, but perhaps the greatest change was in her eyes. Formerly they had been so dim, so sunken, so haunted by terror that they were like those of a thing dying from torture. Now they seemed to get deeper every day, and to gleam brighter under the beautiful curve of the lids.

Olaf found himself wondering about the colour of her hair, which none of them had ever seen, so close did she keep her hood drawn about her face, but the brows were a delicate tint of red-brown, as were her lashes, which, starting dark at the roots, gradually paled in their upward sweep until they ended in a red-gold. Olaf considered them to be quite remarkable lashes, and a fitting frame for the brown amber of her eyes. Morven looked like one brought back from the very brink of death, and recovering life by slow stages. She passed well for a delicate youth, for she had an air of arrested development, a strange sexlessness combined with an effect of remoteness of the spirit which was not so much purity as an absence of some essential quality necessary either to good or evil.

In reality, this was but an immense weariness set up by an experience which had been beyond the capacity of body and spirit to absorb. Olaf was too young to comprehend all this, but he felt it vaguely. All that he was capable of understanding was the effect of persecution, and the consequent social isolation attendant upon this obsession of the Church with witchcraft. He did not know it, but he had won to the great boon of spiritual fearlessness through his experience in Thur's magic circle. In a matter of minutes had been born in him spiritual and intellectual courage, and with it had come that dangerous emancipation of the mind against which the Church fought with all its power of might and subtlety. It was this mind-freedom which the Church regarded as its most dangerous enemy, and these four people had it in a marked degree. Olaf recognised the fact in a flash of insight far in advance of his years. Morven had it through inheritance and by education and persecution. Thur had it through mental ability, acquisition, and growth. Jan possessed it in its lowest form through rebellion against what he regarded as personal injustice; through sullenness and stubbornness of temper ... through resentment, in short; and Olaf, through ordeal.

In the last week he had grown from a child to a thinking man, and had been ruthlessly kicked through the dividing gate by his sympathy for a fellow. He was haunted by the necessity to protect and succour Morven, or, at least, to perform his full share in it; and in this he was urged by compassion alone, for, at the moment of its inception she had appeared as repulsive as she was forlorn. That she should daily become more attractive was rather the reward of virtue than the cause of it. Certainly, as she now smiled at him, there was no connection between her and the foul Witch of Wanda.

They had planned to keep to themselves and to retire immediately after they had supped, for they wanted to start on the road early the next day, and neither did they wish to make themselves in any way remarkable, so supper and the ensuing hours passed without note, and they woke with the sun and started off the following morning in fine weather, their spirits raised by this and the fact that they were, seemingly, beyond pursuit. They were thus in a mood to see every novelty through a rosy haze. The villages scattered around London were many, and the beauty of the countryside both great and varied, so that the capital seemed to be set in a large garden.

From the heights of Hampstead they looked across the fertile valley to the splendours of the great Cathedral, revealed sharply by the crystalline air of that clear day, its surface glistening here and there as the sun caught upon some facet in the newly-cut stone. They gazed at it in awe and wonder that man could devise and raise such an edifice, for in grandeur of conception and beauty of craftsmanship it had not its equal anywhere.

There it stood, softened by distance and the peculiar English atmosphere to a pearly hue. It rose a mass of piled and carven stone. So solid ... yet appearing airily poised as it soared into the intense blue of the sky, so that it indeed looked like the very Throne of God Himself.

"It is a marvel!" breathed Morven, breaking the silence into which they had fallen as they feasted their eyes.

"It is the very symbol of God. Why cannot Mother Church be as holy and gracious in her deeds towards men as she manifests herself in that great temple?"

"'Tis not Church!" jeered the elder Bonder with supreme scorn. "'Tis the Master-mason, and the men who build under him."

"Nay, there is more. 'Tis the eyes with which we see, and the grandeur of vision in the mind of the master ere ever he begins to build."

Jan stared at this, uncomprehending, while Thur smiled in satisfaction and Morven nodded agreement. Even from that distance the city showed as a soft blur of colour set amid green. They could see the sun glinting on the surface of many little streams, flowing through lush meadows, and spinning numerous little mills, while belts of woodland smudged the skyline with soft shadows. It was a goodly and cheering sight to look down upon.

At the inn where they dined the house was thronged with a gossiping, good-humoured company. It seemed that the London citizens were much given to walking out in the fair meads surrounding their city, and taking their ease at the inns. In their own country round Clare, in Walden, the people were tongue-tied and dour, smiling seldom, but here the folk were merry, and a rough jape found a ready laugh, song came easily to their lips, and they lilted many catches and ballads. Some were gay, others dismal, but they all sang in company, so that the Bonders were amazed. Colour ran riot everywhere. In clothes and horse-trappings, in the costumes of the peasants (especially the women) and even in the speech of the people. Every village seemed to have its pipers and knot of dancers, while only the aged crones seemed content to sit spinning on the sunny side of their cottages.

But in the villages there was not such an all-pervading air of contentment, for the living conditions were pitiful and wretched here also, as in most parts of England; but they had a general cheerfulness and disposition to make the best of life, to laugh away trouble and be jocund while the sun shone. Indeed, there was everywhere an almost pagan glee in this warm, bright sunshine which gladdened all the earth. Truly the winter was past, and the voice of the turtle was heard in the land.

After dinner they came down through Finchley to St. Pancras and Bloomsbury, where they found broad meadows spangled with cowslip and oxlip broidering the little streams and merry mills they had seen above from Caen Wood. The interlacing hedges were snowy with hawthorn, whose heavy fragrance mixed with the bubble of running water, chatter of mill-wheels, and the sunlight pouring down from the unclouded sky, until the whole earth seemed to find expression in light, sound and scent. No wonder the people walked abroad in it, thought Olaf, who seemed never to have lived until that moment. Then, coming to a spot where the almond-scented bloom gave place to a row of elms, they had a closer view of the city, and nearer to hand, of some of that city's denizens.

A very splendid lord, with his lady, their servants, and a fine company were hawking. The lady carried her falcon on her wrist, hooded and tethered by a jess. One bird was in the air, pursuing a heron which had taken wing from the brookside. The falconer stood by, a frame hanging from his neck on which perched four others, also hooded. The lady was young. Her lord not so young, but he was a great dandy, and strove to vie with his wife in the colourfulness and youthfulness of his clothes. His bright green tunic was heavily embroidered in red and gold, as was his lined cloak, while his braies were cut very full, falling about his knees like a skirt, and made of the same chequered material as the lining of his cloak. Soft brown leather shoes with cuffs turned over at the ankles, and stiff with embroidery in red, gold and green, shod his feet. He wore a Phrygian cap to match his shoes, terminating in a point. He was altogether an imposing and handsome figure, with his fine gay clothes and curling beard, and hair rolled back in curls above his ears. The country visitors contemplated him with some admiration, for they were used only to sobriety and utility in dress, and he was neither unaware nor offended by their attention.

The lady was a great beauty, a fact that she could not for a minute forget. She was as dark as night with a skin like a nectarine, and enormous eyes, unfathomable as a pool in winter. Her hair was of that blue-black quality rarely seen, plaited and wound heavily about her ears, not hiding, but enhancing, their loveliness. Over all she wore a fine silver net studded with pale jewels of a kind they knew not, and a silver gossamer of a veil outlining her forehead.

Her dress was of some shining yellow material closely spotted with silver, its voluminous folds confined about her waist with a jewelled girdle. Her neck was uncovered to the base, and a dove-grey and silver cloak was flung back over her shoulders and lined with soft white fur.

Jan eyed this beauteous vision surreptitiously and with sheer amazement. Never, in his most ardent moments, had he imagined anything like this. It was stamped plain upon his ingenuous face for Morven to read. She too, marked the lady well. Not a detail of that fascinating exterior missed her critical scrutiny. But the picture was not complete without the page, and it was on him that Olaf's eyes were fixed. He was a youth of eighteen, tall, supple, and clad from head to foot in scarlet embroidered with gold. He was, in truth, in the very pink of fashion. His yellow hair tumbled about his shoulders in corkscrew curls, from under a pointed cap. He minced as he walked in his pointed shoes as though the beflowered grass was an affront to his tread. He minced in his talk, hesitating here and there as though words which came voluntarily were not good enough for his tongue. In short, he was insufferable. His lord treated him with an affectionate, good-natured contempt, as being too youthful for serious consideration, but his mistress had eyes for nobody else, and whenever opportunity offered (which was often), her lord being much occupied with his sport, the two whispered together and exchanged lovers' glances.

"Holy Saints! Did you ever behold such beauty?" Jan demanded of Morven when speech returned to him.

"Yes," she answered. "Many times. Is she a Jewess, think you?"

"That is not a Jew's yellow but some wondrous dye I've never seen before in all my travels."

Had they but known it, the lady was, in truth, Irish, and the colour was saffron, and being safely wed, seemed about to put into practice that proverb of her people which says, "Nobody misses a slice off a cut loaf."

"Were I her lord, I would keep an eye on Master Page," Thur added. "Nay, I like not such tawdry gear in a man. Were he mine, I'd clout his ears soundly and teach him to play in the tilt-yard."

"And I," Olaf agreed, for he envied the fellow and longed to see himself in such gorgeous array, though with a difference. He could not imagine his own locks so tortured, or his manners either.

"I speak of the lady," Jan assured them, so earnestly that Thur laughed outright.

"Oh, *her*" Morven ejaculated provokingly. "Is she not a wonder?"

"A wonder of mischance, the swarthy hussy! Were I her lord she'd lie face down across my knee to teach her where to look, and my hand should point the way."

Thur burst into a guffaw at this picture, and Jan was offended at its crudity. They rode on, the cry of the falconer in their ears, their eyes fixed upon two distant specks high up in the blue, the one so rapidly overtaking the other.

"Poor bird," sighed Morven. "I know not which I pity most, the heron, or the lord."

As they drew nearer to the city they encountered still more people walking in the spring sunshine, and showing off their fine new clothes, bought for Eastertide. Though there was great uniformity in style, for the cut of the cloth differed only from that of the hawking party in length of points, they noted the diversity, richness and colour of material, the beauty of design in embroideries and jewellery. The citizens of London, obviously were very wealthy and fond of display. Every apprentice and serving-wench, romping and laughing on the broad grass verges of the road, sported bright ribands, or a gaily embroidered badge of Guild or Master.

"Home will be a dull place after this jaunt," Jan lamented, as they rode through Holborn. "I wish we had returned forthwith."

"Right about face, then," cried Thur, and even Jan joined in the laugh, but he consoled himself with an added determination to win back all his grandfather had lost. He too would strut with the best ... one day, and, for the first time in his life Olaf too saw what that loss, which he had hitherto secretly deemed unimportant, represented in terms of living. His love of all things in nature, its life and beauty, its variety, had proved themselves a compensation for discomfort and privation, which, without pondering on them unduly, had seemed to him to be the common lot and therefore unavoidable. Now he was being shown another side of life, which was typified in this rich and gay city. He had imagined London to be but an enlarged version of their little home-town in St. Clare ... but how utterly different it was. St. Clare in Walden was dominated first by the Church, as represented by the great Abbey but sixteen miles distant, and its satellites, the Chipley Abbey and the Priory of nuns just outside the town itself. Secondly, it was in thrall to Esquire Walter Upmere, henchman of Fitz-Urse. Under the combined exactions of Church and feudal lord, St. Clare was suitably sobered and subdued. The Lord Abbot was an educated sensualist, seeking only his own ease and pleasure. Esquire Walter was himself but a lout, rough, unlettered and undisciplined; part farmer and part soldier, but wholly a robber, ruling the town with an iron hand in a glove of triple brass. He was homely of appearance and not so well clad as Thur.

Therefore was their astonishment all the greater when the two Bonders realised that their little world was but a grain of sand in an hour glass, like fifty such other towns scattered over the face of England. Whereas, in this great city, dwelt the King and his nobles, and lived a life far beyond the conception of the lads and their neighbours. Olaf felt that his native world was very narrow indeed, and here was something very spacious.

They entered the City by Newgate, and the jollity and independence of the people obsessed Olaf to all else's exclusion. They appeared to care for no one, to fear nothing, as though they had an equal right with the best to the riches which life could offer.

When my Lord Abbot paid a visit to St. Clare, such townsfolk as were abroad lined up and waited his passage with bowed heads before his upraised three fingers. If Esquire Walter went abroad he had the street to himself, the townsfolk seemed to smell him from the moment he decided to leave his stronghold until he returned, and scuttled into cover. Only the brothers and soldiery laughed publicly and sang songs in St. Clare. Yet here was a crowd of people thronging a narrow street along which a party was passing seeking an inn, and coming towards them was a lady in her litter, escorted by her husband and retinue of six servants marching before and behind, all clad in the gay, rich clothing which seemed so common here. But instead of the crowd standing humbly to give passage to their betters, the servants had to push their way through the throng, which they did good-humouredly. It was not until the litter and the lady were sighted that people stepped casually aside, commending freely the beauty of the lady passenger, who smiled and thanked them civilly for their courtesy.

They gaped at two Knights of the Temple.

"I have heard much of these," said Jan. "They spit on the Cross, and adore an image, but they always fight bravely for the Cross, across the sea. What is the truth, think you, Thur?"

"There be many tales," he replied. "'Tis said that the Church loves them not, for they confess not to the priests, only to each other, being scourged meanwhile. 'Tis said that they are initiated at midnight, stripped, and with unholy kisses, and they trample on the Cross. They are said to have an idol which is half-man and half-goat, called Baphomet, and that they practice Magic and are unchaste.

"But do they not tell the same story about half the Abbeys in England? We do know that they are rich and powerful, and therefore hated, but they are ever the bravest in war, and, also, I have heard that 'Baphomet' simply means, 'The Father of the Temple of Universal Peace among Men,' and it is written backwards *Templi Omnium Hominum Pacis Abbas* to disguise it, but who this Father of the Temple is I can't say."

They had not gone far along the main street when they heard ahead of them the insistent barking of dogs, accompanied by a ringing of little bells, combined with the shrill skirl of a bagpipe and the singing of a very bawdy song. A knot of villagers had gathered and stood idly by to watch a sight as common as daylight to them, and of no more interest than to serve as an excuse for gossip.

"Is there a fair?" asked Morven.

Thur shook his head. His persuasive: "Way, good friends," soon won them a path through the crowd, and presently they came up with a little company of six, trudging over the cobble-stones in single file. They were sorry enough on the surface, foot-sore and limping. Their leader clung to his staff in utter exhaustion. His beard was long and matted, and his eyes were hollow in his gaunt face. His weeds consisted of a long hair-shirt reaching down to his calves, and which was worn over his naked flesh. A heavy iron chain girded it round his middle which clanked as he moved, and a cloak of sackcloth hung down his back. His body was so wasted with fasting that these hung about his spareness like the bedraggled rags of a scarecrow. He did not tell his beads, nor toll the bell, for he needed both hands to grasp his staff, or he would have fallen. As he doddered forward Morven saw that his feet were bleeding through their covering dust. His thin and shrivelled hands were dirty and like walnut shells, the nails long, blackened and bent inward like talons. From time to time he muttered, harping on a single chord, his lips too parched and strained for distinct utterance:

"Holy St. Alban sustain me. Blessed Jesu be my strength! Sweet Mary have mercy!"

"What are these?" asked Morven, in wonder.

"Pilgrims," Thur told her, while Jan sniffed loudly, and Olaf muttered, "Blessed Saints, what discomfort." Thur turned in his saddle to give them a warning look and laid a finger on his lips significantly at which the two had the grace to blush. The sight was new to Morven who had not even heard of such things in her narrow life. Therefore she observed this group of devotees with close attention.

The woman who trudged next to the leader was in no such sorry case. True, her weeds were of sackcloth, but she wore them not next her naked skin, nor did a chain encircle her waist, but a neat girdle outlined it, and her feet were shod in sandals which contained no parched peas, and, as she went, she sang lustily her bawdy song. The other four men of the party were equally cheerful, dirty and dishevelled, healthily weary with their day's tramp, yet for all of well-fed and prosperous mein. Morven gathered from their talk (which was entirely secular) that on the morrow they would set forth for St. Edmundsbury, there to visit the blessed shrine. Apparently they spent the summer thus in perpetual holiday, journeying from place to place and shrine to shrine, combining piety with pleasure in a most commendable way. Again Morven smiled, casting a satirical eye at Thur, but he was, for once, unheeding, his professional attention being riveted upon the woe-begone leader of the band. He, with face sunk deep in his cowl, wavered forward~ his fanatical eyes fixed ahead, heedless alike of his companions, the crowd which his stressful appearance was fast gathering, and his ears deaf to the licentious ditty and the skid of the pipe.

Thur thought that every step would be his last, and doubted his awareness of anything from start to finish of the pilgrimage.

"In truth, he must be a great sinner, poor soul," a woman close to Morven commented with intense satisfaction.

At that moment he fell, staff, beads and bell making a great clatter. He lay with his face pressed to the cobbles as though they were his last refuge. Thur's horse snorted and started at the noise, sensing disaster, and was quieted with difficulty.

Instantly the woman was down beside her leader, her arms about him, her song dead on her lips. The piping died in a dismal wail. The crowd stared agape, and Thur flung his reins to Morven and dropped from the saddle.

"Nay, Sir Thomas. Good Sir Thomas!" crooned the woman, striving to raise him.

"Let him lie," said Thur. "Fetch water."

A woman, watching from her doorway, vanished, to re-appear with a cup and water in a bowl.

"Thank ye, Mistress," said Thur. "God reward you," breathed the song-maker, sitting on the cobbles and cradling the fallen head in her lap.

"He needs rest badly," said Thur, damping the dirty forehead and lips with his own kerchief dipped in the bowl, "we must seek him shelter."

"Nay, that he will not until the pilgrimage be ended," she replied, troubled.

"Lie his sins so heavy upon him?" Thur murmured, moistening the lips with water.

"Sins?" she echoed, in horror. "No greater saint outside Paradise than good Sir Thomas."

Thur silently pursued his ministrations and presently succeeded in getting a little water down his patient's throat. Some minutes passed. A hush fell upon the crowd who already had learned that a great saint was departing hence, so that, when he presently moved and stared up in Thur's face, the fire of his resolution undimmed, there was a murmur of disappointment. When, with the help of those two, he rose and stood between them, faint but dauntless, the crowd swallowed its chagrin and veered to approbation. After all, he might pass hence to Paradise at the shrine, and what could be better than that?

Instantly the piper blew a merry lilt to cheer the afflicted, and, with all the impedimenta restored to his enfeebled grasp, Sir Thomas trembled forward again. The woman cleared her throat preparatory to breaking into song again, when she was stayed by her shrewd and roving eye.

From an alley not six paces ahead there issued a procession of monks solemnly chanting, the priest bearing an elevated crucifix. The woman grasped the piper by the sleeve urgently and gave his ribs an angry nudge, accompanied by a warning turn of her eye in the alley's direction. He saw with dismay, and a sort of strangled howl came from the instrument as he descended with dexterity into a dismal chant, which she also took up with gusto. That it was a different chant signified little to their agitation.

The crowd fell on its knees in company with the pilgrims. The piper crouched as a compromise. The priest, who had missed nothing of this manoeuvre glanced sourly at the woman for an instant before turning left towards the Abbey. The little band of pilgrims rose and followed on at the tail of the procession, decorous and with chastened mien, the piper droning, the five chanting, Sir Thomas muttering his eternal incantation, "Holy St. Alban sustain me, Blessed J esu be my strength. Sweet Mary have Mercy!"

Thur and the others rode slowly on behind them. Hardly had this procession passed when they saw in the distance the banners of another. First came priests carrying a huge cross, then more priests with banners, then a procession of people, men, women and children, all mother-naked, walking two by two. Everyone held in his hand a leather scourge, and with tears and groans they lashed themselves on their backs, down which the blood poured, all the time weeping and imploring the forgiveness of God and His Mother.

"What in God's name be these?" asked Jan.

"'Tis the sect of the Flagellants," replied Thur.

"I have heard of them but never seen them. They started in Peruga, then in Rome, and spread all over Italy. They do this for their sins and for the sins of others. Or so 'tis said."

"'Tis an evil sight," said Morven. "They do it to excess. 'Tis true that we of the Witch Cult are taught that water purifieth the body but the scourge purifieth the soul, but we love not to bring blood."

Olaf watched everything in silence and turned it all over in his mind. He was seeing an aspect of life far removed from his birds and the seasonal beauties of the wild-wood, yet seeming in some strange way to supplement them, as though viewing the whole of a sphere instead of one of its sections.

Jan, for his part saw as much as Olaf or Morven, for he was naturally shrewd and observant, but he had the obsession of him who succeeds. He saw these things as something which supported his own ambition and views. Freedom, ease of life, fine clothes, all these were his by right of birth, things which he would presently recover. As for Morven, she had the aspect of a looker-on. She was one set apart by the cruelty of the world's most powerful body of men, and if they could not break her will they had done their best to break her body. Only her youth and natural resilience saved that. In its complete recovery from harsh usage she began to find the re-birth of other faculties, but faith in humanity as a whole had been destroyed. Faith in individuals she had when they had proved their worth, as these three had, but she knew these laughing, good-humoured crowds about her, these gay lordlings and their women. At the first cry of "Witch!" they would turn and rend her, and would be as laughing and gaily clad at her burning, which they would flock to behold. The thought set her apart. She looked at the women and marked their clothes, especially did she observe those of the nobility, with their poise, manner, tricks of speech and intonation, and all the nice details of their attire, but the ready jest, the quick wit and swift retort, the spontaneous laughter, made no impression on her consciousness as expressions of character.

Rather did she occupy herself with other questions. For what purpose had these three sought her out and rescued her? In what manner had they heard of her? These questions remained unanswered. Thur had promised to tell her all when she reached the safety of his home, and with that she was content. She knew too that he would retard their return as long as he could.

She knew that Thur was a physician, she suspected that he was an unusually clever one, and that her recovery was his chief consideration. Before he could present her to her future home, he wished her to look like a maid of nineteen years ... or as much of that as was possible in the circumstances.

That night they lay at the Blue Boar.

# CHAPTER VIII
## LONDON IS A FINE PLACE

HE next day, being one of the many Saints' days, was also a London holiday, and marked by the great jousting at Smithfield. It seemed to Jan and Morven, who were especially sleepy, that the city was astir at dawn. By six o'clock the bells of the many churches were mingling with those of St. Paul's, and further sleep being impossible, they all arose and went to Mass.

The interior of the cathedral was one of the most impressive in the world. Its rare length, with flanking pillars soaring clean-cut to the remote dimness of the roof, gave an austere nobility which seemed that the hand of man alone could not have achieved. The swirl of incense and solemn chanting heralded the procession of priests. Sonorous Latin rose and fell, swelled and echoed beneath the sweep of the arches; while under them a vast mosaic of yellow, green, blue, scarlet and gold swayed like a field of many coloured poppies in the wind as the people fell to their knees, rose again, and knelt yet again on the bare stones. All was eloquent of the mingled voluptuosity and austerity which characterised the time. The climbing sun pierced the east window and cleaved the dusty atmosphere in a level golden shaft which reached to the western door. To Morven it seemed to be God's gift to the ceremony.

As the clergy filed out and their chanting died away, the citizens pushed and jostled their way out into the narrow streets, where the eaves were so deep that the sun could scarcely penetrate between the houses, and only a strip of blue betrayed the existence of the sky. Morven, watching their haste to be gone, wondered whether these people went to Mass for the love of God or the fear of the Church. Was there a pin to choose between these and her own people who gathered at the Sabbath; was not the ad of worship performed there more sincere? If left to their own devices, would not these same citizens fall back upon the religion which was easiest to follow and which gave them the most pleasure? The people of London appeared to be most worldly, given over to the pursuit of wealth and the acquisition of temporal power, aggressive, and swift to fight in the protection of their rights … in direct opposition of the teaching of the Christ whose name came so readily to their lips, and Whose Mass they had just celebrated in no spirit of humility.

The great excitement of the day lay at Smithfield, and there they made their way. No need to ask direction, for everybody was talking loudly of the joust, and all going to see it. They had but to follow the crowds. The lists were set up hard by the village of Holborn, in a broad, flat mead whose grass had been recently shorn so that there was a pleasant smell of hay-making.

The lists occupied the middle of a great field, and rough wooden stands were raised on either side to seat the women of the nobility. Each contesting knight had his pavilion, above which flew a banner bearing his coat-of-arms embroidered on a silken ground. His attendant armourer, horsemen, and six other servants occupied themselves or lounged about while waiting for the joust to begin. These pavilions were beautiful, striking a merry note with their pennons floating out on the gentle wind and blossoming like great flowers in pure white, or stripes, or even chequered. Thur knew a few of the devices flying overhead, but was ignorant of most, although the people about knew them well and frankly expressed their opinions of the bearer, his character, his chances of success, and their hopes of him, whether they were well or adverse. It was yet early. The nobility and rich merchants had not arrived, and the crowds wandered off in search of other sights.

Away from the lists the ground was like a fair. Booths had been set up in a great circle at a respectful distance away from the lists, and there was food, drink and light merchandise on sale of a kind likely to tempt buyers by its novelty. Pedlars were everywhere, their packs lying unstrapped on the ground and open to display every form of fairing in ribbons, badges, embroidery, mock jewels and religious medals. Pipers, singers, dancers, tumblers, dwarfs, beggars, monstrosities displaying their oddness … all a bounded. Here and there knots of dancers gathered round a piper, who would hire himself out by the day or hour to any party willing to pay for his services. There were two cock-pits in opposite corners of the field from whence came the crowing of birds in a constant raucous clamour. There were bouts of single-stick, a form of contest to which the London apprentice was much addicted and brought considerable skill, and, for others who fancied themselves with the bow, there were targets for archery.

Brawls were frequent, especially among the rival teams of entertainers, and these were usually settled by an appeal to the audience, who displayed a fine impartiality and exercised a kind of rough justice in trying to give to all their good-humoured attention. Fresh crowds kept arriving. Whole families with their children and animals, and all squatted on the grass, each party equipped with a huge basket of food, which, in the way of Londoners since London began, they attacked voraciously the moment they arrived, and continued to eat the livelong day through without any apparent diminishing of their inexhaustible supplies.

A group of jongleurs had their pitch near a target set for archery, and among them was a dwarf with a very deformed back, who performed some very grotesque yet highly skilled tumbling, and who collected quite a good private income by letting certain members of the audience touch his hump for a consideration. When this was over, some none-too-melodious singing followed, and the two Bonders turned aside to watch the archery, and were soon joined by Morven and Thur.

A tall, stout youth of about twenty, who seemed to be the leader of a dozen fellows of his own age and interests had just released his shaft to land within an inch of the bull's-eye.

"Oh, well shot!" cried Jan, so heartily and spontaneously that both Thur and Morven stared at him, then at each other. Jan and Olaf clapped heartily, and the youth, who was hailed as Kit by his companions, at first stared arrogantly, as became a senior London apprentice of a master goldsmith. Others of his party then shot in turn with very indifferent success, and stepping forward with apparent nonchalance and a very condescending smile, Kit released another shaft. It struck a fraction of an inch nearer the centre.

"Oh, excellent!" cried Jan again, and this time the lordly youth smiled acknowledgment of the applause.

Jan was, by now, standing close to Kit and involuntarily stretched forth his hand for the bow, which Kit graciously yielded to him, supplying also an arrow from his quiver, which Jan took with thanks. Morven and Thur saw that Jan was a changed man. His impatience and habitual discontent with life had induced a slouching gait, but he now held himself erect. His eyes became alert and bright, his mouth good humoured, his manner easy and open. Morven noted that the pose of his body showed to advantage his tall, muscular figure, and at that moment she realised that, in his way, he was quite as handsome as Olaf.

Jan fitted, then released the shaft, and it struck in the exact centre of the target, and then he handed the bow to Olaf with an apologetic, disarming smile to Kit, who nodded and produced another arrow. Olaf's landed beside Jan's.

A contest now took place between the three in which Kit was hopelessly worsted. Perhaps he was not popular among his fellows, md assumed a leadership which was not willingly followed. However it was, they seemed glad of the Bonders' success, which Kit liked less and less. At length Olaf, seeing how matters lay, pulled Jan by the sleeve, indicating with a look that the bout should end.

"Many thanks, friend," said Jan, still with his new smile. "It is an honour for a countryman like me to shoot against so excellent a marksman."

Morven had not imagined that Jan Bonder ever could be gracious, and she gazed at him with appreciative eyes and softly parted lips, while Thur wondered too at this difference. The matter would have ended happily had not Thur whispered mischievously to Morven: "If that is our true Jan, for God's sake let us make an end of Fitz-Urse and come into our own."

Her spontaneous laugh rang out, long and full-throated.

Kit, smarting under two afflictions, defeat in what he had hitherto reigned supreme and the defalcation of his followers' allegiance, supposed the laugh was provoked by his own discomfiture. He ached to vent his discontent on someone. He plucked the remaining arrow from his quiver, and holding out the bow to Morven said in a very ugly way: "Come, young 'un, do *you* shoot. Since you laugh, doubtless you excel us all."

Many women could at least make some show at archery even though skill be denied them, but Morven did not know the elements of the craft. She stepped back a pace and made no attempt to take the weapons, but stared at Kit in dismay.

"Come on, young 'un. Prove yourself … even though your looks belie you," Kit jeered. Morven swiftly leaped to meet possible danger. She recovered an appearance of composure and waved aside the bow and arrow.

"Such is not my weapon."

"No?" inquired Kit, silkily polite. "Is anything your weapon?"

This encounter was recovering him some of his lost prestige among his friends, and Kit was in his element when baiting the defenceless. Thur, Jan and Olaf looked on with outward nonchalance and inward disquiet, wondering whither this would lead. Thur was cursing secretly the awkwardness of the encounter when Morven stepped forward in front of a near-by target, snatched her dagger with surprising suddenness, and, without apparent effort, hurled it to the centre of the bull's-eye. Jan and Olaf stared at it goggle-eyed, and Thur blinked rapidly once or twice. Kit was disconcerted, and showed it. He seemed to have taken an active dislike to Morven.

"Pretty work," he ejaculated. "More by chance than by good cunning, I fancy."

Morven glared in anger and made a swift clutch at his own dagger. Kit stepped back, but not before she had it and had sent it to quiver beside her own. Then she turned and looked him straight between the eyes. Without a word he strode to the target, plucked out the two daggers and returned them to her. Presenting her own hilt forward, he said:

"That's a good trick, young 'un. You'll pass." Morven took the dagger and put it up, smiled her thanks, but made no remark and, with his hand to his cap in a general salute, Kit rejoined his companions.

Morven's own party closed in around her, pressing her with eager questions in lowered tones. Where had she learned such a feat?

"Oh," said she. "The shipmen taught me, and practise has given me skill. 'Tis easy, needing only a steady hand and accurate eye."

"I have seen that done often in Spain, but seldom in England," Thur assured them. The Bonders declared that they would most assuredly try their hands at it, and Morven instructed:

"Make ye a straw target and practise at that, for if you throw unskilfully at anything hard, such as a tree, you risk breaking the point of your knife."

A fanfare of trumpets cut short the discussion by announcing the first knight to arrive. He was a splendid figure in full battle array, riding a great charger almost enveloped in trappings of blue and silver cloth. Two squires rode behind, one carrying his helmet the other his shield and spear. He was greeted with shouts of applause from the people, who left their various amusements to line each side of the entry to the lists. From thence onward there was a continual influx of spectators and contestants, nobles, lesser gentry, merchant princes and commoners until every place in the stands was occupied and tilting ready to begin.

Jan noted with excitement that his lady of the hawking party sat in the very centre of the principal stand beneath a large crown of gilded wood, from which streamed festoons of flowers and rows of little banners fastened to cord, forming a sort of bower. The rough wood of the stand was covered with cunningly stitched tapestries and carpets brought by the Crusaders from the East, and valuable beyond all price. These gave a very sumptuous air, while overhead floated banners and pennons bearing coats-of-arms and devices worked in every known colour, almost dimming the radiance of the clothes of the audience. Like some gorgeous Limoges enamel they shone forth, these lists at Smithfield, set in the vivid emerald of the spring grass against the deep blue of the sky, and lit up by the sun.

To-day Jan's lady was dressed in gleaming white and silver, the material shimmering in the sun with every movement. A chaplet of white roses wreathed her night-dark hair, and a silver veil streamed beyond it. They learned that she was to bestow the prizes, and that she was the lady of Lord Jocelyn of Keyes.

"She is indeed a wondrous beauty," sighed Jan, and, as though she heard him, she turned upon him the blue-black depths of those unfathomable eyes, so that he blushed scarlet, while a little smile twitched her lips. Among all the ladies there she was easily the loveliest, and amid all that riot of colour and positiveness she was a pale emblem of the elusive, and in consequence all the men's eyes were turned upon her in longing ... which was exactly the effect she had set out to achieve.

When the actual jousting began, however, they discovered that this was a spectacle for the privileged few ... for those seated either side of the list. They could see each knight as he rode to opposite ends of the tournament field, they could see him wheel, and spur his horse to the charge, with visor .down and spear couched, they admired the thundering advance and heard the shock of the encounter, which seemed to shake the very earth. They heard the plaudits of the spectators, and the jubilation of the victors, but all the excitement of the actual *seeing* was denied them, and after half a dozen repetitions of the same scene they grew weary, especially as they had no personal knowledge of the contestants and no inter-est in their fate.

So they wore away their day in dancing, singing, archery, feast-ing and admiring, and when the Bonders left the field early in the afternoon the majority of the crowds were still at it and would carry on until late nightfall.

The four strolled across the pleasant fields until they came to the city of Westminster. The beautiful Confessor's Abbey was still sadly in need of repair, and as they stood looking at it, one of the brothers came to them. He was an old man, with a gentle face, and kindly, short-sighted, peering eyes, and, as they entered the church he followed them in, and soon became their guide. He told them its history, pointing out its perfection over every other building, as he avowed in his enthusiasm. It was through him that they had their first sight of Canute's Palace, which stood nearby, and which, owing to his friendship with one of the stewards, they were ena-bled to inspect. They were not greatly impressed, though the old brother, immersed in the past and full of old traditions, pointed out certain details with an enthusiasm born of long acquaintance.

But Jan had his own notion of what a castle should be, and this was nothing like it, and Olaf by far preferred his wild wood, so alto-gether Canute's achievement paled into insignificance beside the splendour of Westminster Hall, the Banquet Room of the Red (the greatest room in the world unsupported by pillars), as old Brother Carol pointed out with pride.

Afterwards they wandered down to the riverside, where, coming from a little row of shops was a most appetising smell of cooking. It was long past midday, and they were hungry. Drawing nearer, they discovered that these shops sold cooked food of every descrip-tion, suitable alike for rich and poor purses. Servants were coming with covered dishes and going away with roast venison and birds. Housewives with baskets bought according to their means.

They bought a meal without further ado, learning that these cook-shops were a night and day service, so that travellers at any hour might be satisfied. They ate the excellent fare with content, watching the Thames flow by, and made their plans for return on the morrow.

"My little stock of money is finished," said Thur, "and you and Olaf must go, Jan, if I am not to make an enemy for life of your mother." Reluctantly, they agreed.

Accordingly they left the Blue Boar at sunrise and took their breakfast at one of these same cook-shops, then made their way to the eastern gate of the city.

"'Tis a pity we should separate," said Olaf, voicing the feeling which animated all.

"Could we not return together as we came?" asked Jan.

"Better not. A few more days will work true magic in Morven, and each day remove her further from we know whom. We will travel at our leisure, making our way slowly homeward"

They parted; the two Bonders mounted and continued along the road, leaving Morven and Thur still seated on the grass. Many times they looked back until a bend in the road hid them from sight.

# CHAPTER IX
## RIDING TOGETHER

T was the last day of Thur and Morven's return journey, and they expected to reach St. Clare in Walden by noon. The weather still held fine, and the two rode very close together so that their low-voiced talk could not possibly be overheard. All these days she had questioned him incessantly about Jan Bonder and the tragic story of his house, his mother, Thur's adventures, and lastly, on the greatest subject of all, Art Magic. Thur was now speaking earnestly, almost as though talking to himself, recounting his first attempt, the ordeal of Olaf in the magic circle, and the command of the invoked spirit coming through the boy's lips: "Seek the Witch of Wanda."

"And that was your first trial of strength?" she asked.

"My first because I lacked the needed instruments and the means to make them. You have the two knives, and therefore was I bidden to seek you. With those knives I can make the Burin and Magic Sword, Pentacles and Talismans. They are the precious keys which open wide all doors."

"And may not I help in the great work?"

"I need your help. You tell me that you worked no Magic at the Sabbath."

"Some did, but not those with whom my mother and I talked," said Morven. "We talked much of herbs and cures, of the means to overcome sickness, and there was a great book in which we recorded all our experiments."

"No more? I deemed men of every sort were there."

"And truly so. We were all brothers, but when many are gathered together, like seeks like, in thought and talk. Thought is free. I would linger on the fringe of learned men who talked much of the great ones of old."

"Saracens?"

"Greeks. 'Twas said these Greeks worshipped a thing called Democracy, which they interpreted as the brotherhood of man."

"But the Greeks had many slaves."

"So 'twas said, and only at a Witches Sabbath was there ever a true democracy...a strange word, Thur."

He explained its meaning to her.

"What else said they, child?"

"That the Greeks had more knowledge of love and beauty and goodness than any men since or before their time."

"Aye. They were learned in many Sciences, and there has been little joy or beauty in the world since Holy Church crushed the old gods out of life and turned them into devils."

"They also said that the witches' learning came secretly from these same old gods. The Greek witches could draw down the Spirit of the Moon."

"Artemis?"

She flashed him an admiring glance.

"Truly you are a learned man, Thur. Yes, Artemis. She could reveal the future and help gain the love of men. We used to invoke Ardrea, the daughter of Artemis."

"How was that done?"

"By sitting in a circle with a little drum we used for dancing. This was placed in the centre, and we laid our fingers lightly on the skin and asked questions of Ardrea. She answered Yes, or No, by tilting the drum. We had warnings of danger and much good advice that way."

"But you pushed it." Thur laughed.

"No, no! Truly we did not move our hands, but not for all people would she answer. Many had to try often before she would heed!"

All this seemed very small beer to Thur with his wider knowledge, and involuntarily he frowned. A little timidly she said:

"Some witches there were who could read the hour of death on the face, or the future fate. Always they promised me sorrow, to be followed by joy...and sorrow I have had aplenty."

"Aye, poor wench."

"Others there were who would fall into a sleep and the spirits would enter their bodies, speaking with the lips but not the voices of the sleepers. Women would speak with the voice of a man, and men with a woman's pipe."

"Ah," cried Thur, more hopefully, "and what said they?"

She shrugged. "Little, I fear. Warnings of danger or sorrow. What they foretold would come to pass, but me thinks how to *avoid* direness would have been more to the purpose. When they wakened they knew naught of what they had said."

"I have heard of such, and they have their uses."

"Some there were who would look into a pool of water or a magic stone, and see visions of what was happening at a distance, and so we would be warned of approaching danger. By these means we escaped for long, though yearly, as we grew weaker, so did the hatred of our enemies increase, so that they came with armed men to our gatherings to take us … but, being forewarned, we would disperse ere they arrived. They said 'twas the Devil who warned us."

"Have you those powers, Morven? We need them sorely."

She shook her head mournfully.

"No, Thur. I would give I know not what to possess them, but they said that I helped by giving power from my body. My coming was likened to the opening of the sluices of a water-mill for the power it gave to work marvels."

He turned his head and considered her long and earnestly as she rode beside him with hood thrown back. Her burnished hair seemed a living thing in the strong sunlight, its golden-red-brown seeming to ripple and wave in answer to the planet of life.

"Tell me the truth," he said suddenly, "this altar used at your gatherings … in Spain I saw the living body of a woman, and they practised abominations on it."

"Yes," she replied simply. "At the Great Sabbath the living body of a priestess does form the altar. We worship the divine spirit of Creation, which is the Life-spring of the world, and without which the world would perish. Are we then so abominable? We count it not so. To us it is the most sacred and holy mystery, proof of the God within us whose command is: 'Go forth and multiply.'"

"'Tis a phallic religion," said Thur, "and the broomstick symbolises the phallus."

After that he was silent for a while, and seemed to have forgotten Morven in the stress of his own thoughts. Essentially fair-minded, though having no love for the church, he well knew that when a natural act becomes distorted into a religion, as in this instance, it assumed a menace. He saw it all … the reason, the authority given by Scripture, leading to the seemingly senseless cruelty and persecution. Not that way could evil be stamped out and body and spirit be released, rather would he 'Draw folk to Heaven by fairness and good Example.'

Morven broke in: "Such rites may be done in a holy and reverent way, or fall to a depth of beastliness."

"In all their actions are the beasts clean and wholesome as man is not," he assured her sententiously.

At which she laughed, and then sobered to add:

"It is our sacrament. The Church has a sacrament of flesh and blood, or, as she prefers to call it, of bread and wine. To her it is a holy act to eat of it in reverent manner as a symbol of her great truth. But men can be seen grovelling in food and drink as swine in a trough, among them many priests. Yet, should that sacrament be described as a drunken orgy because of these malevolents?"

He shook his head, smiling at her earnestness.

"'Tis naught to me," he said. "I did but seek to learn the truth."

"When the great time comes, may I be there to help, Thur?"

"I need your help for the making of instruments and all the gear necessary to the great event, but for that I fear you are not yet fitted."

"What do I lack?" she cried, in disappointment.

"The perfection of good health and strength, child. We are to perform dangerous work, indeed, so perilous is it that long hours of fasting and prayer, with the mind concentrated on that one thing alone, are needed. If not, we perish by forces we know not how to control. And for this prayer and fasting, perfection of bodily health and strength are needed; for if the body is frail, there is the risk that the mind may wander away from its fixed point. You, who for years have been ill-nourished, may not endure the rigours of fasting and prayer until your body has recovered from its privation."

"These be mysteries indeed," she sighed. "I perceive that they must be obeyed lest I bring danger upon you. A man who would follow them must be dedicated in every way to his Art. Health and strength of body and mind ... the flame must burn in him with purity and steadfastness. Tell me of those instruments, Thur."

"In all magical essays things must be especially made. He who makes them must bring to bear all the powers of a trained mind concentrated on his work, so that no other mind or influence bears upon it in any way that can lead the mind astray. The whole force of his being must be centred on that work."

She nodded understanding, and Thur continued:

"So, when the great Work is performed, everything in every way leads the Magician's mind forward, and concentrates it into a stream which flows onward directed by his will, until its force tears aside the Astral veil, releasing the Forces which lie beyond."

"I will bind myself apprentice to you, Thur. Will you have me and teach me these wonders?"

"Willingly," he laughed, "but there are other matters more pressing. Morven, you are a witch. Lend me your aid."

"I can do very little, good Master Magician."

"*You are a witch*," he repeated. "You should have wisdom. At least your power can move knives to fly far."

She smiled a little secret smile.

"Often my mother spoke to me of a deed from the Far East. It was of a rope flung up into the air, and of a boy climbing to the top until he disappeared. There is an answer to seeming impossibilities, but they are nothing. What need has Thur Peterson of wisdom?"

With every mile bringing them nearer to home, Thur had yet to

make his mind up on the possibility of Morven's future relation-
ship to himself. Should he establish her as his leman, in name, if
not in fact ? He loved her, and marriage with her would have been
his delight. That being so he shrank from a lesser status for her,
but he knew that she loved Jan, and that one day Jan would waken
to love for her ... if all went well. For that reason alone he must act
wisely for them both. A fine screech Mistress Bonder would raise
if her darling Jan proposed to marry Thur Peterson's erstwhile mistress. His ears shrank in anticipation of her voluble and forcibly
uttered objections. After a brooding silence he turned to Morven
again.

"There is another matter for your wisdom, O Witch of the
Mere."

"Let me hear it, Master Magician."

"Are you my niece or my leman, Morven ?" She was silent a long
time, considering.

"I have a daughter's love for you only, Thur, no other."

"I know that, otherwise I would ask you for my wife, but if you
are not my niece, men will say you are my mistress."

"I would thankfully be niece to you in fact, Thur, and thought
you had so decided. If we have it so, does it not raise the least
question ?"

"I am full of doubt this morning."

"Be not so, my friend. Do but consider. Had we hid in the bushes
and swiftly returned to your home, I would indeed have been your
triple danger. The good people of St. Clare, my Lord Abbot, and
Sir Walter Upmere ... all of them would have then seen the miracle of what seemed to be an old witch turning into a young girl
before their eyes. Would that not, to them, have been proof plain
of sorcery ? Need men have looked further for the missing witch ?
We could not have hoped to escape the closest questioning ... and
then execution. But the time we have loitered on the road home
has restored my looks and youth, and I look not the same old witch-
woman that you rescued."

"That is as I see it," answered Thur. "As you are now, but recovered from the raging fever which slew your mother ... "

"My mother?" she questioned.

"Yes. It is best that you be my sister's child, your father dead long ago in the wars. As a leech, I am free to go without hindrance or question, and, I think, they will accept my story without looking further. Ere I left I spoke to one barber's son, a youth well-skilled in blood letting, who had long plagued me to take him as apprentice, and he was glad enough to play physician in my absence."

"Then why doubt? Could you have planned more wisely?" asked Morven. He did not reply to this, and for a while they rode in silence then Morven declared unequivocally:

"Jan loves the Lady Jocelyn of Keys."

Thur laughed explosively.

"Calf-love. 'Twill pass like winter snow, so icy is its purity. Better be a man's last love than his first."

She frowned dissent.

"Why, Morven, you should bless the day he set eyes on her. Jan had never looked upon a woman to see her until that hour. Now he is wakened, he can see. Soon he will look beyond her ... the dream ... and see you, the true thing."

She exclaimed with astonishing emphasis: "Would that you had left Jan at home, Thur. Had he been absent, or had I but looked past him to you, behind, why, then I should have loved the better man."

Thur lost colour in a spasm of deep emotion.

"Your words are hard for a man to hear, Morven."

She offered nothing further, and for a while rode with a darkened face, her mind occupied with negatives and jealousies of the Lady of Keys, seeing again her scarlet-clad page, his fripperies, and the shimmering elusiveness of the vision in the lists, like the sun shining on mist in a dewy meadow. She started as Thur's deep voice cut through the tangle of her thoughts.

"Foolish, foolish wench! What have you to fear? This is no preparation for the great matters that lie before us."

She coloured faintly at his words and roused herself.

"When do we make the Burin?"

"As soon as may be. There is much to do but peace, wench, yonder lies St. Clare in Walden. Now ride in silence."

The sergeant at the gate grunted surlily. He had a long, thin, narrow face, covered almost entirely with hair, and from out of this bush his eyes gazed like those of a famished wolf. That gaze reached Morven and lingered. Unconsciously his tongue came out and slipped over his lips, which shone blood-red out of the tangle.

"Well, 'tis Master Peterson, returned at last and not alone," he observed morosely.

"Alas, good friend. Barely had I ridden half a mile...I went to visit Mat the Miller's wife, brought to bed with twins, an' you remember..."

"Nay, I know not," was the surly retort.

"'Twas so, well, not a mile out I met one coming in haste to summon me to my brother, stricken with a raging fever."

"So?" groaned the man, who had drunk heavily the night before and whose suffering head seemed to be cleft in twain.

"Aye, in London...he died in my arms, and this his daughter Morven, stricken down through ministering to her mother, who took sick after her husband."

The man made a rough salutation to Morven, who gave him a smile which lingered long in his memory in a teasing, nagging manner. "I bid you welcome, Mistress Morven," he said. "A winsome maid is thrice welcome. In this god-forsaken hole-in-the-woods the women are as ugly as sin, as old as Satan, and as stale as a weed-grown pond."

Thur laughed. "Be not so jaundiced, Sergeant Byles! A very good day to you!" and they parted in mutual satisfaction.

"We are in safely," breathed Morven, as their horses picked their way among the pot-holes of the town's single street, and she looked around eagerly at what was to be her new home. St. Clare was happily situated among woodlands. Strips of the forest had been cleared for farming, and many sheep were reared in the district. It was a land of little streams, tributaries of the river on which it was built, whose flood made its sluggish passage to the sea forty miles distant. It was not a walled town, being entirely surrounded by water, whose windings were so tortuous that it enclosed it as a defence. Thur's house was situated on the banks of this stream which flowed through lush water-meadows where the town's cattle grazed and citizens walked in fine weather. At the convergence of river and stream there stood a mill whose race chattered pleasantly year in and year out.

The leech's house was old, and larger than most, being built with heavy beams of oak and rough stones of all shapes, kinds and sizes, held together by mud mortar. One storey jutted out well above the lower facade, with deep eaves beneath the shaggy thatch. A circular stone staircase built outside the back wall gave access to the floor above. The upper storey consisted of one large chamber, embracing the whole of the house's area, and whose floorboards were huge oak planks hewn from the neighbouring forest. It was warm, dry and comfortable (as comfort went in those days) and strong and well-isolated.

To the back and side of the house a strip of garden sloped to the water's edge. Along the margin of the stream grew osiers and withies, which became so dense in the spring that the town's folk could collect as many as they needed for weaving into baskets, of which many were made and sold in the local market.

Each year the stream's bed was then cleared and deepened by gangs of labourers, as a double precaution against flooding and providing footholds for any possible enemy.

On Thur's side of the stream the steep bank was turfed and crowned by six large bee-skips. The garden was planted with herbs and such poor flowers and vegetables as were indigenous to the soil. This was the house to which Thur returned with Morven, and as they dismounted and threw their bridles over the hitching-post Morven looked about her, ever with an eye to the strategic position, and saw that the alley ended in a cul-de-sac not fifty yards away. She saw too that the stream made a right-angled turn at that point, and that the ground attached to the house lay all along its right bank. They had no very near neighbours, but were shut away in this backwater on the town's verge, and surrounded by a garden wall ten feet high, crenellated at the top, with a strong gate about three-quarters of the way down its length. Above this wall she could see the roofs of a barn and a stable.

They stood before the great oaken door, with its solidity heavily fortified with iron studs that would take a ram to batter down, and three windows on the left of it were too narrow to admit even a child's entry, and set deep in the four-foot wall.

Though these windows were tall, beginning a floor from the ground and ending almost at the ceiling, they were no source of weakness, for strong oak shutters, iron studded like the door and fastened by huge bolts safe-guarded them from inside.

To the right of the door was the shop, rather like a large booth, whose open front was clamped by another shutter of solid oak, which lifted up from the outside, but whose pegs and staples were fixed from within, and which was now shut. A veritable fortress in miniature was this home of Thur's, which Morven saw with satisfaction while they waited admittance to their knocking.

At length there came a great unbolting of bars, and she could see the huge bevel of the key turning silently in its lock. Her heart unaccountably beat a little faster. What would she encounter on the other side of that door from one of her own sex, the hostility she had always known, or an unaccustomed friendship and sympathy? She closed her eyes, and her thoughts had the intensity of a prayer.

Slowly the door swung open, and a woman stood looking at them. She was tall and angular with an unexpected round and plump face as though she had somebody else's head fitted on her shoulders. Her brows were very arched, and from beneath their exaggerated half-moons a pair of mild grey eyes looked out innocently upon a wicked world. Altogether she was an odd-looking woman, her face at odds with her body, her eyes at odds with mankind and his works, and her character at odds with all three, for she seemed entirely without personality, to be as lifeless and colourless as a lump of dough.

"Good morrow, Alice."

"Lack, it'll never be you, Master!" she greeted him, her eyes skidding off him to linger on Morven.

"Oh, but it is ... and with a sick child for you to cosset ... my niece and adopted daughter, Morven Peterson."

"I knew not that you had a niece," she began, acidly, her eyes still raking Morven.

Morven's heart sank.

"There is much you know not, good Alice," Thur assured her lightly but with a quelling look.

Morven smiled at her and she herself was utterly ignorant of how much that smile conveyed. Suddenly the woman before them seemed to come to life and blossom. Her face kindled into warmth and she too smiled in such a kindly way that it was pleasant to see, and comforting as a fine fire on a snowy night.

"Will you be pleased to enter, Mistress Morven," she said submissively, pulling the door open, not without effort. "Indeed, you look but frail."

"I have been very near to death. Were it not for my good uncle here I should have died. I am not yet recovered, Alice."

"Aye," Thur confirmed. "The fever which slew her parents laid hold on her." .

"Ah, there has none lived, or ever will, who has the skill of Master Peterson," peaned Alice.

"You'll mend, wench. Alice will see to that," Thur assured Morven, and he told Alice the same tale that he had spun to Byles, but adding some biographical details and an anecdote of his youth. Alice was flattered, and not sure in her heart that the advent of Morven would not brighten up her own life.

"The lass favours you, Maister," she said.

"And so she should," boomed Thur. "She is the living image of her mother, God rest her soul!"

"Amen," said Morven, crossing herself.

"Amen," echoed Alice, with the same devout action.

And so they entered the shop. Its floor was of beaten earth, and two benches and a rough table formed the furniture. On the wall was a curious drawing of a human body, with astrological sigils making the parts of the body which came under the ruler-ship of each sign. Aries, the Ram, on the head. Taurus, the bull, on the neck. Each organ had its zodiacal symbol, and shelves fixed to the walls were laden with jars which each bore an astrological sign as well as the Latin names of the contents. Each set of jars under the "rulership" of the same planet were kept together, and the shelf devoted to the Moon held thin, fat, tall and squat jars which jostled each other, and contained all plants fleshy and full of sap, such as cucumber, mushroom and moon-wart, and these had to be kept well away from the jars containing plants which came under Saturn, like hemlock and nightshade, and from those ruled by Mars, such as garlic, mustard, hemp, horehound, wormwood and sulphur.

Venus's herbs, white poppy, elderflower, myrtle, violet and colts-foot also had to be kept well away from that planet's zodiacal antipathy, and Thur explained rapidly that a physician must ever take note under what planet the patient was afflicted and make choice of herbs and compounds accordingly.

A door on the left shut off the shop from the living-room, which was a big L-shaped place covering the remainder of the ground floor at the side and back of the shop. The hearth was at the north end, with no chimney, but merely a large hole in the sloping roof, through which the smoke escaped. At the east end there were three more windows overlooking the garden and the streams and fields beyond it, with the result that there was more light and air than was usual in those close times. The spiral staircase, built outside the wall, but enclosed in a semi-circular structure led to the single chamber above, and beside it another door opened into the garden.

The floor of the living place was of beaten earth strewn with rushes, and the air was clean with their faint acid-bitter scent. To Morven this home seemed luxurious as a palace, for, though the furniture was rough, it had a certain rude comfort in that it was plentiful and spacious, and bore the stamp of a mind which had given much thought to the best way of improving existing conditions.

A huge oak settle stood at angles to the fire, and, like every other stool and bench there was width in the seat, to make of sitting on it an act of rest rather than a penance. There was a slope to the back which gave ease, and many fine wolf skins were thrown over the benches and chairs.

Again Morven smiled on Alice as she said to Thur:

"You are well served, Uncle. Do you note in what good order your house is kept? Will you teach me your craft, Alice? I would fain be as excellent a housekeeper as you."

Alice Chad did not know that she possessed a heart until Morven's smile reached it. Now was she conscious of strange feelings, of an unwonted excitement stirring in her mind. There was gladness at the advent of this stranger, of the utter loss of that jealous dread which had been her first sensation when she opened the door and saw her. She was aware of increased energy and vitality which made her life seem full of interest, so that she looked about her with eyes which saw something new everywhere. All of this was novel and intensely exhilarating, though her only means of expressing herself lay in the thought: "Fifty is no great age, when all's said and done, and thank the blessed Saints I have my health and strength." Then, finding herself in this entirely new mood, came the wondering question: What's come over me? but she took command of the situation, and said: "Master, you must sleep down here, and the demoiselle shall have your chamber."

"Indeed yes, but we shall soon make her a chamber of her own, Alice," Thur agreed heartily. Then to Morven: "I will take the horses round and bring in your gear, child."

"Come your ways above, Mistress. 'Tis but a rough place, but master will see you in comfort yet. He is a rare one to devise, as you can see for yourself."

"He is the kindest and best man in the world," Morven answered with intense conviction, and Alice assented.

They climbed the spiral stairs, chattering amiably. Morven was almost naively content at the success of her power. Alice could have proved a formidable enemy and was well worth the friendly conquest.

"I have power," Morven told herself, "yet it is hard to define and not always to be directed. Why will it not serve me with Jan? Is it because I would have him turn to me with a free mind? I want not a bond-slave. Yet now he is full of the Lady Jocelyn, and I an out-caste who may not approach."

An unbidden thought darted into her mind which she instantly ejected. "Nay, I will not. I never will! Yet, if it is my fate never to ... None may alter fate. Am I so poor a thing that I dare not meet mine?" With an effort she put the gnawing query aside, and resolutely fixed her mind on what Alice was saying.

The large chamber they entered had none of the comfort of the place below. There was a rough bed, like a big box, containing straw stuffed mattress and blankets. A great table under the front window was covered with parchments and other writing gear. A long shelf held bound books, and another table bore a basin and ewer for water. There was a big chair by the writing table and several stools were scattered about, but they did not seem to furnish the room, which seemed all bare oak board, huge beams and sloping roof, and the light poured down through another smoke hole. While Morven took stock of these things Thur came pounding up the stair, and led her to a table on which were spread his special tools ... the lancets to bleed or open abscesses, and various knives and saws for operations. A silver spatula for spreading plasters, and boxes of powders, pills and potions that were too potent to be left in the shop. Another shelf, above this table, held rolls of parchment.

"1 have brought up the saddle bags," he said. "Nay, Alice, you need not unpack them. There are instruments of surgery that could do you ill if you were to handle them wrongly."

He was mindful of the magical knives that were hidden there, but Alice merely said: "Then, Master, if there is naught else for me to do here, I will be about my work below, and the maid shall call me if she needs me," and with a smile to Morven she went downstairs.

Thur grinned at Morven. "You have captured the citadel, O Witch of …"

"Sh!" she checked him. "'Tis no miracle. I would not bring a sword into your house."

They found the knives wrapped in their white cloth and Thur hid them in a secret place under the eaves, showing her the mystery of their concealment. That done, Morven began to unpack, and soon Thur's bed was strewn with the clothes he had bought for her in the various towns they had traversed. Among them were garments of white linen, the new sword and other articles. While she was so engaged he was busy planning out the new room for her, which was to be constructed at the hither end of the top story, but presently a call from below interrupted them both.

"Morven," he said softly, as she was about to descend.

"Yes, my uncle?"

"'Tis Jan and Olaf. You should know that here their name is Hugh, never Bonder. Their father was called Hugh, and he dropped all but that for safety's sake after his ruin and flight."

"I shall remember," she whispered.

"Come then down to dinner. Alice will have done her best, though she did not expect us," and he took her hand and led her down.

\* \* \* \*

"How went the world in my absence, Alice?"

Thur asked, his eyes twinkling, breaking the silence of their meal.

"Well enough, Master Peterson. Such as came for you I bade to go to young Tom Shooks, but 'twas little but scalds and blood-lettings. Thomas has a pretty way with a wound, and I helped him, and bleeding is his delight. Together we contrived. Sickness dies in fine weather, and 'tis mercifully so."

"Thou art a treasure, Alice, both thou and Thomas promise finely."

"Mistress Hugh came riding in some days ago. A fine to-do. She was up behind Snod and the poor beast was put to it to carry them both, I promise you. She demanded Jan and young Olaf as though I had them in my pocket, and swore she would be the death of you for carrying them off from their work. Did they ride with you?"

"Aye, they went to see the sights...needed a holiday from her tongue, so they said."

"And small wonder. I asked her would she like to look in my pot for them, lest she thought I had killed and carved them up. At which she was sore furious and vowed she'd tell my Lord Abbot of my insolence and complain to Esquire Walter of you. I offered her your bed to sleep in, and Snod the stable, thinking that she must be weary with her long ride. She accepted with as ill a grace as I ever beheld, and I staid alone to minister to her."

"That was a true Christian charity, Alice."

"Yours, Master, I fear, but she went next day in a better grace. Ah well, I can't stay chattering here. I must to market."

"May I go with you?" Morven asked.

"Aye, and welcome, my dove. 'Tis many a long year, since I had a companion."

"Go first to Smid the wright, and bid him come hither to do some carpentry. Let him bring his best oak boards and tools for two. We will get to work, and your chamber shall be ready by the morrow, wench."

Morven helped Alice to clear away the meal and put the house to rights and Thur watched the two with quiet satisfaction and much relief, then watched again as they went down the alley each with a big basket.

"Clever child!" he ejaculated to the empty air, "and she declares she has no power!"

He went above to assure himself that his manuscripts were safe in their hiding place.

* * * *

Later that night, when Alice Chad had departed reluctantly for her home in Parson's Lane (for she did not sleep in the leech's house) Thur and Morven sat talking over the fire.

"I have been looking at thy books, Thur. Tell me of them. Some have pictures of plants, and I think, tell of their virtues. Wilt thou truly teach me the art of reading them?".

He laughed, and showed her his small stock, which was a mighty library as things went in those days. There was a Latin work of Apuleius Platonicus with drawings of plants, also a Grateuss, two books on astrology and several classical works, among them the poems of Sappho, with other Greek works. He read a little from a Herbal:

"'For colds in the head, or if phlegm will not clear, take Horehound, which the Romans call Marrubium, seathe it in water, and let them take, and it will clear them wonderfully .... For lung diseases seathe the wort in honey and the patient will heal ....

"'For sore teeth take roots of henbane and seathe it in strong wine. Sip it warm and hold it in the mouth, and they will speedily heal. ... For dizziness let them run three times, naked, after sunset, through a field of flax, when the flax will take unto itself the dizziness. For ague, eat nine sage leaves fasting, nine mornings in succession and you shall be healed.' "

"Truly thou art a wonderfully clever man," she sighed, "but canst tell me that I want to know? Canst search the stars for me? When will Jan and Olaf come?"

"All in good time," answered Thur.

"They are in no danger of discovery?"

"Their safety lies that perhaps Fitz-Urse knows not or even suspects their existence, but he is a suspicious man and knows that many wish him ill around here."

"But is there no danger for them?" she persisted. "If none recognise their likeness to their father there is none."

"Then why all this mystery? In this town, may not friend visit friend? If not, how do the townsfolk live? Do not the country folk bring their goods for sale? Is there no market?"

"There is a market, for thou hast been to it, and many outlanders bring their goods for sale, and come without question, in sight of all."

"And why should they not?" she argued. "And if so, why not Jan and Olaf? Cannot they bring butter and eggs to market and then visit their good friends Thur Peterson and his niece? What should stay them and who should question them?"

"Nay, pester me not with questions," he laughed. "'Tis all as you say."

"Then what do you fear?" she drove him remorselessly.

"A Fitz-Urse hath the wits of a louse, he knoweth that Sir Hugh may have left a child, and be ever watching for him to turn up, well knowing that many men would favour any claimant against the hated Normans."

"'Tis naught," said Morven. "I well know the folly of fear. I have lived too long alone, with no soul to whom I could turn or speak my mind in safety, and so I start at shadows. Fear is a danger for the fearful mind knows much unease and betrays itself, so that men ask, 'What is there to hide? and from asking, they turn to searching. If the reason cannot be found then would men rather invent a reason than suffer defeat of curiosity."

"Morven, you have an old head on those young shoulders."

"Do not mock," she entreated. "No one knows fear better than I, and in our first encounter my terror was abject, as you know. But since I have been with you I am a changeling. When we were all riding together I sat silent in my saddle, but my thoughts were full and I saw my folly, how fear raises suspicion, and now I am all for boldness. You have given me new life and courage, Thur. I would not have you suffer as I have suffered."

"Dear child, you had reason for fear, God knows."

"But where there is danger I could change their faces with walnut juice to make them swarthy. With paint I could alter the shape of their eyes and mouths, and with pads inside swell their cheeks so that they look fatter in the face."

"H'm," he said. "For such cantrips a ready wit is needed."

"Or I would teach them to walk differently, for a man may be known by his walk before his face is seen. They may then come openly and buy herbs at your shop, to visit you as a friend. Man surely may have friends in this town of St. Clare … or is that against the law?"

"Not that I know, Wisdom. But Fitz-Urse will speedily have killed any that he even suspects. He is the law here."

"Again you mock, but you should make some small spell for Jan's especial safety … a spell of invisibility."

"So?" said Thur, amused.

"'Twill soon be the hour of Venus, and her day, Friday. Make the figure of wax and write the spell on the skin of a toad. Thus do we witches, ever bearing in mind that invisibility is not a lack of sight in all beholders, *but lack of observation.* Any but the blind may see, but he who carries the spell is not marked by all about him."

"Your witchcraft, it seems, is very much a thing of the mind … the dominance of the witch's mind over her surroundings."

"Truly. A thing of much accurate observation, and knowledge of what people do and may do in certain events. The witch holds the mind of those she would influence. 'Tis simple. An old woman with a load may come and go un-noticed, so long as her behaviour is that of an old woman with a load."

"So, if she hurry, or stop to glance about her, she would be marked?"

"Yes, always one so disguised wears the charm of the Talisman with such confidence that she knows none may note her. As she sees herself in her own mind, so do others see her. But if she trusts not in the powers she wears and lets fear taint her mind, then does she impart fear to those about her. They see her furtiveness, mark her, remember her, question her, and take her."

Thur was minded to drive her argument home by applying her theory to her own cirumstance at Wanda, but had not that cruelty. All he said was, "There is a vast gulf between theory and exact behaviour," and then fell silent, considering not so much her words as the subject of witchcraft in general.

"May I not go to Jan and tell him of this...show him how to change his walk by a parched pea worn in his shoe?"

"Jan, nor any man, welcomes a parched pea as a walking companion," he laughed. "Besides, as we have seen, there is no danger."

"In the event of there being one we have not seen, dear Thur, may I go to him? I love the greenwood."

"Doubtless, when Jan Bonder shares its enchantments! When we are fugitives, or when Jan is lord again, then may you. But for the moment you bide here. Thur Peterson's niece cannot roam at will like any *jongleuse*. I need your help on the morrow."

"Willingly. What is our work?"

"We compound spices. Gum and nutmegs, aloes and cinnamon and mace, with incense. We need much, for, from the smoke of such compounding do the mighty spirits draw the material to form themselves into Bodies when we summon them. Without them they cannot become manifest."

"Blood can also be used," Morven said eagerly, "that, or the fine essence drawn from the body of a man."

"Never!" snapped Thur, with such a passion of anger that Morven was startled. "Spirits who require blood or sacrifices are evil devils, and such art is the Black Art, if they are summoned by those impious means. 'Tis as evil as if I made a wax image and roasted it to slay someone."

"But, Thur, what if you made one of Fitz-Urse? Then Jan might get his rights."

"Speak not to me thus. No Magus may do ought of that evil thing. I am a soldier and I slay with the sword. Never by the Black Art!" For once he was deaf to her voice or her distress, his whole being centred in the force of the denial of the thing most abhorrent to him. He went on with the increasing vehemence of denunciation:

"In the True Art Magical we call only good spirits.

We summon them and reward them with incense and sweet odours. As for giving substance from the living body, the parchments say naught of it, and I deem it akin to giving blood … so evil a practice in itself that it will summon naught but evil and lies."

She sat in silence, downcast at this storm she had raised so unwittingly, but Thur had more to say.

"Nay," he went on solemnly, "let us abide by the known ways, that of the ancient days. He taught them to King Solomon and they ever have His blessing."

Morven accepted the rebuke in all docility and Thur sat staring into the fire. Presently she ventured to slide her hand into his. He grasped it kindly and reassuringly.

"It grows late, so get you to bed. You are a good child, little Morven. You hate our religion and Mother Church, and with good reason. Yet are you a better Christian than the many who have escaped her iron hand.

"Some of His servants are not so, and serve Him not at all. Yet is God a Great and Good God. May He keep thee in all thy ways.

"Good night, my child. Blessings be upon thee."

# CHAPTER X
## WORKING TOGETHER

"IT was on the fourth day of their return that Thur said to Morven: "The heavens are propitious, and Mercury's day-dawn approaches. To-night, when Alice Chad has gone, we begin our work. Rest this day, be tranquil, and prepare yourself, as I shall do."

Therefore all that day Morven lay idly in the long grass of the bank by the stream, watching the swallows skimming the surface for insects too minute for human vision, and the martins flitting in and out of their nests under the eaves. The air was laden with the scent of growing clover, and the hum of swarming bees. Morven, in seeming idleness, gathered water-grasses. These she joined and plaited into a long strand with loops at beginning and end and at certain intervals in its length.

It seemed, in her impatience, that Alice would never depart, so long did she linger on one pretext or another. The truth was that Alice now found all her contentment in the girl's company and would with delight have taken up her residence in the house; but she went at last, and Thur and Morven hastened upstairs. He and Smid between them had made her chamber in the western end of the house, shutting it off with oaken boards, and a strong door fastened with an iron bar. Thus, between the two sleeping rooms there was a large space. It was here the circle was to be prepared. Thur and Morven stood considering it.

"'Twill do very well," he asserted.

With infinite patience they fetched a large tub, and coaxed and manoeuvred it up the spiral stairs. Meanwhile water was heating in the fire below and when they had carried it upstairs and half-filled the tubs, Thur, immersed in the rising steam, thus exorcised it.

"I exorcise thee, O Creature of the Water, that thou cast out from thee all impurities and uncleanliness of the spirits of the world of phantasms so they may harm me not, through the virtue of God the Almighty, Who reigneth in the Ages of Ages. Amen.

*"Mertalia, Musalia, Dophalia, Onemalia, Zitanseia, Goldaphaira, Dedulsaira, Ghevialaira, Gheminaiea, Gegropheira, Cedani, Gilthar, Godieb, Ezoiil, Musil, Grassil, Tamen, Puri, Godu, Hoznoth, Astachoth, Tzaboath, Adonai, Agla, On, EI, Tetragrammaton, Shema, Ariston, Anaphaxeton, Segilaton, Primarouton."*

And he stripped, and washed himself thoroughly, bidding Morven to do likewise. She obeyed him, and. he poured water over himself and then her, saying:

"Purge me, O Lord, with hyssop and I shall be clean. Wash me, and I shall be whiter than snow."

When Morven was out of the bath Thur took salt and blessed it, saying: "The blessing of the Father Almighty be upon this Creature of Salt. Let all malignity and hindrance be cast forth hencefrom and let all good enter in. Wherefore I bless thee and invoke thee that thou mayst aid me."

Casting the exorcised salt into the bath, they both entered and washed again, saying:

*"Imanel, Arnamon, Imato, Memeon, Hectacon, Muobii, Paltellon, Decaion, Yamenton, Yaron, Tatonon, Vaphoron, Gadon, Existon, Zagveron, Momerton, Zarmesiton, Tileion, Tixmion."*

Morven, as she emerged, asked him gaily:

"Why are Magic and Witchcraft better than the teachings of the Church, Thur?"

"Nay, I know not," he said idly.

"Because they teach cleanliness of body, while Mother Church persecutes for the same reason. Therefore is she a foul old hag."

"Truly all saints love filth, as witness Simon Stylites. Cleanliness smacks of the Devil. The reason is not far to seek. Many churchmen practise Art Magic and those who do not yet know of it. They know the insistence upon cleanliness of the body before entering the Circle, and so to them dirt must be holy because Magic and Witchcraft are unholy."

Something like a snort came from Morven.

"Did you ever hear of that tale of a Becket? 'Twas said that England knew not how great a saint she had lost until they came to take the under-shirt from his body, so foul with lice was it that it moved."

"Small wonder King Henry called him, 'This turbulent priest,' and cried for his removal. He must have been affected with that shirt."

Thur's laugh roared out.

Morven said: "In my home town folks talked much of the Valley of Holiness."

"I have not heard of it."

"A tale of an Abbot and his monks. None so holy as they in the land of Egypt, giving themselves to the reading of pious books, denying themselves speech, both among themselves and with the outside world, lest the member offend God; eating only herbage, living in every discomfort, praying always and washing never, wearing one garment until it dropped off them from decay and old age, or crawled away, like Becket's. They became famous throughout the civilised world for their learning and Holy Austerities."

"In short, a nest of Beckets."

"Interrupt not with your levity, Thur Peterson. Now, there was a great scarcity of water, so that the Holy Abbot prayed for relief, and lo! ... in answer there burst forth a great stream of purest water by miracle in that desert place. Then were all that community tempted by the Fiend, and they besought their Abbot to build a bath, that they might cleanse their bodies."

Morven broke off to shake down her hair, and Thur called:

"The tale is not told?"

"Peace, impatience, while I comb my hair. Well, the bath was made, the monks bathed, and the outraged waters shrank away until not one drop remained. Neither entreaties, tears nor flagellations, neither lamentations, processions, nor rich gifts, neither many candles or promises of amendment prevailed. And all the land marvelled. Then did they make humble surrender and destroy the iniquitous bath, and behold, the waters gushed forth again!"

"And this is credited by all, of that there is not a doubt."

"There was a poor woman at Hurstforth who was seen at a stream, washing her gown. She turned her pocket inside out, and washed it clean, as would any woman. One watched her and laid information against her. She was not a witch nor of our brotherhood in any way; no good Christian would wash a thing that was not visible ... it must be to please the Devil, they said, and they burned her at the stake for it."

"Have done!" cried Thur. "Such tales sicken and torment me. Yet do you not see the befogged reasoning? No Magic Circle is entered until the body is purified of all dirt and clad not at all, or in an immaculate garment. Therefore is dirt holy, and a condition of perpetual filth a condition of everlasting holiness."

Another snort came from Morven, who was not concerned with the fairness of understanding.

"'Tis the same with healing. A witch will first cleanse a sore or wound, then salve it with a healing herb and bind it with clean linen. A priest will apply an old bone of some saint, which has touched other hundreds of dirty wounds in the same manner, and bind it on with a filthy old rag. Then do they scowl, though in secret they wonder, that a witch may heal her hundreds, where the Church heals one more by chance than good cunning. Because the people know this and go to the witch with their ills and not to the Church, then do the priests hound and persecute her."

"Aye, 'tis a rivalry which will end only with the extinction of one or t'other."

Silence fell, during which Morven combed her hair with savage energy, tugging fiercely at each strand as she came to it as though garrotting some persecuting maniac about to set forth on a witch hunt.

"Art prepared, Morven?" called Thur.

He stood there, perfumed and covered from head to foot in one of the white linen robes he had brought from London. He looked like a priest. Morven stood there, her body rosy, scented and vibrant from water and hard rubbing, holding a knife in each hand, the black hilted Athame and that with the white handle.

The space between the two rooms was designed for the ritual. The night before it had been swept and dusted, so that it was free from the slightest speck of dirt, and while Thur busied himself selecting and tabulating the work to be done that night, Morven went rapidly over the floor again with a damp cloth. When she had finished she washed her hands and rejoined him, and together they solemnly perfumed the area.

"The Heavens are propitious," he murmured contentedly. "The Moon is in an Ariel sign and in her increase, the sky is clear and serene."

Meanwhile Morven thrust her Athame into a chink in the floor boards, looped the strand she had plaited that morning over it, and, fitting a piece of charcoal into a loop five feet six inches down its length, she marked out a circle, leaving an entrance north nor-west in it. Shortening to the next loop six inches nearer the centre she described a second circle, and shortening again to four feet six inches, described the third circle, thus making an inner circle nine feet across. The outer circle was then divided into the four points of the compass. Beginning at the east, Thur marked in Hebrew "Agial", at the south point "Tzabaoth", at the west "Jhvh" (which in English is spelt Jehovah), and at the north, "Adghy". Between each point of the compass he drew a pentacle or five-pointed star.

Morven then took the Athame and with its point went over again all that he had drawn in charcoal, while he placed a lighted brazier of the same fuel at the due eastern point within the smallest circle. This he lighted, then placed a table before it exactly with its centre to the middle of the brazier, and then set out there on the various articles for consecration, among them the wand and the cord he had used for marking. Two stools were placed before the table. Slowly the clouds of fumes rose from the brazier. The triple circle was now complete and he closed the door to it with two pentacles, one inside the third circle and the second in the space between the second and third.

All was now ready. Thur stood in the centre, facing east, tall and solemn, his immaculate robe giving him added majesty. Beside him stood Morven, serene as an alabaster statue. Clasping his hands loosely before him he began to recite in a low, clear voice Psalm CII, which begins:

> "Hear my prayer, a Lord
> And let my cry come unto Thee
> Hide not Thy face from me,
> In the day when I am in trouble incline Thine ear unto me
> In the day when I call answer me speedily."

And when it came to an end, he continued with Psalm XIV.

Then Psalm VI, and ending with Psalm LXVII. When the impressive words died away there was a moment of silence before Thur took from the table a vessel of brass, varnished within and without, having a lid pierced with holes which fitted exactly and tightly, and a convenient handle. This he filled with clear spring water from a jug. Then he took salt and cried in a firm, ringing voice:

"Tzabaoth, Messiach, Emanuel, Elohim, Eibor, Yod, He, Vou, He! O God, Who art the Truth, and the Light, deign to bless and sanctify this creature of salt, to serve unto us for help and protection and assistance in this Art experiment and operation. And may it be a succour to us."

With this prayer he cast into the water the salt, and then he took herbs, vervain, mint, garden basil, rosemary and hyssop, nine in all, gathered in the hour and day of Mercury in the waxing moon, and bound them with a thread that had been spun by a young maiden … Morven. These he steeped in the water and, reaching for the white-hilted knife, with it he engraved upon the sprinkler's handle characters, on the one side:

and on the other side:

When this was accomplished he spoke to Morven for the first time.

"After this ceremony we may now use this water in the sprinkler when necessary, knowing that whatever we shall sprinkle with it will be sanctified by its power to chase away all phantoms and depriving them of the ability to hinder or annoy us. With this water we shall make our preparations of Art."

Morven bowed her head in assent but did not speak. So awed was she, so deeply impressed by the solemnity of the occasion and of what she had heard that she dared not use her voice in case she marred the spell. Thur seemed far removed from her into a realm of mystery whither she could not follow him.

His second operation was to make the pen. He took up a quill from the table, plucked from the right wing of a live male gosling and shaped it with the white handled knife. The exhortation was: "Aurai, Hanlii, 'Thamcii, 'Iilinos, Athamas, Zianor, Auonai! Banish from this pen all deceit and error, so that it may be of virtue and efficacy to write what I desire."

Upon the brazier he cast a handful of dried herbs and with the same knife sharpened the pen, sprinkled it and held it over the brazier in the cloud of perfume which rose from the herbs, then wrapped it in a new white linen cloth and laid it aside. In a like manner, with their appropriate invocations and prayers he consecrated the cords and laid them aside in the linen cloth.

It was late, and he became aware that Morven was looking white and exhausted. He broke up the seance for that night, since he could do no more without the Burin, which must be made in the day and the hour of Venus.

"You are tired, good little Morven. Get to your bed and sleep sweetly."

He kissed her on the brow, turning away and busying himself with clearing away the impediments of their night's work.

In a few hours Morven was wakened from a deep sleep by a loud and continuous thumping on her door, followed by a vigorous shaking. She opened reluctant eyes to encounter the gaze of Alice Chad.

"Why, child, 'tis little short of seven o'clock and you sleeping and looking like one dead. What ails you? Master bid me let you lie, but you must eat, and food has been waiting this hour."

Morven smiled upon the careful soul and yawned.

"I come, good Alice. I was late to bed last night. Your master was talking, and we marked not the passing of time."

"Oh, him!" sniffed Alice. "While he sits reading and talking all night, heedless of all mortal things, you should get your sleep, child, for your strength is yet frail."

Morven laughed reassuringly.

"I shall do excellently well in your good keeping, Alice. I come."
Alice went down again, shaking her head. It was not natural, nay, it was sinful for folks to sit up after darkness had fallen. Did not the good God especially design it for the repose of man and beast? Why, otherwise, should darkness fall? Why should sober, God-fearing people like her beloved Thur Peterson behave so? And talk! What on earth was there to talk about that men should lose their sleep for it? Drink, yes, and conspiracy, yes again, and witchcraft. These dark doings required the night to hide their blackness, but Thur was a creature of light if ever there was one, and his niece more so ... that Lily girl, his precious niece!"

Alice Chad adored the leech, in her partial eyes he could do no wrong. The wonder and delight of him unconsciously possessed her quiescent soul night and day. Her feelings for him were an undiscovered mystery to her. She stood in such great awe of his learning that she was aware only of her willingness and delight in serving him. So selfless was this devotion that criticism was rare, yet Alice felt strongly that Morven should get her night's sleep and not stay awake in wild talk. She was trying to screw up her courage to the point of telling him so.

A few minutes later Thur appeared as usual, followed by Morven, and they all sat down to breakfast together. Thur was addicted to much night study, but Morven was no night-bird, and on the occasions when the Sabbath commanded attendance she was her own mistress to sleep the next day. Now, with the solicitous eye of Alice Chad continuously upon her, she was under the necessity of appearing her normal wide-awake self when she wanted to yawn until her head split in half. The prodigious effect of swallowing made her throat ache. Thur appeared to be swamped in thought, and the meal was a dismal one because the serving-woman tied up their tongues, preventing the talk of absorbing interest which they were so eager to exchange.

Morven was slowly eating bread and honey under the doting and proprietory eye of Alice. An earthen beaker of fresh milk was beside her, and every now and then Alice gave it a suggestive little push nearer to her. Morven did not know whether to laugh or cry in her exasperation. She had put the spell of enchantment upon Alice and the consequence was not to be escaped. Alice was so deep a bond-slave that her enchantress was for ever before her, nor could she endure her out of her adoring sight, so that each was enslaved to the other in a magic circle from which there was no escape. Much as she liked the woman, and enjoyed the novelty of solicitous care from one of her own sex, yet enchantment had its drawbacks and gave her pause for solemn thought.

At length Morven spoke. "Those were words of a rare wonder you spoke, my uncle !"

"H'm ?" murmured Thur, abstractedly.

"Like solemn bells they have been ringing in my head. Never have I heard the like. 'God be merciful unto us and bless us, and cause His face to shine upon us, that Thy way may be known upon earth, Thy saving health among all nations.' Was not that the way they ran?"

"You have a good memory, child," he smiled.

"Nay, Master." Alice burst forth, no longer able to restrain the will to speak her mind. "Such learning is not for a young maid, and to keep her from her bed to listen to it. 'Tis for our good priests and not you, Master Peterson, to prate to her of God and nations. In the small hours, too! Just when she should be sleeping the sleep of honest Christians. She is no great man, to be burdened with such gear...she is a maid but late recovered from the very jaws of Death himself."

"Plague take the woman!" thought Thur, seeing himself as much involved by Alice's amity as her enmity, but he said:

"I hear and mark your wisdom, good Alice. Away with you, Morven. Into the garden, and keep death at bay amid the butterflies and bees."

Later, when Alice had gone to market, he joined Morven and they sat close together on the grassy bank talking in undertones.

"'Tis one hindrance after another," he grumbled impatiently. "No sooner do I get the aid that I require than I have to contend with prying in the very heart of my home." He laughed vexedly. "Alice will be a very dragon in your defence, Morven. Devil take the notion that the day was made for work and the night for sleep. They who sleep by day are necessarily the limbs of evil. O Liberty!" He flung his arms above his head as though bursting under intolerable bonds. Morven soothed him with quiet words, assuring him that all would be well, urging him not to aggravate the situation by wounding Alice's feelings, which were all kindness and tenderness for them both, and not to germinate antagonism in a faithful heart by a senseless contradiction and repudiation, but to agree with her in all she said. "So will she tire the more quickly, for nothing wea-

128

ries the spirit 'like a complete agreement," said Morven. "And I will snatch a sleep where I may, to fortify me for the night's work."

That night they slept in peace, but the following, being the day of Venus, again the two prepared the water for their personal cleansing and, with this accomplished, again they drew the triple circle in exactly the manner of the former occasion. Their work was now to make the all-important Burin.

Thur recited anew those same Psalms of David, then, throwing the herbs on the brazier, he waited until the clouds of incense ascended, and took up an engraver's awl. He purified it on the live coals and, with the white-handled knife, whose office was that of a tool as distinct from that of the Athame used by the witch to control spirits and work magic, he carved on the handle of the awl, which was to become the Burin, these characters:

The invocation followed, solemn and commanding. *"Asphiel, Asophiel, Asophiel! Pentagrammaton, Athanatos, Eheieh, Asher, Eheieh! Qadosch, Qadosch, Qadoschl"* And thus he prayed: "O, God Eternal and my Father, bless this instrument prepared in Thine honour, so that it may serve only for a good use and end, for Thy glory. Amen."

He censed and sprinkled it and folded it away in the linen napkin, and that was the end of their night's work, since before continuing they must wait again for the day and hour of Mercury. Progress was slow and there was much to do, much to prepare before they could begin the great work of helping Jan.

As Morven helped Thur to wipe out the Kabalistic characters from the floor, she asked him soberly: "What are those names, so strange sounding, which you invoke?"

"They are the names of Angels and great Spirits, but their origin is wrapped in mystery. Some are Egyptian, others go farther back in antiquity to Chaldea and Phoenicia, others again are Hebrew.

All we know for certain is that they are words of power. I have pondered upon their meaning for many years, and sometimes I am tempted to believe that they have no meaning, but, because they are resounding, like beaten gongs, they serve the purpose of binding us all together, so that all who hear are caught as in a great net, all feeling alike, all thinking alike, all desiring alike, until the force of each one present sweeps upward, like a cloud of incense ascending, and unites with the concentrated will of the Magus and forms one great pivot upon which the whole wheel of the Circle and all its potentialities turn.· Do I speak in riddles, Morven?"

"No. Do you mean that when two or three are gathered together, especially with one general object in view, that all thought becomes interwoven and so helps to bring about the fulfilment of the object for which they assemble; and that these high-sounding words, in themselves meaningless, by their repetition of certain sounds then changing to another sound and repeating that, beat upon the mind and shape it as the Magus would have it go. Thus does it think what he would have it to think, so that it sees what he wishes it to see, and so can he derive power from those who call upon his service?"

Thur nodded, but added hastily:

"Forget not that I am a novice in the Art. I do but tell you my secret thought about these incantations."

* * * *

When the day of Mercury came round again it found them again in the Triple Circle. Thur again recited the three psalms, which seemed to Morven more wonderful with each repetition, so that she listened with closer attention and increasing understanding.

He would need wax in the making of the Magic Sword, and that to be used was fresh bees-wax taken by Morven from the hive at mid-day. She had proved herself extremely skilful in the handling of bees, which she feared not at all. The creatures seemed to like her.

Holding the wax in his right hand, Thur invoked: *"Exabor, Hetabor, Sittacibor, Adonai, Onxo, Zomen, Menor, Asmodiel, Ascobai, Conamas, Papuendos, Osiandos, Spiacent, Damnath, Eneres, Golades, Telantes, Cophi; Zades!* Angels of God be present, for I invoke ye in my work, so that through you it may find virtue, Amen."

He paused and then exorcised it as follows:

"I exorcise thee, O Creature of Wax that, through the Holy Name of God and His Holy Angels, thou receive blessing, so that thou mayst be sanctified and blessed to obtain the virtue which we desire, through the most Holy Name, Adonai, Amen."

So praying, he sprinkled and censed the wax and wrapped it in the white linen cloth. In a like manner he consecrated strong acid, to be used for engraving upon the tempered steel of the Sword. When this was done and set aside in readiness, Morven took from the table an ink-horn made of baked earth in the hour and the day of Mercury, and gave it to Thur. With the Burin he carved round the base in Hebrew characters these sacred names.

*"Yod He Vau He, Matatron, lah, lah, lah, Qadosch, Elohim Zaboath,"* and filling it with ink he exorcised it thus:

"I exorcise thee, O Creature of Ink, by Anaireton, by Simoulator, and by the name Adonai, by virtue of Him through Whom all things are made, that thou be unto me an aid and succour in all things which I wish to perform by thine aid."

This he sprinkled and censed and laid up with the wax. Work for that night was over. They cleared away all traces of their occupation and went to bed.

There now remained the great event, the creating of the Magic Sword. This was an ordinary blade in common use as a small-arm, and he had bought it in London. When in despair of ever being able to help the Bonders, he had formed the desperate design of obtaining guidance through Olaf, as was shown in the opening chapter. That attempt was more in the nature of a Spiritualistic seance than a true exercise in Art Magic. Olaf had proved a good medium through which the needed guidance came. The command he had received, "Seek ye the Witch of Wanda," had provided him with the Athame and the white-handled knife, the means to the end they desired. The purchase of each article separately constituted no danger, it was the articles in the aggregate which made the menace. Any knowledgable person, viewing them as a whole, would know immediately for what purpose they would be used. Rumour had it that my Lord Abbot was interested (in his holy way), in the Art, and what was known in the town was known almost as quickly at the Abbey, and any gossiping brother could put the Abbot on his track. Thur was convinced that he might as well transcribe his circle, recite his Psalms, invoke his Angels and exorcise his instruments in the open market at mid-day as buy the necessary articles in his awn home town, so he had gone to London for them.

He was thinking of these past difficulties as they prepared the Triple Circle in the hour and the day of Mercury for the making of the Magic Sword. Bathed and perfumed in symbolical accord with the nature of this weapon, both Thur and Morven were as naked as the drawn sword. After the Psalms had been recited Thur took up the cleaned and polished sword, and with the Burin he engraved the name of Power "Elohim Gibur" on the hilt. In the heat of the brazier he mellowed the consecrated wax, smoothed it upon the blade and wrote there on with the Burin, *"Yod He Vau He, Adonai, Eheieh, Yauai."* He turned the blade, smoothed the hither side with wax and inscribed "Elohim Gibur". All these characters were written in Hebrew, then, using the acid they had formerly consecrated, he engraved all these characters deep into the tempered blade.

When this labour was done he turned to Morven. She, holding her Athame in her right hand, brought the point down upon the sword's blade and held it there to communicate increased power, while Thur cried in a strong voice:

"I conjure thee, a Sword, by the names *Abrahach, Abroath, Abracadabra, Yod He Vau He,* that thou serve me for a strength and a defence in all my magical operations, against all my enemies, visible and invisible. I conjure thee anew by the name Shaderai Almighty, and by the names *Qadosch, Qadosch, Qadosch, Adonai, Elohim, Tzabaoth, Emanuel, Azoth. Wisdom, Way, Life, Truth, Chief, Speech, Word, Splendour, Light, Sun, Glory, Virtue.* By these names and by the other names, I conjure Thee, a Sword, that thou servest me for a protection in all adversities. Amen."

Thur sprinkled it with consecrated water and Morven censed it. Again Thur spoke a conjuration:

"I conjure thee, a Sword of Steel, by God Almighty, by the virtues of the Heavens, of the Stars, of the Angels who preside over them, that thou receivest such virtue that thou mayst obtain without deceit the end that I desire in all things wherein I shall use thee, through God, the Creator of the Ages, and Emperor of the Angels. Amen."

Morven perfumed it with the perfume of Art and Thur recited: "By virtue of *Dani, Zumech, Agalmaturod, Cadiel, Pani, Caneloas, Merod, Camedoi, Baldoi, Metrator,* Angels most Holy, be present for a guard to this Sword."

He wrapped it in clean linen and laid it aside, and they followed with the consecration of the sickle. Lights were needed for the great circle, and since nothing might be used which was unconsecrated, Morven had made a number of wax candles in the hour and the day of Mercury in the waxing moon, each weighing eight ounces. The wicks, required to be made by hand by a young maid were her work. For this consecration of Light there were three new Psalms. The first, CLI; of which the beginning is:

> *"Praise ye the Lord,*
> *Praise God in his Sanctuary.*
> *Praise Him in the firmament of His Power."*

and the last verse:

> *"Let everything that hath breath praise the Lord.*
> *Praise ye the Lord."*

Then Psalm CIII and Psalm CVIII with its ending:

> *"Whoso is wise will observe these things,*
> *Even they shall understand the loving kindness of the Lord."*

Thur then took the Burin and on each candle he engraved signs, praying as he did so: "O Lord God who governest all things by thy Mighty Power, give unto me, a poor sinner, understanding and knowledge to do only that which is agreeable to Thee. Grant me power to fear, adore, love, praise and give thanks unto Thee with true and sincere faith and perfect charity. Grant O Lord, that before I die and descend into the Purgatory below that Thy Grace may not leave me O Lord of my soul. Amen."

Then he said: "O creature which is wax, by Virtue of Him Who is Pure Truth, by Him Who alone hath created all things by His Word. That thou cast out from thee every phantom, perversion and deceit of the enemy and may the Virtue, Truth and Power of God enter into thee so thou mayest give light and chase far from us all fear and terror."

Then he sprinkled and censed them and wrapped them in clean linen and set them aside. Thur, in the same manner with the help that Morven's power as a Witch (or as nowadays we would say as a medium) gave him, consecrated every article, no matter how small or insignificant, which was to be used within the Great Circle.

For, to aid that extreme concentration of mind that would be necessary it was essential that everything he should use should already have the Magical will directed into it, so that on the Great Night everything should assist to guide his will to that one purpose.

When all was finished, Thur, who had already blessed so many articles that night, also blessed Morven, saying: "Get thee to bed, beloved child. Sleep and may all Holy Angels guard and preserve you from harm, both in this life and in the life to come."

# CHAPTER XI
## MUSIC MAGIC

HUR and Morven were again in the triple circle, in the day and hour of Mercury. Work that night was making Talismans for protection.

The brazier was glowing. Upon the table were consecrated pens and ink, dried frog's skins, bees-wax, herbs and spices, the sprinkler and consecrated water, the Burin and the white-handled knife. Taking prepared candles Thur placed and lighted them, exorcising them thus:

"I exorcise thee, a creature of Fire, in the name of the Sovereign and Eternal Lord, by His Ineffable Name, which is Yod-He-Vou-Hee. By the name of Power, EI: that thou mayest enlighten the hearts of all the Spirits which we shall call unto this circle, so that they may appear before us without fraud or deceit, through Him Who hast created all things. Amen."

Followed the reciting of the three psalms of David already quoted. Then this invocation.

"Adonai, most Powerful, EI, Most Strong, Agla, Most Holy. On, Most Righteous, Azoth, the Beginning and the End. Thou Who hast established all things in Thy Wisdom. Thou Who hast chosen Abraham as Thy faithful servant and Who hast promised him that his seed shall in all nations of the earth be blessed and multiplied as the stars of Heaven.

"Thou, Who hast appeared to Thy servant Moses in the midst of the Burning Bush and hast made him walk dry-foot through the Red Sea and gavest the Law to him on Mount Sinai. Thou, Who granted unto Solomon these Pentacles by Thy great Mercy, for the preservation of both soul and body, we most humbly implore and supplicate Thy Holy Majesty, that these Pentacles may be consecrated by Thy Power and prepared in such a manner that they may obtain virtue and strength against all adverse spirits and creatures, through Thee, O Most Holy Adonai, Whose Kingdom Empire and Principality remaineth and endureth forever without end. Amen."

Morven was so uplifted by this impressive invocation that she felt power grow and magnify within her and so knew that what she made would really protect the wearer. Taking a piece of consecrated wax and warming it in the brazier she deftly moulded it into a tiny figure, using the warmed white-handled knife to form details. When ready, she cut off the top of the head. With the knife's point she inscribed magical characters, as though writing them on the brain itself. These symbols thus becoming part of the wearer's organism, the knowledge of protection from danger would become part of his mentality and the instinct for self protection increased a hundred-fold, with increased ingenuity in evasion and enhanced perception of threatening danger springing from the very centre of his brain.

She replaced the scalp and carved further characters (emphasising the need for caution and watchfulness) on it. Altogether she prepared four figures in exactly the same manner. While Morven was so occupied Thur wrote Kabalistic signs on the frog skins; when he finished he glanced at Morven.

"We need the hairs of one well disposed. I am well disposed so here is hair from my head for thee, Morven; but I think for the others and for me, we shall need yours." So saying he pulled red gold hairs from her sc~lp, and softening the waxen heads in the brazier, he pressed a hair into each and one of his own into the figure for Morven. Then he sprinkled and censed them all, pronouncing the spell of invisibility.

"Melatron, Melakh, Beroth, Noth, Venibbeth, Mach, and all ye. I conjure thee O figure of wax, by the living God and by the Virtue of these Characters and Words, that thou holdest the eyes of all beholders and renders him who carries thee invisible whenever he beareth thee with him."

Then each manikin was wrapped in a frog skin as a garment, and carefully laid away till wanted. Morven looked at him longingly, wonderingly.

"They may help," she said, "at least they will do no scath, but my heart misgives me."

"Be not so dismal, child, did you not tell me 'twas our own fears made danger real to us?"

"I did, but I fear that against danger my powers fail, I quail myself as I never did before."

"Come, child, never despair; you have power, but you must learn to concentrate it. Remember, 'tis the hardest thing of all to do; to concentrate when a beloved one is in danger, but it can be done."

"You think I have power; that gives me hope, Thur."

But all the time she was thinking: "Am I but saving him for the Lady of Keys who has so much beauty? And beauty is her power. I too have beauty, but what was the use of that when he never looks at me?"

She sighed, then started.

"Someone is at the door, Thur."

Thur cocked his ear: a scratching noise came from below.

"Friends," he said laconically.

She hurriedly slipped on her dress as he went down and soon returned with Jan and Olaf. The very presence of Jan drove her spirits deeper into the mire. Why had he come at this time of all others? She smiled at him; but he scarcely noticed her. Olaf greeted her warmly, pressing her hand in both of his.

"Why, Morven, how … how … " He broke off shyly.

"We looked for you long ere this," said Thur. Morven set about getting supper, moving lightly; listening to the talk.

"We dared not," said Olaf. "Even now we are here more by chance than by good cunning, but mother has gone to a neighbour for the night and someone had to come, so we risked it."

"What said she at your long absence?" Thur asked. "What did she *not* say?" said Jan.

"She will wipe the earth with you, Thur, when she catches you," Olaf warned him.

"Catch me first," said Thur. "What reason did you give for your absence?"

"That we were dutifully returning to the fold with you on a visit to her when one came after you to summon you to your brother's death bed, and as there were many robbers and masterless men abroad and not safe for a single man to travel, we went with you," said Jan.

"And she said she knew not that you had a brother, so did not believe it."

Morven having finished preparing supper slipped out into the garden, but Olaf ran after her and almost dragged her in, so reluctant was she to face Jan and read the indifference in his eyes.

"Look, Jan, behold our Witch ... this miracle of beauty we knew not of when we rode through the waters of Wanda by the mere."

Olaf had lost his shyness and found his tongue. Jan looked; but his mind's eye could only see the dark, shining beauty in Safran who entranced him. Morven knew it, though he bowed courteously saying how glad he was to see her in such good health ... His self-possession hurt her; she knew that had he been confronted by the Bride of Jocelyn he would have become scarlet with tongue-tied adoration. She turned away and spoke to Olaf, saying she knew not what: words coming from her in little gasps of irrepressible dismay.

"Thur, I ... we ... were talking of power."

"Come to supper, try this pasty," Thur enjoined, cutting liberally.

"Speak no more of power." Jan's vehemence was marred by a full mouth.

"Olaf shall go no more into that accursed triangle, my heart fails when I think I nearly had him slain."

"So," Thur retorted, "you give up?"

"Give up," said Jan, startled. "Give up!"

Morven watched him across the table, her lambent eyes seeming to grow twice their size. Jan marked their fire and her parted upper lip lifted from small even teeth.

"No," he protested. "Go on I must, never will I withdraw while life is in me." Morven's sigh of relief was audible; her mouth closed to its normal curve of firm sweetness with its extreme fullness of lower lip. Jan drank deeply of his ale cup; set it down with a bang; then emphatically: "But not with my brother, I alone and you with me, and you with Thur, but not Olaf."

"And Morven?" asked Thur.

"Morven?"

"Were we not bidden to seek her?"

"True." Jan agreed, then went on ungraciously; airing his grievance: "What hope have we? I thought we would get a powerful old witch; full of malice and evil who could bewitch Fitz-Urse and his cursed following to death and damnation; but *what* do we get? A terrified, starving woman who turns out to be a slip of a wench ... harmless ... useless ... " Again, Morven's grey-green eyes dilated; the fire in them flamed, the lip lifted.

"I, useless. Harmless?" she shot a queer, sly glance into the corner where Thur's harp stood. "At least I can play the harp."

The remark seemed so inconsequent that Jan ignored it and went on:

"Aye, harmless, Morven. If you have malice in your heart and strength in your mind, you keep them well hid, I have seen nought of them."

"Canst see this?" she cried. In a flash she was round the table, flinging herself unexpectedly upon him as he sat sprawling sideways. Perching herself upon his knees, her arms around his neck, she kissed him full on the lips, then, drawing herself away, her arms still on his shoulders, she scanned him narrowly beneath her lowered lashes.

"So did Mistress Delilah with her power overthrow the colossus Samson," laughed Thur, highly amused.

"Do you mean you would so use Fitz ... Urse steal into his castle, play the harp, subdue him so, then open to us? 'Tis a wonderful idea," said Jan wonderingly. He placed a huge paw on each side of the slender waist to hold her steady on his inexpert knee and looked at her with kindly interest: "Is that your plan?"

"The Gods be good to us. I mean, Christ and all the Holy Saints," commented Thur.

Olaf guffawed: "Even the High Gods and the Holy Saints can't mend a dolt."

Morven rose slowly; ignoring them superbly.

"Yes … if needs be," she muttered in a dull tone, I will do even that to further your ends, Jan."

"My thanks, Morven."

A silence fell, which all felt in their bones … save Jan. To break this Olaf cast about in his mind.

"What is all this story about Fitz-Urse, why rode he hither?"

"O, he oft comes here, to see the Esquire; 'tis in his Lordship after all."

"Have done with all this gossip about Fitz-Urse, his taxes and marketing," cried Morven. "Him we need not fear, for is he not to be brought low after the manner of Samson?"

The men nodded puzzled assent, and Morven continued: "Then it is to this that our minds must be turned, especially as Alice told me (ere she left) that he had gone, taking his Esquire and half his men with him.

"Here is the very voice of wisdom," Thur admitted admiringly. "Speak on, O Witch of Wanda, for it would seem that yon comely head of thine bursts with knowledge."

"I have discovered that certain members of the Witch Cult live in the forest hereabouts, and 'tis said that some be stout lads who shun not a fight. I may have power to move them to our service, could I but reach them."

"How many are there?" queried Jan eagerly.

"They may number fifty, I know not for certain," replied Morven.

"But who are they? What are they?" asked Olaf.

"People of the old Faith are everywhere. By force they are made followers of Christ (at least externally) but in their hearts they love the Old Gods, and them they serve, in divers ways, when the call comes."

"Said I not that she had power?" Thur demanded proudly. "Power to think and plan wisely in our cause? O Bartzebal, we owe thee much!"

Seeing that she had captured Jan's attention, Morven hastened on: "If, on the morrow, I donned boys' clothes and rode with you and Olaf, wouldst thy mother give me shelter for the night? Thus would I meet thy mother, Jan, and with the dawn I would depart, saying that Thur had bidden me to meet him at a certain hour and place. I have heard that the people of the Witch Cult band together at St. Catherine's Hill, and that is but a league beyond thy mother's farm."

"An you could get us help that way, 'twould be a godsend," said Thur. "But will they help you?"

"I can but try," she answered.

"Then I will meet you in the forest where the main fork of the Stour crosses the track. Olaf will show you the Place, you must not ride alone into the town, I will bring your woman's gear with me. What say you, Jan?" But Jan looked woefully doubtful.

"Our mother..." he hesitated and looked at Olaf uncomfortably.

"Yes, our lady mother..." said Olaf, rolling his eyes heavenwards. Morven could not help but laugh.

"You mean she would not welcome me?"

"She will not," Olaf affirmed, and Jan gave a short, gusty laugh.

"In effect, our mother, who would try the patience of every saint in heaven, wore out mine long ago!"

"And mine," echoed Olaf. "One more hearth-storm like the last, and I am off to the greenwood. Would thy people welcome me there, Morven?"

"Nay, lad, we speak of serious matters," Thur expostulated.

"I did not speak in jest," replied Olaf, who suddenly looked older and more resolute than his years warranted. Thur glanced at Morven, who queried: "Does your mother ride?"

"She does not," answered Jan. "Did she so, she would be a wiser woman."

Morven smiled. "There be more ways than one of dealing with a shrew, so say that you will ride with me to St. Catherine's Hill (as they call it now, though better is it known as Kerewidens Hill) and I will risk the night there."

"My thanks," said Jan, "but as we came here with farm wagons, we must away with them, so we start at dawn," and with that he rose, lifting his empty platter. All followed his lead in tidying away, and then, as they sat round the fire with the consciousness of labour done, Thur brought the harp from the corner, and brought a stool, to which he led Morven, saying:

"Play and sing to us, child."

Well pleased, she lovingly tuned the instrument, and as she drew her fingers across the strings, ripples of melody jewels fell from them, followed by a few careless chords that had in them the sweetness of the sistra shaken by priestesses in the ancient temples of Isis; sounds which held all magic in them, and then Morven began to sing:

*"Beneath a tree she danced alone;*
*The Crescent moon on high*
*Kept watch and shed a silver zone*
*On mime and sanctity.*

*Her gestures were of Holy shape,*
*Her smile all saintliness.*
*Her red-gold hair let down to drape,*
*Her form in loveliness.*

*She swayed and as her body bent,*
*She poised, now high, now low,*
*As piety and fervour spent*
*Her passion's fiery glow.*

*Her soul was loosed upon a quest*
*Of ancient, tragic worth.*
*She proffered all her skill and zest*
*To bring a thought to birth.*

*She came, devoid of wealth and caste*
*To dance beneath a tree,*
*Shunned by the world, a lone outcast*
*A happy witch was she."*

Before the sound of her voice had died away, there was a loud knocking at the door. "Open, open, in the name of the law."

Sergeant Byles had been left in charge of the castle and town while the Esquire was away, and was as trustworthy as any of the band of villains gathered round him. In any case there was not much danger of attack; much of the surrounding country belonged to the Church and the Barons to the south were peaceable men. Strolling robbers were few and the town's defences were proof against any attack they could make. So Esquire Walter's absence made it possible for Byles to put a long-cherished scheme into action. From the moment he had looked into Morven's eyes at the guard house, she had inflamed his blood; he could neither rest nor sleep because of her. He had tried several times to contact her in the market or elsewhere, but she never stirred abroad without Dame Alice. He dare not molest women in the market place; Esquire Walter ruled his men with an iron hand. No trouble with women in town was his rule, enforced with branding iron and gibbet. So Byles burned and brooded, now came his time, ready and ripe for his purpose. He had been drinking, but not heavily, but enough to raise his courage to the height of his purpose. All day he had brooded over his plan. As night fell he placed trusty men on guard and set forth with five cronies who would do what he wished. At the castle he told his second-in-command he was going to patrol the town, searching for possible outlaws who might filter into it, as Esquire Walter had taken half the small garrison away with him. To keep up this pretence, he searched half a dozen houses, earning nothing but sullen looks and a few mugs of ale. Finally he came to Thur's house and thundered at the door, calling: "Open, open, in the name of the law."

"But this is the house of Thur, the leech," objected one of his men. "A well favoured man and not one to cross."

"Peace," roared Byles. "Are not my commands enough? Knock I say." Morven meanwhile had dropped her harp and ran to the staircase, beckoning the Bonders to follow. Thur lingered only to throw two tankards into the cupboard before he went into the shop.

"Coming, coming," he called, slowly unbarring the door. "What's to do, Byles?" he demanded.

"Orders, Master Leech. Orders to search."

"For what?"

"No offence, there was some trouble and 'tis said some miscreants have got into the town."

"Do you suppose I would hide criminals?"

Thur's brows gathered in a frown and he looked menacingly at Byles.

"Not so, good Master. No offence, but duty is duty, your house is on the town's edge, and without your knowledge they might steal inside."

"And I bear the blame since a householder is responsible," Thur grumbled, his mind tussling on the problem; for Byles had a right to search.

"Ah, very well, search an' you must."

Morven and the Bonders were in Thur's sleeping room; the wall of the end gable was four feet high, topped by a heavy beam, the wall plate, supporting the roof beams. Morven pulled out two huge nails and showed that one end of the wall plate was false and moveable. Inside were the magic instruments: parchments and the manikins they had just made; snatching two, she gave one each to the astonished brothers.

"Here, take these, wear them always, they will protect you from harm. Now, in with you both, creep along, it runs the whole length of the wall, push the instruments in front of you, 'tis narrow quarters, but you may lie snug."

One after the other the Bonders crawled and wriggled into the hole; Jan pushing the instruments before him. When they were safely in, Morven replaced the false end and the nails that secured it in place, and returned to the room below. She descended the stairs; a vivid figure, her low cut green dress slipping from her shoulders and red hair glowing in the grey stone staircase, lit by two flickering lamps. Slowly she lifted her right hand and brushed back her hair; a sign agreed between her and Thur that all was safe. Relieved, Thur turned to stare at Byles, reading in his eyes as they roved over the girl's face and figure the secret of his visit. In the tense silence Morven sensed the cause of the disturbance; she was well aware both of Thur's anger and helplessness and his anxiety for her and the Bonders' safety. Byles made a gesture, part greeting, part conciliation: "Give you good even, Mistress," he said civilly, passing the tip of his tongue round his lips.

Morven inclined her head in acknowledgment, moved slowly across the room, and sat down, taking up her harp again. Byles followed her with famished, wolfish eyes. Thur looked at him as though he would joyfully strangle him, his fingers itching to squeeze his throat.

"Now, Byles," he called in a tone that made Byles jump. "You came to search? Away with you and search; all is open to you." He stood in the centre of the room, while a farce of searching the cupboards and outhouses was carried out.

"What, nothing?" he jibed. "Well, there remains the upper part, so up with you." Revolving in his mind, meanwhile, all the hideous possibilities, should they see the magic circles, would they report them and Morven? He was one unarmed man against six in armour, he was her only protection; should he attack them, or they turn on him, he would be killed, and each man could have his will on her in turn; it was more than a possibility that Byles would carry Morven away, or even kill her, and if so Jan and Olaf would perish miserably; fastened in their cramped hiding place. There was silence. The six men-at-arms standing about awkwardly, they had no wish to search upstairs; no criminals could be there. Morven sa t resting her elbow on the harp, gazing into space; the looks of all were on her. Byles could not speak, his wits had deserted him. He wanted someone else to provoke the quarrel.

One of the men yawned. "Thirsty work," he commented.

"Aye," another supported him. "Aye, aye, 'tis thirsty work," added a third.

Thur flung some money on the table. "Get ye to the Lion's Head and drink to a better search."

The men grabbed the money and were making for the street when Byles interposed: "Not so, my orders were to remain and watch, the town be in danger, and this house most likely to be raided. Orders are orders, Master Leech."

Thur saw an opportunity. "So," he commented and went to the cupboard, producing tankards and a six-pint pitcher, which he set down on the table with a bang, at the same time deftly emptying a small packet of powder into it. "The cask is in the kitchen, draw and drink."

But Byles was watching him narrowly. He snatched the pitcher and upended it. The powder fell out. "Rare dusty, your pitchers be, Master Leech. Here, wash this ere you draw the ale," he said to one of his men.

Thur thought quickly, the men were crowding around the ale butt. He called: "Morven:, fetch thy cloak."

"What now, Master Leech?" Byles protested threateningly.

"My niece is in danger. I am taking her to the castle to place her under the protection of Dame Upmere who hath a kindness for me. Send one of your men with me, if you fear for my return."

"Not so fast," retorted Byles sullenly. "My master has ridden with Fitz-Urse leaving me in command. The young mistress is safe enough here ... we will see she comes to no harm," Byles leered.

Morven's voice broke the tense silence. "I am in no danger, good uncle." Thur, warned, relaxed. He wanted to tell her at a given signal to run from the house. Surely he could hold the doorway until she got to a neighbour's house; but how to get his sword was the first problem and then how to tell her ? The men returned with the pitcher slopping over and set it on the table with a splash; tankards were filled and they fell to drinking.

"Your health, Mistress. Thur, you are a lucky man; such beauty to brighten up your dark house."

Morven smiled and drew her fingers across the strings of the harp. "Canst sing, sweet Mistress ?"

"Aye, when I have a mind."

"Canst tell stories, Mistress ?" one of the men asked. "Of witches, hobgoblins, werewolves and such ... ?"

"Nay, of witches I know not, 'tis no talk for Christian folk. We speak not of such in this honest house, sir. Know you of any such ?"

"I, the saints forbid," was the hasty disclaimer.

Then came a knock on the door. Thur strode to open it. Whoever the intruder he could not well worsen the situation. Two monks stood there, Brothers Stephen and Hobden. Thur greeted the former with profound thankfulness:

"Brother Stephen, you are indeed welcome, and I give you good even, Brother Hobden. Stephen, I have a search party ... Byles came with evil intent after my niece, on pretext of searching the town for outlaws. He means mischief without a doubt. If you will conduct her to safety I will hold them in check as long as there is life in me."

"The Saints be good to us?" exclaimed Hobden. "Is the wench then so squeamish?"

"She is my niece, Brother," said Thur.

"Aye, aye, have it your way," grumbled Hobden sourly.

When Morven saw the two ecclesiastics enter, she experienced the first pleasure she had ever known at the sight of a churchman. She acted the part of a young maiden to perfection; laying aside the harp and rising; standing meekly, with eyes modestly lowered and hands clasped before her. Such a picture of delight and desire did she make that Hobden's sourness and discontent increased. Byles eyed her with his famished look. When he saw Hobden he grinned with relief, but when he recognised Stephen the grin changed to a snarl.

Thur said: "Good Brothers, I have been afflicted by the death of my brother, and my niece has come to live with me to cheer my home. Morven dear, draw some fresh ale for Brothers Stephen and Hobden."

She smiled and obeyed. There was a silence among that ill-assorted company. Normally Hobden, would have caroused and gossiped with the soldiers, but Stephen was neither tipster nor libertine, and most of the monks stood in awe of him; not only because he was the Lord Abbot's clerk and an open and indulged favourite, but because there was that about him which commanded respect and fear. He bore himself with dignity and authority which none dare dispute. He had much learning, and steadily set his face against all laxity. Hobden sat down heavily and set to serious drinking. Stephen remained standing; watching Sergeant Byles, revolving in his mind why God made men so.

"Give ye good even, Brother," said Byles sulkily, when he could endure this calm scrutiny no longer.

"Good even to you, Byles. I did not look to find you here in the Esquire's absence, me thinks the townsfolk were better guarded were you at your post."

Byles turned away, muttering something about strangers and his duty to search. "Tush," was the crisp retort, "you know as well as I do what brought you here." As though the matter held no further interest he turned away as Morven entered, and relieved her of the pitcher.

"Thanks, Brother," she breathed, and went to the cupboard for tankards, filled them with a pretty grace and carried them to the two guests in turn. Byles, watching her slyly, trying in his tangled mind to reconcile this present mien with the malice which had snapped out at him just before. She seated herself, and took up her harp and ran her fingers over the strings caressingly.

"A song, a song," called one of the soldiers, sprawling on his stool.

"Nay," croaked Hobden, resolved upon spoilsport if he could not enjoy himself in his own way. "Songs are unhallowed things. Give us a holy hymn or sing not at all." He hunched himself on his stool, hugging his knees, in a very ugly humour, while Stephen watched him with a mocking smile. Morven knew no hymns, but feared to admit it.

"Do *you* sing your favourite, Brother," she murmured submissively, leaning forward, to peer into his sulky face. Whereupon Hobden began to bellow like a cow in labour, wherein there was neither rhyme nor rhythm, with Morven striving to pick out an accompaniment. The din was appalling, then stopped, each participant looking accusingly at the other.

"No hymns, or we go mad," cried Byles, reasonably enough. "Play to us, Mistress, play !"

Morven complied. At first she struck into a popular ballad, beloved of all Jongleurs, then, without stopping, she glided into another less familiar, and again into a third.

Thur and Stephen talked in undertones until the brother saw his companion gradually becoming absorbed in the music, as did the men-at-arms. They were silent now; drinking in the music with open ears, and Stephen, who was tone deaf (and to whom all tunes sounded alike) did not listen but fell into an equally absorbed contemplation of the performer.

Thur was amazed at her proficiency; she seemed to make the harp speak. He recognised that her first tentative playing had gone. With every passing moment she gained an assurance as of one who, having long been deprived of the means, comes again to execution and self-expression with joy and exaltation. Imperceptibly she had stolen away from the ballad and seemed to be improvising; a steady, monotonous beat and yet incredibly sweet. Thur was struck a new pang by her loveliness; the faint apple-blossom tints in her face set against the glancing lights of her hair; the grey-green eyes with golden sparks burning with a strange intensity. The steady throb went on. All the men were fascinated, watching her hands, her arms, curved and slender like the necks of swans in the dusk. She had true musician's hands, capable yet artistic and sensitive, with wide-spaced, supple fingers, beautiful in their agility. The music throbbed on, infinitely sweet, yet. incredibly exciting, as the beat increased in tempo.

Thur watched and heard in the same breathless silence that held all save Stephen, to whom it was of no import, and who sat thinking his own chaotic thoughts, though watching the performer.

What was happening? Thur asked himself. The flashing pink-tipped fingers brought to his mind small, white crested waves lapping over yellow sands. Was that throbbing undertone, the beating hooves of a distant horse at a gallop? No, it was the beating of a heart, his own heart beating steadily, pulse for pulse 'with those vibrating strings, "but surely faster than a heart should beat". A thought somewhat terrifying. He darted a look round and saw with a chill through his spine, the similar effect there ... all faces were flushed red or almost purple, eyes starting from their sockets. All save Stephen, so obviously deep in his own dark problems. And now it seemed that Morven was aware of this consciousness in Thur, her eyes warned him. But of what? "Keep still, keep still"; a message seemed to hammer in his brain, but he was as still as death. What could she mean? The throbbing gradually grew more insistent, until the tension seemed as if it would snap the strings asunder and the hearer suffocate. Thur dragged his gaze away from Morven's and looked at the others. All were still, fascinated by the white arms moving so caressingly. She made a lovely picture; the gleaming ivory shoulders, the lovely glowing hair. She was most desirable. The throbbing went on, beating at his brain and heart; he could feel it pounding as no heart ever should; in exact time with the music. But he was a leech and knew no heart should ever beat as fast as this. Were these waves of passion thrilling through him? He would be happy to sit so for ever listening to her playing for him. It must be for him alone. Bursts of rage almost stifled him with an uncontrollable urge to rise and drive all others from the house, so he could be alone with her. Her eyes caught his again, with the message: "Keep still." Then, he noticed, Brother Stephen was watching. Watching for something to happen. He realised she was doing something to them, and Morven too was watching and waiting for it. The throbbing quickened slightly and Thur realised his heart was responding, beating ever faster and faster. He moved to rise, but Morven frowned, so did Stephen. He sank back again.

Morven was doing strange things, making them mad, and Brother Stephen knew it! The music quickened again, rising almost in a snarl, and his heart leapt with it.

"Suddenly Hobden leaned forward and smashed his great fist between Byles' eyes, roaring: "Take thy wolves' eyes off her, thou hairy ape." Simultaneously one of the soldiers sent his tankard hurtling at the head of another across the room. It struck the target squarely. Then all was bedlam. Thur and Stephen got behind the settle and watched. Morven darted with her harp into a corner, still playing triumphantly. Everyone had sword or bill in their hands, slashing furiously, rushing wildly at each other, weapons raised to strike, but the points caught in the low beams. With what seemed one accord they debouched into the shop, battled there, sweeping the jars off the shelves, and finally got out into the alley. Byles was leaping about like a scalded cat. They were screaming at each other in high-pitched rage, steel ringing against steel. Brother Hobden swinging a huge bill-hook with the best.

Thur and Stephen ran to the street door, peering into the darkness. Gradually the tumult died away, and the breathless combatants looked at each other in amazement; thanks to good armour little damage had been done.

Morven, still playing, was peering out of the door too, but it was a soothing tune; calm and peaceful, like a balm to the mind, and concluding with a soft chord. Thur looked at her in silence.

Brother Stephen spoke with conviction: "That be witches' knowledge. Knowledge is useful. They will not return. I give ye good night," and he stepped out into the darkness. Thur barred the door, as Morven, dropping the harp, flew upstairs to release the two brothers.

# CHAPTER XII
## SPURN HEATH

HE sun was breaking through a dense haze as Thur, Morven, Jan and Olaf rode out of the town next morning. After their experience of the night before the two Bonders were a little distrait and Morven could hardly stifle her gapes, so tired was she. So much power had she put into her strange musical interlude that it had left her in a state of exhaustion. After releasing the captives they had sat talking until late, .then had ransacked the pantry for food and stored it in their saddle bags. Thur rode with them to see them safely through the gates, and seemed to be the only unscathed member of the group. Before them laboured the two heavy wagons which had brought corn to sell the previous day.

Thur said: "Well, my merry men all, were I you, I should seek a good clump of bushes and sleep my fill, 'twill do you good, and you can catch up with the carts easily. Morven, be prudent I beg! I shall meet you at the stricken elm, by the Stour, at the fourth hour to-morrow, an' you be not there by night, at high noon on the morrow again. Farewell, and God be wi' ye."

"I would the leech were twenty years younger," said Olaf with a gusty sigh, as they watched him gallop away.

"Wherefore?" Jan demanded, yawning widely and crossing himself lest a devil should pop down his throat, as was popularly believed at the time. "So we should have more of him. Death will steal him from us and where shall we be then?"

"The Gods be with us; what talk is this? Truly do we need sleep," yawned Morven. "Why sits your mind in that quarter?"

"Because, had I my way, I would be always with him."

"Hm," grunted Jan. "Would you be a leech then?"

"Nay, I would be a great Magus," was the modest reply. "I would probe into all hidden mysteries, and popes and kings would wait breathless at my nod."

"More like to nod the breath out of thee," jeered the other. "There is no more sense in thy head than a cracked pot.... Better awaits you; you shall be captain of all my men when I come into my own and you shall marry Morven here."

For some reason this annoyed Olaf.

"A soldier, I, never! I like not the shedding of blood without reason, but I will fight to reinstate you. As for marrying Morven, that is for you, the elder, I lack three years of her age. No, 'tis for you."

"Between you, I shall not get a husband easily, as neither will have me," said Morven dryly.

Yet, for all her sharp words, she could not stay her eyes from wandering inquiringly to Jan's face. Jan looked at his brother, then at Morven and frowned. Here was a cherished scheme frustrated at the outset. A suitable reward for Morven's services and Olaf honoured for his loyalty.

"Nay, marriage is not for me yet ... when the time comes I must seek a powerful alliance."

"You would wed an heiress?" Morven asked with a dry mouth. While Olaf stared at his brother in disgust.

"Nay, money means naught to me for its own sake, though it has its uses. What could we not do if we had a peck of it?" thoughtfully. "Hire men-at-arms."

"So, instead of seeking the witches kin shall we seek the fairy crock at the rainbow's end?" this from Olaf, ironically.

Jan ignored this and his reply was rather to the question in Morven's eyes. In them he saw some sort of reproach, the cause of which he was ignorant, a hurt of which he was innocent, both in act and intent.

"When we have overcome Fitz-Urse, by magic or otherwise, we will be still weak," he explained in the gentle manner habitual to him and which made him lovable. "My only way to strengthen us is to wed the daughter of some family well established and powerful; by asking a small dowry, or none at all, the path to it would be eased."

"You do not ask for love in your marriage? it means nothing to you?"

Jan hesitated. "What *is* love?" he asked, his eyes growing abstracted as though he searched some inward part of himself for an answer. "An unsatisfied longing for a lovely face … a vision which never can be mine? It is but a dream, a man falls into it unknowingly, as a pit dug by an enemy. One moment he is gay and his own man, the next he has seen the unattainable and has fallen never to rise again the man he was. The blackness of the pit has closed over him and his only star is the memory of her who has plunged him into ruin."

Olaf stared harder than ever. Was this Jan the tongue-tied? Surely love had made him mad as it did some men, and everyone knew madmen were fluent!

Jan came out of his trance and shook his head as one emerging from water.

"Nay, Morven, be not too tender-hearted for us. My wife and I will be fond enough when occasion rises, but, we first have to snare our hares."

Morven made no answer, Olaf jogged along on her other side, thinking his own thoughts about Jan and his affairs. Hitherto Olaf had thought of this business of regaining their heritage more as a story of adventure with themselves as the heroes, than as a serious matter of life, such as digging their farm. Even the experience of the triangle was entirely unlifelike.

But Jan's talk revealed to him how very serious the matter was; and had brought the clouds down to earth with a rush, revealing undreamed of difficulties; the storming and taking of the castle; the slaying of Fitz-Urse, was but the beginning of the story and not the end, as he had always imagined it.

Did his brother really believe in magic and pin his faith in it, or was he using it to mask something else? Jan, whom he deemed he knew as one brother knows another, had in a few words proclaimed himself a stranger, of whose inner mind he knew less than nothing. He kept glancing at him seriously, trying to reassure himself that he was not some alien being.

As for Jan, his mind was clouded for wan t of sleep; he could neither think nor plan, and was acutely aware of the edginess of himself and his companions, but was aware of a spirit of opposition stirring in Olaf and Morven; and though unaware of its cause, was alive to the danger of this hostility to his plans. Surely there was enough to trouble him? His mother's perpetual nagging; and resistance to anything he proposed, and her set resolution not to acknowledge the growth of her sons to manhood, he thought: "No longer are we children to be scolded and slapped into obedience, am I not the rightful owner of the farm?" As he ambled glumly along behind the lumbering wagons, he tried to invent some reasonable pretext for his absence from home for the next twenty-four hours. He felt it was beneath his dignity to seek aid from the quicker wits of his companions. He clicked his tongue impatiently against his teeth and shook up his mount to overtake the two men ahead. "Wat," he bawled through his hollowed hands. "Wat, Samkin." A rising wind dispersing the haze, was blowing against him, and the handsome bay teams plodded on unheeding.

"What is Jan doing?" asked Morven, rousing from her abstraction.

"Sending the teams on by road; we are nearing the forest track."

"Oh," she responded, and fumbling in her pouch, brought forth two lengths of scarlet ribbon.

"What ... "began Olaf curiously as she quickly bound the ribbon beneath each knee; tying them in conspicuous knots on the outside, then laid her fingers warningly against her lips. This done she quickly picked up her reins and pushed forward to join Jan, who had galloped ahead and come up with his men and was arguing with them.

"Wat," he was saying. "Speed you on! Bid my good mother be

156

at ease about us till we return. I have some matters to transact which ... "

"Look, Master Jan, ye canna do tha-at," the man drawled with a grin.

"'Wat,' say Mistress, 'see that they two,' meaning you-ur worship and Maister Olaf, 'come back wi' ye. No junketing wi' Maister Peterson,' ses she, meaning his honour the leech. 'Once they get wi' him thers no seeing them again, so bring them back along o' 'ee,' says she. 'Or I'll be the death o' 'ee.'"

At this Jan was so outraged that he bent from his saddle and dealt the man a sharp backhander across the mouth. "Insolent swine, speak more respectfully to your betters! Be off, or I'll be the death of you here and now. Am I a child to be brought home like a bundle of hay by a hind?"

"No, zur. Yes, Maister Jan, I means no disrespect, zur, Oi du but speak wha'-rt Miss-ess ses."

"Very good, now speak what thy master says to thy mistress, begone."

"But, Oi der'ner, Mas' Jan, Oi der'ner, Miss-ess will sure break ma skull."

Here Morven made her horse plunge, thus drawing attention to herself; after some prancing she had the satisfaction of seeing Samkin staring at the scarlet ribbons, he seized Wat by the arm:

"The bonny red garters," he gasped, pointing. "Wha-at ails ye, man?" objected Wat surly from his chiding.

"Behold, Bumble wit; The Messenger, The Bonny Red Garters come again."

She put her finger to her lips with a warning look, then making a secret sign with thumb and forefinger, she drew into line with Jan and sat waiting beside him. The two men grew alert. After a whispered word between them and another steady look at her, they made clumsy bows and walked to their respective teams, and managed to rouse them into a display of speed, which soon took them out of sight round a bend.

The sun was hot, and in a nearby field a half demolished straw stack offered inviting rest. Jan pointed to it. "Thur's advice is good, shall we sleep awhile? My wits have gone wool-gathering and my head burns for want of rest."

They tethered their horses, removed the bits, and left them to graze. Taking the side of the stack, hidden from the road, each found a comfortable bed. Jan was quickly asleep but neither Morven or Olaf were so blessed. In spite of her aching eyes Morven was filled with wretched thoughts, and was too intent in thrashing out the problem of herself to find rest. She, too, had been brought face to face with reality, and in a way most wounding to her self love. Jan had revealed his mind with all its stark preoccupation with the harsh facts of his destiny.

Not only had he no love for her, but he had no thoughts for her save as a possible wife for his younger brother. She savoured the full bitterness of this knowledge, with a mental pain which was almost physical in its sharpness and far more tormenting. Thur had been so sure she had only to wait in patience for Jan to turn to her as inevitably as the sun rose each day; but now she knew the vanity of such imaginings. Had he not spoken of his own luckless passion in terms which lifted him high above his usual self? Yet there were ways and she knew them. As mistress of the Art, she could compel his awareness, waken it and centre it upon herself for as long as she cared to retain it.

She could, had she wished, have enslaved him. She lay with closed eyes; so still that it seemed she slept, wrestling with the temptation; but as she strove with one part of her nature, she knew the other would never be satisfied and happy with a love evoked by spells and held by bewitchment ... She could, had she desired, have a besotted slave; but her crying need was for a deep and passionate love; voluntarily given because it could not and would not be withheld. She would not shame her love by stooping to encirclement. She wanted a lover and a mate, not a helpless victim. This was a decision, so hard in the circumstances as to be almost heroic.

Mercifully she slept a little, worn out with excitement, grief and suppressed tears.

Olaf did not sleep at all. He suspected Morven's love for Jan and had until an hour ago, supposed that when his calf love for the Lady Bride had spent itself, Jan would inevitably turn to Morven; but that dream had been rudely broken. Jan, unsuspecting the turmoil evoked by his simple scheme for all their good, would not marry Morven though she had a King's ransom for dowry. Because Olaf too loved Morven, he guessed much of what was in her mind, and her consequent suffering. Plague take people who were so busy with the lives of others! First his mother, now Jan, with their everlasting: "Do this," "think that," and "believe t'other." Olaf impatiently kicked at the straw. "Be my captain."

"Marry Morven." As though they were bags of corn to be carted hither and thither. And yet ... to marry Morven; that was a destiny to quicken his head with an undreamed-of happiness.

Olaf loving as imaginative boys love; shyly, secretly, delicately, savouring sweets with little or no thoughts of their carnal fulfilment, felt there was time enough for talk of marriage when love in Morven had died of starvation and neglect; only then might she turn to him. When by their united efforts they had raised Jan aloft, what would become of Thur, Morven and himself?

Would it be his fate to return to the farm; forever thrall to his mother's domination and nagging tongue? Nay, *that* would he not do; for though he had spoken lightly of becoming a Magus, there was underlying truth in his declaration. He wished ardently for learning, the ability to think clearly and concisely, for the means of self-expression and in the achieving of this ambition two ways lay open, the hard, slow, safe way through the Church and the dangerous difficult, swift way which Thur could teach him.

The thought of entering the Church revolted him. Olaf's mind, for all the glancing gaiety of the surface was an abidingly serious one and he had the eyes of an artist coupled with a love for beauty and an artist's expression of creation. In the opinion of his mother he was born lazy; he would rather lie hidden watching the creatures of the greenwood than take his turn at the plough. Olaf's dislike for such work lay not in its hardness or monotony, but the inescapable fact that to do it well the thought of the workman must be centred on his work, else would the work suffer. If a man could plough and also ponder on the relation of God to the universe there would be no more willing ploughman than Olaf, but the business of plough-ing was to break up the soil in a straight furrow, and he who thinks of God instead of his work ploughs a crooked one. So, for any man who has to earn his bread, yet who wished to live the life of the mind, the only answer was the Church.

Olaf would lie on his back on a sunny bank, watching the chang-ing sky, the sun and wind playing in the tall, wavy grass, and it seemed to him that God and His Blessed Son were part of all this wonder.

He was filled with the joy of God; with an abiding sense of His mercy and love, also with a knowledge of his own inadequacy and unworthiness. He was full of a humble adoration and an intense desire for service. He knew the presence of God in his heart and mind. He wished to feel it every hour of the day throughout his life ... just the love and wonder of God; manifest in all his works and in all his creatures.

Yet, when he entered a church, all this ecstasy vanished and could not be recaptured until he was outside again. This was a fact which troubled him greatly. Authority was not unpalatable to him; on the contrary: he was capable of extreme veneration. No, it was the Church's interpretation of God and Christ which Olaf found irreconcilable with his own, and from which he would be forever alien. All the dogmas of the Church seemed to narrow God to the dimensions of a narrow stone. God, who made the world and life, was associated only with death and the grave, and for death and the grave humanity was compelled to live. The comparison between the simplicity and avowed poverty of Christ, His lack of worldly goods and the greed of the Church for wealth, and her arrogant assumption of power and might were things he could not reconcile. The perfect freedom of will which Christ gave mankind found no echo in her teaching. The Church had made God in its *own* image, but Olaf was convinced, how, he knew not, that God was infinitely greater than any father of the Church; however learned, however sainted, had the power to conceive Him. He pondered over all this; gazing at the sky and seeking inspiration; for he was deeply troubled by his own attitude. The Church showed an easy way for the sincere seeker after truth and learning. To one of his mettle, venerating only where he could respect, undisciplined, unyielding, disliking all control in thought, he was bound to come into conflict with the Church at a very early stage ... her orders: "Think this, think that. Dare to think otherwise at your peril," roused profound revolt. Her arrogant dictation to humanity of what it might think; her intolerable restrictions upon the greatest of all God's gifts; the ability to think at all, was an assumption of infallibility which no honest scholar could accept unquestioningly. Her persecution of those who dared to think boldly, was an abomination which filled Olaf with hostility. To persecute a man in the Name of God, because God had omitted to endow him with the gift of faith (the safest and most useful of all gifts in the medieval world); could bigotry go further? At sixteen a healthy youth has little of the stuff of martyrs; he was no fanatic, rather would he sneer and resist passively. If burning at the stake was the reward for sincere thinking, he would keep his thoughts to himself, confiding them only to those whom he could trust. The Church should not get *his* body to burn. Yes, Thur was his only safety valve and his mentor. By the time Olaf had relieved his feelings with these disgruntled reflections, Jan was stirring and stretching. "Truly could I eat a house."

"We must ride ere we eat," said Olaf squinting at the sun. "It lacks an hour of noon and if we are to reach Maldrums before nightfall we have little time to waste. Morven still sleeps."

"She seems frached this morning," Jan added. "She is a strange creature ... what think you of her? What will our mother think of her if she knows of this trip?"

"What will she? I fear all this trip will do is embroil us further with mother, and all to no purpose."

"But Morven may help us by her power."

"What power? We be but mocked by the spirit that bade us seek her."

"But she had what Thur lacked, two knives."

"Aye, and beyond that, to my way of thinking she is but a danger and a hindrance."

"You speak sourly, disappointed because she is no foul hag, ugly enough to scare the devil himself."

"Well, fancied you witches were like her?"

"Fancy hath naught to do with fact. I could fancy her as a water sprite, with her rare pale face and green eyes. I have seen lilies lying still on the surface of ponds; white and pink tinted like Morven."

"I need no lily-white wench but a ... "

"You had no thought of a witch till the spirit bade us seek her." Olaf cut him short with some heat.

"Nay, we will not quarrel over her, that would indeed give her power for unwanted evil," Jan answered, laying his arm on his brother's shoulder.

"Disarmed," Olaf laughed. "Strange things happened last night, unbeliever."

"What did happen? I could not make top nor tail of it, Thur says she played the harp and the soldiers drank and fought, 'tis but what they ever do. It needs not a harp to make them fight when they have ale, but I heard not a note of music, didst thou?"

"Not a note, and God knows we had naught to do but lie and listen. I vow we slept not. I was too full of cramps." Jan shrugged; the mystery had not greatly enthralled him, he was disappointed with Morven; even in their present mission he had no great faith. He was naturally hard-headed and sceptical, and though he had asked Thur's help by summoning spirits to his aid in a moment of passion, it was as a drowning man clutching a twig. He respected Thur when in his presence, but his mind soon reverted to preconceived notions of the kind of help he wanted; a band of devoted followers, professional soldiers well armed, gold to pay them; all magically produced from nowhere by wave of a wand. Of the steady step by step, the linking up into one big whole which Thur and Morven envisaged and followed with patience, he could form no conception, as is the case with so many in this world.

"Jan," said Olaf slowly. Unable to put into words what he thought and felt of the folly of invoking supernatural aid, and not believing in it when it came, and piqued because it did not follow preconceived lines, he broke off.

"What?" growled Jan ungraciously.

"No matter."

"But you must have meant something."

"Jan, you lack patience, you lack judgment, you lack the grace to band men together to follow blindly such a forlorn hope." Olaf burst out in temper.

"Why should Thur, and Morven and I, to say nothing of a hundred others risk life and limb for a dunderhead who will not look an inch beyond his nose?"

"You call me a dunderhead?" Jan flashed, stung by the contempt.

"I do, every act and word proclaims it."

"How?"

"By ugly manners, discourtesy, disbelief and other follies unworthy of you. If there be such beings as spirits know they not your disbelief? Is that the way to propitiate them? Can you not be content to be led step by step in their way? Or must they plunge straight headlong into an abyss which perchance they can see though thou canst not?"

"There is pith in what you say," Jan admitted after a moment of consideration. "But, how may a man check his thoughts?"

"Have some faith in Morven. Do as she asks, indeed she is

friendly as Thur himself. If she is acting for you under the guidance of the spirits let her be."

"By the powers, you speak sense, but I see no sign of her doing so."

"Saw you not how Wat and Samkin obeyed your orders only when she made them?"

"I'll make my hinds obey me or know the reason why," growled Jan.

"Nay, brother, they obeyed mother, till she showed them something; red garters I think, then they obeyed Morven."

Olaf took breath and continued. "Be it witchcraft or what, I saw with my own eyes. My rede is, let us take her to our mother without delay. We should not deny her the chance to be kindly and hospitable, an she will, and perchance Morven may put magic on her as she did to Wat and Samkin?"

"What debate you so solemnly?" Morven had wakened and asked.

"Whether we push on to Meldrums or take you to Spurnheath to our mother, 'tis for you to say," said Jan.

"To Spurnheath, an' your mother be willing, but I would not vex her by my coming."

"She is kittle-cattle, Morven … One knows not how it will take her."

"Those two men of yours are of the brotherhood, or they know of it, if I could get word with them alone, I might learn much," she said.

"Enough! To horse," said Jan.

Through the forest glade they rode to the spot Thur had appointed as a meeting place. Here Olaf dismounted and cut a big cross on the trunk of a beech. "Thou canst not mistake this," he said. Then they hurried on until they were clear of the forest and entered a lane fringed with pine. The way was densely overgrown, a mere track; trails of bramble starred with blossom snatching at passers-by and making a sharp tangle, it was really the bed of a dried-up torrent, long used as a path which wound up the side of the hill, terminating in a plateau of coarse grass-land; marshy even in dry weather. It was very green high up, with a wide view of the country below; forest and farmland and a distant shining line, which was the sea, on the horizon. The hill on the other side had a gradual descent and from a spring a wide brook ran swiftly down, about whose grassy banks grazed a flock of geese, tended by a barefoot goose-girl, whose young body was barely covered by her rags. A wild mane of yellow hair straggled over her shoulders to her waist, covering her brow like a thatch, from which her eyes, bright as a rabbit's and as inquisitive, peered out at them.

Jan and Olaf hailed her blithely as they passed.

"Give you good day, Truda."

"Good day, Masters." The girl stared wildly, then made a sign, which Morven answered. They cantered over the springy grass down the hillside and along the edge of the stream. A spur of the forest grew into well tilled lands in which cattle grazed. From the woodland came the squeal of swine, rooting in the beech mast, and beyond stood a farmhouse, with outbuildings towards which a cart piled high with wood moved deliberately. Such was Spurnheath. At the foot of the hill was a road giving access to the farm. Morven, looking keenly about her saw everywhere evidence of thrift, orderliness, good management and prosperity, backed by a hard driving mind. They reached the gate; the wood wagon arriving simultaneously, and they drew aside to give it passage. Morven did not ask why Jan and Olaf chose to bring up the rear of the procession instead of heading it. The house door stood open, and from it emerged a woman, who crossed to the nearmost barn and stood leaning against the wall, tilting on her heels as though to relieve the soles of her feet. Her hands rested on each ample hip, and her arms were covered with flour, while a smell of baking bread bore witness to her recent occupation.

She was a comely woman, big and strong, covered with good firm flesh, and standing six feet in height. A clear white skin threw into relief handsome regular features, to which very dark brown hair arranged in two thick plaits made a frame. She was dressed in a woollen gown of glowing crimson, which well became her. Bright, dark, intelligent but irate eyes watched the approaching wagon balefully. The wretched driver affected a nonchalance he was far from feeling, knowing that as yet she had not beheld her offspring who were hiding behind the piled wood.

"Now, Chinnery," she hectored. "Hasten wi' that wood! On to the pile wi' it! Hi, Tomkin! Come ye and lend a hand. Stack the small trunks yonder where they can dry in the sun … why … what's this?"

A sudden stride brought her to the wagon, where the removal of the top logs revealed that part of the load was not cut, but only gathered wood, some of which was rotten. Chinnery quaked as she snatched a near-by cudgel, and strove to dodge, but she fell on the wretched man and belaboured his backside heartily.

"Thou dog!" she yelled, her arm rising and falling like a flail. "Thou adder of corruption, thou spawn of evil, thou knavish cheat! I'll have the hide off thee for this," and pursuing the yelping Chinnery round the wagon Hildegarde came face to face with her truants and the stranger. She was taken aback, and lowered her cudgel with surprise.

"Well!" she cried indignantly, "and who art thou, Mistress?"

"I am Morven; my uncle Thur the leech sends you greetings and felicitations, Mistress Hugh."

Hildegarde, becoming calmer, opened her mouth, then shut it again abruptly. Her angry eyes had encountered those of her two sons and there was that in their steady gaze which she had not seen before, and which gave her pause.

Meanwhile Morven had slipped from her saddle and rummaging in her saddle-bag produced an earthen jar. "Alice Chad sends you this. She begs you will taste it .. 'Tis a confection she hath devised of pounded nuts and honey, flavoured with almonds."

Hildegarde's eyes slid over the slim figure clad in a youth's clothes of brown cloth, and though her lips tightened she refrained from comment. She was angry and must voice it in violent speech or remain silent.

"You look at my dress," Morven continued. "My uncle deems it safer I ride clad thus, less danger for Jan and Olaf. I come to seek my mother's people who are said to live three leagues hence, and my uncle bade me ask you shelter for the night."

Hildegarde swallowed hard, and by this action arrived at a measure of civility.

"You may have it and welcome, Morven. My sons are sad gadabouts and leave me to play the man's part, aye, and do the man's work too while they junket abroad with the leech hither and thither, but I knew not that Thur ever had a niece."

"He knew it not himself till he saw me," Morven assured her with wide-eyed candour. She held out the jar which Hildegarde took as graciously as she was able. Chinnery stole from beneath the wagon and began unloading. Jan and Olaf came to his assistance, while the two women stood watching the proceedings with feigned interest to cover the awkward minute and the silence which had fallen between them. There was no genuine cordiality from Hildegarde, and Morven felt the lack of it, so she stood docile, waiting the elder woman's pleasure. The wood was almost stacked when Chinnery saw Morven clearly for the first time, and his eyes encountered the red ribbons.

"Oh, the bonny red garters," he exclaimed excitedly, and dropped his log as if unaware of what he was doing, but receiving a warning glance from the wearer he slapped his great paw over his mouth as if to stem further speech.

"What ails the clod?" cried the exasperated Hildegarde. "Hast not had enough of the cudgel that ye must yammer about red garters while ye stack rotten wood? About your work if ye would keep a whole skull!" A diversion arose at this juncture by the arrival of Wat and Samkin who had brought back with them various articles from the market. Seeing their mistress, cudgel in hand and a blacker frown than usual on her brow, they assumed a bustling activity in unloading their goods, when they suddenly saw Jan, Olaf and Morven. The bucolic mind is not a fast worker, especially when for hours it has been dwelling on witches and witchcraft. Their masters in company with the red gartered stranger, had declared their intended absence from the farm. Therefore they ought to be truly absent, and now they were confronted by their wraiths! They promptly dropped what they carried with a yell and an exclamation of which Hildegarde caught but the words "Red Garters." Morven, reading their minds, spoke calmly and clearly before the storm broke.

"We outstripped you through the forest," she explained. Her serenity restored their lost senses and they knuckled their foreheads and picked up their burdens, looking foolish as they met the baleful glare of their mistress.

"Red garters," quoth Hildegarde. "Hast come here to bewitch all my men-folk with thy gauds? They might be Barbary apes with their senseless chatter of red garters."

Morven simpered. "In London they be the very pink of fashion, an they please you, I beg that you will accept them."

"I? Deck my legs with such? Who would see them? I am no strumpet to show my legs for all the world to see. Now, if ye possess any woman's gear, get ye into it. Into the house with ye!"

As Hildegarde led the way the goose girl came down the hillside, driving h'r flock before her, her eyes on the women entering the door.

The houseplace consisted .)f a large room with a hearth in the middle, and the usual hole to let out the smoke. Small slits of windows let in a modicum of light, which fell on a floor of beaten earth strewn with rushes, and a flight of wooden, ladder-like stairs leading aloft. A serving-wench was busy at a long narrow table, setting out mugs and wooden platters. Another girl was stirring a huge pot slung on an iron crane over a fire, and not far from it a door led to another room where the women slept after Hildegarde had locked them in.

Hildegarde herself enjoyed the luxury of a separate room, in the loft over the hall itself; while the men of the farm slept round the fire in the hall.

"You will sleep here, with the women," said Hildegarde, pointing. "An' get ye into decent women's weeds ere any of the men folk see ye again," said she, her mind making note to lock up Morven safely that night.

# CHAPTER XIII
# RED GARTERS

OON came a summons to a meal, but a dismal one. Farm hands trooped in; each to his seat in silence; Chinnery easing himself down gingerly and with a pained grimace instantly suppressed. Hildegarde sat at the head of the table with Morven (now clad soberly in a green gown) on her left, Jan on her right and Olaf next to him. The maids served all before taking their places at the board. The food was good; wholesome, ample and well cooked, lacking only the salt of good fellowship. Like all tyrants, Hildegarde deeply resented the effects of her own tyranny. "Why must her folk always be so sulky and silent?" she brooded, feeding the embers of her wrath with fresh fuel. She smarted under the inury of her capitulation, forced into it by she knew not what agency, prevented somehow, from flaying her sons alive with her tongue, for slipping away without her leave and then (the crowning insult of all) cozening her into receiving this red-haired, white-faced chit into her house. She glanced sourly at Morven from time to time, telling herself spitefully that she sat there like a princess, eating as though her food had no honest acquaintance with her belly, but must come by some backstairs route of mincing manners with dainty finger tips. As for the Bonders, cats on hot bricks were immeasurably more comfort a ble. They ate stolidly, avidly, their minds blank, conscious only of fires being stoked against their inevitable roasting by their mother. When the silence became so marked that even Hildegarde felt it to be a reproach on her hospitality, she turned to Morven and spoke as civilly as she might:

"You say you seek your people, wench."

"Truly, mistress."

"How are they called? I know of none here who might be thy kin."

"Robin Artisan, sometimes known as Robin-with-the-Hood.

Janicot, better known as Little John, Simon, called Lord of the Wood and Kerwiddeon."

Morven spoke clearly, watching Wat, and she saw him nudge his companion on either side and they drew their heads together and whispered: "Well, I know of none so called in these parts, you must seek further afield. I wonder at Thur sending you on such a wild goose chase, mayhap he would be rid of his responsibility for your guardianship."

Jan glanced up angrily at this but did not speak.

"'Twas I that wished to find them," Morven answered demurely.

She glanced at the men who were all looking at her with pathetic expectation. She must get speech with them and quickly, but how? She knew if she could get free from the family the men would find a way of approach, but how to do it?

"The names are outlandish. Who was your mother?"

"A good woman whom my father loved dearly. She died when I was a little child."

"Aye, the good die young, I ever tell Jan and Olaf here they will make ancient bones."

At this Olaf giggled: "An' I ever tell you, Mother, I trust I will indeed."

A long silence ensued, Hildegarde brooding on Jan's action in bringing this girl home. Doubtless the great oaf fancied himself in love with this chit and was looking forward to hours of free inter-course with her denied to him in her uncle's house. Soon he would be marrying her and bringing her here, and would then try to set her up as mistress of his home, and she would try to lord it over his mother and perhaps turn her adrift. Hildegarde forever com-plained loudly and bitterly of the work she was left to do by her run-agate sons; but the bare thought of a daughter-in-law coming, even though it meant relieving her of some irksome tasks drove her into a welter of opposition. She would see to it that Jan got no chance of as much as one word alone with his doxy.

She was interrupted in these pleasant ruminations by Morven:

"Mistress. I am stiff with riding. I pray let me dig your garden, 'tis good to get the stiffness out of my back." As she spoke she looked at the three men.

"Perhaps Jan can get me a spade and show me where to dig?"

Jan honestly voiced his protests:

"Nay, Morven, that you shall not, and you a tired guest. Think you our mother will suffer it?"

"Aye," said Morven stolidly, "an' you when you know 'tis necessary."

"How necessary?" snapped Hildegarde.

"That I should give aid where aid is needed, but I cannot give aid without tools, Jan."

Her use of the word aid pierced the fog of his mind; remembering his talk with Olaf, he made no more objections. "I'll get you a spade, an you may dig where you will, if you must dig."

"You'll stay wi' me, Jan," commanded his mother, who saw in this an artful ruse for the two to creep away anti be together.

"I need you. Olaf will go."

Olaf was only too happy to follow Morven outside. "What's this, Morven?" he whispered.

"Cannot tell yet, but get me a patch right out of sight of the house, then beguile your lady mother with sweet words ... and keep her away."

Olaf frowned: "She will be too busy keeping Jan beside her to spy on you."

She laughed sardonically: "Little she knows how needless are her pains to keep him from me."

"Does it trouble you greatly, Morven?" he ventured.

"Trouble and I have been close these many years. I should be lost without my fellow, I ween."

He said no more but led her to a patch he had started to dig himself and handed her a wooden spade edged with iron.

"Here you may work in peace, unseen. Shall I work with you, Morven?"

"Were that wise?" she asked, smiling ruefully.

"Most unwise," he responded, stifling a sigh.

"Morven, counsel me; for I need it. My mother is my mother. That can I never forget. When I am away from her she has very many of my thoughts and my love, yet when I am near her, love flies, leaving but rebellion behind. How long should a man suffer thraldom?"

"Not a moment after he can throw it off. Be courageous, Olaf, speak thy mind with firmness, be kind and reasonable, but steadfast. No man or woman has a right to dominion over his fellow save where such dominion be freely granted."

"You speak wisely and truly and echo mine own thoughts, yet do I hesitate."

"'Tis natural. Now, begone, ere you draw down wrath upon me."

He wandered away, Morven girded up her skirts and worked with a will; it was many weeks since she had dug a patch, and the smell of the new-turned earth was good to her nostrils. Digging is satisfactory work and she knew how to adjust her body to its rhythm. She had come to the end of her second row when she saw three men crossing the fields, going towards some huts, with many a backward glance at her. She watched them disappear, her mind troubled. Would the Red Garters produce no results beyond useless stares and whispers? Were the men too afraid of Mistress Hildegarde to venture near her? The fourth row was nearly finished when she suddenly found that Wat, Samkin and Chinnery and three others-each armed with a spade-were standing behind, watching her with considerable attention.

"What seek you?" she asked. "Who are you?" to the three new men.

"Simon Pipeadder an' his sons, Peter and Garge, Mistress," said Samkin.

"Be it true, Mistress?" Simon asked anxiously. "Is what true?" she demanded cautiously.

He hesitated and mumbled: "My Truda, up on hillside yonder..."

"Aye, she came running wi' a tale that one bearing the sign o' the messenger was riding wi' the young masters."

"What sign? I was taught caution in a hard school."

"The Bonny Red Garters he means, Mistress," Wat thrust in impatiently.

"Be it true, are you the Messenger, are the good days coming to earth again?" said Samkin.

"We corned fro' town quicker nor ever before, an' when we sord Mars' Jan and Mars' Olaf an' you here when we deemed them leagues away, us thought ye all wraiths."

She lifted her skirts, showed the red garters and dropped them again. At the sight of them the men fell on their knees, chanting in a sort of chorus.

"O Blessed Day. Maiden, when do we meet?"

"Not so fast," she said, "we must not be seen talking and idling here; spread yourselves out and dig backwards."

"Th-aart no wa-ay tu dig," protested Chinnery, who had a conventional mind.

"No wonder you take beatings," said Morven. "Peace, fool, du as Maiden says or I'll clout 'ee," cried Wat.

They dug as Morven directed while she faced them and talked: "I seek aid. The good old days may not come again just yet, but your help may bring them. Now, heed me closely. I need men. Fighting men armed with bows and bills and swords if you have any; men who will come when I call and go where I bid them and who will keep silence."

"Be it to fight wi' the King's Majesty?" asked Simon.

"No," Morven assured him. "'Tis to fight for justice against one whom all hate and whose rule for years has been black; an outrage against men and God ... the Old Gods I mean!"

"A fight be ever a good thing so it be short and sharp an' we win, when a man can take much loot. 'Tis your marches and counter marches, your defeats and retreats, and winter inside and out that eats into a man's guts. I know, I soldiered wi' good King Richard," said Wat.

"There will be no such," Morven assured him. "Victory must be ours at the first assault and much plunder or we swallow black failure. We must plan well ere we strike."

"I like not failure," argued Simon. "I mislike your failures most damnably."

"Come, come, Granfer, be not disputious and swaresome," his son thrust in. "We come to hear Maiden and not thee."

"We waste time," said Morven. "How many of the faithful do you muster?"

"Some six score men and women, old and young," Wat informed her.

"Others be scattered far in forest, they will come an' there be good loot," put in Chinnery.

"Will you not come and speak to thy people, Maiden?" Simon suggested. "There be many who love not the new ways, an' be sorely put to pay the dues and tithes Church ever calls for."

"I will, but when?"

"Whoy, tu-night, at Dearleap, there be meeting, 'tis full moon. The way is clear."

"'Tis but a meeting, we have no priest and no coven, 'tis ten years an' more since we had a Sabbath, we du but meet and feast and talk o' the good old times," grumbled Simon.

"I was at last Sabbath," chuckled. Chinnery, "Lord, an' Misstress knew; she ever loves the priests and her hand is as heavy as Lord Abbot's."

"You should know," Samkin laughed.

"Aye, we all knows, an' that says summat," said Simon pausing to spit on his hands. "Plague take the woman; a man might work all night as well as all day and yet not please her; yet she was not always so. Faither du say she were a comely, fair-spoken lass when she married maister."

"So the old folks du say," Chinnery corroborated, "but her temper ever were high and quick."

"Yet you abide when you all might flee?" Morven commented. "The forest is nigh."

"But we be Jan Bonders' men, every man Jack o' us, we abide by him as our faithers stood by his faither."

"Aye," Simon recalled, "we stole away an' after him, good Sir Hugh, as good as his faither before him."

Morven was amazed at what she was learning, but wisely concealed her surprise; obviously these men credited her with supernatural powers of acquiring information and she must not undeceive them. She wished to hear as much as she could from this unexpected source and encouraged them by her attentive silence.

"My da' tells tales o' him o' winters nights," said one, Cant by name. "'Tis God's pity he went to wars again, once he was safe back."

"I mind him well," put in old Simon, "Maister Olaf was then a babe, stumble-walking, and his faither came to me wi' the child riding on his shoulder, behind barn yonder. Ther'd been a turrible todo that morning... morning is ever a bad time for Miss-es... she's a sour bed riser."

"Aye, tha-rt be true," Chinnery interjected feelingly.

They loved a gossip and their tongues wagged freely.

"What happened, Simon; I never rightly knew?"

"Whoy, there'd been high words atween them and Miss-es up wi' her cudgel and beat him afore all o' us."

Cant swore a fierce oath, declaring flatly: "I would wring my wife's neck an she took stick to me."

"And he?"

"Took stick from her an' flung it far an' walked away."

"Wi' her screaming arter him as ever," Chinnery supplemented.

"He made us all swear to always bide by the child," Simon resumed.

"Me an' mine to aid him recover his own when day should come as surely should be."

"When we had sworn, by the Old Gods, Maister was not O' the brotherhood hisself, but he knew all about it, so when we had all sworn he set child within house an' rode away, an' we never saw un more."

"Knows Jan Bonder of this ? Knows he you are his father's men ?"

"Maister swore us to speak not a word so we kept Maister's secret, but Oi think he must know summot and Maister Thur may ha' told him."

"Does Mistress Hildegarde know ?"

"Not a word to her, Maister ever feared she would scream it in her tantrums and so 'twould come to the ears of Fitz-Urse, then the two young Maisters would be in peril o' their lives."

"Oi," said Cant, "Oi pity Mistress, she've had a hard and grieving life, knowing as 'twas she druv her husband to his death; not but that he meant to come back … 'twas only to larn her."

"So, how stands the matter now, Simon ?"

"We awaited a sign, Maiden."

"What sign ?"

He scratched his head. "Some word from Mars' Jan."

"So, when we saw Bonny Red Garters riding wi' he we thort it might be the sign," said Wat.

"Aye," Simon agreed, "an' when our Truda came running wi' the same tale Oi said to Peter here: 'Our times come la-ard, 'tis the sign.'"

"And you were right," said Morven with a tone of authority.

"Praise be to you, Maiden. The good old days will come again."

"Not in my Lord Abbot's time," Peter warned him.

"Who can say, afore the Norman took away the land many monks and brothers came to our meetings; 'tis said the last Abbot but one, led the dance hisself, masked as a gert stag. But now 'tis all changed, all changed," the old man mourned. "I were just new wed when priests came wi' men-at arms and crossbow-men and broke up our meetings. Many were took to Abbey prison and never returned. Those who escaped the fire rotted thar and died."

"So my da' tells O' winter nights," Cant joined in. "'Tis a sad an' evil tale, an' those who were left fled. Priests all said 'twas wicked an' idolatrous to try to make crops yield more, an' to make the beasts an' women too, strong an' fruitful."

177

"But why wicked?" Chinnery asked.

"We ha' dun it ever since the All-Father taught us, many a thousand year ago," Stammers protested obstinately.

"Think you the Horned God will return to his people and drive all these priests away?" Peter asked wistfully. "Will he, Maiden, will he?"

"Like all Gods He will only help those who help themselves. I am fighting for it, but the Church of these Christians is strong and haughty and brooks no rival. It commands castles and soldiers, emperors, kings and courts are subject to it. It has all learning and knowledge in its grasp and denies learning to all but Churchmen." Morven paused, to be answered by hollow groans of assent. "In the old days all knew where the Sabbath was to be held, and who would attend it, so when a few were taken and tortured it was easy to find out all who went to the meetings, their leaders and priests, and often even who represented the God Himself."

"Aye, I know of such," lamented Simon. "Thus was it ever easy to take them, the Church commanding all soldiers. If we would restore we must first take some castles and man them with our own people. This must be kept secret. We must pass as Christians and only officers must know who are the leaders of the Covens, and especially, who is our God. All must keep favour with the Church, repay treachery with treachery, give lip service and be unpersecuted."

"Surely you breathe wisdom, Maiden," Cant said admiringly.

"Yet, Oi likes no truck wi' church," Peter resisted. Though silent he was the one fanatic among them.

"'Tis necessary," she assured him. "I like it not myself, yet in this way only may we survive. Restoration can only be brought about by prudence, patience and slowness. We be as travellers in the dark; we must feel every step of the way, lest we fall into an abyss. Now, wilt help me?"

"Aye!" came the chorus.

"Meet us to-night at Dearleap and ask the brethren, we will tell them you come. Mars' Jan and Olaf will bring 'ee. Ah, here he comes," as Olaf ran up.

"My mother comes with Jan. Off with you, men."

They saluted clumsily and loped off with their spades, disappearing behind a hedge. Morven shouldered her spade and went to meet them.

The intervening time had passed unhappily between mother and son, he grew restless beneath a ceaseless fire of questions. The more troublesome to answer because there was really nothing between Morven and himself, so his mother accused him of lying at every turn. He wanted to stop Morven from labouring; his sense of hospitality was revolted at a guest so occupied. He quickened his pace to escape, but his mother laid a firm hand on his shoulder and kept up with him. Thus it was in no sweet temper that she saw Morven, the work abandoned.

"Whither away, Mistress? 'Tis not dark yet that you leave your work. We keep not city hours here, back to your work."

"You will have your jest, Mistress, the patch is dug."

"Dug!" screamed Hildegarde. "Nay, Jan, I will speak my mind, be silent." Seizing her skirts in both hands, Hildegarde agilely hopped over obstacles and ran to look, thrusting her stick into the ground to test the depth.

"O, Morven. I am so abased," cried Jan wretchedly.

"And I am uplifted. Tell me, Jan, dost know a place called Dearleap? We must be there this midnight."

So much could she say before Hildegarde came hopping back; her long plaits flying, her comely face wreathed in smiles.

"You are a great worker, dear child," she burst out, "you have indeed helped us well this day. Six of my lazy hinds would scarce have dug it in the time," and she beamed on Jan, thinking: "He has some sense after all, though he has been lying to me all the time."

"Olaf, take her spade, and you come along in to the fire, Morven. It grows dusk and chill, and your labours must weary you. None so welcome as you to bide with us for a season if your good uncle will spare you."

They went inside, Jan and Olaf only too gladly, relieved from apprehension at this most unwonted geniality.

"There, sit you down and rest, Morven," Hildegarde urged, motioning her to a stool. "For my part I always say, 'new work bringeth ease', and you have sewing hands I see."

Ere Morven realised it she was engaged upon a huge pile of garments awaiting mending; but as well sew as idle. She was willing enough.

"Me, I am ever spinning at my leisure," said the lady, giving the spindle depending from her girdle the first twirl it had known that day. "I would ever rather spin than patch." A fact the pile of garments she allotted to her guest proved. The serving maids came in, silently seated themselves and each taking a garment from the pile. Their mistress chattered fluently, repeating such scandals as she had heard.

How various parish priests had taken to themselves wives (concubines she called them) and much disappointed that Morven knew no dainty little bits of gossip of the town. She did not want to hear about London; it was too far away to interest her. It might (she felt) be in another country and the maids' questions on the subject were sternly repressed. It was over the supper which followed that Morven whispered to Jan about the projected meeting at Dearleap. He was dismayed at the news.

"How will you get there?" he demanded. "You have to sleep in the room with the serving wenches, and mother ever locks them in securely, lest they should be out with the men, or the men into them."

"Oh dear," whispered Morven agonisingly. "An I go not, all our trouble will be less than vain, and the people think I have no power at all if I can't get through a locked door. Thou must steal the keys for me, Jan."

"My mother keeps them always about her person, but there is a way out, an' you will dare it... by the smoke hole in the roof. If I and Olaf climb from the barn, 'tis easy, we have oft done it as boys. We can drop a rope to you with a loop in the end, and so pull you up but," he eyed her, "leave your gown behind, for there is much soot. We will have your boy's clothes with us. You can ride with us and return the same way. Be not afraid of the maids. They sleep like logs until mother turns them out."

Morven nodded her understanding. Outside the last light was fading, and the moon rose red in the summer sky.

"Come all!" cried Hildegarde. "To bed. There is work to be done on the morrow. Olaf, you bolt every door. Jan, see to the shutters. Women, come over here. Men, over yonder." Thus dividing her flock she shut the women in their quarters like cattle in a pen, and turned the key on them.

"Lud," agonised Sue, the dairymaid, her mouth one great yawn. "Know you where there be any wars, Mistress Morven?"

"I know of none," replied the astonished girl.

"Nor I," answered Sue sardonically. "Else I would be off... camp following," at which the others laughed heartily.

Some bawdy talk followed, but the raised voices and laughter brought a thump at the door, and Hildegarde's stentorian voice bawling:

"Silence there. Get to your prayers and to sleep like decent Christians," so the conversation had to be resumed in whispers and suppressed giggles, but soon all fell asleep.

Morven's pallet was of sweet-scented heather, which she had placed in the centre of the room beneath the smoke hole. Already her keen eyes had seen a birch broom in the corner, and as she lay waiting she was devising means of turning this into a dummy. When the deep breathing of the serving wenches told her that they were asleep she crept from her pallet, and with her blankets made the broom into a dummy that would pass muster, for a sleeper in the dark. This she set in her bed.

She waited quietly until a scrambling on the roof overhead told her that Olaf and Jan were above, and soon she saw a rope snake down through the smoke hole. She caught the end of it deftly, so that it would make no noise, and as the end of it was fashioned in to a loop she placed her foot therein and tugged as a signal that she was ready to be hoisted, and so was drawn up. She scrambled through the hole, and presently stood up on the roof. Olaf and Jan averted their eyes from her undress attire, murmuring that her boy's clothes awaited her on the ground.

These she donned.

Softly they stole to a clump of trees where their horses were guarded by Old Simon's son, Peter, and in silence they mounted and rode away.

# CHAPTER XIV
## DEAR LEAP

UIETLY, following the taciturn Peter on what seemed a very maze of a path, in and out of giant beeches they wound, blanched in the pallid moonlight, past rocks casting gaunt, terrifying shadows, through glades from which deer fled silently at their coming. The moon was full, the sky cloudless, the night sultry, even with the breeze which kept the heavens clear, heat lightning constantly stabbed a course from zenith to horizon; momentarily and vividly illuminating branch and leaf and tree.

Peter steadily pursued this apparently aimless journey for upwards of an hour without once faltering; guiding himself by what were invisible landmarks to them until they saw an outcrop of high rocks at one end of a big clearing. On closer view it proved to be a natural amphitheatre, grass grown, wide at the base, upon whose boulder-strewn sides many people were assembled.

"This is the place, Maiden," said Peter; "a few are wont to meet here at full moon, but we have sent riders out and called all for many a mile. The farmers will stare and say their horses have been ridden by the fairy folk, when they see them all sweating and tired out in the morn." He dismounted and helped her down, tethered the horses, then led the party where they could look down on the hollow from whence half a dozen fires burned and the smell of roasting venison rose appetisingly.

There they were greeted by Old Simon, who placed the brothers among their own men, then he said to Morven:

"Maiden, I have talked to many, but as yet they be uncertain. You must give them a sign, and show them that you are truly a priestess." She nodded, and taking her by the hand he led her towards the high rock they had first seen. It was plain that he wished Morven to appear before her people as priestess of the old faith. Leading her up the path into the centre of the rocky outcrop, he knelt, kissed her hand and retired. Morven understood, and slipped out of her boy's clothes, and drew her Athame.

"This be an odd place and a strange time for you and me, Jan," Olaf whispered.

"I like it not," Jan, equally low, answered with intense conviction. Then he added more hopefully, looking round: "There are some likely stalwarts here. What a plague! Cannot a man have these fine fellows without all this flummery?"

"Whatever you call it, 'twas you who first sought magical aid, and gladly too," Olaf retorted, adding, a moment later: "Look, Jan, didst ever see so lovely a sight?"

Divested of her clothes, Morven found before her, when she stepped from behind the rock, a grass-grown semi-circle, shaped like a platform or pulpit jutting out high above the amphitheatre, showing clear traces that the hand of man had wrought it in some prehistoric time. With solemn steps she paced to its edge, holding her precious Athame erect in her right hand. With it she solemnly blessed the assembly.

Jan grunted, eyeing her askance. Olaf sighed in ecstasy at the beauty she made there. "See how the moonlight falls upon her, as though it loved her and acknowledged her as its kin. She gleams there as a pearl of great price."

"But, why must she stand there as bare as God made her?" Jan answered his brother's rhapsody.

"Can you not look on God's handiwork unabashed?"

"My eyes can suffer as well as most, yet it pleases me not, nor does it help me. I need men-at-arms, not a stark wench, anticking with a knife. As for God, I think he hath little to do with it."

Olaf said: "I would not be so sure."

As Morven raised her Athame in blessing there was a murmur from the people below: "Ahha! Ahha! Evoh! Ahha!"

Suddenly an unseen harp behind her began to play. For a while its solo rang out with weird effect, as though plucked by faery fingers, seeming to heighten the strangeness of that strange scene. Gradually other harpists in the body of the arena took up the theme and people began to sing a low crooning air, harmonising with the harps. This air, gaining confidence, swelled superbly into a fine open chant.

The familiar scene, the fires, the singing, brought all too vividly to Morven memories of her mother, of her childhood, of comrades who had suffered torture and death because of their faith. For a moment she was choked by tears, but this was no time for display of emotion. She was there as the messenger of the gods. With an effort she recovered her poise, swallowed her tears and forced herself to join in the singing to the end. There was a pause and afterwards a pregnant silence. Once more she raised her hand and Athame in magical blessing. Again came the murmured response and silence.

The strings of the harps began another air: a song of welcome to her, The Messenger, The Maiden; a warmer, richer, more human air, where the silver tones of young girls' voices mingled with the sweet soprano of the boys, backed by the louder and deeper notes of the elders in all their variety of tenor and bass. When that, too, died away there came a loud, ringing cry of welcome and salutation.

"Evoh Ah! Evoh Ah! Greetings, O Messenger!

What tidings have you of the Good Gods who have forsaken us for so long? When will they come again to rescue us from the evils we suffer and when will they save us from our bitter foes? Come, O come back to us, O Bright and Happy Ones."

Far and near they took up the eager cry. "What tidings? Speak, O Messenger."

Morven waited until the cries died down, then she spoke slowly, in a medium-pitched, clear, carrying voice which penetrated to the end of the arena.

"Good people, my own dear people, I have come to bring you comfort, to bring you hope, and the promise of the return of all you love, to bring you joy."

At this a mighty shout went up, which died away as she raised her hand.

"Peace. Let Maiden speak," called Old Simon. "But though I come with good tidings, nothing can be won without striving, as you well know."

"Aye, aye, we know well, blest messenger. Tell us our striving."

"Before I may aid you, we must first overcome our enemies. And you know their number and strength."

"We know, we know," they answered in a kind of mourning chant.

"But though they outnumber us we have one advantage, an' we use it. We have nimble wits and can use them to cunning twists and stratagems. With but one of their strong castles in our hands, with one who is with us, as its Lord, then would he grant us protection. Once more would we have freedom to worship as we will. Once more could we make the earth fruitful and plenty would fill the land. Once more would pleasure be ours, dancing and feasting, security and the joy of the old days would come again."

A perfect babble broke out, at first the words indistinguishable, but resolving into cries of "A leader. We follow a leader! Where is our leader, O Maiden?"

"The Good Gods have raised you up a leader, and I am come to proclaim him to you. But ... before I reveal him to you, first will ye grant him all the aid ye can give?"

"We will aid. We will fight. We will be faithful and swear fealty."

"Spoken like bold spirits and true. But, men of the wild, above all, be secret unto death; for if our foes get wind of us we lose the priceless advantage of surprise. All our efforts will be vain and we shall be overthrown. from such ruin shall we never rise again, and never again shall the Good Gods visit us or the old days return!"

Amid the murmurs of assent which followed these words, Olaf spoke to Jan. "What think you of Morven now? Could a foul and ugly old hag, for whom you pine as a lover for his mistress, could *she* so move the people? Standing there, with her gleaming weapon in her hand, is she not the soul of freedom and revolt incarnate? Would not any man follow her to death, aye and beyond that were it possible?"

"You prate like a bear-leader at a fair. Can her nudity charge with me in battle? What I need is a band of fighting men."

"Well, you look like getting such a band. Already has she roused them to a point of accepting a leader. Listen."

"But I want men in armour, not woodsmen."

"Take what you can get and render thanks. Listen."

Morven raised both hands above her head. "Men and women, children of the wild! Swear to hold secret unto death all I have said to you this night. Swear to hold secret unto death who 'tis I shall presently reveal to you as your leader, or that ever you have taken a leader, and to this you shall swear." And she administered the great and terrible oath in use among them.

They swore, repeating the familiar words after her, but even as they did so she reflected, a spy might be among them. That the forest people had elected a leader might be no great thing, but if it were known he was a Bonder, grandson of the good Sir Edgar, it would be clear what was his objective, and all precautions would be taken against attack, so Jan's identity must be kept secret till the castle was in their hands. She racked her brains for some high-sounding name by which he would be known among them.

Why had they not talked it over and agreed upon it earlier? Plague take that screaming woman and her tantrums. Never had she supposed such a state of thralddom existed on the farm. Jan ... Jan-o'the-Sword? No! Jan-o'-the-Flaming-Pine? What pitiful rubbish! Jan-o'-the-Fiery-Cross? Fiery Crosses conveyed nothing. Jan-o'-the-Red-Hand? Jan-o'-the-Bloody-Hand? There was no time for more, to hesitate was to lose.

The oath was sworn.

Raising her voice, she called with a note that thrilled all present: "Stand forth, O Nameless One. Stand forth with me as appointed leader of our cause."

"Now must you go up and stand beside Nakedness," grinned Olaf. "She awaits you, Jan, and it is for you to take command now."

"As leader of all that flam-jamery? Me—a leader of a lot of witches and hobgoblins of the forest?"

Morven wildly asked herself: "Why does Jan not come forward?" She dropped her aching arms while she waited a response, but she could not linger too long. Again she raised them and called: "Stand forth, O Nameless One."

"'Tis you who are crazed," Olaf spat, almost beside himself with excitement and apprehension.

"All that is required of you is to shut your eyes to their meetings … they are harmless, never need you take part in them."

"But—"

"Clever wench, she is making a Rite of this summoning, go while there is time, she may only call three times."

Morven dared not look round to see if Jan was there, but she listened intently. There was no answering sound and she knew she stood there alone.

The people before her were gripped in a profound hush of waiting.

She flung up her arms again and cried with desperate appeal:

"Stand forth, O Nameless One. Stand forth as appointed leader of our cause. Thus thrice do I summon you."

"If God only granted you wit to match your towering ambition," Olaf lamented in desperation. "An' you go not, I go myself. Someone MUST answer that call."

As Olaf half rose to carry out his threat, Jan sprang to his feet and leapt like a deer for the rock. Though his feet made no sound on the grass, Morven knew she was no longer alone. She stepped backwards, keeping her right hand with the Athame raised above her head, her left hand outstretched. He placed his right hand in it and she led him forward.

"Why did you delay, fool? you almost ruined all," she whispered as they approached the verge.

"Behold your leader, Jan-o'-the-Sword-Hand!"

Her voice had the tones of a silvet trumpet, her mien heroic. A shout answered her as they noticed his fine height and handsome bearing, his bold assurance and the set of his stern young jaw. They acclaimed him with deep satisfaction. At that moment of intense exhilaration Jan looked and felt like a born leader. As they cheered him again and again she spoke to him in an exhausted voice yet with almost contemptuous authority; for she knew his mind.

"I have done my part, now do yours. All lies with you now, be it success or failure. Here do you play Sir Jan Bonder, though name-less. You have yet to win your knighthood, but your gentle blood will speak and guide you. Be their leader. First make them your friends, your comrades, and so more than servants. You have a gift for leadership, I believe. Follow it, for I can do no more."

"I ask forgiveness, Morven. My debt to you never can be paid."

"Never heed that. Speak to them, Jan, forget all your doubts, cast away all foolish prejudice, unbend to them. Be easy, speak to them fair and you will win them to your cause."

The shouting died as he raised his hand. "Good people! I am a simple man and have few words, rather would I act."

Yells of applause showed him the way to popularity through mild self-deprecation. "I come among ye because I, too, am oppressed by the same enemies that oppress you; I have been driven forth from my home as you have been driven forth from yours; by the same violence. My grandsire and father have both been foully murdered as have been your grandsires and sires. I have been stripped of all, as you have been stripped, and by the same people. I seek venge-ance as you seek it, and restitution of my rightful heritage as you seek yours. Let us then join forces since we have a common enemy and a common injury to avenge. Aid me and I will aid you. I, your leader, know all you have suffered and will avenge you and lead you to victory."

Wild cries greeted this speech. "Lead and we will follow," they called, and then: "Come down amongst us O Jan-o'-the-Sword-

Hand. Come down and eat and drink with us; for to-night we make merry. Come down, O Blessed Maiden, and lead us in the dance."

"We must go down among them. I, for one, am famished," she told him. "You have won them, Jan, but you must *keep* them. Be merry with them and they will love you and serve you."

"I am more than willing," he declared, "I will wait till you get into your woman's gear."

"I am in my woman's gear and so must I remain ... for I am Priestess, and so must appear as their Priestess, or I lose my power, so clothes are forbidden me. Accept me as I am, Jan." Then, imperiously, as he would have spoken: "Nay, no more; your eye is too narrow. Come, let us go down."

As they left the platform together they were joined by Olaf and the men from Spumheath, and went among the people. Boisterous were the greetings as Old Simon led them from group to group until all were acquainted. This friendly act endeared them to Jan.

Soon Morven clapped her hands. She was wearied by the rough endearments of the good-natured crowd. "Come, let us dance," she cried.

To their wild assent the harps began to play, reinforced by bagpipes, drums and flutes. A long line formed behind Morven, who led them in what can only be described as a follow-my-Leader dance. Often she had danced it and knew every step and gesture, though the honour of leading it usually reserved for great and privileged persons only, had never before been hers. In and out of the boulders scattered over the arena they wound their course.

Jan, immediately behind Morven, copied her steps and gestures with faithfulness and thoroughness. They were simple, and he was a great dancer, but, being no great lover of girls, he preferred this type of single chain which involved no taking of partners, which gave him considerable pleasure. He danced well and unselfconsciously, surprised to discover how much delight lay in the simple self-expression of these movements.

Unknown to him, the people watched him critically, and he won anew their liking by the pleasure he took in their merrymaking. They admired his good looks, his health and activity. The girls and women approved him as much as the men. Altogether it was very much Jan's hour. At the end of half an hour, something had happened to him. He lost some of his prudishness which hitherto had held him iron-clamped, he found his place, his natural activity and ease, which, in this company, would never abandon him.

When the dance ended and it came to feasting, he could eat and drink, laugh and quip with the best; for the wit was bucolic and of familiar guise. Ale flowed freely. They ate of venison, cut in strips and roasted on sticks on the great fires, also there were many kinds of wild fowl, fish and pastjes. So they feasted and danced. There was some coarse love-making, but naught surpassing any he had often stumbled upon in odd nooks of his own farm. There was no orgy of licentiousness, such as he had expected and dreaded. So Jan had not to purse his lips and avert his eyes from any unhallowness. Beyond the fact that many threw off their clothes and danced, there was no difference from any village merrymaking. There was so little to offend, that at the end of the assembly he was almost persuaded there was a distinction in young bodies of which clothes robbed their wearer's beauty and that the flames flickering upon and lighting those white young limbs as they danced, proved an enchantment altogether innocent.

As for Olaf, he was never in doubt of their beauty. Unlike his brother, he had not first to reconcile morality with loveliness and its enjoyment. It was true, as the ale went down and excitement rose, the scene became more wildly boisterous; the most part of it expressed itself in shrieks and yells, in frantic leaps, exaggerated gestures. As the fires sank, couples danced and jumped across them, but the greater part ate, drank, danced and were merry; laughing at the kissings, gigglings and tickling and antics of the others with good-natured tolerance.

Olaf watched Jan critically and saw his adjustment to his new circumstances. It was as though he blossomed before their eyes; and that, with the coming of leadership, some oppressive weight had been lifted from him at the chance of his life's hope being realised. Jan had a solemn conclave with various elders; as to means of communications and future meetings. Beyond that, neither he nor they could go at the moment.

In two days his destiny had changed. He was now the acknowledged leader of a goodly body of skilled bowmen, and though they were not the men-at-arms for which his soul craved, they were men.

The moon was sinking in the west as the Bonders, Morven and Old Simon returned to the farm. They scrambled up the rope, hauling Morven after them, and crept along the roof.

"Best strip off thy boy's clothes," said Olaf. "The smoke hole is small and they'll get covered with soot, and the maids well know you took them not in with you last night. They will talk if you have them there in the morn, and mother is always on the look-out to cross-question folk."

Morven did as she was bid, slipped through the hole and was lowered into the room. She sank on her couch with a sigh, thoroughly exhausted with riding, excitement, nerve tension and anxiety. All she wanted was to rest in bed; lie there for days, and it was with no blessing that she found her couch occupied by the broomstick dummy of herself. With an exclamation of disgust she threw it out and sank into bed. Then the thought came: "They'll see it in the morn, and ask silly questions." With muttered curses, she rose and replaced the broom in its corner, returned and soon fell into a sound sleep.

Unfortunately for all concerned, Hildegarde overslept. She had talked more than usual the night before, and becoming excited instead of falling to sleep at once, her brain repeated scraps of her talk with wearing monotony. She wakened long after the sun had risen; and ought to have been up at dawn. Hildegarde opened her eyes suddenly to stare incredulously at the red sun. She flew out of bed with one wild spring, only to stub her toe against a chest. Trembling with rage she hurled herself at the maids' door, unlocked it, and flung it open with a screech. "Up! up! you lazy bitches! Would you snore all day, as well as night? But for me, never would you tumble out of the straw. Morven, up, I say; Jane, Sue, Marian, once I come to fetch you you'll rue the day you were born."

"Every time we see and hear you do we rue it," Sue spat out at her, not afraid to speak her mind, and rudely awakened from some delectable dream not unconnected with her expressed wishes of the night before. She was in a mood for rebellion.

"Insolent slut; do you dare bandy words with me?"

Sue, by now scrambled into her clothes, advanced to the door insolently swinging her hips, and Hildegarde, seeing her in this truculent mood, returned up the ladder to her room, for she wore but a shift, and bundled some clothes on. But her eyes flashed vengeance, battle and murder. Morven, still dazed with want of sleep, followed the three girls into the yard, where they took turn to sluice face, shoulders and hands in a bucket of water set on a chopping block.

"If war comes not soon, I'll raise rebellion and make it. Lord, what a life," grumbled Sue.

"La, Mistress, you're all over soot," exclaimed Marion. Morven suddenly realised her hands and arms were covered with black streaks where she had climbed through the smoke hole. Assisted by the girls, she was soon tolerably clean, and they trooped in for a hasty breakfast. The Bonders looked glum and sullen, their mother had been at them already. Hildegarde herself looked furious. Morven softly echoed Sue's words: "Lord, what a life." She thought: "Let me get my horse and ride away from here, I have done all I came to do and but make matters worse by staying. O for somewhere where I could really wash me clean and then sleep."

But Hildegarde had other plans, and Morven found herself again with spade digging an enormous seed bed. As soon as the mistress had departed Morven sat down to rest her aching back, but had barely found a comfortable position when Old Simon, Wat, Samkin and Chinnery, stole from behind a stack and gathered round her; she rose to her feet with a groan.

"Maiden, your orders!" Ere she could answer, Chinnery made a clucking noise of dismay. He was a tall man and could see over the others' heads.

"Drat the day … ther's na' luck in it, here comes miss-es and the two maisters. We all be in for a fine tongue wiping, I lay."

"Why, Mistress Morven, what do you with these men?"

"They have brought me news of my people, good mistress, for which I am heartily grateful."

"Thy people indeed," sneered Hildegarde, beside herself with a dozen vexations. "If the search be an honest one, why did not Thur accompany you? If indeed you are a niece of his and not some vile strumpet picked up in God knows what vile stews to corrupt the flesh of him and my boys."

Jan and Olaf were breathless, their faces flamed, then Jan quietly slipped away. Morven sprang forward with passionate energy. "Peace, woman, lay not your lewd tongue on me!" she commanded, her face deadly white with anger. "Is not Thur the best of men, has he not befriended you and yours for twenty years and more? Must you say such monstrous things of him? Are you out of your wits, Mistress?" The women confronted each other, one flaming red, the other deadly white.

"She must not harm Maiden souls," Simon murmured apprehensively.

"Maiden can blast her to hell, an she be so minded," Chinnery whispered in his ear.

"What are you men muttering about?" Hildegarde demanded, shifting her attack. "Back to your work." They stood their ground stolidly, staring at her like beasts in a pen.

"Begone, I say!" she cried with an enraged stamp.

"Nay, Miss'ess, we bide," Simon assured her succinctly.

But she was already attacking Morven: "Do I not find you in

the midst of my hinds? Did you not come riding astride rigged in men's clothes against the Holy Scripture? Flaunting red garters, so my men nearly lost their senses when they saw them girding thy shameless legs? If that be not the mark of a strumpet, then I am no judge of one."

"Mother, have done," Olaf interposed. "You shame us by your ugly brawling and your tongue says monstrous things and evil lies."

"Hoity-toity, I must not speak? I am a liar to boot and how will *you* stop me, pray?"

"I'd like to seal thy mouth with honeyplaster. So you might learn sweetness in silence."

"Nay, Olaf…" Morven expostulated, but Hildegarde turned on him fiercely.

"I'll manage my own oafs without any aid from thee."

As she spoke, Jan returned leading two horses, saddled and bridled, and entered into the fray.

"Mother," began Jan, with a new firmness. "You will manage us no longer. I am a grown man and Olaf is coming along. Such thraldom is unseemly, and, good mother, we will have no more of it."

"And, pray, what is your vast age?" she demanded. "Scarce twenty-three years. Oh yes, you strut it like any manikin and visit your stews, and bring back your strumpets for your mother to house."

"Mother, your mind stinks like a midden. Morven is here to help me get my rights."

"Your rights," she spat, "so we come again to your 'rights'. I thought we would come to them soon. Your 'rights' are to bide at home and till the land and get a hand's turn out of these scurvy knaves that batten on us."

"Na, Miss-ess, we be na knaves." "We be honest, hard-working folk an' faithful." "We work hard for 'ee." They all spoke together.

"Mercy on us, what a clamour," she scoffed.

"Night and day we work for 'ee, Miss-ess, and get no thanks but curses and blows," Simon said with stolid dignity.

"You speak truth, Simon. No man or woman was better served, I know your loyalty," said Jan. "Mother knows it in her heart of hearts too."

"Aye, there is no end to what your mother knows," she vociferated. "I am sick to death of hearing of your rights knowing what they are, or if you ever had any."

They all gaped at her; for they all thought she had a good notion.

Jan and Olaf supposed her informed by some natural process of what they all knew so well.

Hildegarde saw on all hands staring eyes and sagging jaws: to her it was incredibly stupid.

"Well," she jeered, "now I ask, you cannot give it a name."

"Mother, in truth, do you *not* know?" Olaf asked incredulously. "Didn't father tell you?"

"Your father told me he was a soldier sick of the wars. Unlike you, he was good and kind and a hard and honest worker, he had no 'rights' to keep him like a kitten chasing his own tail."

"But, Mother, he had! Castles and lands, knew you not *he* was Sir Hugh Bonder?"

"He was of Bonder kin, I knew, but naught else, and I believe not a word you say. Should not I know all that concerned my husband? Would he leave me, his wife, all unknowing?"

"Aye, if our lives depended on it."

"There's not a word of truth in the whole story, I smell some evil here. Some vile witch cantrip has bereft my poor lad of what little sense he had; what vile bewitchments are these?"

The men, prepared to declare themselves, were effectually diverted from their purpose by that dangerous word.... Instead of speaking they hesitated and exchanged uneasy glances.

Instantly Hildegarde saw her advantage and seized it. "Are you too bewitched?" she demanded in a high tone of moral indignation.

Morven walked close up to her and fixed her eyes on the accuser compellingly, holding the other's eyes with all the power she possessed.

"You use dangerous words, Mistress Hugh. What know you of witches and witchcraft, of strumpets and stews, that you speak of them so glibly? I like it not. You seem over-well acquainted with both."

"What mean you, vile hussy?"

"I like not much I have seen here; I like not this locking in each night. Why is it done?"

"Why? Because 'tis my will."

Morven advanced a step further and pointed her forefinger straight between Hildegarde's eyes. Their baleful light flickered and the pupils dilated a little with the acute discomfort she experienced.

"So that *you* may go from the house in secret when you will! So you may attend midnight gatherings beneath the moon when you will; so you may strip off your clothing and practise unbelievable abominations an' you will. Is this how you know so much about witches and witchcraft, strumpets and stews, that they are for ever on your tongue to fling at me?"

Somewhat out of breath, Morven stopped her torrent of words.

Hildegarde, who was no fool and whose wits worked like lightning, saw at once whither her unbridled tongue had led her. She was appalled to realise how any innocent act could be distorted to a semblance of abysmal guilt; how easy an accusation could be made, and how well nigh impossible to disprove it.

"Nay, nay," she retracted in a veritable panic.

"Say not so, dear Morven. I spoke in anger. Forgive me, say not such things! They are hard and dangerous words! Forgive me, child. I spoke in anger." Hildegarde was overwrought and burst out sobbing, and ran back to the house, leaving Morven, the two Bonders and the men staring at each other.

"Said I not, Maiden can blast her to hell an' she wills?" chortled Samkin.

All the men were grinning widely.

"Thou hadst better get to work, friends," said Jan, and, as the

197

men moved off, he said: "Olaf, go and fetch Morven's saddle bags, I think she had better be off, ere mother sees her again," and, as Olaf obeyed, he continued: "I think you hadst better go, a witch of the Mere; you certainly have scared my mother for a time, but I fear, when she recovers, she will be back, and perchance worse than before, for, if she hath a wish in her heart, if checked one way, she ever tries another. Ah, here comes Olaf," as the boy ran up with the bags, and began fastening them on. But as he spoke, Hildegarde appeared again, hauling along the serving wench Marion by the arm, followed by Jane and Sue. All with wild excitement in their eyes.

"Hear, my sons, hear *this* tale, then see how you have misjudged your mother," she ejaculated. "Come, wench, tell your masters what you saw," and she shook the girl savagely.

"I waa-knd this morn, by aa skuffing noise on roof, an' I la-y an wun-erd, a-n' I seed sum-mot white come thr-ugh sma-ok hole, sort O' glide slow like to ground, aa tho-rt 'twas a boggart, aa-n' I lay moidered wi' fear, the-n it moved, and there was aa patch o' moonlight, aa-n' I saw clear 'twas Mistress Morven here, bare as a bone, carrying a broomstick, aa-n she put un back in corner, and went and lay down again, I thort, 'tis well 'tis no boggart, but aa wand-red wa-at er war doing wi' broomstick, climbing on roof, th-een wen aa wer washing in morn, aa seed 'er wer aal over soot, a-an a told Jane and Sue here. An Jane ses witches rub 'em-selves aa over wi' soot ari' fa-at O' unbaptised babes, an' th-en fly through air on broom, so we knowed wa't she'd been up to, so-o we looked at broom, and there be soot on 'un, and there be soot on 'er blankets. So-o we a-ll to-ld missus 'ere."

"What have you got to say now, sons?" demanded Hildegarde. "This spawn of hell thou hast brought to my respectable house lives not here a minute more!" and she turned and ran to the house again, leaving all looking at each other in dismay.

"Mount, Morven, mount, she will do you a mischief, I fear she brings a pitchfork!" cried Jan, holding out his hand. Morven put her foot in it, and he threw her up, she seated herself and took the reins, just as Hildegarde returned at a run, clutching some things, but to their relief they were small, and she had no pitchfork. She charged up to Morven, holding up a crucifix, crying: "Swear, swear on the Holy Cross that thou art no vile witch. Kiss it and say, 'May my soul be damned to hell for ever and ever if I went in or out of the smoke-hole last night.'" Pressing it up towards her lips, Morven recoiled. Though the crucifix meant naught to her, she would not swear a lie.

"Ho," cried Hildegarde. "So you dare not take the oath? Then take this!" and she flung a pint pot of Holy Water over her! The noise, and this sudden cold bath was too much for Morven's mare, which reared and plunged, kicked out and bolted, scaring Jan's horse, who pulled away and followed.

For a minute or two, Morven's whole attention was on keeping her seat, but as the mare set down to a steady gallop, she looked back. Jan was running wildly, chasing his horse, and the maids were all on their knees, fervently crossing themselves.

Mistress Hildegarde was doing a sort of savage war dance, wildly waving the crucifix and pint pot, alternately shrieking out prayers and curses at the top of her voice.

# CHAPTER XV
## CHARGING THE PENTACLES

**M**ORVEN lay on a grassy bank ten yards distant from the forest track. Close by her little mare peacefully cropped a patch of grass. She was a docile creature, and Morven was much attached to the beast, and every now and again she spoke a soothing word to her to help erase the memory of that morning's fright, which indeed both mare and rider had endured.

Curled up in a nest of fallen leaves, Morven had slept sweetly and deeply for some hours. The spot was secluded and shady, and she felt the sun come out and touch her eyelids with his beams. This awoke her, and there she lay, arms clasped behind her head, idly reviewing her recent experiences.

"The Talismans worked," she mused. "We came boldly through the gates of the town without hindrance or question, and, looking as farmers, why should folk take us for aught else. In the main, folk have bad memories. If a man but looks *and feels* his part, will the Talismans give him the confidence necessary ? May' be … and yet the danger lies in Hildegarde's tongue. She hath wit, and knows that should any hint get abroad, she will be the first to be taken and put to the question; first about her husband, and then concerning her sons. *That* should stay her tongue, tantrum or no tantrum, for certain tortures long continued are great muzzles. I know none stronger. Yet we must hurry the work, for rumours may spread of the meeting in the forest."

She got up and shook her clothes free from twigs, and wandered among the trees towards a glade wherein lay a woodland pool, dark and clear over a pebbled bottom. Its waters were tawny and still, half gleaming in the sunshine, and part shadowed by sloping willows. Her mare had followed after, and snapping her fingers to the beast she motioned it to drink. The widening ripples from the mare's muzzle seemed to beckon her, and slipping off her gown Morven washed it as well as she could without the use of soap, and hung it on a bush to dry.

Then, slipping into the pool she bathed her white body, rubbing hard at the sooty marks until the waters reflected only pure ivorine flesh. With red-gold hair outspread like a faery net she swam thrice round the pool, emerged, and lay on the grass to dry, shaking her hair free from wet, aided by the sun and wind.

In the middle of the glade there grew a solitary silver birch, and between this tree and herself she felt an affinity. Not only did they share their pliant grace, but both had an evanescent quality of other-worldliness, an ethereal beauty that while satisfying the eye, reaches beyond the mere physical gratification to touch some slumbering emption of rarefied pain … the perfection of loveliness.

The song of the nightingale has this quality of perfection and beauty in the realm of music. It is the mystery of fairyland, the apotheosis of the elusive, a sense of peril, indefinable yet alluring, lurking in strange paths where such beauty has its habitation.

The drift of the gentle breeze through the branches of the birch tree set them swaying, each delicate leaf vibrant in the sun-glow, and the darker tones of the dappled bark seemed wrought in bronze and silver. The tree was not only living and dancing, but it sang as it danced, as an act of worship, obeying a law and performing a ritual that was ancient even when the world saw its first dawn.

Drawn to the silver birch, Morven paced a wide circle in which she began to dance, full of the wild exhilaration of being alone and the mistress of herself for the first time in months. Yet there was nothing Bacchic in her revel, rather was it a pattern postures, in which her young body bent and swayed in rhythm with that of the tree; a slow wreathing of arms as though they were branches, and an intricate pattern of her feet as if she wove a spell about the Dryad of the Birch.

She did not sing, but hummed gently, with head thrown back and throat curved like the sickle of the moon, the sun drenching her in a myriad tones of rose and pearl, and the wind playing in her glowing hair.

Suddenly she stopped. Some exterior consciousness impinged on her mood, and she knew that she was not alone, and also that the secret watcher was Jan. She did not betray her knowledge, but quietly sought her clothes and dressed.

As for Jan, he had encountered some trouble in capturing his runaway horse at the farm, and when he had succeeded, Morven was far out of sight, but he knew that she had gone in the general direction she wished.

Still, she had not kept to the path, and this had meant hours of patient tracking, but at last he had sighted her waving arms as she performed that pagan dance around the tree. Jan was disquieted, not only for Morven's safety, but for Thur's inevitable displeasure, and so he had kept secret watch while she danced, scanning every possible approach lest some danger should appear. He was not prying on her, though he did ponder whether the wan diffusion of the moon or the radiance of the sun produced the lovelier effect on the perfection of the nude witch, but found it impossible to decide in favour of either, since each gave a different aspect of beauty. Jan felt that he was committing an unwarrantable intrusion upon her ... yet, so ardent was his desire to continue watching this lovely sight, so fierce the temptation to gratify desire, so resolute his determination not to yield, that so much stress of mind could not fail to reach Morven ... and, as he watched, she stopped her dance, and he knew that she was aware of his presence.

To jan's relief she did not attempt to discover his hiding-place, but quietly went to where she had left her clothes and donned them, recaptured her little mare, mounted her, and rode away as though entirely oblivious of Jan's presence ... a subtle manoeuvre that left the way open for Jan to follow her and re-encounter her under conditions less embarrassing for them both.

Jan waited for awhile, until the figure of mare and rider had passed out of his sight, and then he too re-mounted and followed in Morven's wake, so timing it that he should overhaul her only gradually, and thus give his own feelings, and hers, a space in which to re-orient themselves. In his case this was easier than it was in hers, for the knowledge of Jan having witnessed her dance had brought Morven's ecstasy in the simple joys of life to an abrupt end, and face to face again with the stern realities of life. She brooded again on her love for him, and him for the avowed Bride of Jocelyn, and disappointment with the fact that he had been disappointed not to find her an ugly and evil old woman. Had ever a man harboured such a resentment against a girl before ? At the thought she laughed sardonically, startling a magpie, which flew chattering from the overhead branches.

Yet that fact remained, and the nauseous draught must be swallowed. Women meant nothing to Jan Bonder, and even his impossibly romantic love discomforted him. It was but the fashion of knighthood to love some unobtainable star. His wife would be a means to an end, and in no wise his heart's desire. He would be gentle with her, and even fond of her, and would beget many strong sons ... and even if his children should prove only to be daughters, even so they would represent an advantage to Jan, who would marry them to the heirs of important families, until at last this half-peasant lad might become one of the strongest lords in England; and, once re-established, his whole life would be devoted to preventing a repetition of the disaster that had fallen to his grandfather.

"Once bitten, then twice shy," quoted Morven, "though my aid can guard him against all his enemies, 'twould only be in ways he can't comprehend and which he likes not, for he can follow the ways only known to him. So of what use to torment myself with these mortifying feelings of being passed over ? Jan loves not me. He hardly notices me, and doubts the aid that I can give him, even, as at times, he doubts Thur's. He realises not that stout men-at-arms can spring only first from the imagination. His did, and now, I have got for him the men, and the armour and swords will follow in some way, I know, as will the training that will make of them not peasant hinds, but soldiers of Jan's desire … yet he cannot see the purpose, or the thread that connects his dreams, as a string holds beads together. He can only be disappointed that I am not an old witch who can sow Dragon's teeth, and from these should spring, as he thinks, most miraculously, fully armed men to aid him in his fight." She fell to musing again.

Had she herself so little strength that she could not overcome a wayward fancy for a man who plainly wanted her not? Was her pride so poor a thing? Was it not rather vanity suffering, because her beauty, which turned the heads of other men, could not enslave him also, blind him to his ambitions, and reduce him to besotted adoration? Shame upon her for such a paltry desire, such miserable cowardice. So did Morven take the scourge to love and apply it vigorously. A turn of the track revealed the trysting place, and there was Thur halted beneath the tree, awaiting her. So static. were horse and rider that they might have been wrought of bronze. He was a magnificent horseman, and clad in his well-cut, close fitting russet clothes (for Thur was enough of a dandy to have care of his appearance), his head uncovered in the strong sunlight, he made an imposing picture.

He was looking for her in the opposite direction, for she had come out on the other side of the trysting place, so she viewed him in profile. She marked his fine brow sweeping up broadly to meet the crisp, abundant flaxen hair, almost white, the strong suggestive nose, indicating an inventive mind, the clean-hewn lines of mouth and chin. How glad she was to see him again, how long it seemed since she saw him, though scarce a day and a half-almost before he knew she was there, her head was on his shoulder. "O, Thur, how I have missed you," she whispered. He started at her touch, and put his arm around her caressingly. She felt all the woe of her misplaced love most poignantly, she wept because Jan half ruined her efforts to help him by his sullen opposition and disbelief in her.

"Why tears, Morven?" said Thur, lifting her chin with his fore-finger and looking down into her face. "Has aught gone wrong? Why are not the boys with you?"

"Never heed, Thur, Jan has but this moment departed and all goes well. Except for Mistress Hildegarde."

"Then why tears?"

"Because, beside you, all men are dwarfed to nothingness."

"Oh," said Thur, puzzled, then smiled down on her tenderly. "So, then no more tears, dear wench."

"I have missed you so," she sighed.

"And I you... more than ever you can know, but now, 'tis over!"

Soon they were cantering home, and she told him all their hap-penings, and the success of their mission. "This be fine news, Mor-ven, but I like it not about Hildegarde; she will see that any talk will harm her own sons more than any and herself to boot, but her tongue clacks; we must act ere it puts a noose round our throats."

"And the brethren. They accepted you?"

"Yes, they gave us a great welcome, and accepted Jan as their leader."

"And how did Jan bear himself?"

"Handsomely... a veritable lording."

"Aye, twill suit Jan very well... and you, Morven?"

"Our Jan has devised the course of his future life for many years to come, Thur, we had it from his own lips, not only his but ours, Olaf's and mine. He will seek an alliance with the daughter of the most powerful man he can approach and who will have him. Olaf is to be his Captain and I, I am to marry him."

Thur stared, marking her reddened eyelids, and knew their cause.

"What folly is this?" he demanded angrily. "No folly, but a device to which he hath given much careful thought. 'Tis useless to frown, Thur, he will not change his mind!"

"But," exploded Thur, indignantly outraged at what seemed to him a piece of monstrous ingratitude. "The unnatural young jack-anapes! Hath he no eyes?".

"Yes, but only for the Bride of Jocelyn. He saw her, and she filled them, and so, he hath never seen me, Thur. Let us be satisfied and speak no more."

Thur was unheeding. "I'll bring him up with a round turn, I promise you."

"Thur, you'll do no such thing."

"The young upstart; not yet has he reached his ambitions, and now he makes his terms. I'll have a word with Master Jan. What the plague! What has he devised for me, pray, do I wear cap and bells and sit at his feet?"

"Thur, be reasonable, 'tis his life he arranges, by what authority do you or I say he shall do this or do that, or you will know the reason why?"

Thur fidgeted in his saddle. "He has never seen you? Why, did he not see you last night?"

She bowed assent, biting her lips. "And it made no change in him?"

"None, why should it?"

"God help us; what is he? What lacks he?"

In spite of her vexation Morven burst into so merry a laugh that Thur's exasperation vanished and his good humour was restored in a vast sense of relief. Morven had opened this matter with him because she wished to silence once for all Thur's only too patent expectation that she would become Jan's wife sooner or later...now she saw, that though he would no longer speak of it, he still clung obstinately to that conviction, but to have secured his silence on the subject was a point gained, hence her laughter, which was wholly sincere. "Would not long association with Hilde-garde cure any man of any fancy for woman?"

It was Thur's turn to laugh. "There be much in that, poor wench, she hath borne a great sorrow."

"Because she parted with Hugh in anger?"

"Even so... she drove him forth, though she loved him much and he died."

"He should have mastered her, not run away from her."

"So did I tell him oft, he was like Olaf, discord was an abomination to him, though he was a fine soldier. But this makes it clear, we must start at once, make all our Talismans ready, and strike the Great Circle as speedily as we may, for who can tell when Hildegarde's tongue will be clacking."

"Yes," and they rode in silence.

Then Thur spoke again: "Brother Stephen came again last night, we talked late."

"Of what."

"Almost everything."

"He will not always be an obscure brother, clerk to a profligate Abbot in an English by-way."

"Why wastes he his time here, was he not in Paris... as gossip says?"

"Aye, he had a school of theology, and will return thither no doubt, though men say, his pupils have been taxed with heresy."

"What he seeks here I know not, but he is not here for naught."

\* \* \* \*

The next day, being Tuesday, Thur and Morven prepared to make some of the Talismans, Sigils and Pentacles they needed in the Great Circle. Though these names are often used indiscriminately to describe each other, there is an important difference between them. A Sigil means a sign, on parchment, or a medal, made with the object of controlling one particular spirit, usually to summon him up to the Circle, and it bears his own peculiar design. The knowledge of these designs is one of the great secrets which the Magus must master, because a spirit will strive his utmost to keep this sign of his individuality hidden, to prevent mortals obtaining power over him. If a certain spirit is particularly favourable to him, a Magus may make use of this Sigil as a Talisman, but this is not common.

When a Sigil is written on paper or parchment it is often described as a seal, whereas if a Talisman or Pentacle is inscribed on parchment, it is not a seal, the difference being, that a Sigil or seal belongs to one individual spirit, who in Jan's case was Bartzebal, while a Talisman or Pentacle belongs either to one human being, or in a general way, to all the spirits serving one Governing Spirit, like Mars, Saturn or Venus, as the case may be. A Pentacle is also a medal used to evoke a spirit and command him, it is in addition a figure like a five-pointed star, and should always be drawn and used with one point uppermost, and never with two points uppermost. From their nature, certain Pentacles can be carried outside the circle and worn with a view to bringing good fortune, such as the Pentacle of Venus for love. Of Jupiter for success and prosperity. A Pentacle of Saturn will induce his good qualities of steadiness, perseverance and loyalty, but this can only be carried by one born under Saturn; to anyone else it would bring disaster. A soldier born under any sign could wear a Pentacle of Mars, with advantage, which might produce quarrelsomeness in a merchant, while the latter would be well advised to wear one of Mercury. While a medal such as described above is sometimes called a Talisman. This name should more properly be kept for articles made especially for its owner, with the express intention of bringing him success in what particular object he has in view, and are made in accordance with the owner's horoscope. They are usually made by an expert, in the proper day and hour, with the special object in view, with protection and safety. Or Prosperity, gain, and success for the subject firmly fixed in his mind. The Talisman is then consecrated with magical formulae. In some such way Thur and Morven had made theirs.

Bathed and consecrated, the two prepared their small circle at midnight on the Monday following Morven's return, so as to start the work in the day and hour of Mars, viz., between twelve midnight and one o'clock on Tuesday, the day of Mars (each planet rules the first, eighth, fifteenth and twenty-second hours of his day), but, at any other hour they would be liable to intrusion, with subsequent denunciation of sorcery, so midnight was the safest time for this operation. Thur placed in the centre a small table, to serve the double purpose of Altar and work-bench. Beside it was a glowing brazier of charcoal. Morven's duty was to keep this brazier fed and at an even high temperature, also to serve him generally as an acolyte serves a priest. She had, however, a much more important part to play in the actual ritual, which was to fix her mind unwaveringly on the work, to do her best to make it fluid, so that by welding it with his as it were, he derived added strength. For this concentration of the will upon the object of the ritual there must be no means of distraction. Everything used must have been made with this object in view, so everything used brings to the brain of the Magus, the reason of the work. Therefore was Thur clad in the symbolically pure, clean white linen robe, signifying light, strength and purity, also, this is important, bearing no colour or pattern that could distract the mind of the wearer or his acolyte. For the same reason the girl was nude, this signified purity unsullied, and the natural magnetism in the human body could flow unhindered to the support of the Magus. Here would be no temptation, no distraction for him in this beauty unadorned because a Magus must be immune to such conditions, ere he may become a Magus, for if he cannot at all times prevent his mind from straying, failure in his enterprises would be inevitable; rather was such nudity an added strength to him, for by its presence it signifies the strength of his will and the power of his self-control. For a Magus must ever work with a naked woman till nudity is naught to him, lest an evil or mischievious spirit should appear thus, and distract his mind at the critical moment and so ruin an operation.

Throughout the practice of High Magic, or Art Magic as it is often called, the emphasis is upon purity and strength, and through

209

purity, strength of will and self-control. Without these no man may become a Magus, though by trickery and self-deception he may become a great "rogue, but with them, even in a small degree he may go far along the road in his search into the hidden mysteries, for by a rigid self-discipline, self-control can be extended and strengthened almost to any limit, and by patience and rigorous exercise the will can become such a dominating factor and obtain such power that nothing can withstand its impact. Therefore a great Magus should also be a great man. By the habit of self-control which is the essence of Magic, he attains to abstinence, which, in its turn gives him health and vigour. The habit of faith, which is essential to success in the Art, faith in God and His goodness, faith in righteousness, absolute faith in the ritual he performs, in its efficacy and in the success of its object, through the ritual; and finally, supreme faith in himself, firstly as a willing servant of God, and secondly in his power as a Magus; such faith is in itself a purifying element in any life. The application to close study through long hours of poring over intricate manuscripts, the patient repetition of obscure rites until success is obtained, indicate high qualities of mind. The fact that no Magus can work for himself and his own advancement, or work for another with solely evil purposes, imposes a certain rectitude of conduct upon him. If he fell from his high status of being a helper and benefactor to others through his Art, descending to use it for harmful purposes, the reaction upon himself would in the medieval mind be in proportion to the magnitude and wickedness of his success, and dire retribution would swiftly overtake him for having corrupted his Art. Therefore, by all the laws of his Art, such good qualities as a Magus possessed are developed to their utmost. Indeed, one might say that without a number of good qualities in his character a man could never become a Magus. There have been many charlatans who have claimed the title of Magus by hypnotism or by plain trickery; they imposed upon the credulity of thousands, also sometimes they may have possessed powers of clairvoyance which they have misused for gain. It is these tricksters and glib rogues who have brought the Art into disrepute, and for which they have afterwards suffered.

It is the fashion to-day to laugh at the Magus and his pretensions, to picture him as either a charlatan or a doddering old fool, and bearing the slightest resemblance to the men who were in fact, the scientists of the day, who gave us alcohol, but not the Atom Bomb.

Four other braziers were in their appointed places around the Circle. Upon the altar-table lay the Athame, the Magic Sword, the Burin and the Sprinkler, also materials for their work, four iron discs, two-and-a-half inches in diameter, already purified by fire, had been prepared previously. There were writing materials, lengths of cord, some black cloths and a scourge, laid ready. Before the bench were two stools. The inner circle, seven feet in diameter … was already drawn on the floor, surrounding it was a double circle eight feet in diameter, with names of power between the two. Thur took the Magic Sword and retraced all the markings with its point, for the painted circle has no power of protection, which comes from Power of the Magic Sword or the Athame. It but serves as a guide to the latter, to ensure they draw the Circle perfectly. The Circle drawn, Thur recited appropriate Psalms, and began to make the Talismans and Pentacles. Iron is the metal of Mars, the spirit of War under whom Jan was born, and as it was for a warlike purpose, Thur proposed to summon his spirit Bartzebal to Jan's aid. Taking one of the iron discs Thur described a circle on it with the Burin, inside this circle he scratched the mystical characters of Mars and outside, between it and the edge, he wrote in Hebrew the names, EDIMIEL, BARTZACHHIAHE-SCHIEL and ITHUREL; this was for invoking the spirits of Mars in general.

On the second he engraved within the Circle an equilateral triangle surmounted at the apex with a pentacle. Within this triangle a smaller inverted triangle was drawn with a great Vau, and round it the name ELOH.

Between the circle and the edge was written in Hebrew: "Who is so great as ELOHIM ?"

This Pentacle was for the purpose of exciting War, Wrath, Discord and for the overthrowing of enemies. The third Pentacle, the Circle was divided into four equal parts with a star pentacle above, it had in the centre the word AGLA IHVH, repeated twice, above and below, (was EL). All was in Hebrew, as were also the words of the text written between the circle and the outer edge. "The Lord is my right hand, and he shall wound even Kings in the day of his wrath." This was to give power in war, and would bring victory. The fourth had inside the Circle, written in the secret characters of the Malachim script, the words, Elohim Quibor. "God hath protected me." Outside the Circle was written a text from Psalm XXXVII, 15; written in Hebrew, "Their swords shall enter into their own hearts and their bows shall be broken." This Pentacle was to give strength and courage in fighting and ultimate victory. Upon the reverse of each of these Pentacles was engraved the Sigil of Bartzebal. Having finished engraving them, he purified them anew in the incense smoke which arose from the herbs and spices Morven cast upon the centre brazier. Each planet has its different and appropriate incense and for Mars they used euphorbia, bedellium, ammoniac, lodestone and sulphur. This matter of incense is of the greatest importance in the ritual, as it must be of the nature of the spirit, not only does it influence the spirit conjured, but all surrounding objects; it lies heavy upon the air and the Magus breathes it deep into his lungs, making him of one nature with the spirit, the fragrance and density attracts and draws the conjured spirit, partly because it is of his nature, and partly because of the pleasure it gives him. It is from its density he obtains the means to build up a body and so materialise. To increase the affinity, the brazier which was used for heating was fed with sticks of dried thorn and wild rose. When all were censed and purified, Thur took a strand of cord and bound each, winding it round thrice, and tying it with three separate knots, then wrapped each in a separate black cloth and laid them in their order on the west side of the Circle, sprinkled them with consecrated water, baptising them and saying, "I hereby consecrate thee, O creature of Mars and of iron, Bartzebal." Then he held each in the smoke of the incense, saying: "By fire and water I consecrate thee. Thou art him, and He is ye, in thought, in feeling, and in sight, as I bind ye, I bind him, as I loose ye, I loose him. By the sacred name Abracadabra. Amen. I consecrate thee for the especial purpose of bringing victory to Jan Bonder, to obtain vengeance upon Fitz-Urse and to regain all the castles and lands stolen by Fitz-Urse from his grands ire, Sir Edgar Bonder." From thence onwards the table served as an altar. Upon it Thur now placed the four Pentacles, he repeated over them the words he had just spoken, the words of consecration and dedication, and then announced solemnly, in a loud and clear voice, that all these purposes would be accomplished. Still using the same firm and distinct utterance he declared: "All has been prepared and is in readiness to charge these Pentacles with power, I summon all ye spirits of the nature of Mars, and command ye to attend." The critical moments of the ritual were approaching, Thur took the Magic Sword, Morven took her Athame, and while they held the points of their weapons on the first Pentacle, Thur recited slowly and with the utmost intensity he could summon. "Adonai, Most Powerful; El, Most Strong; Agla, Most Holy; Oh, Most Righteous. Azoth, The Beginning and the End. Thou Who hast established all things in thy Wisdom. Thou, who hast granted unto Solomon Thy servant these Pentacles by Thy great mercy for the preservation of both soul and body; we most humbly implore and supplicate Thy Most Holy Majesty that these Pentacles may be consecrated by Thy Power in such a manner that they may obtain virtue and strength against all spirits, through Thee, O Most Holy Adonai, Whose Kingdom, Empire and Principality endureth without end. Amen."

With the point of his sword Thur traced in the air above the first Pentacle the symbols engraved on its disc.

This ceremony with the points of the weapons, the above invocation and consecration together with the aerial tracing of the symbols, was repeated without variation of any sort over each Pentacle in turn. When all this was accomplished, with equal intensity directed upon them, Thur took each in turn in his left hand and smote it thrice with the flat of his sword. Coming again to the first Pentacle, he took it in his left hand and with the sword erect in his right hand he circumambulated the Circle, holding up the veiled disc to the four quarters, west, north, east and south; this procedure was followed without deviation with each in turn. Each time placing the Pentacles on the floor, this time in the south, and repeating the former consecration with fire and water, adding: "O, creatures of Iron and Mars, twice consecrated, thou may est approach the gates of the south." He circumambulated the Circle again. Then taking the first Pentacle he carefully unwrapped it, not removing the veil, but leaving the disc covered with the ends hanging down. He smote it once with the sword then held it at arms' length while he elevated the sword above it. Thrice he stamped with his right foot, addressing it. "Thou canst not pass from concealment to manifestation save by virtue of the name ALHIM. Before all things are chaos and darkness, I am he whose name is darkness. I am the exorcist in the midst of the exorcism. Take on therefore manifestion from me." He circumambulated again, re-wrapped the Pentacle and replaced it on the Altar, repeating the ceremony with each in turn. When all were assembled on the Altar, he again partially unveiled the first and summoning Morven with a gesture, she held her Athame above it; while he held his sword in a like manner, he conjured it saying: "By all the Powers and Rites, I conjure Thee, render this Pentacle irresistible, O Lord Adonai." When this had been repeated over each he reveiled the Pentacles and carried them to the north, laying them on the ground, opening each veil completely, saying: "Thou canst not pass from concealment to manifestation save by the name JHV (Jehovah)."

Reveiling them he passed to the south, and laid them on the

ground, and entirely removing the veils from each, but leaving them bound, this done he invoked: "O Bartzebal, too long hast thou been in darkness. Quit the night and seek the day. As light is hidden in darkness, yet can manifest itself there from, so shalt thou manifest from concealment unto manifestation."

The words, "So shalt thou manifest," were spoken with such a degree of concentrated will, that Thur's tanned face took on almost a greenish hue, so great was the concentrated effort he made.

Reveiling them he took the Pentacles from the floor and replaced them on the Altar, again invoking he held them in turn towards heaven, saying: "I conjure upon thee power and might irresistible, by the Powers of DANI, ZEMUCH, AGATMATUROD, EODIEL, PANI, CANELOAS, MERoD, GAMODI, BALDOI, METRATOR."

Now he laid his sword down and taking the scourge, smote each in turn, saying over each as he did so: "By, and in the NAME of ELOHIM, I invoke into thee the powers of Mars and the powers of War," and released the cords binding them. As he said this over the first of the Pentacles, a chill crept up Morven's spine and over her scalp. Witch and believer in Witchery as she proclaimed herself, here was a manifestation of power she had never seen; for the Pentacle glowed with a sullen redness, infinitely menacing and terrible. In its small circumference it seemed to hold all the cruel, remorseless wantonness of war. On each in turn as he invoked, he bore down upon it the whole might of his highly-trained mental strength, so was each infused with the same smouldering red fire, and Thur realised his prayers had been answered, the consecration had been successful.

After a moment's pause, as though to gather his faculties which had been strained to a snapping point, Thur stood erect and prayed:

"I thank Thee, O LORD OF HOSTS, for the favour Thou hast manifested to me."

Standing so, with his face to the Heavens, he looked truly

inspired. Then he relaxed, sinking on one of the stools before the Altar-table. His head sunk forward on his breast, his whole pose expressed acute physical exhaustion, and he panted quickly. Morven watched him in silent solicitude, not daring to speak. Presently he was sufficiently recovered to make a sign towards the Altar, where the Pentacles lay. Understanding, Morven wrapped the newly consecrated Pentacles in a clean cloth and put them with other articles in the casket, this she stowed away in a hiding place. Then she collected the tools they had used, from time to time stealing anxious glances at Thur, who still sat upon his stool, his robe hitched up showing his bare legs and feet, his hands hanging listlessly between his knees.

The two had presented an embodiment of perfect service and perfect leadership.

Suddenly she felt a glow of happiness and contentment, a sense of peace such as she had never known.

# CHAPTER XVI
## MAKING THE GREAT CIRCLE

ORD was sent to the farm and the brothers arrived in time for supper. All were tense and excited, for the stars were well aspected, and that night they were to attempt the great experiment, making the Great Circle.

Between the upper floor and the roof was an attic reached only by a ladder.

This Thur decided was the best place, so he and Morven spent many hours sweeping down cobwebs and years of accumulated dust, and then scouring it.

As the hour drew near, Thur said to the brothers:

"Much depends on you two to-night. You have come here braving your mother's wrath when she finds out. So waste not the works which I do on your behalf."

Jan looked puzzled.

"You mean?" he asked tentatively.

"I mean the adventure of the Great Circle, for, make no mistake, I rise mighty forces and there is danger."

"How may that be, Thur? Are you not a Magus? and do you not command spirits by your mystical lore?"

"My mystical lore, as you call it, is but half the tale, knowledge of rites and incantations I have learned, but I have never yet practised the Art. When all is said and done, it is the mind alone which is the true worker of wonders and of this wonder in particular."

Jan looked and felt harassed and mumbled: "Yet I understand you not."

"By powers of mind, I mean self-control ... the power to keep them fixed immovably upon the object of your purpose, procuring the downfall of Fitz-Urse, the capture of the castle, and through that the restoration of your lands, titles and revenues. You must think of that and nothing else, Jan."

Jan laughed, mightily relieved to find so little was required after such solemn warnings.

"There is little difficulty in that," was his careless reply. "What else do I think of, day in, day out?"

But Thur found this over-confidence ominous.

"Day in, day out, 'tis not enough, such bat-like flittings have little to do with true concentration of thought. They are common to all men, you must do much more; what is wanted is for you to dwell on it with a frantic intensity for at least an hour and not to let thought slip from your mind for a single instant all the while that we are in the Circle; nor let the slightest glimmering of another thought intrude. 'Tis not too easy... make an image of the castle before your mind's eye till you actually believe you see it before you."

Jan promptly assumed a stony stare. "I have it, I see it as plain as a pike staff perched on that villainous rock, the sea slavering at its feet and gulls screaming round its battlements. Oh, I can see it well enough."

"Good, but keep it there when the time comes, and you too, Olaf. What I say to Jan is for you too, lad. All who enter the Circle with me come as my helpers, and must help me by thinking correctly, to give me strength and so increase my power, for if there are any in the Circle who lets his thoughts stray from the matter in hand, he not only' weakens me and so defeats his own ends, but brings danger upon us all."

"Danger?" Jan exclaimed, startled.

"Aye, lad, for our lives."

"From what?"

"Blasting," said Thur grimly. "Nothing quicker than a spirit to detect weakness in a Magus or a slackening of the powers that summon him. For I must summon the power of war and revenge. He is not evil in himself, but his powers are dangerous if not controlled. He will not want to come, he would never come of his own free will. I may command him to come and cover such command by enticements, and blind him, puzzle him and bring him

218

by sweet incense such as all spirits love according to their nature. Then, when I have got him within hearing, command him by the power of the Holy Names, and so force him to obey my will. But if he sense the slightest weakness in the Magus, or anyone present, straightway will he become unruly and disobedient, and his power, clashing with our wills, might end by destroying us all. If you make the slightest gap in a mill dam, the imprisoned waters may rush forth destroying both dam and you. The water wishes you no ill, it will work willingly for you, an you control it. So remember. As this is the power of the spirits we loose forth. Our weakness is their strength. If we lose control, it may mean our destruction."

"But why do they not work for us willingly?" asked Morven.

"Dear child, an we could go cap in hand and ask them, perchance they might. But remember, we have to get in touch with them first, and the only way we know is to trap them, blind their eyes and mind and speech, till they may see and hear us only. Would you not be angered if, say, a flock of sheep surrounded you and forced you to labour for them, enforcing their demands by jostling and biting? I have to summon the spirit by force and apply more and more force till he comes, willing or not, and all I can offer in return is sweet odours, courtesy and respect. So remember, I need your wills to aid me, all your strength and your fixed mental images, because our combined strength is their weakness and through that we may force their obedience."

Awed, all replied: "We will indeed, Thur."

"My thanks. I ask no more, let us up and the blessing of God be with us."

With some soberness of spirit, because of the great things before them, they mounted the stairs to the chamber above where stood the tub of water, each man carrying a bucket of hot water which they mixed with the cold already in the tub. Thur stripped and exorcised the water thus:

"I exorcise thee, O creature of water, that thou cast out from thee all the impurities and uncleanlinesses of the spirits of the world of phantasms, so they may harm me not. Through the Virtue of God the Almighty, Who reigneth through the Ages of Ages. By the names of Mertallia, Musalia, Dophalia, Nnemalia, Zitanseia, Goldaphaira, Dedulsaira, Gheninairea, Geogropheira, Cedahi, Gilthar, Godieb, Ezoiil, Musil, Grassil, Tamen, Puri, Godu, Hoznoth, Astroth, Tzabaoth, Adonai, Asla, On, El, Tetragramaton, Shema, Ariston, Anaphaxeton, Segilaton, Primeuraton. Amen." Then he washed himself thoroughly, saying as he did so:

"Purge me, O Lord, with hyssop and I shall be clean. Wash me and I shall be whiter than snow."

Then he took salt and blessed it, saying:

"The blessings of the Father Almighty be upon this creature of salt, let all malignity and hindrance be cast forth there from, and let all good enter therein, wherefore do I bless Thee, that Thou mayest aid me. Amen."

Casting this exorcised salt into the water, he washed himself again, saying as he did so:

"Imanel, Arnamon, Imato, Memeon, Vaphoion, Gardon, Existon, Zagverinm, Momerton, Zarmesiton, Tilecon, Tixmion. Amen."

As the invocation ended he stepped out, dried himself and donned a clean white linen robe.

While all this was in progress, Jan was obediently fixing his mind upon Fitz-Urse and his castle, but Olaf's attention was fixed upon Morven, who had now entered the bath and splashed about.

Then Thur poured water over her, saying solemnly:

"I conjure thee, O creature, being a young girl. By the Most High God, the father of all creatures, by Father Elohim and by Father Elohim Gebur and by Father Elion, that thou shalt neither have the will or the power to hide anything from me, and that thou shalt be faithful and obedient to me. Amen."

Then he poured water over again, saying:

"Be thee regenerate, cleansed and purified, so that the spirits may neither harm thee nor abide in thee. Amen."

Then he had the two Bonders strip and get into the tub together; silently they obeyed, watching him covertly as they scoured their bodies with an earnestness that made them glow. Thur smothered a smile at this cleansing, accomplished as never before. Taking water from the tub and pouring it over their heads so it flowed in a cascade to their feet, saying as he did so over each: "Be ye pure and regenerate, cleansed and purified in the name of the Ineffable, Great and Eternal God from all your iniquities, may the Virtue of the Most High descend upon you and abide with you always, so that you may have power and strength to win the desires of your heart. Amen."

When they stepped out and dried themselves, much subdued by the solemn strangeness of this unusual stress upon purification, Thur pointed to two clean white robes and motioned to them to don them. Then he said: "It is needful that you wear these Talismans upon your breasts," and hung about Jan's neck a Pentacle of Iron for Mars, and upon Olaf a thin disc of beaten gold, for Leo. Morven already had her own, the Pentacle of Jupiter of silver. Each of these Pentacles was engraved with the Kabalistic signs appropriate to its ruling spirit.

Upon his own breast Thur then suspended three of the Pentacles of Iron he had made for Bartzebal, together with his own individual Talisman of Mercury, formed of brass. The Pentacles of Bartzebal he covered with a kerchief. He then censed the three disciples and himself, then censed again the Talismans upon their breasts and upon his own, saying: "These are the Talismans and Pentacles, perfumed with the proper fumigations, by which being assured and encouraged ye may enter into this matter without fear or terror, and shall be exempt from all perils and dangers provided thou obey my commands and do all I shall ordain. All things shall go according to my desires."

After a moment of silence he spoke again. "Jan and Olaf, you will need your swords; Morven hath her Athame. Each weapon hold in your right hands when in the Circle."

As he spoke he picked up the lighted lantern and turned to ascend the ladder leading to the loft above. They all followed. The rays of the lantern faintly illuminated the great loft. Thur lighted a great candle upon the Altar, placed in the midst of the Great Circle, saying: "I exorcise Thee, O Creature of Fire, in the Name of the Sovereign and Eternal Lord, by his Ineffable Name which is J HVH, by the name Jah and by the name of Power which is El, that thou mayest enlighten the heart of all Spirits which we may call into this Circle, so that they may appear before us without fraud and deceit, through HIM who half created all things."

Then, going sunwise, he lighted other candles round the Circle. When he had finished there was a soft and steady illumination; meanwhile Morven had been following him around lighting the charcoal in braziers set at the four cardinal points, and putting incense thereon.

As the candles were lighted, details of the place of experiment leapt into being, the vast oak beams, springing from the floor, and sloping upwards to the peak of the roof, wisps of reeds from the thatch increased in shadow to fingers of clutching hands; Kabalistic signs chalked on beams, which as they sprang to their attention, struck the mind with all the force of a physical blow by reason of their mystery and the awfulness of their import. As the little points of light grew, the creamy satin-smoothness of Morven's body, like a fine pearl, concentrated them and drew them to itself to send them forth again in iridescent lustre at which Jan. resolutely refused to look. The markings of the Great Circle could now be seen in all its complicated detail. In all there were four circles, the outer, a double one, was fifteen feet in diameter, a second was drawn a foot inside this, and a third a foot within this ,again. Thus the inner circle was eleven feet in diameter.

Outside the Great Circle but just touching it were four small double circles, two feet in diameter, around the braziers at the cardinal points. A triangle was drawn outside the Circle at the south. A doorway was marked into the Great Circle by drawing two parallel lines two feet apart, from the outer to the inner circle. The three disciples stood waiting his pleasure. To Morven, Thur gave a censer and a basket of incense. In her right hand she held her Athame, and she slung the handle of the basket on her arm. Jan was given a mighty parchment and a flash of perfume; to Olaf a pen, parchment and a small horn of ink, which, together with his sword, he clutched with a desperate firmness of determination not to drop them.

Meanwhile Thur, standing in the centre of the Circle, facing eastwards, crossed himself, saying: "Atoh, Malkus, ve Gevurah, vr Gedulah, le Olam."

Then, going to the eastern side of the Circle, said:

"I summon, stir, and call thee up, thou Mighty Ones of the East, to guard this Circle." He then made the same proclamation to the Mighty Ones of the South, West and North in turn. Then, with the point of his consecrated sword, he retraced every line of the Great Circle, but carefully raised the point of his sword in the form of an arch each time he passed the doorway, so the Circle was left incomplete at these points. Then he wrote names of power between the circles. In the south-east he wrote JHVH (Jehovah); in the south-west, AHIA, at the north-west, ALVIN; and in the north-east, ALH. Within the second and the inner circle he wrote at the east, AL; at the south, AGLA; at the west, JA, and at the north, ADNI. All in Hebrew characters, Pentacles were traced between these names around the circumference of the Circle. All this accomplished, Thur went to each brazier in turn, from the east passing southwards, the way of the sun, fanning up the coals, followed by Morven casting upon them fresh incense of aloes, nutmeg, gum-bengerman and musk. Before the Altar was a larger brazier, this. was now lighted and incense set on it.

Thur, leaving the Circle by the door, followed by Morven, then marshalled his disciples, and led them inside the Circle. Closing the door, by drawing his sword across the uncompleted lines, saying as he did so: "Agla, Azoth, Adonai," and marking three pentacles to guard the doorway.

Then, assigning to each of the disciples a position, Thur said: "Whenever I move, you will follow me with decorous steps and woe betide him who steps outside the Circle, for I call up mighty forces."

This speech put the finishing touch to the Bonders, the space was so confined it was like trying to circumnavigate a farthing, their feet seemed not only to be enormous and unwieldly, but almost clamped to the floor. Olaf cast a look of mute protest at the Magus, but already he had begun to intone a prayer in his rich, sonorous notes.

"Zanaii, Zamaii, Pindamon most powerful, Zidon most strong, El, Yod, He Vou, He. lah, Agla. Assist me, an unworthy sinner who have had the boldness to pronounce thy Holy Names, which no man should name and invoke save in very great danger. Therefore have I had recourse to these Most Holy Names, being in peril of both soul and body. Pardon if I have sinned in any manner for I trust in thy protection. Amen."

So praying, he censed them all anew, then himself.

It was now midnight. In all the braziers the embers glowed, and dense clouds of perfumed smoke rolled up to the thatch, and curled along the beams in fantastic shapes, their strangeness augmented by the under lighting from the fierce fires beneath, so that already the loft seemed to be peopled by other-world phantasms. Thur stood by the Altar, facing the East, and cried in a loud voice:·

"O ye spirits, I conjure you by the Power, the Wisdom, and by the Virtue of the Spirit of God, by the Greatness of God, by the Holy Name of God. EHEIEH."

Upon the Altar lay the remaining Pentacle of the four he had made for Bartzebal. Also cords, black cloth and other things which he would want for the operation. Taking this Pentacle, he bound it with a cord and shrouded it with a cloth. He then passed sunwise round the Circle, followed by the others, to the west, where

he baptised the Pentacle with consecrated water, saying: "O creature of iron, I consecrate thee in place of thy master, I name thee
Bartzebal. Thou art Bartzebal. . . . "So saying, he censed it in the
perfumed smoke of the brazier, fanning the flame so it licked it
without firing the cover, then placing it on the floor in the west,
and standing with his sword point on the Pentacle, he declared in
incisive tones:

"I, Thur Peterson, hereby evoke the Great Spirit Bartzebal to
come to my aid, so that Jan Bonder here shall regain his lordship,
his following, his lands and his honours."

Taking the Pentacle he placed it on the Altar and called
thrice:

"Bartzebal come, Bartzebal come, Bartzebal COME. Come to
the aid of Jan Bonder that he may attain his desires."

Thur then announced with intense conviction:

"Bartzebal WILL APPEAR."

Jan's eyes searched wildly for the approach of Bartzebal, expect-
ing to see a fearful apparition of immense martial strength, probably heralded by a deafening clap of thunder. To his inexpress-
ible relief none of these things occurred, only the familiar, and
to him comforting, voice of Thur was heard evoking the spirit
again: "Come, O Bartzebal, by the Indivisible Name of God, IOD
by the name Tetragramaton Elohim, by El, Strong and Mighty, by
the name Elohim Gibor, wonderful, I conjure thee by the Name,
ELOTH VA DATH."

A moment's pause followed, as though the whole Universe
waited upon these great names and held its breath in suspense.
Jan's breath seemed to have died away in his breast and would
never come again to sustain him.

He moistened his parched lips with his tongue, and glanced at
his brother. Olaf, his eyes bright and shining, had his gaze riveted
on Thur's face in adoring wonderment, his white robe, with his
fine hair folded on his head like the petals of a hyacinth, and that
glorified worship illuminating him so that he glowed from some

inner radiance like the fire in the heart of a diamond, looking like an archangel, lacking only the splendour of rainbow pinions to complete the illusion.

Olaf, lost in God knows what paradise that the human mind was capable of creating for itself, had no place for his brother in it, and Jan felt all the desolation of the fact in that moment of his own need of human contact.

He looked at Morven, quietly attentive, watchful of the Magus. Compared with Olaf, her face was void of expression, but she caught his roving eyes and held them with hers, and anxiety marked her clear forehead.

She frowned and shook her head at him warningly. Jan understood her and made a frantic snatch at his vagrant thoughts. He forced himself to see the castle, even to the point of seeing a helmeted head on the battlements, which he labelled Fitz-Urse. He riveted his attention and, seeing this, Morven relaxed her frown.

Thur was now at the east of the Altar and had placed the Pentacle, still bound and veiled, upon a triangle marked on its centre. In his right hand he held his magic sword, raised at arm's length, with the pommel above the Pentacle, saying:

"O Bartzebal, I conjure thee by the Most Holy Name, SHADDAI! I have bound and veiled this thy symbol, which is thee. Thus I bind thee so that thou canst not move, nor see, nor hear aught but according to my will. So do I conjure thee to visible appearance.

"Come swiftly to obey my will, by the Most Holy Name of El Ghai I conjure thee, through the virtue of the Most Holy Name of God, ADONAI MELAKKI. Through the virtue of Methratton His Image. Through the virtue of his Angels who cease not to cry by day or by night, Qadosch, Qadosch, Qadosch, Elohim Adonai Tzaboath!

"And by the ten Angels who preside over the Sephireth, by whom God communicateth and extendeth His influence over the lower things, which are Kether, Chokmah, Binah, Geburah, Tipereth, Netzach, Hod, Yesod, and Malkuth. I conjure and command thee absolutely, O Bartzebal, in whatever part of the universe ye may be, by virtue of these Holy Names. Adonai, Yove, Ha, Kabir, Messiachionah, Mal, Kah, Eral, Kuzy, Matzpatz, El Shaddai, and by all of the Holy Names of God, which have been written in blood in sign of Eternal Alliance.

"I conjure thee by the names of God, Most Holy and Unknown, by virtue of which he may tremble each day, Baruch, Barcurabon, Patachel, Alcheghek, Aquachai, Homorian Eheieh, Abbaton, Chevob, Cebon, Oyzroymas, Chaialbamachi, Ortagu, Maleabelech, Helechyeze, Sechezze.

"Hear ye, come quickly and without delay into our presence. I summon thee, Bartzebal, spirit of Mars. Bartzebal, COME. Bartzebal, COME. Bartzebal, COME."

Thur uttered the last "come" with all the. strength of will and voice that he could command. Then, flinging more incense into the centre brazier and motioning to Morven to replenish the others, he resumed:

"As the voice of the exorcist said unto me, 'Let me shroud myself in darkness, peradventure thus I may manifest myself in light.'

"Come, O Bartzebal, come! Come, O Bartzebal, come! Come, O Bartzebal, come."

Again the command was issued with stupendous force of will. A dense cloud of smoke from the big brazier leapt up to the thatch to mingle with the equally heavy fumes rising from the lesser braziers. Thur motioned to Morven, and she went quietly round, putting on more spices.

The smoky clouds began to descend with a plunge and the whole loft was full of a whirling smother of shapes, misty and contorting, none of which came into the Circle, however. Jan watched this development with a kind of interested disgust. His sensations were many and complicated and confusing to himself. He lacked entirely the long patience of the seeker after hidden mysteries, and after that breathtaking moment when he had expected he knew not what in the way of awfulness, the present moment savoured of anti-climax, and he found himself disliking the whole business with a fervour equal to his one-time desire to seek its aid. Not in any way given to introspection, he was troubled and puzzled at his reaction, at this recoil, which he knew to be deeply instinctive. How could he understand in his simplicity of disposition and outlook, that for some natures there is no affinity between them and the occult, that there is not the smallest channel of approach, and if, for them the veil is torn aside momentarily, the vision vouchsafed will be of a contrary order to that experienced by the devotee.

Jan, though a realist of the first water, was yet a casual believer in marvels, but typical of the common sense of the day, he disliked being too much mixed tip with them. He believed because he never thought about them. "Go to a magician, seek a witch," were commonplace actions of people in difficulties ... words tripping lightly off the tongue, and accepted with the same light thoughtlessness, but with the implication: "Let them do the work, you yourself keep out of it"; and now he found himself in the midst of it ... He himself should be clear of anything. It was in such spirit that Jan, prompted by his own angry desperation, equally thoughtless, had sought the aid of High Magic, and being committed to it, had continued in it with much reluctance. It was not what he expected, the witch was not foul and hideous, the rites of the Magus had nothing to do with a menagerie of snakes, spotted toads, efts and black cats, and, like many another, Jan was now faced with the difference between the dream and the business. He did not know why, but the more he saw of the business, the more he felt inclined to wash his hands of it.

To his simple troubled mind, all he wanted was a stout army of honest fellows, who would follow him into a good, honest, ding-dong fight, that he might slay his enemy in a hand-to-hand encounter and take back what had been filched from him, and it was only right the world should furnish him with such, without for a moment wondering why such an army should risk their lives fighting for his cause. It was an intolerable impertinence that this Bartzebal, whoever he was-and who needed so much coaxing-must have his smoky finger in the pie. Naked women and stinking smoke, while he, Jan Bonder, instead of training his men at Dearleap, must stand rigidly in an eleven-foot circle, or be following Thur Peterson around, with a slow and stately pace, until he was dizzy and numb with the strain, and all through his own daft folly.

So thought Jan. But Thur regarded the scene with satisfied approval. Things were going as the old Spanish Doctor had taught. He took the Pentacle from the Altar, and paced with it around the Circle, holding it up to all four quarters; this done, he went around again to the south, and again baptised it with water and fire, repeating: "O creature of iron and Mars, twice consecrate, thou mayest approach the gates of the West." As he spoke he passed around to the west and opened the veil of the Pentacle without discarding it, at the same time exposing the three other Pentacles on his breast.

Dropping the veil over his breast again, he smote the Pentacle in his hand with the flat of his sword, saying: "Thou canst not pass from concealment to manifestation save by virtue of the Name, Alhim. Before all things are chaos and darkness and the Gates of the Night. I am the Great One in the lands of the Shades. I am He whose name is Darkness. I am the exorcist in the midst of the exorcism. Appear therefore before me, FOR I AM HE in whom fear is not. Thou knowest me. So, come, Bartzebal. COME! Come, Bartzebal, COME!"

The smoke from the centre brazier became violently agitated, forming a pillar, rising and falling with spasmodic energy. Faces came and vanished. Morven, at a quick gesture from Thur, threw a handful of incense on the brazier and, passing to the smaller ones, replenished them. From all this heavy feeding, the smoke grew denser and more fragrant.

Again the Magus passed to the east of the Altar and faced west. Again he smote the Pentacle with his sword and spoke with gathering forcefulness. "Thou canst not pass from concealment to manifestation save by the virtue of JHVH … After the formless and the void and the darkness, cometh the light … I am the light that ariseth in darkness. I am the exorcist in the midst of exorcism. Appear therefore in harmonious form before me, for I am the wielder of the forces of the balance .... Thou Knowest Me, So Appear."

Thur then removed the veil entirely from the Pentacle but left it bound, he also withdrew the veil from the Pentacles on his breast, then replaced it. Loudly he declared: "O Creature of Iron and of Mars, too long hast thou dwelt in darkness, quit the dark and seek the light."

He replaced the Pentacle on the Altar and, holding the sword erect, with the pommel above it, said:

"By all the Names and Powers already rehearsed, I command ye to a visible appearance, in the names of Herachio, Asacro, Bedremuael, Tilath, Ierahlemi, Ideodoc, Archarzel, Zopiel, Bla-q.teel, Baracata, Edoniel, Elohim, Amagro, Abragateh, Samoel, Gebrurahel, Cadato, Fra, Elohi, Achsah, Emisha, Imachedel, Dama, Elamos, Izachel, Bael, Sergon, Demos. O Lord God, Who art seated in the two Heavens, Who regardeth the Abyss beneath Thee, Grant unto me Thy Grace, I beseech Thee, so that what I conceive in my mind I may accomplish through Thee. O My God, Sovereign Ruler over all. Amen."

"Come, I conjure thee. Come, O Bartzebal, come!"

The agitation in the pillar of smoke became more marked, and grew in violence. A face of wild and unearthly beauty, many times larger than life, appeared at the western side of the Circle, the body of which was unstable, coming and going. Upon its face was an expression of sulky annoyance mingled with astonishment that was almost comic, a frowning amazement at having been snared and compelled into this manifestation. Thus was Bartzebal.

A booming sound like that of a great gong, struck in a place of vast dimensions at some immense distance, echoed through the loft, and they sensed rather than heard an angry demand: "What seek ye?"

Did Bartzebal speak or was he really soundless? Was it in truth a voice, or merely a hollow vibration resounding simultaneously in every head?

Jan could not determine, he saw that the atmosphere of the loft was becoming clear because the smoke had collected and resolved itself into a crowd of shapes, writhing in endless contortions. They seemed to have definite substance, pushing and jostling in an unruly endeavour to peer into the circle, as though they were curious about the people therein.

Jan was no coward and was not aware of fear, but his spirit quaked and he was aware of strange and unusual thoughts acting in his mind very much like the people of the smoke before him, thrust forward, clamouring for attention. He was no thinker, but one great thought materialised in his mind. As Bartzebal had materialised from the smoke of the incense, grown from all the emotional reactions of the past hour's events, and the thought which persisted and grew in strength was that God was a reality of the greatest moment to him, Jan Bonder. Hitherto he had only associated God with the Church, because of what the Church was to him, he had dismissed God as no better than the Church, which called itself his. Jan had heard Thur solemnly pray that God would aid him, and here, before his bewildered eyes, God had manifested Himself. In all His Power and Goodness, manifested Himself through this thing of air, Bartzebal. Gone were his thoughts of Morven, and her beauty, and all his dislike for that particular form of manifestation. All were swamped in the astounding revelation. That God willed it … and so it was Right!

The Church denounced what Thur was doing, declaring it to be sinful, punishable by death, and forbidden by God. Yet it Was God who was aiding Thur. Jan knew that Thur was not working through the Devil, as the Church said, all sorcerers worked, because one cannot invoke the devil in God's Sacred Name. That evil would surely blast a man where he stood. No, Thur had worked through God with the uttermost reverence, and God had answered his prayers. So clearly it was God's Will! In this creation of Bartzebal, Jan saw the hand of God in answer to solemn prayer, and Bartzebal sent by God's hand was there, though he frowned and so was there unwillingly, and the thought came, he himself was there unwillingly, to gain his own ends. Was this not sin? and God in his infinite Goodness and Compassion, had plainly worked this thing, performed this wonder that he might understand.

Meanwhile Thur, seeing the form of Bartzebal materialise, drew aside the veil covering the Pentacles on his breast. Bartzebal looked at them, and averted his eyes uneasily, but inevitably was drawn to look at them again. For the Pentacles, by the rites in their making and their consecration, had become an integral part of his nature. While they remained veiled he was blind and deaf, wherever his locality, he was conscious only of the words of the Magus, by the incantations and the incense he was pulled towards the Circle, and as they grew he was compelled to materialise. Once there, and the Pentacles were unveiled before him. He could hear and see the Magus clearly and was being forced to do service by the repeated incantations, even though he was angry at being so trapped. Angry or not, he could not escape until his hour was past. But in his mood of annoyance he would do his best to avoid action, to palter and delay in order to gain time, and to try conclusions with the will of the Magus. This he prepared to do. Thur threw more incense on the brazier and Morven replenished the outer four, Bartzebal tried to counter these tactics by closing his nostrils to the enticing perfumes quite uselessly, they were too seductive and he gave up the attempt, trusting to events for aid, and he inhaled the grateful mixture long and prodigiously.

As the dense smoke arose, Jan saw it was drawn, as if by a strong wind, towards the throng outside the Circle. He was curiously intent upon them; he saw they grew in distinctness, seeming to build themselves up as it were, from the fragrant fumes. In their eagerness to assemble their bodies, they pressed forward to absorb the smoke, while never passing the outer circle. This circle was as a protecting rampart to those within, charged with some stupendous force which repelled all invasion. He saw that those shapes, too roughly jostled by their neighbours that they almost touched the Circle, were violently hurled backwards, and several who actually touched it were disintegrated into wisps of smoke, which were instantly absorbed by their neighbours. Again the atmosphere inside the Circle was clear, only the steadily rising columns of incense from the braziers mounted half-way to the thatch then curved outwards to the countless throng who, couched in every variety of positions, silently watched. Jan felt as if all the eyes of a million years watched him, saw into his soul, asking the voiceless question: "What seek ye?" Again it seemed as if a great gong-like voice reverberated through the loft. "What seek ye? I would be gone."

This Bartzebal impressed upon their minds with simplicity. Thur removed the cords from the Pentacle lying on the Altar. He spoke with a courteous authority: "Greetings, O Bartzebal, I do invoke upon thee the power of visible appearance and of speech, by the power of the Almighty God, Lord of the Ages of Ages. I conjure thee, O Bartzebal, to tell me truly how may Jan Bonder here obtain his desires?"

Bartzebal, articulate, replied in no uncertain terms: "Ye have no power to force my answer." Thur held out in turns the Pentacles hung round his neck. Bartzebal looked, his eyes starting from his head. With an effort he turned his eyes away, but something drew him, and he looked again as if fascinated. Thur gave a sharp command: "Enter the Triangle." Bartzebal stiffened and stood still defiantly. Thur beckoned threateningly with his sword, holding out the Pentacles on his breast, saying: "Here are the secret things, the Pentacles of Mars, thy Lord. They are the Standards of God, the Conqueror, the Arms of the Almighty One, to compel the Airy Potencies." Bartzebal sulkily moved into the Triangle, as if he knew not what he did. Thur continued: "I command thee absolutely by these Powers, by the Virtue of God, the Almighty One. So answer my questions and tell me truly, how may Jan Bonder gain his wishes?" Bartzebal rolled his eyes but stood sullenly mute.

Thur said: "I exorcise ye anew and powerfully command thee, commanding thee with all my strength and violence by Him Who 'Spoke and it was done'. By the Names of Power, El Shaddai, Elohim, Elohi, Tzabaoth, Asser, Eheieh, Yah, Tetragramaton, which signify God, the High and Almighty, and by His Holy Names we shall accomplish our work."

"Wherefore should I help ye, ye who are nought to me?" Bartzebal asked, betraying a close affinity to humanity.

"Again we command ye with vehemence and we exorcise thee with constancy, by virtue of these names: Ahai, Aetchedad, Iransin, Emeth, Chaia, Iona, Profa, Titach, Benani, Briah, Theit, and all whose names are written in Heaven in the characters of the Malachim. By the Living God, Whose Dwelling is in the Ineffable Light, Whose Name is Wisdom, and Whose Spirit is Life, before Whom goeth forth fire and flame, Who with fire fixed the firmament, the Stars and the Sun, and Who with fire will burn thee everlastingly, as also all those who contravene the words of his will. So swiftly execute our command."

An expression of shy malice mingled with the mutiny on the face of the spirit. "How may I, Bartzebal, answer thy questions, when thine own man knows not what are truly his desires?"

Jan spoke with almost contemptuous directness "I know my mind well enough, thou rebel. It is to get . .." He paused, stayed by a gesture from Morven and the look of intense warning in her eyes. He thought swiftly, so Bartzebal knows what passes in our minds. Thur turned to him swiftly.

"Tell this contumacious imp what you desire."

But Jan stood as in a dream. Olaf prodded him sharply to attention; Morven closed her eyes, expressing despair; and Bartzebal grinned wildly. "I desire two things," said Jan with a crisp clarity. "First to do the will of God, and secondly to regain my grandsire's lands and fortune and following, filched from him by Usa Fitz-Urse, and to re-establish my family." But as he said this, swift came a thought in his brain. "I want Morven."

Bartzebal shook his head. "I am Bartzebal, the spirit of Mars, I can give deeds of war and revenge, aye and of treachery too. Power and success are within my gift, at a price. But thy desires must be single, clean-cut as a naked blade. Thy will must burn clear and steady as a guarded flame. Thine does not. Therefore, I cannot grant thy wish, for I cannot give love of woman."

"Thou hast no power to contravene the will of God," said Jan doggedly. "And if it be His will, I shall succeed, because my own will burns bright," and he strove to see the castle again.

But even as he spoke, the form of Bartzebal began to disintegrate into vapour, as did the bodies of the crowd outside, only their strange eyes glowed in watchful anticipation, as they waited upon this unpropitious event.

"He is trying to evade me, and the hour of Mars is passing swiftly, and will soon be gone and he beyond my power," Thur whispered to Morven. "Should he go ere he obeys me, never again may I evoke a spirit, so, shall I ?"

"Aye, hasten," she urged, holding out a piece of parchment. Thur took a pen from Olaf and rapidly drew on it the Sigil of Bartzebal, meanwhile Morven was throwing evil-smelling gum-resin, rue and asafoetida upon the brazier, and Thur held the parchment into the dense fumes that rose, saying:

"I conjure thee, O creature of fire, by Him who removeth the earth and maketh it tremble, that thou burn and torment this spirit so that he feeleth it intensely, so that he may be burned eternally by Thee," and he put the parchment into the brazier, pressing it against the live embers, saying:

"Be ye eternally damned and eternally reproved, be ye tormented with perpetual pain, so ye find no repose either by day or by night, if ye obey not instantly the Command of Him Who maketh the universe to tremble, by these names and by the virtue of these names, which being invoked, all creatures obey and tremble with fear and terror. These names which can turn aside lightning and thunder, and will make you perish instantly, destroy you and banish you. These names which are: Aleph, Beth, Gimal, Delath, He, Mau, Zayan, Cheteth, Teh, Yod, Kapath, Lam, Med, Mem, Nuns, Mekh, Ayan, Pe, Tzaddi, Quopth, Resh, Shin, Tau." (Note. These are the names of the letters of the Hebrew alphabet, but they were used in Magic for this purpose.)

Thur continued: "By these secret names therefore, and by the signs which are full of mysteries, and by virtue of the power of the three Principalities, which are Aleph, Mem, and Shin, by air, fire, and water, we curse you."

Thur came to an impressive pause; Bartzebal was wavering as if a strong gale had invaded the loft. His face grew contorted with rage and pain, fire darted from his eyes, his form grew denser and in height, till he towered over them menacingly. His voice beat upon their afflicted ears, till they feared their drums would burst ... "Seek Even Gull's Egg. He alone can guide you up the secret path. Kill. Kill. Kill there in My NAME. Let me go. LET ME GO."

Thur snatched the shrivelling parchment from the brazier. The form of Bartzebal dissolved in a cloud of thick oily smoke.

Outside the Circle the watching eyes vanished, and the smoke of which their forms were embodied eddied into the Circle in a suffocating smother half-choking them.

"Leave not the Circle at your peril," Thur commanded.

"I will dismiss them." He put sweet incense into the brazier and, holding forth the Pentacle which had lain on the Altar, and making a Pentacle in the air with the point of his sword, beginning at the lower left-hand corner and going upwards, he chanted:

"By virtue of these Pentacles, and because you have been obedient to the commands of the Creator, feel and inhale these grateful odours, and afterwards depart to your abodes and retreats. Let there be peace between us and you. Be ye ready to come when summoned. May the blessing of God, as far as you are capable of receiving it, be upon you.

"Camiack, Eome, Emoii, Zazean, Maipiat, Lacrath, Tendac, and Vulamai.

"By these Holy Names and by the others which are written in the book of Assamaian Sepher Ha, Shamaiimin. Go ye in peace. Amen. Go. Go. GO."

The Circle was suddenly invaded with black, choking smoke.

Thur waved his sword before him in a final gesture of dispersal and strode from the Circle, followed by the others; with a rush they stumbled down the ladder, half stifled, drawing in great panting breaths as they reached the clear air below.

# CHAPTER XVII
# THE WITCH CULT

EXT morning they all crawled sleepily down to breakfast, weary eyed, half disappointed, half intrigued, and wholly puzzled.

Their hopes of a speedy finish to their difficulties were shattered.

"Seek Even Gull's Egg," was but a poor result from their mighty magical operation.

Jan, who realised it was all his fault, looked downcast and ashamed, also puzzled and worried, he kept looking at Morven in a half hopeful, half frightened way.

They all ate and drank in silence till Morven spoke.

"I want to talk to you seriously, Jan, and it concerns you too, Thur and Olaf. The people at Spurnheath have been talking. Not yours, Jan, but mine, I'm sorry to say.

"When the idea was put to them at Dearleap the other night, they were filled with enthusiasm. They thought the good old days would come back at once. Jan of the Sword Hand was a mighty leader, and all they had to do was to follow him shouting, and they could take all the castles. But in cold daylight, they think again, they see how strong the castles are, and the men in armour who guard them, they think of the torture cells, and the gallows tree, and the men blinded and maimed who drag out their lives begging. Then they think, we have no weapons, and they find their leader is but a farmer with no skill in war, so they cool off, and would wait and see. Now, up to last night I thought we would get magical aid to win at least one success, and then the people would follow us without question, but I fear. now that Bartzebal having once got the better of us we may never enforce our power on him again."

Here Jan looked abashed. "But it was not the fortune of war, and all we got was a piece of advice. I doubt not that we will find Even

Gull's Egg in time and he will give us good help or advice, Bartzebal dare not cheat us there."

"An the advice be good, it will help us," said Thur.

"True," she said. "But we want speedy aid, to make the people follow us to success, before Mistress Hildegarde's tongue spoils all."

"You are a priestess, the people will follow you," said Thur.

"'Tis true, I have assumed the dignity of a priestess. I have been through the Triangle, and through the Pentacle, and so have the right to assume it, if there be none present elder, and with a better claim, but I have never held that office, and I fear I lack experience and personality to hold men together in battle, and if we meet checks. That is the reason I want you to have authority, Jan, and you too, Thur."

"Aye, fighting is a man's game," from Thur.

"I'll take authority all right," said Jan. "Nay, you have it not, yet," she replied.

"I think Morven means something," said Thur.

"Yes," she replied. "I want you all to join the brotherhood. Then all will trust and follow you to the end, be it what it may."

"What, me! Worship devils?" gasped Jan.

"Nay, they be not devils, Jan, that is but a priestish lie, they be but the old Gods of Love and Laughter and Peace and Content."

"What exactly do you want us to do?" asked Thur.

"Sometime, soon, to-night an you will, I will use your circle upstairs, I will put you through the Triangle, that will make you all priests and witches."

"Do we ride broomsticks?" asked Jan suspiciously and Olaf hopefully, at the same instant.

"Nay, that be but a silly chatter, you are each in turn brought into the Circle, there is an ordeal to go through, but 'tis slight, then you will swear to be faithful and ever help thy brothers, then you will be told the powers of the working tools, that is all."

"But, will you not call up devils, or your Old Gods?" asked Jan.

"1 will in sooth call up the Old Ones. The Mighty Ones, to be present and witness your oaths, and to give us their blessing, but of them you will see naught," she answered.

So, after much argument, it was agreed, and Thur finding the stars favourable, that night they went to the upper room, where Morven became Directoress of Ceremonies. After all had bathed in warm water, she said:

"Put not on your garments, for to be witches you must be as Witches. Now, I initiate Jan first. Wait here till I call you."

She and Jan mounted to the loft, here she redrew the Circle with her Athame, leaving a doorway, then circumambulated three times sunwise, with a dancing step, as she did so calling on the Mighty Ones of the east, south, west and north to attend, then after dancing around several times in silence, she chanted:

> "Eko: Eko: Azarak. Eko: Eko: Zomelak."
> "Bagabi Lacha bachabe
> Lamac cahi achababe
> Karrellyos
>
> Lamac lamac Bachalyas
> Cabahagy sabalyos
> Baryolos
>
> Lagoz atha cabyolas
> Samahac atha famolas
> Hurrahya."

She then left the Circle by the doorway, and going to Jan said: "As there is no other brother here I must be thy sponsor as well as priest. I am about to give you a warning, if you are still of the same mind, answer it with these words. "Perfect Love and perfect Trust.' "

Then placing the point of her Athame to his heart said:

"O Thou who standest on the threshold, between the pleasant land of men and the domains of the dread lords of the Outer Spaces, hast Thou the courage to make the assay? For I tell thee verily, it were better to rush on my weapon and perish miserably than make the attempt with fear in thy heart."

Jan answered: "I have two passwords. Perfect Love and perfect Trust."

Morven dropped the knife's point, saying:

"All who bring such words are doubly welcome," then going behind him she blindfolded him, then clasping him from behind with her left arm around his waist, and pulling his right arm around her neck and his lips down to hers, said: "I give you the third password: 'A kiss'."

So saying she pushed him forward with her body, through the doorway, into the Circle.

Once inside she released him, whispering. "This is the way all are first brought into the Circle."

She then carefully closed the doorway by drawing the point of her Athame across it three times, joining all the circles.

Then leading him to the south of the Altar, whispered: "Now there is the Ordeal."

Taking a short piece of cord from the Altar she bound it round his right ankle, leaving the ends free, whispering: "Feet neither Bond nor Free."

Then with a longer cord she bound his hands firmly behind his back, then pulling them up into the small of his back, tied the cord round his neck, so his arms made a triangle at his back, leaving an end of cord hanging in a cable tow in front.

With this cable tow in her left hand and the Athame in her right, she led him Sunways round the Circle to the east, where saluting with the Athame she proclaimed.

"Take heed, O Lords of the Watchtowers of the East. Jan, properly prepared, will be made a priest and witch."

She then led him in turn to the south, west and north, where similar proclamations were made.

Then, clasping him round the body with her left arm, Athame erect in right, she made him circum ambulate three times round the Circle with a half run, half dance step. Bound, blindfold, running round and round in so small a space, Jan's brain reeled giddily, tightly bound as he was he could do nothing but strive to keep his feet.

Suddenly he was pulled to a stop, at the south side of the Altar, where he stood swaying, his head reeling.

Morven struck eleven strokes on a little bell, then knelt at his feet, saying: "In other religions, the postulant kneels, as the Priests claim supreme power. But in the Art Magical, we are taught to be humble, so we say:

> *Kissing his feet.*
> *"Blessed be thy feet that have brought thee in these ways."*
> *Kissing knees.*
> *"Blessed be thy knees that shall kneel at the Sacred Altar."*
> *Kissing phallus.*
> *"Blessed be the Organ of Generation, without which we would*
>     *not be."*
> *Kissing breasts.*
> *"Blessed be thy breasts, formed in beauty and in strength.*
> *Kissing lips.*
> *"Blessed be thy lips, which*
> *shall utter the sacred names."*

She then made him kneel at the Altar, tying the cable tow to a ring so he was bending forward, and could scarcely move. She then tied his feet together with the cord on his right ankle.

Then, ringing three knells on the little bell, said: "Art ready to swear thou wilt always be true to the Art?"

Jan replied: "I will."

Morven struck seven knells on the bell, saying:

"Thou first must be purified."

Taking the scourge from the Altar, she struck his buttocks, first three, then seven, then nine, then twenty-one strokes with the scourge (forty in all).

They were not hard, but blindfold and bound as he was, their effect was startling, they helped to rouse him from the dazed condition he was in from running around the Circle.

As he came more to his senses he realised how utterly helpless he was. In Morven's power, he belonged to her, he was part of her, the blows that were raining on his buttocks gave her power over him, but he did not resent it, she had power over his mind, but that was as it should be, all he wanted was her, if he was hers he would be part of her, and that was all he wanted.

Then the blows ceased, and Morven's voice came. "Art always ready to protect, help and defend thy brothers and sisters of the Art?"

Jan: "I am."

"Then say after me: "'I, Jan, in the presence of the Mighty Ones of the Outer Spaces, do of my own free will most solemnly swear that I will ever keep secret and never reveal the secrets of the Art, except it be to a proper person, properly prepared, within such a Circle as I am in now, and that I will never deny the secrets to such a person, if they be properly vouched for, by a brother or sister of the Art. All this I swear by my hopes of a future life, and may my weapons turn against me if I break this my solemn oath.' "

He felt the cords loosed from his feet, then the cord from the Altar, the blindfold was whisked off, and hands still bound, he was assisted to his feet, where he stood, blinking, dazed and yet somehow, he felt so happy.

Morven knelt before him; he heard her voice as in a dream.

"I hereby consecrate thee with oil.

"I hereby consecrate thee with wine.

"I hereby consecrate thee with my lips, Priest and Witch," and he felt the touches, first the phallus and then right breast, then phallus again, forming a triangle. Then she rose and loosed his hands, saying:

"Now I present thee with the working tools of a witch."

Handing him a sword from the Altar, and motioning him to touch it.

"First the Magic Sword. With this as with the Athame, Thou canst form all Magic Circles, dominate, subdue and punish all rebellious Spirits and demons, and even persuade the angels and geniuses. With this in thy hand thou art the ruler of the Magic Circle," and she kissed him.

"Next I present the Athame. This is the true Witches' Weapon, it has all the powers of the Magic Sword." (Again a kiss.)

"Next I present the White Handled Knife. Its use is to form all instruments used in the Art. It can only be properly used within a Magic Circle." (Again a kiss.)

"Next I present the Censer of Incense, this is to encourage and welcome good spirits and to banish evil spirits." (A kiss.)

"Next I present the Scourge, this is a sign of Power and Domination, it is also to cause suffering and purification, for it is written: To learn thou must suffer and be purified. Art willing to suffer to learn?"

Jan: "I am." (Again a kiss.)

"Next and lastly I present the Cords. They are of use to bind the Sigils, the material basis, and to enforce thy will, also, they are necessary in the oath."

Morven again kissed him, saying: "I salute thee in the name of the Gods. Newly-made Priest and Witch."

They then both circumambulated the Circle, Morven proclaiming at the four quarters:

"Hear Ye, Mighty Ones, Jan hath been consecrated Priest and Witch."

Then Thur and Olaf were in turn consecrated with the same ceremonies, but when Morven at last announced to the Spirits of the Four Quarters that Olaf had been consecrated, she added: "I thank ye for attending, and I dismiss ye to your pleasant abodes. Hail and farewell."

That night, for the first time in his life, Jan could not sleep. His brain turned with the thought: "Morven, I want Morven." What a fool he had been, the idea that he should only marry a wife to bring him wealth and power. It was love he wanted! Yes, he thought, perhaps at one time I might have had her love and I have rejected it. Fool, what a fool he had been, and at last he dropped off into a troubled sleep, where Morven, Brother Stephen, Fitz-Urse, and various spirits danced, grimaced and mocked at him till dawn.

\* \* \* \*

The next day Jan was silent and thoughtful, as was Thur; Olaf was excited but disappointed. "I feel just the same," he complained. "You say that now I am a priest and a witch, but I don't feel any different. It's all a fraud.

"All priests feel different from other men, they all tell me so, and they all act so, as if they were so much better and wiser and prouder than mortal men, see how they even threaten great nobles, and get away with it, even kings have to bow down to them."

"Not so our present noble King," observed Thur wryly. "He ever hath a short way with them, and 'tis said that Lackland hath not shown too great reverence for our Father the Pope himself."

"No," said Olaf, "but if I be a witch surely I should have some power, and I feel none."

"Nay," said Morven. "Many men are made priests by the Christians, but didst ever know a case when priesting a man made him a great preacher, or a sweet singer? Nay, the power always lies within. Yet by being priested a man is put in a way of life where he may learn to develop his powers, and learn to preach or sing, which he would not have done had he stayed at the plough's tail all his life."

"When the brotherhood was strong, they ever picked out those who had a little natural power and they were taught, and practiced one with another, and they developed their powers. But I have ever told you, we have not the wonderful powers that men speak of, though we have some. We only seek to live quietly and worship our Gods in our own way, to enjoy ourselves in our own fashion and be content and at peace. But men ever harrieth us, so 'tis little wonder we strike back at them sometimes.

"Then every time there is a thunderstorm, or a bad harvest, the priests say the wicked witches cause it, and they spread awful tales of our secret meetings, where we eat the flesh of newborn babes. But, long ago they told the same tales of the Gnostics, and did not the old Romans tell the same tales about the early Christians? Nay, Olaf, thou art now of an ancient brotherhood pledged to mutual aid. If thou wantest, thou may study Magic, and where canst find a better teacher than Thur here? But it only comes by developing thine own powers, and by no stroke of Magic Wand."

"Nor by stroke of Scourge seemingly," said Olaf, wriggling reminiscently.

"Thou spoke of higher degrees. Dost beat them in all degrees?"

"Aye," said Morven. "Canst not understand? 'Tis for thine own advancement 'tis written. Water purifieth the body, but the scourge purifieth the soul.

"1 think Jan felt something of it," she continued.

"Aye," said Jan. "Somehow I feel a different man, as if much dross was sloughed off. What felt you, Thur?"

"Aye, I felt it too," said Thur. "'Tis a strange, mystical experience, but, I had heard of it before, and 'tis a dangerous tool in the wrong hands, but in the right ones it works wonders, so you see, you are learning already, Olaf."

"Hum," said Olaf. "Learn that a man's soul may be cleansed like a carpet by beating."

"Thou hast seen and heard of the sect of Flagellants," said Thur. "They beat each other, cruelly, and 'tis said they work wonders thereby and even raise the dead. And does not the Holy Mother Church prescribe it for so many cases. Did not our King Henry, the second of that name, be flogged at Canterbury at a Becket's tomb, five strokes from every bishop and abbot present, and three strokes from each of the eighty monks, he was in a sorry state bodily, but his soul was in a state of grace afterwards. And did not King Henry of France, the fourth of that name, be flogged by the Pope himself? Nay, the rod is an evil thing, but it may have its uses, the Blessed St. Theresa ever used it and caused it to be used in the Carmelite Order, and they get many wonderful visions thereby and again, does not everyone speak of the wonders wrought by the Holy Birch of the merry St. Bridget?"

"But what about these higher orders you speak of," asked Olaf.

"All I have got so far is a whipping and been shown some swords and knives, all of which I had seen before; I want to get on, to something that works."

"Nay," said Morven, "I think you will never advance, if you feel not the old secrets of joy and terror, 'tis useless for you to go on."

"I would go on," said Jan, "I felt things which seemed to brush against my soul, how was't with you, Thur?"

"I know not, but there seemed there was some mystery of worship, delicate, but as a dream, the queer thing is, I can scarce remember what happened, I was as if in a trance, but I think of it with joy."

"When may we advance, Morven, and how many degrees are there?"

"There is but one degree more," she said. "Where you take an oath and are made to use the working tools, but after that, there is what is called a degree. There is no oath, and all who have taken the second degree are qualified to work it, but 'tis the quintessence of Magic, and 'tis not to be used lightly, and then only with one whom you love ,and are loved by, may it be done, all else were sin. To misuse it were the greater death, in this world, as in the next."

"Do you get whipped there?" asked Olaf. "Don't ask silly questions," snapped Morven. "I almost wish I were putting you through the second, the Pentacle. I'd like to scourge you hard, though I must not, for a reason I can't tell you now. Meanwhile I'll put Jan and Thur through the Pentacle, whenever you will, the sooner the better."

"And further?" asked Jan.

She blushed. "Nay, Jan, when you are' past the Pentacle, 'twill be my duty to tell you further mysteries, the Mystery of Mysteries, when you know what it consists of, we will speak further. 'Tis not a thing to be lightly done. But now, there are many things to speak of, Even Gull's Egg for one."

\* \* \* \*

The next day Thur who had been consulting the stars all night announced: "This day is bad for operations abroad, but good for those at home. So seek we not Even Gull's Egg to-day. But I wit there is an operation at home we can do well," and he looked pointedly at Morven.

"Aye," cried Jan, as the sudden idea came to him, Morven blushed.

"Aye, make us high priests," said Thur.

Olaf scoffingly offered to whip them both soundly without waiting for night. And Morven blushingly protested that many men waited for years for advancement, but agreed that it would give them greater power over the Brethren, few of whom ever advanced beyond the triangle.

So that night the three of them (for Olaf, despite his protests, was locked out as a scoffer) ascended to the upper room.

Again they washed themselves thoroughly, Morven again consecrated her Circle as before, but this time around Jan who had to follow her round, and join as well as he could in the evocations and chantings. Then he was bound as before but not blindfolded, and led around while she proclaimed to the four quarters: "Hear, Ye Mighty Ones. Jan, a duly consecrated priest and witch, is now properly prepared to be made a high priest." Again he was made to run around, led by the cable tow, circumambulate, and be bound to the Altar as before. Then Morven said:

"To attain this subline degree, it is necessary to suffer and be purified. Art ready to suffer to learn?"

Jan answered: "I am."

Morven said: "I prepare thee to take the Great Oath," and struck three knells on the bell.

Then with the scourge she struck him as before, three, seven, nine and twenty-one strokes (forty in all) as before.

Then said: "I give you a new name, Janicot, repeat thy new name after me saying:

"'I, Janicot, swear upon my mother's womb and by my honour among men and my brothers and sisters of the Art, that I will never reveal to any at all, any of the secrets of the Art, except it be to a worthy person, properly prepared, in the centre of a Magic Circle such as I am now in. This I swear by my hopes of Salvation, my past lives and my hopes of future ones to come, and I devote myself to utter destruction if I break this my solemn oath.' "

Morven knelt and placing her left hand under his knees, and her right hand on his head, said: "I will all my power into thee," and exerted her will to the uttermost, then she loosed his feet and the cable tow from the Altar, and helped him to rise as before.

She then with her thumb wet with oil, touched his phallus, then right breast, across to left hip, across to right hip, up to left breast, and down to phallus again (thus marking him with a reversed Pentacle) saying: "I consecrate thee with oil." Dipping her thumb into wine she repeated the motions, saying: "I consecrate thee with wine." Then dropping to her knees, she again marked the Pentacle with her lips saying: "I consecrate thee with my lips, High Priest and Wizard."

Rising she unbound his hands and said: "You will now use the working tools in turn," and prompted him to take the Sword from the Altar, and redraw the Magic Circle around them, then she kissed him.

Then she prompted him to do the same with the Athame, another kiss.

Then she prompted him to take the white hilted knife, incise a pentacle on a candle, again a kiss.

Then prompted, he took the Wand and waved it to the four quarters, again a kiss.

Prompted he took the Pentacle, and exhibited it to the four quarters, again they kissed.

Prompted he took the censer and circumambulated the Circle with it, and they kissed again.

Then she took the cords, and prompted him to bind her as he had been bound, then she spoke. "Learn, in Witchcraft, thou must ever return triple. As I scourged thee, so thou must scourge me, but triple, where I gave thee three strokes, give nine, where seven, give twenty-one, where nine, give twenty-seven, where twenty-one, give sixty-three. (For this is the joke in Witchcraft, the Witch knows though the initiate does not, that she will get three times what she gave, so she does not strike hard.)

Jan was nervous but she insisted, and at last he gave her the required number, but struck very lightly.

Then she said: "Thou hast obeyed the law. But mark well when thou receivest good, so equally art bound to return good threefold."

Prompted he released her. Resuming her Athame, and he carrying the sword, she led him round the Circle, proclaiming at all four quarters.

"Hear all ye Mighty Ones, Janicot has been duly consecrated High Priest and Wizard."

Then she went around the Circle, scuffing out the marks with her feet.

Thur was then summoned and Jan made to do his first work of Magic, redraw, and re-consecrate the Circle.

Then Thur was made in the same way, a high priest and wizard.

When this was finished she dismissed the spirits as before.

# CHAPTER XVIII
# THE SPIRIT DANTILION

"NOW you are of the Brotherhood," said Morven next day. "'Tis best that you seek Even Gull's Egg."

"But where do we start?" asked Jan. "To seek you we had at least the name Wanda."

"I think we have a clue," she replied. "It smacks of the sea and near Dunbrand, I think."

"True reed," said Thur, "Bartzebal dare not speak falsely while he was in the triangle, but we dare not go to Dunbrand and ask for Even Gull's Egg without some reason, folk would talk and talk would go straight to Fitz -Urse."

"Nay," she said, "go first to Simon Pipeadder, he is old and I think hath much knowledge. He will obey you now you are of the brotherhood."

So that night Thur consulted the stars, and finding them favourable the three men started out the next morning.

\* \* \* \*

Arriving at the outskirts of Jan's farm, Truda the goose girl soon brought Old Simon. At first he was not helpful: "Na, na, Maister, 'tis turrible risky, and Miss-us be like a demon unloosed these days. She ses as you brought a devil straight from hell, Maister Jan, and she skeered 'un away wi' her Holy Watter, tha-at she du, so she beats us all who had truck wi' 'un."

"Yes, yes, Simon, but how may a castle be stormed unless we come to it?"

Simon shook his head with vigorous obstinacy:

"Na, Maister, it be turrible risky."

"But you do know Even Gull's Egg?"

"Aye, Maister."

"Well, to take the castle we must fight. We may not fight without risk, would you have us cowards?"

"What want you wi' Even Gull's Egg? He be an outlander and turrible unchancy."

"Would he betray us think you?"

"Nay, perhaps not, he hates the Normans. But he loves money and he be not O' the brotherhood."

"But I am," said Jan, describing a Pentacle in the air, with his thumb thrust between his fingers. "O Mars' Jan, Mars' Jan! Thou hast been spying, thou knowest not the way into a circle."

"I was taken," said Jan, "with two passwords, and I received a third."

"And where was he that led 'ee into circle, answer me that?" gasped Simon.

"She led me from behind," said Jan.

"O Mars' Jan, Mars' Jan, this is happiness," gasped Simon. "Truly thou art of the brotherhood, but how far hast gone?"

"I have been through the inverted Triangle and through the inverted Pentacle," was the reply.

"O Joy, I must ever do as thou sayest, you whom Holy Maiden be helping, and who hast been through Pentacle," was the reply. But turning suspiciously to Thur and Olaf. "What of these? You should not speak of such things before outsiders."

"Never fear, Master Thur is as I am and Olaf has been through the Triangle."

"Well, well, I must do as thou bidst me, Maister, but I like it not and Miss-us will sure beat me black and blue when she catches me, I think I derner go back to farm."

"Never mind, go fetch the black mare and send word you are ill and can't come to work; she may believe it," and Old Simon trotted off with a new spring in his gait.

Soon he returned on a powerful black mare, and all four rode steadily till the forest began to thin and gave way to scattered farms. At the edge of the forest Simon drew rein and with an all-embracing sweep of his hand said: "Yonder lies thy lands, Maister, as far as eye can reach and a good bit farder."

"Aye," muttered the dispossessed, "and what is that beyond? Is that the sea?"

Olaf pointed across the flats to a dark smudge on the skyline.

"And that?"

Simon chuckled: "Aye, Maister, that be Dunbrand."

The Bonders accepted the fact without comment; the distance was too great for any details to be seen.

"Have you been there since our father's day?"

"Aye, thrice, while castle was building."

"But my grandsire's stronghold?" Jan interposed hastily.

"'Twere gutted by fire, it were an old, ancient place, built they say in good King Alfred's day, an' folks say 'twere an old Roman castle afore that, and the Bonders came here from the sea, and lived here free men afore the Normans ruled the land, and then, well, you know how it was, wi' the Fitz-Urses, an' the fight."

"And only my father escaped?"

"Aye, and me and others you knows of . . . I were but thirty then. Lord, it seems but yesterday."

"I will deal with them . . . suitably, so help me God," Jan exclaimed in a burst of passion.

"Amen to that," said Olaf and Thur together.

"And the castle?"

"Fitz-Urse's building most on it, nigh twenty years it's tuk him, 'tis bare finished yet. He went to Holy Land wi' Good King Richard, and brought a mort o' queer fashionings back thet say: soft cushions and triflings like that as no Christian man has ever seed afore."

"How far is it from here?"

"A matter o' three leagues, Maister."

They rode on till they came nigh the sea, and a small fishing village lay beneath them.

Simon drew rein and pointed. At first they could see nothing but a jagged line of cliff top through the haze, then the line broke revealing a great naked rock standing alone sheer out of the water which surged around its base. Then they picked out a narrow bridge across the chasm, and what at first appeared to be rugged rocks took the form of battlements.

Simon pointed: "See that black there, 'tis a gert big cave, wi' water for floor, they keeps their boats i' it, there be a way fro' there to a ledge where rock overhangs, an' there be another ledge O' top, were tha be a gert big windlass so be as they haul up stores, an' a postern leads into castle, an' it was always so but none can get in that way unless they be hauled up in basket as they do indeed haul up their boatmen; and all the stone for building did come that way."

As the castle stood, it looked as if one man could hold it against thousands, so inapproachable did it seem. They realised also that on the mainland side of the bridge rose twin towers of a barbican.

"Well," said Thur. "A tough nut to crack, lead us on to Even Gull's Egg, good Simon."

"Right, bide ye here, Maisters. I go seek un."

\* \* \* \*

"Got 'un, Maister," gasped Simon a little later,
pushing an uncouth looking man. "'E ses wat do ee want wi' ee?"

"You are called Even Gull's Egg?" said Thur. "Aye, so folks calls me," was the surly reply.

"You climb the cliffs for gulls' eggs?"

"Aye."

Thur showed him a groat. "Do you ever get eggs from the castle rock?"

"Na, Master, Fitz-Urse loves not any to climb that rock, an' what he dislikes he shows wi' arrows."

"But you have climbed it ?"

Even gave him a shrewd look but said nothing.

Thur showed him a gold besant.

The man's breath caught in his throat, but he said nothing.

"I would climb that rock. Is there a way ?"

"Master, I ha' a throat and my wife has one and so ha' my three childer; if any go up that rock, FitzUrse will blame it on me and five throats will be slit, he knoweth well none other could do it."

Thur placed three more pieces by the first. The man's eyes glistened. "What's your will ?" he whispered.

"There is a postern that leads to the great windlass; set me with some of my friends outside it some dark night."

"That way be right perilous, but I might on a misty, moonlight night; but I must ha' twenty-five pieces, wi' the King's Majesty's head on 'un. I can climb and fix ropes, so ye may follow safely, perhaps, but, you understand, you pay me the money, half ere we start, half when I set ye on the ledge; what ye do then I know not nor care. I'll ha' ma woman and childer i' ma cobble below and wi' the money I go wi' them, days along the coast ere I' dare put me ashore where I buy me a farm. I dursent live here after."

"Twenty-five pieces of gold ? Impossible," exclaimed Thur.

"So 'tis impossible I go for less," said Even, getting up and making as if to go away. Thur motioned him to stay.

"'Tis a mighty sum, friend, and not easy to come by. But, an' I can get it, wilt do truly as you have said, and not betray me to the Normans ?"

The man spat: "I love not Fitz-Urse an' his brood, I'd do 'un an ill turn an I could wi safety. I'll not betray ee. But I must ha' what will let me settle in a new country far away. Send word by Simon here an' you want me," and he rose and shambled off.

"Twenty-five pieces of gold, 'tis a king's ransom," gasped Jan. "Hast got it, Thur ?"

"Not I, but I might borrow. I have a house, but I know not who might lend. If Good King Richard had not banished all the

Jews 'twould have been easy. I can but try, for truly I see no other way, and Bartzebal clearly said Even would show us up the secret path."

Old Simon rejoined them, all bandaged up.

"What has happened, man?" gasped Jan.

"'Tis naught, Maister. I ha' been ripped by a gert boar. Kit did 'un wi' his knife and tied me up, I'll tell Miss-us. I were 'urt bad and I swooned away like, and only cum to hours arter. I'll get off a cudgeling an' I'll du no work for days like now. A man wat's been half-killed like canna work for many days arter."

Jan goggled. "So that's the way of it? I remember something like this happened to you before, last year, was it false also?"

"I, Maister, I do be too aged tu be cudgelled like..."

Thur and Olaf were roaring with laughter, so in the end Jan laughed too, and they all set out for home.

\* \* \* \*

Morven greeted Thur when he reached the house with: "Brother Stephen has been waiting to see you all day, I fear there is somewhat toward, but tell me how you fared?"

"None too well, none too ill," he replied wearily.

"We found Even Gull's Egg and he may help us at a price, but 'tis a heavy one and I see not the way too clearly as yet, but there will be a way, never fear.

"But what wants Stephen?" (as Brother Stephen rose to greet him as he entered).

"I would speak with you, Thur, alone," and he glanced at Morven. Thur dismissed her with a nod.

"Speak freely, friend, there be none to hear." Stephen hesitated. "What I have to say must be secret for your sake as well as mine."

"As the grave," said Thur.

"Thur, I think you have often wondered what I do here. Thou knowest I have my school in Paris." Thur nodded.

"Thur, thou hast seen my horoscope, Jupiter is in exaltation with the sun and all the other signs show the same thing. I can do great things for myself and others, and my country, in a way that will be ever remembered. Now and in the next month I will have the opportunity, in this little town of Clare, and nowhere else. Now, what may all this mean?"

"How can I tell?" said Thur, "I know I have seen it, but perchance there is an error in the calculations."

"But we checked it by many astrologers ere I came, and they all tell the same tale; from France and Italy, Spain and Almain, Bohemia and the heathen Moor's, all tell the same, and my friend, Lothair di Signi."

Thur nodded. "Lothair sent me to find it. What we must both have, 'tis as important for him as it is for me, his horoscope shows it too. You know, he must have what he wants, to gain power."

"How may I help you, friend?" asked Thur.

"Thur, I have wondered and watched and waited and I think I see clearly now. Thou art working High Magic. Art Magic, somehow. That girl Morven haunts me, I dream of her, Thur, you must work magic for me. Let me gain the power and let me begone."

Thur considered. "Magic is an ill word, what would the Lord Abbot say?"

"He would say: 'Make me young again or thou burnest,'" was the swift response. "And I, Stephen, say: 'Work for me or the Abbot's men raid the house within the hour, Thur.' Didst think thou couldst do what thou didst two nights agone and not be noticed?"

Thur started. "What did I do?"

"Thur, half the town heard, voices calling long after midnight and all."

"May not a man have a few friends in for a junketing?"

"'Twas not the sound of men junketing. The smoke and the smell of incense, thou perfumed half the town and an hour after midnight, and as for that burst of black smoke ... the watchers saw it and trembled in their shoes, saying: 'The Foul Fiend himself has come for the leech and his lamen.' Then, when they saw you both, yestermorn, they said, Master Thur be sib with the Devil himself. So half the gossips of the town have been to the Abbey. I had hard work to keep the old man quiet. He wanted to raid you right away and try what the rack would do. But I lied hard, I said I knew what you were doing and I'd get you to work for him. He is worth helping, Thur, if thou canst, for the sake of thy life and limbs, if for no other reason. But, Thur, you must work for me first."

"But how can I help you? What do you want?"

"Thur, call up the spirits for me this night, or the Abbot's men raid thee in half an hour, two lay brothers wait outside an' I come not soon. They take a sealed letter to the Abbot, so think not to stab me and so silence me that way. You *must* help me, Thur."

"An' I give you what help I may, wilt help me?"

"How?"

"I want money and I want the Abbot kept off me for a time."

"I can keep the Abbot quiet all right, for a time, but I have no money, Thur, canst not make it by magic?"

"Well then keep the Abbot quiet. Money I cannot make, I am no master, but a beginner, I get no more than advice. Wait, I will tell you my tale."

Stephen listened attentively. "I think I begin to see," he said. "Well, call up the spirits for me. I can keep my mind on my desires. As for money, I think I can help there. The Abbey has much gold in store, they may not lend; usury is forbidden to Churchmen. But, you can sell your house for say, twenty gold pieces, and buy it back again in three months for say thirty, the Abbey oft does things like that, and it can be arranged that you may live in it for three months or more. If thou takest the castle you will get gold to repay. If thou dost not, well, I think you will not need any house."

Thur made a wry face. "The terms are extortionate, but borrowers may not be choosers."

Stephen rose. "Well, 'tis settled, I will speak to the Abbot, telling him 'tis but a foolish scare about magic and only a matter of you having some friends in and burning some drugs that had gone bad. Now, what night wilt call the spirits for me?"

Thur pondered. "I must consult the stars and my parchments, but I know thy stars are well aspected. I will prepare things in the morn ... come tomorrow night."

The next night, being Thursday the seventh of the new moon Stephen knocked, and was admitted. After greetings, Thur said: "I have searched the parchments, I think Dantilion is the best spirit for your purpose, he is a Duke, Great and Mighty. His office is to teach all the Arts and Sciences unto any, and to declare the secret councils of anyone; for he knoweth the thoughts of all men and he can change them at his will. Or at least so the parchments say. This is a favourable night to call him. Morven and I have made the Pentacles to summon him, if your heart fails you not."

"I would face the devil himself," came the rejoinder, "and, Thur, I have spoken to the Abbot, you can have the gold an' you sign this parchment, selling the house and its contents for twenty-two pieces, and you may buy it back again for thirty-two any time within the six months. Will that suit you? 'Twas the best terms I could screw out of him."

"Aye, borrowers may not help themselves," grumbled Thur.

"Now, come you up," and he led the way to where Morven waited by a tub of warm water.

Stephen who knew something of the theory of the Art Magical, watched with a critical and interested eye, as Thur bathed, and then exorcised the water, then purified himself, then Morven followed suit, and Stephen was in turn purified. This being done, exactly as when evoking Bartzebal, then Thur donned his linen robe and handing one to Stephen prepared to mount to the loft above.

"Hast no robe for Morven?" demanded Stephen.

"It is not seemly that a woman should stand as God made her in the presence of clad men. It passeth my understanding whither hath fled her modesty."

Stephen voiced his discontent with an austere kind of grumpiness, as he eyed her with an unyielding disapproval. It was not so much her particular nakedness to which he objected, as the fact that the nakedness was divided; if nakedness was needful to the rite, well and good, if not, let all be clothed alike. Such was Stephen's mind; he knew it was the custom that a witch must work naked to attain full power, but, to his surprise, he found himself excessively disliking the fact that this particular witch was obeying the law. He knew they were going to raise spirits; probably through the Power of God, but his natural austerity was such that he made a natural cleavage between sex and God. He did not consider sex as sinful, he had seen too much of it. In the Abbeys there was much wantonness, but he could never admit to himself that things of the spirit had any connection with the flesh. When Stephen Langton approached his God he wished to put from him the idea there could be such a thing as sex. He knew some of the practices of the Art Magical by repute, he knew it was said these things were necessary, but he approached it with some uneasiness. Could not things be so arranged to suit his own notions? More power exerted somehow, to cover the weakness that would be caused by the rites being mutilated? Go through with it he must; he was being driven forward by a stronger mind than his own. He well knew his fate if he returned having failed in his mission especially through his own weakness. Yet he had a lurking sense that he should not seek to attain his ambitions this way. Yet he was amazed and impressed by the paraphernalia, the thoroughness of the purification, the quotations from Holy Writ, the repeated mentions of the name of God. He expected something slightly adverse, if not diabolical, or at least something tending that way, but it was so much a religious service that his mind was raised to a lofty pitch of sublimity only to be brought to earth again at the sight of Morven.

"We meet to worship God," he proclaimed, "to beseech him to permit us to perform marvels. Put on thy raiment, woman, when you enter the presence of God."

Thur paused with one foot on the ladder and turned his head to the speaker, the light of the lantern threw vast shadows on the walls, turning human beings into the semblance of giants. Troubled and doubtful, Thur turned the lantern so its rays fell on Stephen's agitated face, in which the Magus read hurt and shock.

"We must do as the rite bids, Stephen," he said.

"Morven is necessary to me in the Art, I cannot work without her. Thou knowest she is a witch and so must do as ever witches must do, or her power fails. Rid you of your distractions if you would succeed. Keep thy mind on thine own wishes; for if you let the sight of Morven, or aught else perplex you, you loose all your power. You must be used to nudity, 'tis as you well know, the oldest trick of a mischievous spirit to appear thus, attempting to divert your mind from its object; you must be above such things."

"But," said Stephen, "God is an unescapable fact. Nudity is another, both are equally right in their appointed spheres, but they do not meet easily in my mind, it savoureth of impiety, of blasphemy. So therefore do I protest against this blasphemy."

"Stephen," said Thur, "a moment ago you spoke of this woman as being as God made her, then how can it be blasphemy? God cannot blaspheme. We must have Morven, and we must not limit her power. She enters the Circle as my disciple and you as a suppliant of God's Grace. We work as God wills, and if God wills, she be as the rite demands. If he will not vouchsafe to grant our requests, unless the rite be duly performed, who are you, a mortal, to object?"

Stephen swallowed. "I fear," he said bluntly.

"Fear naught, keep your mind on your high endeavour and on he who sent you here; he would have no such scruples. Set your mind on naught but your high desires. Heed not trifles or all will fail."

"Lead on," Stephen said grimly repressing further words; striving hard to overcome his detestation of Morven's beauty. Yes, he suddenly realised; that *was* what he detested. If she was not so lovely, so exquisite!

But as soon as they entered the loft his mind was distracted by the strange signs on the walls. The wonderful ceremony of forming the Great Circle; the consecration of the fire, the lighting of the lights. The incense, which in this case was cedar, rose, cinnamon, sandal and aloes. Then the long evocation and the repeated call: "Come O Dantilion! Dantilion come! Being exalted above ye, in the Power of the Most High, I say unto you, obey in the name of the Mighty Ones, Liachadae and Baldachinensis, Paumachia and Apolgiae Sedes, and of the Mighty Ones Liachadae, and the Ministers of the House of Death. I evoke ye and by evoking conjure thee, and being exalted above thee in the Power of the Most High, I say unto thee 'Obey.' In the Name of· Him Who Spoke, and it was. Him whom all creatures and beings obey. I, whom God hath made in the likeness of God Who is the Creator according to His living breath. Come ... In the Name which is the Voice and Wonder of the Almighty God, Eo, strong and unspeakable. O thou spirit Dantilion, I say unto thee: 'Obey!' In the Name of Him who Speaks and IS. And in everyone of these Names of God. EI, Elohim, Ehyah, Asher, Zabbaoth, Elion, Iah, Tetragrammaton, Shaddai, Lord God Most High. In Thy Strength I say 'Obey.' o spirit Dantilion, appear to his servant in a moment, before this circle. In the Ineffable Name Tetragrammaton, Jehovah. Whose mighty sound being exalted in power the pillars are divided; the Winds of the Firmament groan aloud, the earth moves in earthquake and all things of the house of heaven and earth and the dwelling places of darkness are in torment and are confounded in thunder.

"Come forth, O Dantilion! Dantilion, Come!"

Stephen watched the room fill with the thick smoke of incense.

"Come, O Dantilion!"

The smoke writhed and formed shapes which vanished almost as they were formed. Stephen's heart beat faster, and through his veins surged that occult frenzy of excitement which accompanies the fixation of will upon desire.

Power! To rule kings. To create a new law so that his beloved

England might obey the same law and obtain the same protection. There should be no more serfs, and men would be free to go, and love and worship where they willed, and this the gift of Stephen of Langton.

"Come, O Dantilion! Dantilion, come!"

Stephen stirred uneasily; the strain of keeping his mind fixed wearied him; the smoke of the incense grew denser. The strain began to hurt, but he determined to bear this. Power he must have; power to rule kings. A charter of liberty; idly he watched Morven replenishing the incense. A young girl, no, a flower, a blossom of flesh, her mouth like a rosebud. He shook himself, never must he have such thoughts, he must keep his mind clear and fixed; it must not waver in the slightest. He shook himself more angrily; "Power!"

He looked at the billowing smoke and now noticed that it was flowing in a steady stream outside the circle as if drawn by a strong draught. The room had now vanished from view, though the inside of the Circle was entirely clear of smoke. He could imagine that there were spirits in that dense cloud; but they were invisible. Would the ceremony never end? He must not think of such things; he must concentrate. He knew he must keep his mind fixed, but he felt as though a sword was piercing his brain from the intense effort of concentration. He dragged back his thoughts with a supreme effort and concentrated with renewed vigour. Then the smoke wavered as an elderly man, carrying a big book, came forward and stopped before him, at the very edge of the Circle. For a second Stephen thought it was a man who had come into the room for some purpose, but there was such a look of power in his eyes, such a look of terrible beauty in the awesome face, in which was neither human weakness, pity or mercy. There was a soul-freezing glitter in his eyes, and yet they were kindly. Power radiated from him. Behind him, seen through the billowing smoke, were crowds of faces; men and women, changing, melting and forming anew.

Thur's voice changed from command to the soft'ness of a greeting, but the spirit ignored him entirely. Looking at Stephen, he said:

"A mortal who knows what he wants! Most interesting. Dabblers in the occult who trouble us for what they know not, and seek to entangle us in their petty affairs but weary us. If we were to grant all their boons, as they ask for them, it would almost always bring about the opposite effect to that which they had intended. But you know what you want. Fools often ask to be made kings, though kings have no power save what their ministers give to them, but you have the correct attitude, and so it may be arranged. I notice also that you do not ask for happiness."

"Happiness!" The thought struck Stephen like a blow, he looked at Morven, but now her loveliness entranced him. Her sinuous grace; her full red mouth; the smooth sweet line of her arms; her twin breast buds.

She saw his changed glance and shook her head meaningly.

Stephen started. "No. No. No!" His mind shouted. Happiness was not for him. His was to be a life of Power. To rule men and kingdoms. No time for happiness!

He saw Dantilion was laughing. "You have passed the test, friend," he said. "You want to be a cardinal and an archbishop. It can be arranged, in time. Now learn. Archbishop Hubert Walter died over a year ago and men think no successor has yet been appointed. But the monks of Canterbury, secretly at midnight, have elected their Sub-Prior Reginald and have sent him to Rome for confirmation. But the secret will leak out, and Lackland, in his rage, will force others to elect John de Gray and dispatch him to Rome for confirmation. The Pope will profess that both elections are null, and will demand a new election by representatives of the monks in his presence.

"So get ye to Rome swiftly with what ye wat of."

He paused. "Now, ye have seen how to summon me, with a will as strong as steel, and a mind as clear as ice." He looked round reflectively. "You will need someone; a woman is best, a witch for preference of course; a nun perhaps; a young boy will sometimes do, to form a medium between the world of men and ours. Someone who can give out much power; such as this wench.

"Now, I go. Remember all I tell thee. 'Tis needless to dismiss me. I go," and he dissolved into the intense smoke.

"Thou hast mighty powers," gasped Thur, for as the spirit vanished, the smoke suddenly invaded the Circle. Coughing and spluttering they all dived for the ladder, and rushing to a window flung open the shutters and hung out gasping.

# CHAPTER XIX
## CASTLES AND LANDS

HE beams of the full moon struggled to pierce the sea mist as Jan, Thur and Olaf marshalled their men into several small fishing boats. Olaf was sent with ten archers, to lie outside the Barbican, and stop any messengers who might be sent in or out of the castle, and also though he did not know it, to ensure that if the attack failed one Bonder might survive to carry on the line. All the able-bodied men of the Brotherhood from the forest were there, together with Jan's six men and some fishermen, who also belonged to the witch cult and who were good cragsmen.

Jan and Thur had no illusions; if they failed there was a very small chance of there being any survivors. But, they had a good chance if they could get in undetected.

They had laid their plans well. Fitz-Urse with his lady and second son, Rual, had ridden out that day with twenty men-at-arms and a few servants. Rumour had it they would not return for several days. This meant there would not be more than thirty fighting men and a score of servants left in the castle, of these they knew at least six men would be on guard in the barbican and so unable to aid their fellows in the castle, if they could only gain control of the drawbridge before the alarm went.

Even Gull's Egg was in his little cobble, with his wife and children and much household gear; he got out and slouched over to Thur, saying: "I am here, show me the gold."

Thur showed him the twenty-five coins then replaced them in a little pouch. "On top of the rock," he said.

Even grunted. "'Tis nigh a man's life to seek new homes and companions."

"'Tis your own wish," Thur replied.

Even grunted louder than ever. "Come on an you will." He sulkily shoved the little cobble off.

The other boats followed him with muffled oars, and were soon in the mouth of the cave. There was a rough landing place cut in the rock and some mooring rings. Even pointed out some boats hauled up on the sand inside the cave. "Fitz-Urse's boats," he growled. Silently they moored their own boats and landed. Even led them up steps cut in the rock, to a wide ledge which ran upwards, ending in an open space, about twenty feet wide, and some fifty feet above the sea. The cliff towered upwards till lost in the mist.

"The cliff overhangs here," Even said. "They have the big windlass up there. They carry things this far then haul them up, and the boats' crews too, they also come down that way. Fools," he grunted, half to himself. "They think there is no way, but how else could men have scaled the rock first, if there was no way ere the bridge was built?"

He led them to the far end of the platform where the ledge continued a little way, then ended abruptly and they heard the sea churning beneath their feet. Even uncoiled a rope from his shoulders with a loop on the end, looped this over a nob of rock, and proceeded to climb down till he could scarcely be seen standing on a ledge barely the width of his foot. The others followed cautiously. When they reached him Even moved to the right; the ledge was narrow and slippery, but there were handholds; it led gradually upwards. Then the way was blocked by a jutting mass of rock, but a rope hung down it. Even hauled himself up with the tireless ease of a climber; but though there were fair hand and footholds, the others made but slow progress. Then came another ledge wider and easier than the first, this also led upwards to lead to a cleft in the rock, scarce two feet wide, with a rope hanging down; by aid of this and by pushing shoulders and knees against the sides .they slowly climbed up. On reaching the top a worse peril awaited; they had to crawl slowly and patiently along a narrow ledge where the cliff jutted out above, so they could not stand, nor were there any handholds, and to make matters worse this ledge slanted downwards. It was impossible to fix a rope, and the sea churned hungrily a hundred feet below. A man close behind Jan slipped, for a moment hung by his hands, then with a cry fell into the darkness. "Look up, you fools, or you are lost!" called Even Gull's Egg. But rounding a corner the ledge grew broader, here came another rift, but with an invaluable rope. Gasping and breathless they toiled upwards till with bursting lungs Jan and Thur reached the top; but not without hearing two more cries and crashes from below.

"God comfort their poor souls," said Jan, crossing himself piously.

Even stood sulkily watching as the men came up; as the last arrived he said: "I have fulfilled my bargain, give me my due." Thur silently handed him the pouch. Even weighed it in his hand and without a word swung himself down the rope and vanished.

Jan and Thur looked around curiously; they were on a small platform, about ten feet wide and thirty feet long. A huge timber windlass and a derrick rose before them, and a path led to a wall about twenty feet high with a small tower with a gate in its side.

Thur panted. "This is part of the old castle, and not Norman work, I mind it well."

They stole up and Thur put his ear to the gate; satisfied he returned to the windlass platform and hauled a great sturdy man to his feet. "Here, Smid, canst crack this nut for me?"

Smid, still panting, examined the gate professionally, felt it cautiously and at last shook it. "Fastened by a bar and by bolts at top and bottom, I judge."

They all listened attentively, there was no sound from within.

"Fitz-Urse deems no one could come this way except by the windlass, no need to waste a sentry here, and Bartzebal said we could come this way and slay in his name, so I risked all on there being no one here," whispered Thur. "If there were, we would have had to return by Even's perilous way. We will soon see if Bartzebal was true to us."

Meanwhile, Smid, drawing a brace and bit from his pouch, was methodically boring a circle of holes in the gate. The sharp bit ate through the wood without any sound and then he connected these holes up with a small saw, and a large piece of the door was soon cut out. Smid, inserting his arm, drew back the bar, then making a long arm, he at last succeeded in drawing back the bolts at top and bottom. The door creaked open and the party stole on muffled feet in to a large courtyard. On their right was a large building, doubt-less the Hall. As the Lord was away, probably only maids would be there, this could wait; on the left were stables. About the encircling wall was first a long low building from whence came loud snores and a smell that proclaimed it as the kitchen; this also could wait. There was a larger building, doubtless the barracks, then a round tower and after outbuildings and storehouses, then came the twin towers of the gatehouse, to the right of this again a stretch of wall and a huge round tower, the keep, here the wall joined up with the Hall, completing the circle. Thur observed everything with a soldier's eye. He swiftly placed six men outside the kitchen with strict orders to do nothing till they heard fighting elsewhere, then to enter and kill anyone they found, then rejoin the main bat-tle, wherever it was. Twenty men were posted outside the barracks with similar orders, but otherwise to keep quiet and do nothing. He posted another six men outside the Hall with orders to slay any coming out, but otherwise to do nothing. The Keep he ignored: "There never be any in there, save in case of war," he muttered. The remaining thirty picked men he led to the Gatehouse. He knew there would be armoured men on watch, and none of his men had any armour, and if they had had they could not have climbed the cliffs. There was a door in each of the twin towers, both con-veniently unbarred. Thur led the way up one, Smid Blacksmith up the other, and both simultaneously peered into the guard chamber over the gateway. A torch in a sconce in the wall cast a dim and unsteady light, revealing two men at a table dicing, and vaguely seen beyond was the windlass controlling the portcullis and draw-

269

bridge, and snores proclaimed other men of the guard were sleeping on the floor. From above came the sounds of footsteps, as the sentry on the roof paced about, endeavouring to keep warm. Thur slipped in silently, Smid did likewise, another man and another followed them, then something caught one of the dicer's eyes. "Who be it ?" he shouted, then as he saw more men crowding in, he seized a sword and buckler from the table and rushed forward shouting: "Treason." Thur's sword danced out, swept, parried, darted in again, swept and lunged, up inside the man's mail sleeve, laying hi.s arm open from wrist to elbow, his severed tendons dropped his blade, but he drove at Thur with his heavy shield, nearly crushing him against the wall. Thur wrenched his sword clear, there was no room to cut or thrust, but he drove the heavy pommel against his jaw, and as the man reeled back, thrust for his throat and found his mark. Meanwhile the others fought with intense desperation. The men-at-arms were outnumbered four to one and were dazed with sleep, but they were soldiers trained to arms and had armour, but unluckily they had removed their helmets to sleep and had no time to put them on. Men shouted and thrust, slipped aside, backed and dodged. The heavy blows made the steel thrum and sing. The spring and slash of their blades showed they knew how to handle their weapons. Thur saw the blacksmith was down, his throat bubbling blood, his loose mouth worked and dribbled a red ooze that in the flickering light of the one torch looked like ink. Thur swung madly into the fight, slashing, ducking, whirling, thrusting. Soon all was over, but only twelve of his thirty men remained standing, some were on the floor, groaning, the rest lay still. Thur stood panting, but before he could collect himself, there were sounds of hurried footsteps and a man in full armour burst down the stairs and spitted one of the standing men with his pike. It was the sentry from the roof alarmed by the clash below. Several swords swept, clanged, and glanced from his armour, he withdrew his pike and spitted another man, then someone caught the pike before he could withdraw it, another man caught his arm from behind, there was a furious struggle while swords and axes battered him till a lucky stroke brought him down with a crash. All was still again save for the panting and the groans of the still surviving men.

Thur listened attentively to muffled sounds of shouting from the barracks, which showed that Jan's men were engaged. But there was another sound that worried him. The sentry on the roof before descending had alarmed the sentry on the barbican, and the men on duty there were shouting across to know what was the matter. At all costs they must be prevented from joining in the fight, until Jan's men had cleared all opposition in the castle, Thur looked out of the loophole. Two stone arches had been built across the abyss. A heavy timber bridge had been built on this for about forty feet on the landward side, and a drawbridge let down from the gatehouse and joined up with this. Luckily, the bridge was up. He pondered a moment. If only he could lure them across!

Cupping his hands round his mouth he yelled: "Help! Here, men! The men are drunk and fighting!"

Two men with halberds came out across the timber bridge and called:

"Who summons? Lower the Bridge!" but Thur's men were already at the windlass, and the bridge creaked slowly downwards, while two other men joined those with halberds and all argued furiously. Thur knew that they were perplexed as to why they should be called to help instead of the garrison being summoned. Thur called for help again.

"Who 'st that calls?" they replied. "Show yourself! "

"Come quickly!" bellowed Thur.

"Name yourself!" was the reply, and the men started retreating towards the barbican shouting over their shoulders. "The trouble seems over now, so we come in the morn when we can see you."

Thur swore, but it seemed that the men were still uneasy, for they came forward again, still arguing, while Thur pondered. "'Tis hopeless to lure them. They won't have many men there, but each of them may cost me ten lives ere the barbican can be taken."

He motioned his men to take cross-bows from the walls. These were hastily bent. At this short range it was impossible to miss. The arrows whanged through the air and three men fell with bolts in their faces, while the others darted into the barbican yelling: "Treason!" and slammed the door behind him.

"The rest can wait," thought Thur, and ordered the drawbridge to be raised. Meanwhile Jan, with Wat and Stammers, led their party into the barracks, illumined only by a flickering lamp, but they were armed with torches. It was more of a massacre than a fight. The Saxons had endured many years of oppression, and most of the Normans were cut down before they could reach their weapons, or, indeed, before many could come out of their daze of sleep, and many died in their beds, without ever waking. Noises proclaimed that the same thing was going on in the kitchen. Just then arose a tumult in the courtyard, Jan rushed to the door. A great man with a long sword, accompanied by two squires with torches burst out of the door of the hall. It was Fulk Fitz-Urse, Fitz-Urse's eldest son, who was thought to be abroad. "What is it? What is the matter?" boomed his great voice. "Fighting, ye vermin? Peace, or, I'll flog ye all." He strode angrily, still bellowing threats towards the barracks, but as Jan looked, something jutted out from under Fulk's chin, his knees crumpled up and he fell sprawling with a clatter on the stones, almost simultaneously, his squires reeled and fell. The men stationed outside the hall door had obeyed their orders, and shot them through their necks, from behind, killing them instantly. So by the time Thur had reached the courtyard, there were none of the garrison left alive, with the exception of some servants, all Saxons and a hedge priest who happened to be there, staying the night.

"The castle is ours!" said Jan triumphantly.

"Not quite," said Thur, "listen." There came a creaking from the direction of the gate. They dashed towards it at a tired run. It came from the barbican. "They're lowering their drawbridge," said Thur. "They're sending for help. I wonder will they all go? Probably they'll send only one man, if so, Olaf will settle him. The great question is, how many men have they left? Two men might hold off fifty on those narrow stairs."

"Can't we do anything?" asked Jan.

Thur reflected. "Off you go, with all the men, fetch all the straw from the stables, make it into mighty bundles, get firewood and any oil and grease you can find, take the rushes from the floor of the hall if there be not enough, and bring some torches."

When all was done as he ordered, the gate was opened wide, the drawbridge fell with a crash, and men darted across carrying huge bundles of straw, and piled them against the doorways leading to the twin barbican towers. Ignited wood was piled on this, and oil. Some crossbow bolts were launched at the men carrying straw, but the bundles protected them, and as soon as the straw was fired, the smoke made it impossible to aim, so not much damage was done. Fed with oil and grease the fire took hold, the smoke swirled up, and Thur and Jan could imagine they saw Bartzebal exulting in the flames and smoke. Men went with pikes and buckets of water, and pushed the blazing mass against the doors, while keeping the fire from the bridge; shielded by the smoke, they brought some beams, which made useful battering rams, and the doors, half burnt through, quickly fell, water soon extinguished the remaining fires, but smoke still swirled up as men cautiously ascended the stairs. But there was no resistance, as soon as the doors were breached, the smoke had swirled in as up a chimney, and they found the fouf men left inside had all been suffocated by the smoke. They found the outer gate open and the drawbridge down. A messenger sent out soon returned with Olaf and his party. They had killed the one messenger sent from the barbican, and at last Thur breathed freely. The castle was theirs till Fitz-Urse returned ... The next day, questioning the frightened servants elicited the news that Fitz-Urse was not expected back for several days. So preparations were made to stand a siege. Provisions were got in from the fishing village, and the inhabitants were sworn to secrecy. As their men-folk were mostly implicated, Thur judged they would keep their peace. The burnt doors of the barbican were mended, and Olaf was sent with the good news to Morven, with instructions to take refuge in the forest at Dearleap, with the woodfolk. For as Thur said: "If it gets known that I am in the castle, or had any part in its taking, the Normans will surely take revenge on my household."

Then Thur went back to tending the wounded men of both sides.

All the next day preparations went on. Inspection showed there was a good stock of provisions and warlike materials. A fair amount of silver plate adorned the cupboards of the great hall, and in the lady's bower. There was a fair amount of copper money, some silver and a little gold. On this Thur pounced. "I must have this, to redeem my house," he argued, much to the disgust of the forest folk. They had suffered badly. All the plunder should be theirs, they protested. If the leech wanted gold, why didn't he make it, as all respectable Maguses were well known to do constantly, and there was much dissatisfaction and black looks over this matter. But, the inescapable fact that they held high rank in the Brotherhood counted for much, and in the end, Thur got his way, on promising he would never claim anything again. "I would not loose my house for anything," said Thur.

"But why?" asked Jan. "You must ever live here with Olaf and Morven, in the castle. You shall be my Grand Vizier, as the heathen say, and ever give me good advice, as to how I shall rule the land. For though I rule the castle now, I certainly see not how I may rule the land while Fitz-Urse and any of his breed live."

"I think we must call on Bartzebal again, to know what to do next," said Thur. "If I could only get back to town and bring the tools of Art, and the manuscripts, but I dare not leave till we know where Fitz-Urse is, I might ride straight into his grip."

"That can be done at any time," said Jan, "and they would be little use without Morven."

"Aye," answered the leech. "We can think of them when it is safe for her to come here."

Provisions came in steadily and some volunteers from among the fisher-folk, and the walking wounded were sent away to their own villages. The next day Olaf returned, and with him Morven, and the news that Fitz-Urse was close behind. Morven had insisted in coming with him. No country for her while there was a chance of a fight, and a siege would be a wonderful experience, she insisted. She was there, so they had to admit her since sending her back might mean that she would fall into FitzUrse's hands. Jan was delighted to see her, but torn with grief at her danger. Thur pounced on her and sent her off to nurse the wounded. Afterwards he said to Jan: "If the worst comes to the worst, you can take her down the cliff way, with a few men, and get away in Fitz-Urse's boats at night, while I and Olaf hold out, for, you must raise up more Bonders to maintain the struggle. Go after her, lad, speak her fair, and the hedge priest can tie ye up to-night, safe and sound in wedlock."

"But!" ejaculated Jan.

"But me no buts! 'Tis your duty to the family, and her presence here is a danger, to her at least. It convinces me more than ever what we must do. We are not waging war for glory and renown."

"But," said Jan "may I not win renown if I retake all my grand-sire's ravished lands?"

"Aye, aye," said Thur. "Renown and glory and a great death be grand things, for you, but I think of Morven, it means the stake for her if she is captured, and I myself, have a small liking to keep my throat unsevered. I command here as your general. I aim to make you lord of these lands and castles, so I plan, and you will take orders from me. Now off you go and talk to Morven." So, after some argument (for Thur obstinately refused to disclose his plans) Jan went off, to find that Morven, having duly tended the wounded, had departed. He soon found her in the Lady's Solar, she had never seen such a place since her childhood days at Hurstwyck. The tapestry, the soft cushions, the couches (for FitzUrse had learnt luxury in the Holy Land), the wonderful views from the windows, it all seemed like a glimpse of her childhood's days and ever the thought of her mother carne to her. She looked up as he came blundering in. Jan was not a tactful lover. He looked at her shyly and said: "Morven, Thur says we should get the priest and be married?"

"Oh, indeed? Master Thur hath ever a way of giving orders, but have I not a say in the matter? Is he my liege lord that he giveth me, or selleth me in marriage, without my consent?"

Jan looked confused and sulky. The girl put her hand on his shoulder.

"Jan, you are only a spoiled boy after all." Jan glowered at her for a minute. He, who had taken a castle by assault! Then a thought came to him. Thur once said: "Women and castles are much the same." He seized her in his arms and his lips sought hers, she struggled a minute, then hers were on his, eagerly. Somehow, he never quite knew how, but they were lying on a great cushioned divan, arms twined round each other's bodies, her head nes tling in to his shoulder . "Tell me, beloved, how much do you love me?"

"More than all else," he said. "More than all the world, more than castles and lands. I have loved you ever since that night at Dearleap, but fool that I was, I didn't know it."

"But what of your Irishwoman, the Lady of Jocelyn of Keys?" she said maliciously.

"O speak to me not of her, she is but a flickering torch compared to the stars of heaven. O, Morven, what a sweet and lovely name, Morven; it hath magic in the sound." They lay still for a time, he tenderly stroking her arms and shoulders. "Then, 'tis settled," he said. "I'll call the priest and tonight we will wed?"

She raised herself. "For the first time since I've known you, you are moving swiftly. Why all this haste?"

"Fitz-Urse," he mumbled. "To-night or tomorrow he cometh and we have to stand siege."

"So-ho," she laughed. "First I must wed to suit Master Thur's convenience, and then to suit FitzUrse. Come along, Jan, take me to the top of the keep, so we may spy if Fitz-Urse cometh, and so forceth me to wed, without even a change of raiment."

Jan looked at her, she had changed from her boy's riding suit to her usual town garb, a short petticoat of green serge, a white chemise with shoulder straps, that were always off either one shoulder or the other, the wonderful beauty of her bare arms and shoulders, her flower-like face and billowing red-gold hair, she was wonderful, divine, he thought. But she pulled him. "Come away, horse and hattock, as we say in the Cult. Come."

But he mumbled: "We cannot go to the top of the keep."

"Why?" she demanded. "Does Master Thur forbid, or is it Fitz-Urse? They seem to order all my life nowadays."

"Nay, 'tis not that. We cannot find the key, come see," and he led her out into the courtyard and showed her. The only entrance to the keep was by a narrow stone staircase, scarce two feet wide, that ran round the outside of the tower, ending in a small platform and a small door, plated with iron. Full thirty feet above the courtyard.

"Smid, the blacksmith is dead," he said. "He might have opened it for us. There is so little room to stand on, and men fear to swing a heavy hammer there for to fall is death. We cannot burn through the iron, and we know not how to enter, till we get a clever smith again. Say, Witch of the Mere, hast a spell to charm locks as you charm the hearts of men?"

"Alas no," she said. "But will it not be a great hindrance to you, if you may not use it in time of siege?"

"It will," he admitted ruefully, "but Thur hath a plan, and he thinks he may win, and save lives; 'tis not for glory we fight he saith, 'tis for our lives, before Fitz-Urse may bring others to his aid, so we must ever do as he saith, for he is a soldier, and skilled in ambushments and stratagems."

"So you know not what be his plan?"

"No, he will tell me naught. Now, say, dear heart, shall I summon the priest this night?"

"Jan, I know not what to say, I love not priests. But Thur and Dame Alice have taught me that all Christians are not cruel. So this night an you will, dear heart."

And so, that evening, Father Mathew, the hedge priest said the words that made them one, in the little chapel of the hall, with Thur, Olaf and Simon Pipeadder as witnesses.

The next morning a scout galloped in to say a party of horse approached, and soon these were in sight of the gates. It had been Thur's main object to prevent any news of the taking of the castle getting abroad, and he seemed to have succeeded, as the party came on with no sense of danger. Questioning the servants had elicited what was the usual procedure when their lord approached.

As they drew near the barbican, they sounded a horn, the outer and inner drawbridges were lowered and the gates swung open, and men in captured armour appeared on the battlements. Fitz-Urse led the way across the bridges, the lady Ellenora following, then his son Rual, followed by the men-at-arms, and some servants.

Fitz-Urse was inside the courtyard before he noticed anything strange. Then he started bawling for "Jehean." His lady and the horsemen followed him, and he was still bellowing for "Jehean and Fulk," until the last man of his train was through the barbican gates. Then, at a signal the portcullis of the barbican dropped, cutting off all retreat, and a second later the portcullis of the gate-house dropped, crushing a man and horse beneath it, and effectually cutting the party in half. Then Jan, in full armour, called from a window of the gatehouse:

"Surrender yourself, Fitz-Urse."

Fitz-Urse dragged at his bridle and forced his horse round, striving to see where the strange voice came from.

"Who are you, you cockerel, who crows so loudly, in a man's own castle ? Show yourself, and I'll cut your comb."

"I am Jan of the Bonders, I have reconquered my grandsire's castle." Fitz-Urse stared confusedly at the portcullis that cut his party in two. Then he spurred his horse to the centre of the courtyard and pulled it round, gazing in amazement. "But who in the devil's name be ye ?"

"I am Jan Bonder, son of Hugh, grandson of Sir Edgar, whom your father so foully murdered," was the reply."

Fitz-Urse looked bewildered, he cast his eyes round, noting that bowmen were standing ready at the loopholes in the gatehouse, and more at the door of the barracks, scratched his head. Then suddenly siezing his wife's bridle, and shouting: "To me," he dashed off towards the keep. Horses plunged and slipped on the flagstones. But the next thing Jan saw was some of them were slipping off their horses at the foot of the steps, and the others were forming a circle with their lances pointing outwards. Then he saw Dame Ellenora, holding her skirts with both hands, and with a huge key in one of them, running swiftly up the steps, followed by many men.

Then came Thur's voice from the barracks. "Shoot, shoot swiftly, if they get in there, we'll never get them out." Quickly came a flight of arrows, rattling and rebounding from the walls, but up she sped, apparently unharmed. Some of the Normans on the steps were already bending crossbows and commencing to shoot back. Then she reached the iron door, and turned to fit the great key in the lock. But her back was a steady target. Two arrows feathered themselves in it. She reeled for a minute, the key falling from her nerveless hand and clattering into the middle of the courtyard. Then she fell backwards with a dull thud on the stones. Jan closed his eyes with horror, then opened them again as a dull "Ahha" seemed to come from all, and he saw that Thur had darted out from the barracks, seized the key and turned like a flash to run back, while two of Fitz-Urse's men spurred forward, lances down. A few arrows glanced off their armour, he saw Morven appear like a flash, a knife whirled through the air, and caught one man in the face, he swerved aside and fell over. His foot caught in the stirrup, his horse dragging him over the stones. Thur had nearly reached the door, when Jan saw to his horror a long lance point coming out of his chest. The speed of the horse carried him forward for a few steps then he stumbled, the horseman dropped his lance, dragged round his horse and tried to gallop back to his companions, only to fall, riddled with arrows halfway. Dimly Jan realised that Fitz-Urse and his men were slowly falling under a hail of arrows, and noises from behind him showed that the men trapped between the gatehouse and the barbican were being exterminated with stones and arrows.

But all he could see was Thur's body prone in a pool of blood on the stones, and Morven lying on the body, sobbing her heart out.

# CHAPTER XX
## ALL ROADS LEAD TO ROME

THAT night Jan and Olaf sat in the Solar, while Morven cried herself to sleep in the next room. "I know not what to do next," was the burden of Jan's argument. "I thought that when I had taken the castle, and avenged my grandsire's death, that would have been an end of it. I perceive clearly now that, when the next step came, I ever sought Thur's advice, and now I see not what I must do next."

"Proclaim yourself Lord of Dunbrand and Claire, and the surrounding country. Bid all to pay their dues to you, none dare say nay, and, should they do so, fight them," was Olaf's counsel.

"Fitz-Urse held his land from the King," said Jan. "What of that?"

"Lackland has troubles enough of his own."

"Yet, as Fitz-Urse held the land from him, he will trouble enough about what is his."

"Not so," replied Olaf. "For, as I see it, ever since he murdered Arthur of Brittany all Normandy is against him, and he has not time to bother with such small fry as us. Should he do so, we have the parchments, and we know the trick of magic now, so we'll call to Bartzebal, who gave us good rede last time, and we will do what he says."

"Aye, he told poor Thur what to do, and where is Thur now?"

"Nay, he told us not of Thur, since we did not ask, *but how to take the Castle,* which we did. We trapped Fitz-Urse *without* his advice, and so Thur died, 'twas but the chance of war, which we all took." Olaf's eyes were wet with tears but he continued: "Bartzebal ever gave us good advice, from the day when he bade us seek the Witch of Wanda."

"You mean that we should get the parchments here and try Bartzebal again?" asked Jan.

"Aye, and if thou doubt thy powers, ask Brother Stephen. Morven says he works wonders in the Circle, and he might give us sooth on other matters too, for he is well affected to us ... or at least, to Morven, and men say that my Lord Abbot will do naught without his advice."

So it was that two days later Jan, Morven, Simon Pipeadder, his son and six men rode towards St. Claire. It was a pleasant day, but they were a silent little band, and afternoon found them in sight of the town without many words having been spoken.

With new-found decision Jan said: "You wait here while I go and spy out the land. Post one man here in these bushes, where he can see a mile along the road both ways, and so creep back unseen to warn the others if any come in force. The rest of you take cover back there with your horses, and if you be pursued, ride across country unseen.

"I go to the town. If I return not by sunset, then let Simon and one other come to search, and you others back to the castle with all speed, there to hold it against all comers."

So spoke Jan bravely, but as he came to the gates of St. Claire he was troubled. The guard was more alert than usual and had been doubled, and they were stopping people and questioning them, but most of them were being let go forward unhindered. As he drew near, one of the soldiers recognised him as one who had passed frequently in and out of late.

"Hast news?" the soldier inquired eagerly.

"News of what?"

"Of fighting. Men say that Dunbar hath been stormed and Fitz-Urse slain, but none know who did the deed, whether it be by foreign enemies landed or some nearby Baron."

"We have many wars on our farm," laughed Jan.

"But they be with rats and suchlike pests. Is it true about Dunbrand? 'Tis a mighty hold, and it must be a great warrior who hath taken it."

"If thou knowest naught, then go thy ways," said the disappointed soldier, and Jan rode slowly towards the house. Alice Chad was a doughty gossip, and would tell all she knew unbegged. As the house came into view he saw some mules tethered outside, and thought that Alice and Tom had some patients from a distance, but he was dumbfounded when he saw instead the Sub-Prior of St. Ethelred seated at a table, busy with some of Thur's books and manuscripts. Before him sat two monks, with knives and tapers, erasing the letters and smoothing the parchment with pumice stone so that it could be used again. As he examined one of Thur's treasures, the Sub-Prior was saying: "'Tis but the poems of the Greek woman, Sappho. I thought them amusing when I was young, but now they are not worth keeping. 'Twill do to keep the Abbey accounts in," and with that he pushed the book over to have the lettering erased.

Jan's heart leaped when he saw the books, but quietened again as he remembered that the magical parchments had been kept in a safe place, but his face fell as he saw on the floor Thur's magic sword and other instruments, tied up in a bundle, but there were no parchments with them.

The Sub-Prior turned as Jan darkened the doorway. "I thought you might be Brother Stephen," he said. "Have you seen him?"

"I have not," answered Jan, coming forward. "But what be you doing in the house of Thur Peterson the leech?"

The Sub-Prior answered: "'Twas the property of the late Thur the leech at one time, but now it belongs to the Abbey of the Holy St. Ethelred, but who are you who question me, my son? Were you a friend of Thur? Do you know aught of his parchments? Were any concealed in a secret place?"

Jan considered. Evidently the news of the taking of the castle was known in the town, and perhaps this priest knew more, at least he knew of Thur's death, though how, he could not conceive.

"I was a patient of his, and somewhat a friend. Of his books and parchments I know naught, save I have seen some on his shelves; I know naught of their contents."

"Hum, a pity," mumbled the Sub-Prior, half talking to himself.

"Think again, young sir. Did this Thur ever mention that by his Arts he could restore youth? 'Tis said that he had an old woman here, whom by his Arts he had made young again."

"There were but two women here that I ever heard of, one his niece, who is young indeed, and Dame Alice, who to my knowledge is still old."

"Well, well," grumbled the Sub-Prior. "Men say he was a good leech so he must have had such knowledge, but perchance he feared to use it. Did he not consult the stars, eh?"

"He may have, but I know naught of it," said Jan. "Hey, Master Know-Nothing," said the Sub-Prior, "you have not answered my question. *Who are ye?* What is thy name?"

"Jan," was the reply.

The Sub-Prior cocked a reflective eye at him.

"Brother Stephen said a certain Jan would be coming here, shortly. Dost know Brother Stephen, eh?"

"I know him," said Jan shortly.

"Then no shilly-shallying, answer truly, art thou Jan of the Bonders, whom we look for? Come to look at it, thou art the dead spit of old Sir Edgar. I knew him when I was a boy."

"I am Jan of the Bonders," said Jan fiercely, his hand sliding to his sword. He could easily fight his way out of this handful of monks.

"Glad to know ye, my son. Brother Stephen has told us of thy exploits, and said you would be coming, the Lord Abbot craves thy presence, and right speedily. He will welcome you with great honour, he hath affairs of great import to discuss with you."

Jan felt and looked bewildered. He feared a trap, and yet the Sub-Prior seemed friendly. He felt it was worth while to risk something to find out what all this mystery was about. That Brother Stephen was at the bottom of it he felt sure, and Stephen was well disposed to him, or at least to Morven and Thur. But, Thur lay in his grave. That thought stung him like an arrow. If he only had Thur at hand to advise him. Was he walking into a trap? Should he risk going to the Abbey? But the Sub-Prior wasn't giving him other option, and in a friendly way he was hustled outside and on to his horse, and the Sub-Prior was on to his mule, and two other monks, their mules loaded up with Thur's books and magical instruments. Before he knew it he was shepherded up the narrow street towards the Abbey which, ancient even in these days, lay on their right, a sombre pile whose solid strength dominated the township, seeming rather to menace than bless, and even the glow of the setting sun did nothing to soften its austerity, but rather did it accentuate every line of its stark simplicity.

Jan eyed the frowning majesty of this religious stronghold with misgiving. In its two hundred years of life he knew it had used its power to condemn men to torture and to death. Many crimes had been committed there in the name of God, but on the other hand, it had known as many deeds of goodness and mercy. But, almost as he thought this, they were through the gateway, and before the great door of the Abbot's lodging. Feeling like a rat in a trap, Jan suffered himself to be conducted to the Abbot's presence. He looked around suspiciously, but there was no sign of guards, and he was being ushered, most politely, into the Abbot's presence.

The Abbot was a big, dignified, elderly man, with white hair curling crisply round the temples, surrounding a handsome but much wrinkled face, but his eyes were brilliantly shrewd, and his body was sturdy, though age had bowed the proud shoulders.

"My Lord Abbot," began the Sub-Prior, "I have found Jan Bonder, and straightway brought him to you."

The Abbot looked narrowly at Jan, then smiled. "Aye. Your face tells me who your father was. I knew him, and your grandfather too. Welcome, lad, did Stephen send you?"

Ere Jan could answer, the Sub-Prior put in:

"Brother Stephen has not yet returned. When he does I will tell him you desire his presence."

The Abbot inclined his head, then turning to Jan again, he said:

"Welcome, dear son. We are all interested and gratified to hear of your coming into your inheritance, and we condole with you on the death of your relatives. Ah, in the midst of life ... but have a cup of this most excellent wine, the best Burgundy can offer."

Jan gaped: "I know not of what you speak, reverend Father. 'Tis true I have captured the castle of my ancestors, and killed off a nest of foul usurpers, but I know of naught else."

"Speak not of such things in these enlightened times," said the Abbot, with some meaning in his tone and glance, and with a slow closing of one of those bright, shrewd, searching eyes, and gazing straight at Jan with the other.

Jan was aghast. Surely the Abbot was not winking at him? Mechanically he took the proffered seat, and drained the offered wine cup, which was promptly refilled by a serving brother. The Abbot drank deeply in turn, and had his cup refilled, then, holding it up, he said:

"I drink your very good health, Sir Jan."

Bewildered, Jan responded to the toast, and sat awkwardly waiting.

The Abbot gazed blandly at the ceiling, saying:

"We all know that at times there are little family quarrels, but think back, Sir Jan ... by the way, you are not knighted yet, are you? We must arrange it. It adds an air, I think. Yes. Drink up!"

Jan complied, wondering if he was dreaming.

Blandly the Abbot continued: "Think back, I say. Your grandfather, the late Sir Edgar, had two children, Hugh, who was your father, and Maud, who married the late Sir Ogier Fitz-Urse. Well, shortly after the regrettable little family quarrel, and your revered grandfather's death, your father Hugh, being beyond the seas and presumed dead, your Aunt Maud became heiress. Naturally her husband administered the property and so succeeded to the property on the occasion of her sad demise shortly afterwards. They had only one son, the late Sir Usa, who succeeded on his father's death ... but drink up. Much talking is dry work," and with that the Abbot followed his own advice, continuing:

"As I was saying, the late Sir Usa succeeded by Statute of Mort d'Ancestor and Nuvel Disseisin, in which the Court Christian, in fact, this Abbey Court, being the nearest, decides the claims on land in such cases where a claim is made that, since a certain recent definite date fixed by the Court, a man has been disseised by another. Now, I understand that your two cousins, Fulk and Rual, who would have been the next heirs, unhappily did not survive their father, and since they did not leave any legitimate offspring … then you are the heir at law. Yes indeed! My secretary, a most able fellow, has been to a lot of trouble looking into the matter. Yes, that Statute of Mort d'Ancestor is a very useful one indeed. Come, drink up!"

Dumbfounded, Jan gasped: "And now?"

"Well," said the Abbot, "of course there will be some Court fees. We must call a special meeting of the Court Christian and speedily, before any of those confounded nose-poking fellows of the King's Court get wind of it. *But if the Abbey Court once sits, and decides the case, they dare not try and reverse the judgment.* Mind you, I think we must charge special fees for holding the Court at such short notice. Those farms at Southridge, for instance, and the mill at Walkford, especially as my secretary has done so much work over this case." He struck a bell, and the Sub-Prior entered.

"Has Brother Stephen come in yet? Did you bring what I wanted from the house of the leech?"

"No, my Lord Abbot," answered the Sub-Prior. "We have searched the whole town, but Brother Stephen is not to be found, and Satan is missing from the stables."

"Satan missing!" roared the Abbot. "Fools! Have all the stablemen flogged! Send out mounted men to scour all the roads! He shouldn't have taken Satan without my leave. Well, though, he must come back sometime, and when he does, send him straight to me. I wonder what he is up to," he muttered half to himself; then, to Jan: "Drink up, Sir Jan."

He turned his bright eyes to the Sub-Prior. "Now, what got ye at the leech's house? Didst get what I sent you for?"

"No, my Lord," answered the Sub-Prior, "only these books and what lie in this bundle here. Some instruments of Magic, I ween, and some books on Astrology, and on healing and some worthless poems and worldly books, but naught could we find on Magic and naught on restoring youth or the lusts of the flesh."

The Abbot considered, and turned to Jan. "Tell me, Sir Jan, you knew this Thur. Men say that he brought an old woman into his house and by his Magic Arts made her young again. Dost know aught of this?"

"There was no Magic used," said Jan, "save feeding a starving girl and medicining a sick one, no Magic in that, I ween."

"Well, where is the girl?" said the Abbot to the Sub-Prior. "I told you to bring her to me. I would question her strictly."

"She's not to be found either," said the Sub-Prior.

"Oh, ho, I see!" laughed the Abbot. "Well, well, I see, but he really shouldn't have taken Satan for his junketing, and he always pretended the lasses were nothing to him. I'm very angry with him. Well, well. I only wish I was as young as he."

Turning to Jan, he said: "I crave your pardon, Sir Jan, there are little matters of Abbey discipline. Now I beg you to drain a cup of wine with me, and then perchance, you have some affairs of your own to attend to. 'Tis late. I trust you will do me the honour of staying at the Abbey this night, and will sup with me. We will call the Court Christian on the morrow," and the Abbot started examining Thur's goods like a child with new toys. "More wine. Drink up, Sir Jan. Now, about to-morrow, I wish that confounded Stephen were not off on his junketings, but I think I remember the main points. After all is settled here, and registered in the Abbey Court Records, he advises you take copies of these records to the King's Court and pay a fine on them. Anything will do. If you want money, I will give you a good price for Highcliffe Farm, or Sumerford. They never question anyone wanting to pay them money, not in these days! The King's Receipt gives a legal guarantee and makes the thing final, in case any other claimant should turn up, in which case he will himself be baulked from the start. Have some more wine, Sir Jan. Now, you'll wish to make the usual offerings to the Abbey for prayersh" — Jan realised that for the past few minutes the Abbot's speech had been thickening) — "hic ... and for the soulsh of your relationsh who so unhappily recently died ... hic!"

"Then there need be no more fighting?" gasped Jan.

"My dear boy," deprecated the Abbot, "the lasht thing we want in these times is fighting ... hic ... we are all men of peashe. An old family quarrel has at length been amic ... amic ... happily settled. You will take your plashe in the country, and we hope we will never hear anything more about fightingsh and warsh ... let bygonsh be bygonsh .... "

Jan realised that by now the worthy Abbot was decidedly the worse for the wine he had taken, and looked wonderingly at the Sub-Prior, who chuckled:

"My Lord is always like this about this time O' night, but what he says is sooth. Brother Stephen has bothered himself mightily over your case, and 'tis all clear. The Abbot will be as sober as a judge when he presides in that capacity on the morrow. The parchments are all ready. You will make your claim, and it will be granted, and nobody there to argue about it."

He indicated that Jan should take his leave, but as the Abbot was sunk into a stupor, Jan crept quietly out, and away to seek Morven, leaving the dreaming Abbot muttering about "Eliksher of Life ... the Shtone ... and the non-return of Brother Stephen."

Meanwhile Morven, accompanied by the faithful Simon Pipeadder, lay hidden in the bushes, eagerly watching the road.

Suddenly they heard hoof-beats, and a horseman appeared round the bend from the direction of the town. For a moment she hoped it was Jan, but as the rider drew near she recognised him as Brother Stephen.

Morven ran out, calling his name, and at sight of her he drew rein so suddenly that he nearly pulled the magnificent black horse over backwards.

"I am glad I could say 'Farewell' to you," he said softly, "for I go on a long journey indeed."

"Hast had news of Jan?" gasped the tortured girl.

"Thy Jan is all right," smiled Stephen. "He will have his castle and lands with no trouble, for I have attended to that matter. As for me, I ride to Lothair, Count of Signi. The stars spoke truly. At first I did not understand, but now 'tis clear, and I take him that which I was sent to fetch. I ride to Rome, and there to obtain supreme power for us both!" His eyes gleamed with fanaticism.

"Wilt thou return to this country?" Morven asked.

"Aye, I will return, when I have done all that is necessary to free it from tyrants' grip ... but, though I have settled thy affairs for thee, should there be anything thou needest in the future when I return ... "

"To the Abbey?"

"Nay, not the Abbey! I have seen the last of that place, and have done toadying to that drunken fool. When I return, I say, all England will know of the Great Charter of man's right and liberties that will bring freedom and justice to all. That is my destiny, Morven."

"This Great Charter?"

"Aye. It was foretold in my horoscope, and to that end have I stolen the parchments as Thur did long ago. I take them to Lothair di Signi, whom men call Pope Innocent III. He will be supreme in Europe, as I will be in England, and I trow, the names of Stephen Langton and Innocent the Third will be remembered in this world for a thousand years.

"For this have I, Stephen Langton, forsaken hope of earthly happiness, but I will be for ever remembered as the bringer of the Great Charter, and of the freedom of the Mother of Parliaments which shall bring true liberty to England, and from her shores will spread all over the world.

"And this for thee, Morven. Thou canst remember that once all this, and the history of the world itself, hung upon a shake of thy loving head. Now, blessings on thee, and fare thee well!"

He dug spurs into his horse, saluted her, and leaving her standing in the road watching after him, he galloped like an arrow ahead, to fulfil his destiny with the aid of Magic's High Art as she had fulfilled hers.

THE END

# The Museum of Witchcraft
## Boscastle
## Cornwall
## UK

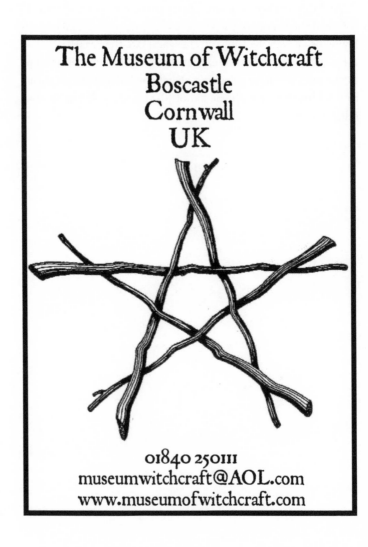

01840 250111
museumwitchcraft@AOL.com
www.museumofwitchcraft.com

# The Museum of Witchcraft

Gerald Gardner has touched and changed the lives of many but he remains controversial some 50 years after his death.

Did he reintroduce witchcraft, or Wicca as he originally called it, to the world or did he invent it? Did witchcraft ever die out, and if not should it have remained secret?

These are just some of the questions that we are often asked at *The Museum of Witchcraft* and these are questions to which there is no simple yes or no answer. However we can all agree that Gardner did introduce the world to a magical system that incorporated many aspects of traditional witchcraft along with elements of ritual magic, freemasonry and nature worship. How much of his Wicca did he inherit from the New Forest coven, how much did Doreen Valiente write, how much did Gardner take from Aleister Crowley and others? I am not going to attempt to answer these questions but reading *High Magic's Aid* is a good starting point on the quest to discover the truth.

Gardner worked at *The Museum of Witchcraft* when it was located in the Isle of Man and later purchased the old mill in which it was housed after Cecil Williamson brought his museum to the mainland. I am proud to be the current custodian of that collection and am especially proud to display some of Gerald Gardner's magical artefacts as a tribute to a very influential man. The Museum also holds a good many letters and papers written by Gerald in the archives along with some excellent books about him including those of Philip Heselton who has done more than anyone to discover the real Gerald Gardner.

For more information visit **www.museumofwitchcraft.com**

Graham King
Curator

**Witches!!**

Come and See the only
Collection of Witchcraft
Relics in Europe!

Shown for the First Time at the

# WITCHES KITCHEN

ARBORY ROAD

# CASTLETOWN

## Restaurant

### and EXHIBITION

Open from 10 a.m. to midnight [Sundays Included]

ALL MEALS SUPPLIED

We are famous for our superb Home Baked Cakes in the
old Manx farmhouse style : : : : : :

**To Drink? What better than the
Original Witches Brew?**

THE MUSEUM of WITCHCRAFT